Teach the Torches to Burn

A Romeo & Juliet Remix

THE
REMIXED CLASSICS
SERIES

Teach the Torches to Burn

A Romeo & Juliet Remix

CALEB ROEHRIG

FEIWEL AND FRIENDS

New York

Content warning: This book contains references to queerphobia
and misogyny in the context of 14th century Europe,
and an instance of blood, violence, and death.

A Feiwel and Friends Book
An imprint of Macmillan Publishing Group, LLC
120 Broadway, New York, NY 10271 • fiercereads.com

Our books may be purchased in bulk for promotional, educational, or
business use. Please contact your local bookseller or the Macmillan Corporate
and Premium Sales Department at (800) 221-7945 ext. 5442 or by email at
MacmillanSpecialMarkets@macmillan.com.

Library of Congress Cataloging-in-Publication Data is available.

First edition, 2023
Book design by Samira Iravani and Maria Williams
Feiwel and Friends logo designed by Filomena Tuosto
Printed in the United States of America

ISBN 978-1-250-82848-4
1   3   5   7   9   10   8   6   4   2

For my sister Debie, the hostess with the mostest. I miss you.

ALSO BY CALEB ROEHRIG

Last Seen Leaving

White Rabbit

Death Prefers Blondes

The Fell of Dark

Teach the Torches to Burn

A Romeo & Juliet Remix

Bright Smoke, Cold Fire

1

THE MORNING IS CRACKED AT THE HORIZON AS I COME TO THE TOP
of a rise in the lane, warm color just beginning to bleed into
dark sky—a band of coral and gold that lifts gently humped
clouds out of the deep gray like bits of driftwood. Ahead of me,
the first threads of daylight are taking the measure of church
towers, rooftops, and the crowns of cypress trees that bristle atop
San Pietro Hill.

It's breathtaking, to see my home this way—this quiet, this
beautiful.

This distant.

There is no Verona without Montague, and no Montague without Verona,
my father has said on more than one occasion, when he feels I
need reminding. For centuries, our family has been synonymous
with this city, my ancestors contributing their blood, gold, and
labor to build and defend it; and, for good or ill, Verona is the
anchor to which my own legacy is tied. From generation to generation, the Montagues have carried a destiny of status, leader-
ship, and public, unflinching piety. My father makes it sound
like an honor to bear the name, but more and more I find it a

crushing weight. My future is one of two paths—knighthood or sainthood—and I must live up to both possibilities, at all times. Or else.

But if there's no Montague without Verona, then why is it that I feel most like myself when I'm finally able to see it from afar? What cruel irony, that it's only from such a remove that I can finally appreciate its beauty—the scattered glow of lanterns, like earthbound stars; the gentle warmth of terra-cotta tile and rosy marble; the spiking trees and looping ivy, so rich in green they're almost black.

Out here, there are no rules or demands. There are no expectations I can't live up to, no ironclad fate that I cannot escape, no future of empty gestures, tedious company, and strategic alliances. Out here, there is no Romeo Montague—there is only a boy and a vault of wild air filled with expanding color and flickering, dying stars.

Only from here, my feet in the dirt and the city's lanterns burning against the rising sun, can I finally understand why my father always calls it "our fair Verona" in his many public speeches.

Even though, in my own experience, it is a deeply unfair place to live.

———

Church bells are ringing the hour as I finally reach the city gates, my legs weak from miles of walking on an empty stomach. I've no one to blame but myself for this suffering, of course, but still

I curse the earth for the distance it forced me to travel. After all, as my father likes to say: If you can't find someone else to blame, you are not trying hard enough.

But then, he never thinks I am "trying hard enough." In fact, my journey from home this morning was prompted by something he'd said to me yesterday, after he let himself into my chambers and found me coloring in a sketch I'd made of some wildflowers.

"*You are not a child anymore, Romeo,*" he declared furiously, snatching the sheet of parchment out of my hands and tearing it in half. I was devastated; it was a piece I'd been working on for weeks. "*You have seventeen years behind you now. One day, you will be the head of this family, and I expect you to behave accordingly! There will be no more of these . . . frivolous pursuits.*" He shook the shreds of my artwork in my face. "*Come the fall, you will either commit to an apprenticeship under me and learn to manage your future affairs, or else you will join the prince's army and learn to be a man.*"

Ever since I surpassed my sixteenth year, it seems I can make no choice that doesn't result in a lecture by my parents, a litany of reminders about my duties and obligations—as if they could be forgotten. Already, the weight of them causes my heart to sink as I trudge up the winding lane that leads to the back of our villa, even though I just spent the better part of the last hour unburdening myself to the wisest man I know.

And, as always, *his* counsel was maddeningly obscure. *At the end of every story is a new beginning.* Whatever that means. But I suppose riddles are what I deserve for seeking advice from someone who talks to his plants.

My bedchamber is on the second story of our home, my windows overlooking the orchard and gardens that supply the kitchen, the stones ribbed with dense veins of creeping ivy. I've always loved the view I have, and in this season, it is especially lovely—a rich green sea blanketing the hillside, in which bob the pastel blossoms of coming fruit.

If I'm being honest, however, what I love most at the moment is that my chambers are on the opposite side of the grand staircase from my parents'—they won't be able to hear me scaling the ladder of ivy to get back inside. Technically, I've done nothing specifically *wrong*; at my age, there's no reason I shouldn't be allowed to come and go as I please from my own home. But my parents rarely need anything as prosaic as a reason to make me feel that I have disappointed them.

As nimbly as I can, I begin the short but treacherous journey up the outside wall of my home. The ivy is probably older than I am, its roots growing sturdier every year. But then, *I've* been growing every year as well, and ominous cracking sounds underscore my progress. By the time I finally reach the ledge of the sill, I'm sweating under my cloak, and I cannot push the shutters open and dive through the darkened window fast enough.

My sense of relief is abruptly cut short as I collide headfirst with something warm and alive and *angry*. There comes a startled yowl, a fistful of tiny claws ripping at my collar, missing the skin of my face by a hair's breadth; and then we're crashing to the ground, a jumble of awkward limbs, tangled fabric, and frantic hissing.

As pain acquaints itself with each one of my tender bones,

a ball of furious orange fluff leaps across my chest, streaking for the shadows beneath my raised bed. Sucking air through my teeth, I sit up, growling, "Curse you, Hecate! You don't even live here!"

To my profound shock, I actually receive an answer.

"I'll say this for Montague men: You love a dramatic entrance." There comes a movement in the darkness, a figure stretched across my bed drawing languorously upright, and the waxing pool of dawn light brings features into focus: ginger hair, freckles, a strong chin, and an upturned nose. The sight is simultaneously familiar and annoying.

"Benvolio?"

"Good morrow, Cousin." He smiles sweetly, but there's a wicked glint in his eyes. "I do hope I haven't caught you at a bad time."

Disconnected thoughts run through my aching head and then scatter like pigeons. My mother's kin by blood, Ben lives on the other side of Verona, and I'm certain we had no rendezvous planned for these early hours. "W-what are you doing here?"

"All right, I suppose we can start with that," Benvolio allows with a patient shrug. "As it happens, I was . . . visiting with a lady friend who keeps house in San Pietro, and on my way home I chanced to cut through your orchard." He smiles, showing the devilish points of his eyeteeth. "Imagine my shock when I spotted someone climbing down the wall from my dear cousin's window and then skulking off into the night like a thief, as quietly as possible and without so much as a lit match to see the way."

The smug way he grins at me makes my stomach roll with

nerves. I have no desire to explain where I've been. Even though he would understand some of the distress I feel over my father's ultimatum, it was not the only matter I sought counsel on—and I absolutely cannot tell him the whole story. Flustered, I delay addressing it altogether. "Ben, that was practically an hour ago."

"It was *more* than an hour ago," he returns easily, stretching his arms above his head. "And I've been waiting here ever since, so I might find out where my prim-and-proper cousin is spiriting himself off to under the cover of night."

It's both question and accusation, and again I deflect. "Please at least tell me that, this time, the 'lady friend' you were visiting wasn't one of our chambermaids."

"That only happened once!" His cheeks go pink, leaving me both guilty and satisfied. "And, I'd like to note, it was *her* idea."

"So then, who is the lucky girl who lives across our orchard?"

"Erm." Benvolio coughs, looking away. "She's somewhat reluctant to let our . . . *association* become known about publicly, and I gave her my word I would keep it a secret—hence our pre-dawn rendezvous. It would be ungentlemanly of me to betray her confidence." With an airy gesture, he concludes, "I'm sure you understand."

"I believe I do," I answer. "You're telling me she has a husband."

He rolls his eyes. "Well, of course it sounds terrible when you say it in that tone of voice! But it's not as though they're *happy*, Romeo. He's twice her age and treats her like an exotic pet. They don't even like each other!"

"You don't need to explain yourself to me." Most marriages

8

in Verona are arranged, and the picture Ben paints is not at all uncommon. "I'm not your keeper, and what your lady friends do, married or otherwise, is no business of mine to judge."

Frankly, I'm hoping he'll take this philosophy to heart before he gets to the point of his creeping into my bedchamber; but, of course, my hopes are in vain.

"I should say not." He folds his arms. "There are only so many reasons the son of Bernabó and Elisabetta Montague would be sneaking out his window by moonlight like a common alley cat, and I am tired of waiting for an explanation."

Thinking fast, my fingers worrying the strap of the leather bag slung across my back, I try, "I was making sketches. Of the countryside."

Benvolio's smug expression collapses into one of disappointment. And suspicion. "You crept out of your bedchamber to go sketching? In the dark?"

"When the sky is clear, the effect of moonlight on the river is really striking," I tell him earnestly, and honestly. "My father doesn't exactly approve of my hobby, so I've had to pursue it covertly."

"Of course he doesn't approve." Ben frowns, and my heart sinks further. "It's a womanly pursuit, Romeo. It's fine to admire a painting or a statue, but drawing little pictures of flowers and trees and things . . . it's what girls do to pass the time and make their homes pretty. It's not a respectable hobby for a gentleman."

My cheeks burning, I lift my chin. "I suppose you're saying that Giotto di Bondone is not respectable, despite designing the

9

campanile for the cathedral in Florence—which has been hailed as a masterpiece."

"You are not Giotto di Bondone," he points out with no hesitation. "You are Romeo Montague, and your destiny is not to design campaniles." Scrubbing his hands through his ginger hair, he sighs. "Great things are waiting for you, Cousin—greater things than most of us could ever dream of—and this is the sort of thing that could hurt your reputation."

"You sound like my father." I cannot keep the bitterness from my tone. A part of me is sorely tempted to reveal the true reason for my moonlit expedition: how I was visiting a monk, because I needed someone to understand *me*, for once—to take *me* seriously. Someone I could be wholly honest with, knowing his vows require him to keep my secrets.

The orange tabby that foiled my entrance chooses this moment to reappear, leaping into my cousin's lap and rubbing her treacherous face against his chest. She purrs, as loud as a millstone crushing chestnuts into flour, and Benvolio scratches between her ears.

"You gingers always stick together," I grumble, weary from my lack of sleep, yet grateful for a chance to change the subject.

"Of course we do." Ben's voice drops into a maudlin coo as he pets the little beast, her back arching with every luxurious stroke. "She's a little angel. Isn't that right? Who's a little angel? Who's my little whiskered angel? *You are.*"

He blubbers nonsense at her in a truly embarrassing way, and Hecate purrs louder. I look heavenward. "I'll have you know that your 'whiskered angel' there eats her own vomit and bites my fingers while I'm sleeping."

"Well, she's a cat." Ben snorts. "Why do you even keep her if you don't like cats?"

"I *don't* keep her!" I exclaim. "Hecate doesn't live here; she just . . . showed up one day, honing her claws on my bedding and trying to flay me alive—and now she won't leave! I have been appointed my own personal demon."

"Well, perhaps if you were nicer to her, you might get along." Ben makes a face at me, relinquishing Hecate to the floor. Then, standing, he begins fastening the buttons on his doublet. "Now get up, wash your face, and shake off some of that road dust. You look like a plow horse, and I shall be embarrassed to have you seen with me."

"Seen with you?" My thoughts are murky with fatigue, but I'm certain he's just started a conversation in the middle. "Ben, what are you talking about?"

"I have some important business in the city today, for which I require a chaperone." He smiles at me deviously. "As you're aware, my father is to be married in six weeks' time, and he has instructed me to have some 'suitable attire' made for the occasion. To that end . . ." With a flourish and a grin, he produces a bulging coin purse from his belt, swinging it like a pendulum. "He has bestowed upon me a rather obscene amount of money!"

"Oh no." It is all I can think to say.

"He expects me to hire one of Verona's finest tailors and

commission a whole new costume to wear on his blessed day; but *I*, smart thinker that I am, have found a man willing to do the same work for less than half the price—leaving *us* a more than ample sum to spend on a day of good food and better ale!"

"You plan to swindle your father by entrusting a cut-rate clothier not to swindle you in turn?" When Ben replies only with an eager nod, I pinch the bridge of my nose. "Listen, as much as I'd love to be involved in this doomed conspiracy, I really—"

"Did I mention that Mercutio might join us?"

I freeze in the middle of my sentence. "Oh. He . . . he might?"

"I thought that would get your attention." His tone is dry, but I read a dozen or more meanings into his statement before he continues, "Yes, *really*. You know, he's not a celebrity, Romeo, no matter how much you worship him. He's just an ordinary person, like the rest of us. Only with much worse table manners."

"I do not 'worship' him!" I protest, heat flooding into my face.

"You do." My cousin shrugs into his coat and gives me a stubborn look. "You always have! Even when we were little, it was always, 'Mercutio *this*' and 'Mercutio *that*.' As if he was the friend you actually wanted and I was the one you had to tolerate."

My heartbeat slows back down as I realize that we are talking more about my cousin's ego than we are about me. "Don't be silly, Ben. Of course I admire Mercutio—despite his bad table manners—but you are my favorite relation, and always will be."

"I'm your *only* relation within a two-days' journey that isn't either ten years older or ten years younger than you," he points out in a surly grumble, "but I accept your apology. Now change into something less filthy than those rags. We have a lot of establishments to visit today, and my tailor won't remain sober for very long."

With a self-pitying groan, I turn to my armoire. "Oh, all right, *fine*. Maybe if I'm lucky, your drunken tailor will sew your mouth shut."

"If you were lucky, you'd have been the one born with my devastating good looks."

As I shake out my cloak and change my admittedly grubby hose, we trade a few more barbs in the perpetual battle of wits neither of us is ever going to win; and by the time we leave my chambers, I have gotten him to forget the reason he sneaked into them in the first place.

2

Any optimism I feel, however, does not even last the trip to the front door of my home. We're only halfway across the central courtyard when my frighteningly stealthy mother appears without warning, bursting from the shadowed loggia that leads to the parlor. I actually yelp a little.

"Romeo? Where are you off to so early?" She frowns, staring at me like she expects to find some guilty confession written across my face. I'm twice as glad now that I risked life and limb on those ivy vines, because it feels almost as if she's been lying in wait for me. "You're not going hunting, are you? That would last all day, and I need you to carry some letters into the city for me. They're terribly important, and these new servants can't be—"

"Good morrow, Aunt Elisabetta," Ben interrupts her with a dazzling grin, making me twice as grateful that he's here. He's always been my mother's favorite nephew. "How wonderful that you're up! I was afraid I wouldn't see you."

"Benvolio!" My mother's pinched expression smooths instantly into a delighted smile. "I didn't even notice you at first. What brings you out this way before the bells have even struck Prime? And, Romeo, why didn't you tell me we were to expect—"

"I'm afraid I rather surprised him with my company," Ben says, taking her hand and bowing over it in an exaggerated show of grace. "My father is set to remarry at the end of next month, and I'm afraid I need help having the proper vestments made, so I thought of Romeo. Who knows fabric and clothing better than a Montague?"

"Oh yes." And just like that, my mother's expression pinches again. "I forgot about your father's upcoming venture. I do hope it's a success."

Her smile is tart enough to make my own mouth pucker. She didn't like Ben's father—a fact she does not bother to keep secret—never believing him quite good enough for her youngest sister, Caterina. And even though her sister died in childbirth, some seventeen years ago, she still sees this new marriage as an act of infidelity.

"I'll be sure to pass along your sentiments," my cousin says, taking me by the arm and maneuvering past her. "But we had better be going. The day awaits!"

"How long do you think you'll be?" Mother regains her composure instantly, falling into step behind us as we hurry over the paving stones. "It's vital that my correspondence goes to the city today, and—"

"Unfortunately, I suspect it will take some time," Ben interrupts again, moving faster. "There are so many decisions to be made, and I'm such a dunce about these things. Besides, my father is insisting that I attend some awful ceremony today at the courthouse, and I absolutely cannot go alone." With a sigh of tremendous long-suffering, he continues, "These ridiculous fetes are invariably swarming with highborn girls on the hunt for a husband, and I will need someone to help keep me out of trouble!"

If he knows nothing else, Ben at least knows how to speak to his audience; in a heartbeat, my mother's attitude shifts. "Well. I suppose I can spare Romeo for the afternoon. Heaven knows it would do him some good to attend a party once in a while with some of the eligible young ladies of our fair city. You know, when I was your age, I was already two years married and—"

"—and heavy with your first child, yes, we know." I try to temper my impatience. "But I'm still younger than Father was when he first met you. Perhaps I take after him."

"Yes, well. Perhaps." She huffs out a discontented breath. "It's different for men, of course. There's no hourglass waiting to run out on you, and you may take all the time you like to grow up and settle down."

"Growing up is a waste of time," Ben interjects flatly, "and our bones shall have an eternity to settle after they're laid to rest. Men like Romeo and I are meant to lead exciting lives, Aunt Elisabetta! Besides, who shall keep me from gambling away my money and fighting in taverns if my cousin abandons me for a wife?"

"You jest far too much, Nephew!" My mother wags a finger at him. "There is more to an exciting life than just games of chance and broken ribs, and you can't remain a young bachelor forever." To me, she adds, "And are such cheap thrills truly more

16

rewarding than giving your poor mother a grandchild before she dies?"

"You are going to outlive us all, and you know it," I reply, eager to cut off that thought. "Besides, I've yet to meet a girl who can hold my interest for more than a season, let alone one I wish to be the mother of my children!"

"It can happen faster than you imagine, my darling," she says, almost fondly. "And better that it happens now, with a young lady of appropriate standing, than if your father elects to make the decision for you."

This is not advice but a warning, and a quick, clammy wave of panic rolls through me. Yet another aspect of my future that I won't be consulted on, a looming choice that won't really be *my* choice at all. I've always known I would be married someday, and always envisioned that stage of my future as an oil portrait: me, looking distinguished, standing with an elegant bride, surrounded by our children. But that future has always felt a long way off, and the woman in my imagining was always hazy and indistinct.

Now the future is coming at me a little faster with every passing day, and I *still* cannot make the bride in that imaginary portrait take on recognizable features. There are plenty of ladies in Verona whose company I enjoy well enough, but not one with whom I can imagine sharing the sort of life, the sort of confidences, my parents share with each other. Their own marriage was arranged—they were practically strangers when they wed—and what affection they share today was bought with years of mutual negotiation.

But what if I'm not built for the same sort of work?

Benvolio talks about girls the way I try to talk to *him* about sunlight—how magical it is, how undefinable, how exquisitely beautiful in all its permutations; at any given time, he is pursuing multiple paramours, and each one is uniquely alluring, uniquely irresistible. But I have never felt that way about any girl. *Why have I never felt that way?*

"Fear not, Aunt Elisabetta," Ben says, shoving me ahead of him into the grand entrance hall. His manner is still just as suave as ever, but I know him well enough to sense his growing impatience. "There will be heaps of delightful and *appropriate* young ladies at the courthouse, and I shall see to it that Romeo is buried beneath them all."

When we're outside again, the morning sky painted bright and decorated with birds, I draw as much fresh air into my lungs as I can. Heat is already gathering in these early hours, warming the golden dust under our feet and drawing a heady, resinous scent from the cypress trees that line the road. I try to let it fill me, to chase away my worries. But there is a sour feeling in my gut, a grim underside to all my thoughts, and it won't be washed clean that easily.

"If Aunt Elisabetta has her way," Benvolio murmurs under his breath as we trudge down the lane, "you will be strapped to your marriage bed for the convenience of producing grandchildren."

"If she had her way, I'd have been married for some three years already." A dull ache has begun to form in my head. "The instant my fourteenth year began, she was pestering my father to seek a match for me."

18

"This world is terribly unfair." Ben shakes his head in frustration. "Your mother is practically *begging* you to woo as many beautiful girls as you possibly can, while my father has all but threatened to castrate me if I don't stop! There is no justice."

"My mother does not care if they are beautiful, or if I have any interest in them; she cares only if they are eligible and of a proper station," I point out wearily. "She wants me to find a wife, not pleasure. If I carried on with girls the way you do, she would be just as tyrannical about it as your father."

"She has given you license to be licentious, and you are sulking about it." He shakes his head again. "Honestly, Romeo, sometimes it is nearly impossible to understand you."

I swallow any answer I might give to this, and feel that grim underside expanding. Although Benvolio is possibly my closest friend, there are still so many ways in which we seem to talk and think at cross-purposes—and, lately, those instances have become more and more frequent.

We were seven the first time Ben fell in love, with a girl who got mad at him for chasing pigeons in the piazza. For weeks, she was the only thing he could talk about. Her shiny hair, the way her eyes flashed when she'd shouted at him—he was infatuated.

By the time he was thirteen, he had a new infatuation every week, one girl after another capturing his attention. At first, I assumed his perpetual frenzy of desire was the result of some overactive glands, but then the same syndrome began to spread through all our friends. It was an epidemic of girl-madness, and somehow I seemed to be the only one who was immune.

But at the same time, I was starting to have a lot of feelings—

confusing, intense, and unignorable feelings—that I didn't completely understand.

And most of them had to do with our good friend Mercutio.

Two years older than me, and the son of a distinguished judge, he was the most remarkable boy I knew. Taller and stronger than the rest of us, smarter and more daring, funnier and more charming, more interesting, more *present*, somehow. Certainly, he was the most handsome of us. There wasn't another person in Verona, boy or man or otherwise, who seemed as good-looking as Mercutio.

I was desperate to impress him, to be his favorite, to gain his respect. I wanted to *be* him, and I used to practice all his familiar gestures and expressions at home in the mirror. In my fantasies, I would wake up to find myself transformed—not into a copy of Mercutio, exactly, but maybe into someone he would recognize as his equal.

And then one night I dreamed that Mercutio kissed me.

I had awoken with a start, hot and cold all over at once. What I had conjured in my sleep was no casual press of lip to cheek, either; it was a true kiss, performed with the same passion Mercutio often spoke of when telling us about his romantic exploits with girls. The dream throbbed in my memory, frightening and exciting all at once, and every time I let myself revisit it, warmth would flood my stomach and pressure would build in my groin.

It was the moment I began to realize that something about me was different.

My condition is not unheard of. For example, it's an open

secret that the prince's brother spends considerably less time with his wife than he does with the captain of his personal guard. But what a relative of Prince Escalus does in private is no one's business—not even his wife's. People will only speak of it obliquely, or in hushed whispers, and always, *always*, with a patina of scandal.

No matter how badly I wanted to know more about why I felt these things, and what they meant, and how I was supposed to make any sense of them, I was also instinctively aware that I should never ask about it directly. To seek information would be seen as a confession—and the prince is no brother of mine. Surely, there was a reason the truth had to be so hidden?

My parents expected me to marry and produce heirs; my friends expected me to chase girls and brag about my successes. And yet no girl made me half so weak in the knees as Mercutio did. And I had no idea what that truly meant—for me or about me.

"I hope you don't intend to be this quiet and broody all day long," Ben comments abruptly, and I glance up, realizing that we've already walked quite a distance while I was lost in thought. "Otherwise, I shall regret choosing you to share my ill-gotten gains. At least your mother was hungry for conversation."

"Sorry." Fighting back my thoughts, I yawn. "I'm a bit tired. I was meant to be taking a nap just now, but someone pestered me into going without it."

"The only thing I've pestered you into is an afternoon of delight and debauchery—and at my father's expense, no less." Gripping my shoulder, he shakes me a bit. "Romeo, you are my

21

best friend, and I love you dearly, but sometimes I think you hate to enjoy yourself!"

I grumble my response, hoping he'll take it for a bit of good-natured complaining—but the truth is that I'm not at all sure how to reply. *You are my best friend.* I've always felt the same way about him . . . but what would he say if he knew the reason I do not care to chase girls the way he does?

He's almost more interested in my romantic notions than my mother is, and every time he presses me about it—about whether I prefer blondes to brunettes, or tall girls to short ones, or this sister to that one—I have to dodge or deflect or lie. It has gradually created a distance between us that seems to spread wider each day.

"I will enjoy myself when you finally say something amusing," I retort, burying my troubled thoughts behind a cheeky facade—an act I've grown quite good at. "Or when this cut-rate tailor of yours gives you lockjaw from a rusty pin."

Ben smiles wickedly. "That will be a price well worth paying, so long as he also gives me the wool I need to fleece my father. Now stop dragging your feet! The longer it takes for us to get there, the less time we'll have for drinking."

With that, he takes off at a sprint up the lane, leaving me to scramble after him.

3

BENVOLIO'S TAILOR TURNS OUT TO BE JUST AS QUESTIONABLE AS I'D imagined, running his business out of squalid quarters in one of Verona's most disreputable neighborhoods. Everything smells faintly of mildew and spoiling food, there are stains on the walls, and the man is already half-drunk despite the early hour.

To his credit, though, the tailor does seem to know what he's doing. He takes his measurements quickly and with assurance, he asks all the appropriate questions, and our visit ends up being surprisingly short. When the agreements have been made and hands have been shaken, Ben leads me back into the street, grinning from ear to ear.

"That's my business sorted for the day. Now let's see to some mischief!" Slinging an arm around my neck, he says, "I've discovered a tavern near the Arena that has adequate beer and exceptional girls. I promise that your father won't approve of any of them."

"Are we going to be robbed?" I'm skirting the topic again, but it's also a serious question; nothing excites Benvolio more than being accepted as an equal by the criminal element, and he's embroiled us in more than one dire situation as a result.

"You need to *live* a little, Cousin," he urges me. "You heard your mother: One of these days, old Bernabó is going to pick a bride for you, and you'll be stuck with her for the rest of your life. If you're lucky, she'll be rich and quiet and decent to look at, but a gilded cage is still a cage." His expression is pointed. "Do you really think he's going to care about finding a girl you might actually *like*? Don't you want to choose at least one girl for yourself, while you still can?"

This is a trick question, deserving of a trick answer. "You make it sound like borrowing a shirt or deciding on a meal. How can you want to . . . *be* with someone you barely even know?"

Ben's answer is swift and decisive. "Familiarity breeds contempt. Witness how relieved I am to finally be free of Maddalena—whom I once loved deeply—because I eventually found her habit of laughing at her own jokes to be intolerable." He spreads his hands. "You'll have a boring wife for *years*, so you may as well have a little fun before the gossips of this town start minding your private affairs."

"You know very well I've already found a girl whose looks please me," I point out, seizing the opportunity to remind him of an elaborate fiction I've been designing. "Rosaline Morosini is the most enchanting girl in Verona—probably on this entire continent—and it is senseless for me to pursue girls who I know will only disappoint me in comparison."

It's possible I'm being a bit too effusive, but it's still true enough for him to believe. There's no denying that Rosaline is uncommonly beautiful—with luminous eyes, a pouting mouth, and warm brown skin that has apparently never known a single blemish. My cousin has himself remarked upon it more than once, so convincing him I am under her spell *should* be an easy task.

But regardless of what he thinks about Rosaline's appeal, Benvolio only groans. "Cousin—"

"I know you refuse to accept my feelings, because you think she's out of my reach, but I can't help it." I affect a manly scowl. "How am I supposed to feign interest in women who possess only a fraction of her loveliness? Her elegance? I'm besotted, Ben, and I have no desire to seek the companionship of weak substitutes."

He rolls his eyes. "The only reason I think Rosaline is out of your reach is because she *is*."

"You lack faith in me."

"She has taken a vow of chastity."

I wave this away. "No one is perfect."

In reality, however, it is thanks precisely to this very obstacle that Rosaline Morosini is perfect for me. So long as she remains determinedly chaste, she is my ideal woman: untouchable. I can pine for her as much as I choose, and no explanation will ever be required as to why I cannot successfully woo her.

Ben has not given up trying to talk me out of it. "She is not just out of *your* reach, she is out of *every* man's reach! You are fishing in an empty pond, and you are guaranteed to come away with an empty hook."

Trying not to sound too ridiculous, I counter, "How can you gaze upon perfection and be satisfied with anything less?"

Ben is quiet for a moment. "I know you think of me as some debauched, girl-mad satyr, but I actually do understand what it means to desire someone special, Cousin."

His solemn tone catches me by surprise. "I didn't mean to imply—"

"Yes, you did, but it's all right." He laughs a little, although he doesn't look at me. "All girls are special in their own way, and I suppose it's just easy to desire them—but it's not as if I wish to be a bachelor forever. Someday, I'm going to be a father, you know? And I hope my future bride, whoever she may be, is someone fascinating."

"That's what I'm saying as well," I tell him meekly, because I'm aware that we're not saying the same thing at all.

"Rosaline will never be yours," he counters bluntly. "Unless her father forces her to recant her oath so she can be married away, there is no future you may hope for." With a heavy sigh, he adds, "This is not a torch worth bearing, Romeo. And someday very soon, your father is going to marry *you* away, and you will lose much of the precious freedom you have to choose companions of your own."

The words fall on me like hail, sharp and bruising, because they are even truer than he knows. "I cannot simply undo my feelings, Ben."

"No one is asking you to!" He thumps my back encouragingly. "The world is filled with girls; and although some of them may not measure up to Rosaline's beauty, you'll find plenty who exceed her in charm and liveliness. There are, after all, more important qualities in a woman than the ability to look glamorous while moping at a dinner party."

"You know that is an unfair assessment of her! She does not simply *mope* at dinner parties." I struggle with a comeback, though—and not only because he actually does have something of a point. In the end, I decide to be honest. "You will not find a woman who holds more appeal for me than Rosaline. I guarantee you that much."

"That's a bet I'm happy to take," he answers. Too late, I realize I've somehow said the wrong thing after all. "Give me one month—during which you will actually go places with me, and smile, and let me introduce you around—and I am certain I can find a girl who will make you forget about Rosaline. If you still think she is the only decent woman in Verona at the end of it, I shall give up and leave you alone."

In spite of myself, I hesitate. My immediate instinct is to treat his offer as a bad joke, to push it aside and distract him with something else . . . but it is impossible to resist that final remark.

Arching a brow, I clarify, "Forever?"

"Yes, yes. I will leave you alone about it forever," he vows theatrically. "I'll never concern myself about your perpetual, brooding loneliness ever again."

I ignore his sarcasm, aware that this is one devil's bargain I cannot afford to decline. As reluctant as I am to spend an entire month flirting with girls to appease my cousin, while simultaneously avoiding any potentiality of an actual romantic entanglement, it may be the shortest—perhaps even the *only*—road to a future free of this pressure for good.

What I want more than anything is for Benvolio to stop concerning himself with my lack of interest in girls, and if I must commit the next few weeks to a more enthusiastic charade in order to achieve it, it's a price worth paying. "You have a deal."

"I'm offering to throw the prettiest and sweetest-tempered girls in Verona at your feet, and you act as if you're doing *me* the favor." Ben tosses his hands up and lets them drop. "Sometimes I truly struggle to understand you, Cousin."

As I turn up one of the alleys that lead to the heart of the city, he suddenly grabs my arm and pulls me back. "Not that way. We'll go to where the bridge crosses by San Fermo, and then cut through from there."

"Are you sure?" I wrinkle my nose, and when he says nothing, I press him. "Didn't you say this tavern of yours is close to the Arena? It is barely five minutes in that direction, but if we walk all the way to San Fermo—"

"It will make us that much thirstier for cheap ale," Ben says, cutting me off and dragging me away from the sensible shortcut and toward the avenue along the embankment. "Trust me, you'll be glad we took the longer journey. That grubby little street you were about to stumble down is rather overrun these days with rats and Capulets—but I repeat myself."

"Capulets?" I echo. "What are you talking about? None of them live anywhere near this part of the city."

"Oh, none of them are living here, but they've claimed this quarter just the same." He tosses a wary glance over his shoulder as a pushcart trundles by, wooden wheels grinding against the cobbles. "See for yourself."

When I look back, it is just as three figures emerge from the mouth of the alley, daggers sheathed at their hips. As they lean up against the walls on either side of the passageway's entrance, like sentries taking up their post, I recognize them immediately: Venzi, Arrone, and Galvano—three of the Capulets' most quarrelsome representatives. Their manner is lazy, but menace hangs in the air, and a frisson of nervous apprehension travels the length of my spine.

"Two weeks ago, Jacopo went down that very street to meet a lady friend, and he was set upon by Tybalt and some of his boys," Ben continues, hastening me along at a brisker clip. "They told him, 'Montagues aren't welcome south of Via de Mezzo,' and left him bleeding in the gutter."

"Jacopo?" I repeat, a bit dumbfounded. Jacopo Priuli, only eight years our senior, was a clerk at my father's warehouse—not a Montague at all, except perhaps by association. "No one told me he was attacked! Why am I just hearing of this now?"

"Well, you've had your head somewhat in the clouds of late." Ben's accusatory undertone is hard to miss. "It's impossible to tell you things when no one can find you."

"This is absurd!" I ignore him, sticking to the safer argument. "The Capulets have San Zeno, we have San Pietro, and everything in between is neutral ground—that's how it's always been. They can't just start claiming parts of the city as if it's theirs to divvy up!"

"And yet they've done just that," Ben counters drily. "If you

29

decide to challenge it, though, I'm sure Tybalt would be happy to let you explain your point to his fists. As for me, if I'm going to have my nose bloodied, I'd rather earn it by getting ferociously drunk and flirting with a married woman in front of her husband."

The Capulets are one of Verona's most powerful families; some even say they are *the* most powerful, much to my father's discontent. Every breath he draws is in service to enhancing the glory and prestige of the Montague name, and he hates to think he has competition. But Alboino Capulet, notorious for his public devoutness and patronage of the Church, is just as greedy for influence as he is for wealth. And he has *astonishing* wealth.

Verona may be our whole world, but it is barely large enough to contain both our lineages at once. The Capulets live in a villa near the San Zeno Basilica, to the east of the old Roman walls. We Montagues reside in the exclusive district of San Pietro, on the north side of the Adige River from the old city. Our paths never cross, if we can help it.

For generations, their bloodline and ours have battled—figuratively and literally—and to this day a bitter rivalry persists between our camp and theirs. According to my father, the Capulets have committed any number of heinous crimes against the Montagues throughout our shared history: theft, swindling, false accusations, slander, murder.

The feud began, as I have always heard it explained, when one of their ancestors—jealous of our family's good fortunes—cut down a Montague patriarch in cold blood, eager to supplant him. The Capulets, of course, tell the tale the other way around; and because there is no one left alive who remembers which version is closest to the truth, both accounts prosper to this day, and hatred's long shadow is cast upon the cradle of every new generation.

My father believes in the Capulets' innate villainy with a martyr's conviction, and he has drummed it into me that I am not to trust a one of them under any circumstances. And I suppose he'd be happy to know that, in fact, I don't. Although that is less because of the folklore he's handed down to me than it is because of my experiences with one Capulet in particular: Tybalt.

Alboino and his wife have a daughter, but as Lord Capulet's oldest nephew, there is no question that Tybalt is their favorite. Destined to be the next patriarch, he's also first in line to inherit the family's profitable business in trading furs, and he has spent his whole life believing this makes him untouchable. The same age as Mercutio, he is the most vicious person I've ever met—the quickest to throw a punch, and the last to hesitate on a violent impulse. When I put some thought to it, I have no trouble believing that he would breach the unwritten treaty that has demanded peaceful interactions within the city walls.

"Wait—so they just . . . *decide* that this quarter belongs to them, and that's it?" I protest. "We start taking the long way around, skulking in the shadows of our own city, and let them do as they please?"

"Exactly what solution do you propose?" Ben arches a brow.

"You're not going to convince Tybalt and his crew of ill-tempered minions that they're being unfair, and I'm pretty certain you're not suggesting we challenge them to fisticuffs. You hate fighting, and I'm approximately half Tybalt's size."

"There are laws against fighting inside the city," I point out, a little vexed by his attitude. We both carry knives of our own, of course, as do most of the men in Verona. But we have never had to draw them before—not on this side of the walls, at any rate. But if the Capulets are shedding Montague blood in the heart of town, it's a new and altogether alarming turn of events. "And that's my point. They *attacked* Jacopo, and evidently right out in the open! Why haven't they been reported to the prince's guard?"

"If Jacopo were to denounce Tybalt and his boys, he would need witnesses to back him up, and I believe you'll find there is a fresh plague of amnesia spreading through the city south of the Via de Mezzo." Resentment curdles Ben's tone. "Only a fool would risk crossing Alboino Capulet for the sake of a lowly warehouse clerk—and everyone in Verona knows what sort of retribution they could invite if they make an enemy of Tybalt."

"But . . ." Only I've got nothing else to say. The injustice of it all is infuriating, but it's also just one more grain of sand in the expanding desert of my troubles.

"It's the prince's fault," Ben mutters, glancing over his shoulder to be sure no one is close enough to overhear. "He should be standing up to them, but he's a coward. Or maybe an idealist. I don't know which is worse."

His boldness has me glancing around as well, but the

embankment is empty. It's a sunny day, the heat gradually climbing, and a sluggish breeze stirs up the thick green scent of the river. "He told my father that he refuses to take sides because he thinks the feud is childish, and that there's no reason for 'ancient animosities' to 'run our lives.'"

"'*Ancient animosities.*'" Benvolio gives a scornful laugh. "As if the Capulets don't make a point of refreshing those animosities once or twice a day. The true reason Escalus refuses to take sides is because he's afraid of being put at a political disadvantage." His cheeks color. "The denizens of Via de Mezzo aren't the only Veronese afraid of getting on Alboino's bad side. If Tiberius were still in charge . . ."

He may simply be repeating something he heard his parents say, but that doesn't mean he's wrong. Prince Tiberius was a committed ally to the Montagues, having married a distant cousin of my father's, and his loyalty to our bloodline removed any possible question as to who Verona's leading family was. But when he unexpectedly died three years ago, the crown passed to his younger brother Escalus—who is unmarried, unaffiliated, and uninterested in acting as an arbiter.

Whether born of idealism or cowardice, his indifference to our ongoing hostilities creates an imbalance in Verona's power structure. And, clearly, Tybalt sees the lack of obvious favoritism as an opportunity to tip the scales in the Capulets' favor.

When we at last reach the bridge that spans the river at the Church of San Fermo, I glance across it, to the district of Campo Marzio on the other side. From here, the far bank is nothing but green trees and rust-colored rooftops. Somewhere beyond it spreads the lengthy and formidable stone wall that protects our city—the same wall that wraps around San Pietro, San Zeno, and the old city, and holds us all in an embrace that's growing far too tight for comfort.

Lately, everywhere I look all I can see is another wall, another limit. For just a moment, I can't seem to breathe. Staring across the bridge, down a lazy avenue that leads nowhere, I can think of nothing besides the dwindling scope of my future. Verona is shrinking, my days to govern my own life running swiftly out, and every door available to me merely opens onto four more walls.

Beside me, Ben turns away from the bridge, heading into the city again. After a moment, I unstick my feet and follow after him—down yet another path that ultimately leads to the same stone wall.

4

THE TAVERN BEN HAS CHOSEN TURNS OUT TO BE JUST AS DANK, dark, and questionable as I'd envisioned; but there is a lively atmosphere, and we both receive a boisterous welcome. The company is seedy but convivial, and I decide I like the place well enough.

As we make our way to a free table, ruddy-faced men clap Ben on the back and greet him by name, and I'm struck anew by how easily my cousin manages to make friends. The ale begins to flow the second he takes his seat—on top of the table, because it allows him the best opportunity to see and be seen—and within minutes he has launched into a performance that commands the attention of everyone around us. First, a little flirting with the barmaid; then, a bit of, "Did I ever tell you about the time . . . ?"; and finally, as a full tankard of beer appears in his hand, he is off on a wild tale that has the room in his thrall.

"And there the cook stands," he says as he approaches the climax of his first soliloquy, "with a basket of broken crockery in one hand and my favorite rock in the other, and she has the flames of hell in her eyes!" His voice jumping two octaves, he does a scratchy impersonation of the woman. "'*Which of you is responsible for this?*'"

"You're telling the story wrong!" I interrupt him at last, unable to abide his inaccuracies a moment longer. For once, he has chosen to describe something that actually happened, and yet he still muddles all the facts—it is very like him.

"I never tell my stories wrong," he rebuts confidently. "If there is a discrepancy, then it is history that is in error, not me."

I cannot help but laugh. "That is not at all how it works!"

He turns back to the room. "In any event, the cook stands there with my trusty rock—the one I had carved my initials into—and says, '*Which of you is responsible for this?*'" For a heartbeat, the tavern is silent as Ben leads them right back to the edge of his story. "And as I sit there, my slingshot still gripped in my trembling fist, I muster my most innocent look and reply, '*Your house must have a ghost!*'"

The room roars with laughter, and another tankard of beer settles on the table beside my cousin—the second he has been served without having to pay, I notice—but I have reached the end of my wits. "No, no, no; all of that is incorrect!"

Ben merely shrugs. "If I have improved on any of the details, it is only because they weren't right to begin with."

"To begin with," I counter, "she was not a cook—she was a nurse. *My* nurse, as it happens." Rising to my feet, I lean across the table. "And I believe your exact words were, 'He *told me it was a ghost.*' And you were pointing at *me*!"

There is a moment as Ben's audience puts these new pieces together, and then they roar with laughter again. But my cousin is unperturbed. When the merriment subsides again, he tosses his hands. "See? My version was better after all."

There is still more laughter, sympathetic hands pat me on the back and shoulder, and a tankard full of ale slides into place before me, unbidden—and, believe it or not, it is only at this point that I realize just how skillfully my cousin has manipulated me.

With very little effort, he has finagled me into being the center of attention—a source of fresh entertainment for the regular clientele, who have long since memorized one another's most interesting stories. Just like that, I'm the most popular person in the room, being coaxed and begged and urged to tell more tales of Ben's outlandish antics; and whenever I get close to the end of one account, my cousin prompts me to tell another.

It doesn't escape my notice that there are plenty of girls in my steadily growing audience, and that all of them live up to Ben's promise of beauty and spirit. The men are all eager to wring me dry of every embarrassing, compromising, or off-color tale I have to tell, but these girls are clearly measuring me for a different sort of entertainment. It makes me terribly uneasy.

It's not as if I'm unused to situations such as this. Every time my parents host a ball or a garden party, I am surrounded by proper young ladies I'm expected to impress, and I've become expert at finessing my way through those conversations. At flirting casually, but never seriously—creating a painstaking ambiguousness that's impossible to openly question by the unwritten rules of our social tier's sense of propriety.

But the ladies at this inn, with their forthright gazes and

ostentatious charms, are not like the girls I'm accustomed to. There is nothing unassuming about them, and they are not under the sway of any sense of artificial "respectability" that I might otherwise rely upon to maintain a comfortable distance.

"Tell them the story of how you once mistook a tureen of chicken broth for a chamber pot," Benvolio suggests, his face alight with impish glee.

"I believe you've just told it for me, Cousin." Setting my tankard down, I glance at the rear door of the inn, sunlight leaking through around its edges, and get an idea. "In fact, I could use that tureen now—I need to go make some room in my body for a little more ale. Don't gossip about me while I'm gone!"

Before I can be waylaid, I duck out of the crowd, scuttle across the tavern, and slip through the door into the narrow passage that cuts along the inn's western side. The air is dusty and hot, and the smell of a nearby latrine spoils whatever else is left to enjoy. Nonetheless I shut my eyes, feeling my shoulders loosen and the knot in my chest unravel. The tranquility here is worth the price my various senses have to pay.

I didn't always feel like this—relieved to get away from my best friend, from the escalating pressures that come with a roomful of people. It wasn't even very long ago that I actually looked forward to making new acquaintances. Once upon a time, I reveled in my popularity, even if much of it was unearned. After all, it's hard not to be popular in Verona when your last name is Montague. But still, I loved how it made me feel to have people taking an interest in me, wanting to know me.

But that was then, and the mask I'm wearing now is one I'm

not sure it's safe to take off anywhere. I have to avoid my parents' inquisitiveness, I have to avoid my cousin's relentless if well-meaning entreaties about my love life, and I have to avoid—by any means necessary—a situation where I must explain to a girl why I do not reciprocate her affections. There are precious few tactful ways of saying, "I do not find you attractive," and I have already used *all of them*.

I miss when an afternoon like this was easy and fun—when I didn't get nervous at the sight of Benvolio, the one person I've always been able to count on. And I don't know how to deal with the fact that the problem is only growing more acute. Part of me is almost hoping my father will choose a bride for me soon, so that I may be done with dreading it, and done with my cousin's persistent meddling.

When I open my eyes again, I could swear the alley has gotten smaller—that all of Verona is finally closing in.

I take my time at relieving myself, extending the silence of the alley as long as I can, trying to think of what I'll say when I'm back inside. And when I can dawdle no longer, I start back for the door to the inn . . . and stop short when I discover a slim figure huddled on the meager doorstep. A boy of only about twelve or thirteen sits there as though he's been abandoned, his knees tucked together, his face blotchy with frustrated tears, clutching a hefty leather satchel that rests in the dust beside him.

"I don't mean to bother you," I begin delicately, unsure what tone to strike but certain I'm using the wrong one. Having no siblings has left me utterly incompetent at dealing with anyone much younger than I am. "Is everything okay? You seem upset."

He scrambles to his feet, clearly embarrassed. "I'm all right. Um . . . sir."

The lie is palpable, but just in case I missed it, he sniffles loudly and turns away—hoping I won't notice as he swipes at his eyes. He's too clean to be one of the orphans who beg in the piazza, but he has such a desperate aspect about him, I hazard, "Are you lost?"

"Yes." He takes a sharp breath. "Maybe." His face crumples again. "I'm not sure."

As he begins to sob—making the most wretched squeaking sounds into his hands—I am frozen in horror. Fortunately, the door bursts open at that exact moment, startling both me and the boy into glancing up, and Benvolio leans into the alley.

"Oh, *there* you are. I was beginning to think you'd ducked out on me." His gaze moves to the boy with the satchel, and he does a double take. "*Paolo?*"

Relief suffuses the boy's face, and I blink my surprise at Ben. "You know him?"

"This is Paolo Grassi. His mother does our washing." My cousin steps into the passage, letting the door bang shut behind him, and puts his hand on the boy's narrow shoulder. "What on earth are you doing out here?"

"I was looking for someone." Paolo gestures defeatedly at the tavern, shaking his head. "But he isn't here. I was so sure . . ."

"Who are you looking for?"

Paolo puffs out his chest a bit. "Giovanni da Peraga. He is a famous condottiere from Lombardy, whose soldiers aided the Milanese forces in the Battle of Parabiago."

The way he says this last bit, it's clear he's repeating something he's overheard; and yet the condottieri—military captains, in command of highly skilled, independent armies—*are* a very distinguished and elite class of men. Ben's eyebrows creep toward his hairline. "I am almost afraid to ask what need you have for a band of mercenary fighters. Or perhaps your mother is looking to eradicate her competition among the laundresses of Verona?"

"I have gotten a job," Paolo returns, puffing out his chest even more. "I'm serving as a page for a prestigious household now, and they've tasked me with making some important deliveries, but . . ." His voice hitches and cuts off, tears welling up in his eyes once again. "I can't find any of the people on the list. It took me more than an hour just to locate this inn, and yet the landlord insists that Giovanni da Peraga isn't a guest here! I don't know what to do." More tears rolling, he whimpers, "I cannot afford to lose this position."

"Well, don't weep, man, it will only cost you valuable moisture!" Ben looks Paolo in the eye encouragingly. "Show me this list of yours—maybe I can help." Dully, the boy nods and then produces a bit of folded parchment from his bag, which Ben examines with a doubtful expression. "I don't mean to question you, but . . . it seems as though all the addresses are written out right here next to the names of those invited."

Turning first pink and then bright red, Paolo mumbles, "I cannot read."

"Oh." Ben takes this in. "Oh! Well." He breaks into his brightest and most disarming smile, clapping Paolo on the shoulder with so much force the boy nearly topples over. "Lucky for you our paths happened to cross today, because I'll bet that me and my cousin can help you track down every person here! For instance, it looks like this da Peraga character is staying at an inn on Vicolo Alberti, while *this* inn is on Via Alberico."

Paolo's face remains scarlet. "That sounds exactly the same."

"Vicolo Alberti is where they hold the fish market," I supply, trying to be helpful. "There's a bust of Prince Tiberius on the corner near the inn."

"Oh." Paolo frowns. "I know where that is. Why didn't they just say all that?"

"So that's this one." Ben flicks the page with his finger. "And then come Ugolino Natale and his wife—and their address is in San Pietro, where Romeo lives!"

"Whatever you're meant to deliver, you might as well let me take care of it for you," I say. "I can practically see the Natale villa from my home."

"They are invitations," Paolo explains, the color already subsiding in his face as we take charge of his troubles. "There's to be a masquerade, and they've arranged for musicians and peacocks and everything."

I appraise the boy with new eyes. There are some peacocks in the prince's royal menagerie, and the occasional boat comes down the Adige with exotic creatures for sale, but to populate a private estate with rare birds for the sake of a party? That meant considerable wealth. "This sounds like a rather grand event."

"The grandest of the season," Paolo replies stoutly. "There shall be nobles in attendance."

"How exciting." Benvolio's comment comes without any

particular emotion, his attention fully wrapped up in Paolo's list. "This *does* seem to be a very . . . comprehensive index of Verona's upper crust. Count Anselmo, Count Paris, the lady widow of Antonio Vitruvio, Lucio and Helena Azzone . . . oh, and look at this, Cousin!" His expression brightens with mischief. "The fair Rosaline is to attend, along with her father and brother."

"How exciting," I reply, my voice thick with wariness.

"She is just about the fairest girl in all Verona, you know," Ben adds for Paolo's benefit, to which the boy merely shrugs. "Have you ever set eyes on her? She has our Romeo here somewhat bewitched—"

"Who else is on the list?" I ask brusquely, not eager to return to this subject again. "The Azzones live south of the old Roman wall, not far from the Cittadella."

Ben turns back to the page, his brow furrowing. "Hmm."

"What is it?"

"Mercutio and Valentine are to be invited as well," he remarks disinterestedly, turning the sheet over to inspect the back side, although it appears to be blank. "And their family is scarcely remembered anymore by the sort who can afford peacocks. How strange."

"Valentine?" It's a name I haven't heard in years, and it takes me by surprise. "Mercutio's brother, Valentine? Is he not still living in Vicenza somewhere?"

"No, Cousin." Ben turns an exasperated frown my way. "Mercutio sent for him last month, when he finally got his apprenticeship and could afford a place with enough room for both of them. It's all he could talk about for weeks!" Shaking his head, he gives the list yet another once-over, grumbling under his breath, "Honestly, where have you *been*?"

Talking to a monk, I almost tell him.

"It'll be nice to see Valentine again," I manage instead, a little weakly. "I've thought of him from time to time."

Valentine is a year younger than us, one of Mercutio's half-dozen siblings—who, until the year Ben and I turned fourteen, were all packed together under the same comparatively tiny roof. When their father died of a sudden illness that winter, seven mouths very quickly became too many to feed; when some well-off relatives in Vicenza agreed to take in thirteen-year-old Valentine, he was shipped off overnight—just like that, bag and baggage—to live with near strangers in a city he'd never seen before. Aside from a letter or two in the early days, we'd heard nothing from him ever since.

We all missed him, of course, but Mercutio had been utterly heartbroken. It was, I think, the only time I've ever seen him cry.

"Evidently, *everyone* has been thinking of him. He's scarcely been back in the city for a fortnight, and already he's being asked to attend the 'grandest event of the season!'" An uncomfortable laugh comes out of him. "Near as I can tell, the only people in Verona who *aren't* invited to this expensive little soiree are you and me."

He thrusts the page in my direction, and at a glance, it's easy enough to see that the list bears out his statement: Almost all of Verona's luminaries and notable figures are represented—with the exception of anyone connected to the Montague dynasty.

With a bad taste in my mouth, I ask Paolo, "Exactly which household is throwing this masquerade, did you say?"

The boy turns scarlet. "It's Lord and Lady Capulet—but I need this job, Ben, you don't understand! They're paying me well, and without it—"

"Oh, calm down." Benvolio waves the boy's burgeoning tears into submission. "I'm not angry, for goodness' sake. Just because you're doing the bidding of our mortal enemies doesn't mean I hold it against you. Or because you're off inviting people to a sumptuous party with food and wine and peacocks, from which we are specifically excluded, and where I'm sure there will be numerous beautiful girls I've never—"

"Ben."

"The Capulets are throwing the event of the season, Romeo!" He looks up at me, and there's a canny glint in his eyes I long ago learned to recognize—and fear. "All our dearest friends and acquaintances will be there, along with nearly every young lady of distinction who lives anywhere between Milan and Venice, including your precious Rosaline! Isn't that just *grand*?"

"*Ben*." I don't know exactly what's cooking in his thoughts, but I'm sure I'm not going to like it. This particular expression of his always precedes a catastrophe.

"Cousin." He smiles beatifically. "I've just had the most wonderfully terrible idea."

5

SCARCELY TWO WEEKS LATER, UNDER COVER OF NIGHT, BENVOLIO and I are venturing cautiously into the San Zeno district against my better judgment. The moon is full and the sky is clear, the air scented with jasmine where we walk a narrow lane bordered by a high stone wall. It's beautiful here, the stars bright and the crickets chirring, and yet I'm hardly in the mood to enjoy it. My misgivings are doubling with each step we take.

"I cannot believe I let you convince me to infiltrate a party thrown by the *Capulets*," I finally hiss, irrationally afraid of being overheard. There is no one out here but us and the insects, and yet I feel as though I've already been caught.

"*I* cannot believe you have lately grown so fatally allergic to having a good time," Ben grouses back. "You used to love sneaking into parties uninvited, and seeing how much wine we could drink before we got caught!"

"Yes, when I was thirteen, and the worst that would happen is we would be scolded by an angry footman." I thrust my hands out at the countryside. "Tybalt and his crew are willing to attack anyone who wanders into his imaginary territory if they even *smell* of Montague! What will he do when we waltz into his uncle's home and start making ourselves comfortable? What do you think *Alboino Capulet* will do?"

Ben shrugs, unbothered. "Nothing."

"*Nothing?*" I repeat, my tone just shy of a screech. "Cousin—"

"To begin with, this is a masquerade." He gestures at my attire. "As long as you keep your disguise on and your wits about you, no one will ever know who you really are."

I'm dressed as a shepherd—one of the few costumes I could devise on short notice—with a porcelain volto mask that will cover my entire face. It still somehow does not feel like enough.

"For another thing," Ben continues, "this is not just some family affair—there will be kin of Prince Escalus at this party. Even Tybalt cannot be foolish enough to do violence right in front of them, with his uncle's reputation on the line. And the same goes for old Alboino. He cares far too much about his public image to let Verona's aristocracy see him acting on an old grudge against two innocent boys."

"That all sounds very reasonable, Ben." I let out a nervous breath. "But you are putting a rather great amount of trust in people who openly despise us."

"Romeo." Ben turns to me, and there's some expression on his face I've never seen before: a mixture of vexation, sadness, and exhaustion. "What's happened to you? You used to live for this sort of mischief, but lately it's as if you don't want to do *anything*. You avoid me, you make up excuses, and I have to negotiate with you like an ambassador forging a peace treaty just to get you to have a little fun!"

I open my mouth and then close it again, warmth pouring into my face. His assessment hews far too close to the bone, and I don't know how to respond—because he isn't wrong. The only reason I'm even with him on this misguided escapade tonight is because, after I summarily rejected his first suggestion that we should trespass on the Capulets' party, he offered to restructure the terms of our regretful arrangement.

"You told me you'd let me see if I could find you a better match than Rosaline," he pointed out that afternoon in the heat-soaked alley, determi- nation sparking in his eyes. *"Well, there shall be no finer opportunity than this. She'll be there herself, and you can try your best to convince her to recant her vow of chastity; and if you don't succeed, there will be dozens of other girls around—and all of them from families your father will approve of!"*

"I don't want to deceive my way into a Capulet stronghold, and I defi- nitely *don't want to do it for the purposes of a wife hunt!"* I tried not to sound too panicked. *"How is my being a stowaway at a masquerade sup- posed to impress Rosaline, anyway?"*

"What will impress her is how you choose to speak to her, and maybe even how smoothly you dance—ladies love a man who is light on his feet." He rubs his hands together. *"Besides, what could impress her more than learning of the lengths you'll have gone to just for the chance to meet with her? You would do well to let her know you came despite being unwelcome; girls find that sort of thing wildly romantic!"*

Again, I hesitated, because this was a very good point . . . almost too *good. Rosaline struck me as someone far too sensible to be persuaded by reckless gestures; but Ben knew way more about this sort of thing than I did. What if she* did *find it wildly romantic? What if it changed her opinion—of both me*

48

and marriage? It would be just my luck to win her love by accident, and then have to figure my way out of that mess.

But after all the energy I put into convincing Benvolio that Rosaline holds my heart in her hands, what possible grounds could I invent to discount his reasoning?

Misreading my discomposed silence, Ben huffed out a breath. "Romeo, I am practically begging you to put aside your worries for one evening and go on an adventure. Instead of giving me a month to help you woo a girl, just give me this night—just this one. Please." He smiled hopefully. "Let's catch some trouble by the tail, the way we used to! Do your best to charm Rosaline, and then dance with five girls of my choosing. Only five, and I shall thereafter leave you to lonesomeness for good."

I hated the way he made it sound: like an ultimatum, or a lost cause. Like one last chance before he washed his hands of me. And yet, for all of that, I felt a sense of pure relief. Rather than a full month of dodging his attempts at arranging liaisons for me, I would only have to endure a single night of decorous flirtations—all beholden to a strict code of moral conduct I already knew how to exploit. In the end, it was hardly a choice at all.

"Very well," I'd said. "I'll do it."

Tonight, of course, as we get closer and closer to the Capulet villa, I am having second thoughts. And Ben, also of course, is making it impossible for me to explain myself in a way that does not make me seem tedious, whiny, or indifferent to his feelings.

"It isn't you I'm trying to avoid," I tell him, as honestly as I can. "It's just . . . sometimes the things my parents expect of me are more than I can manage, and I become . . . I don't know. *Crushed* under the weight of it all." Shrugging, my hands nervous where they grip the mask I'll be wearing tonight, I add, "It's difficult to enjoy myself when all I can think about is what my father will do if he catches me being the wrong kind of happy."

"And that's all the more reason we must have this adventure!" Ben exclaims, resolute—and not listening, either to the words I'm saying or to the meaning I'm trying to convey. "Your parents wish to drain you of your spirit, and you cannot let them. We are going to wring joy out of this night with our bare hands if it kills us!"

"Ben . . . ," I begin, but he stops me.

"You can't change whatever future your father has decided upon for you, but you can set whatever course you like in the meantime." Dressed as a soldier, wearing his own father's old uniform, he looks as though he means to encourage me into battle. "Remember when we sneaked into the reception for Magistrate Stornello's wedding? We both ate too much and drank too much, I knocked down a trellis trying to climb it, and you mistook the tureen for a chamber pot?" Eyes glowing, he says, "That was the best night of my life, Romeo. And I want us to have that again."

"Me too, but—"

And then he rounds on me, his expression so angry and heart-felt that it startles me into silence. "I have *missed* you, Cousin! We used to spend all our time together, but you've practically been a stranger to me since this past winter. I don't know where you spend your time, or who you spend it with; I don't know what you're thinking, because you make a point not to tell me; and you act as if a night of my company is a chore you must endure!" He shakes his head, frustrated, and I begin to sweat through my tunic. "Did I do something wrong? Have I somehow made you tired of me?"

"No, Ben!" I scramble for a reply, praying for a sudden lightning strike or an earthquake—anything to change the subject.

Naturally, I miss him, too, but I cannot say so without encouraging him further. I hate having to avoid him, and I hate that when we *do* see each other, I know him a little bit less than before. But avoiding him is easier than lying to him, than having to talk my way out of corners, having to inventory all my falsehoods so I don't contradict myself later.

It agonizes me to think that I have hurt his feelings, but there are no good choices to be made. Verona's walls will crush us all, in the end.

"I . . . I know I haven't been myself, and I'm sorry for that," I manage to tell him, "but I promise that I've not grown tired of you." Tossing a look at the empty lane behind us, winding all the way back to San Pietro, I mutter, "It is only that I've found it hard to be merry at all for a while now, and I know that makes me a burden when you wish nothing more than to have a good time. But I have missed you, too."

"Romeo, you are rather impossible sometimes." Ben looks down at his feet, shaking his head. "We don't have to always go carousing, you know. When you aren't in the mood for it, you

51

can simply tell me, and we could do something else. I might even go along with you on one of your artistic excursions. Provided you never tell anyone about it, of course," he adds hastily. Then, with a teasing grin, "After all, it is my duty as your friend and kin to bear you—no matter how much of a burden you might be."

"Oh, thank you," I tell him, although I cannot restrain a smile. The matter is complicated, but I am genuinely touched to know how much our friendship means to him. He disapproves of my hobby, and yet he'd be willing to indulge it in order to spend more time with me? Pressure builds in my chest, and I blink a fine mist out of my eyes.

For the first time, I wonder if Benvolio is someone I can trust with my secret.

It is then, as I am lost in thought, that the Capulet villa at last heaves into view. Sitting at the top of a pronounced rise, backed by the milky endlessness of the night sky, it sprawls across the horizon in stacked tiers. The silhouette of it is vast, lanterns glowing at every window and walkway, swaying on hooks and warming the moonlit stone. It's like a net of stars cast down on the hillside, and it takes my breath away.

Their home might be even grander than ours.

"Here, hold this," Ben says, thrusting his mask at me. Then, withdrawing a few steps, he takes a running start at the wall beside us—and leaps, grabbing the ledge at the top, his boots finding purchase among the jasmine vines. Hauling himself up, he leans back and stretches out his hand. "Okay, give me those and come on!"

Luckily, the wall only takes a small bite out of my shin, and then we're both dropping to the ground on the other side, where we find ourselves standing before a phalanx of olive trees that climb the hills toward the backside of the looming villa. The air is loamy and resinous, the grove planted in orderly rows, and I realize that we've been walking alongside the Capulets' property this whole time. Everything on this side of the wall is part of their estate.

Ben takes off through the trees, bright moonlight broken by the leaves into dappled patches, and I hurry after him in order to stay close. I'm panting when we finally make it to the top of the hill, where the olives end and extensive kitchen gardens begin, tidy beds of flourishing thyme, fennel, and rosemary scenting the night.

Ben stops me before I step out into the open, speaking in a harsh whisper. "The door to the laundry should be open and unattended, but we ought to stick to the trees for now. If anyone sees us, our night will be over before it starts."

He ties his mask into place, and with a little difficulty, I manage the same. Lord Capulet might hesitate to throw us out if our identities are exposed in front of his genteel guests, but if we're caught and recognized before we even make it onto the premises, no rules of public decorum will protect us.

As we stalk along the backside of the villa, where darkened balconies and empty arcades make it clear that the party is excluded from this part of the home, the air thickens with the fragrance of roasting onions, grilled fish, and venison on the spit. My stomach growls, and I suddenly hope that if we *are* thrown out, it isn't until I've had time to eat.

"There," Ben murmurs, pointing to a door at the foot of a shallow staircase bordered by rosebushes. It's one of several such doors along the rear wall, all of which are meant for the use of servants. Taking me by the arm, my cousin drags me from the safety of the trees at last, scurrying straight for what is apparently the laundry.

And we almost make it.

6

"WHAT ARE YOU DOING OUT HERE?" A STRIDENT VOICE DEMANDS, a figure lurching suddenly into view from behind a trellis covered with tomato vines. It's a woman, a scullion with a flushed face and a bucket of food scraps under her arm, and my heart lodges fast in my throat as she steps into our path. Ben and I exchange a mute glance, his expression lost to me behind his porcelain mask, and the woman continues, "Lord Capulet said no guests were to be permitted in the gardens tonight—you are supposed to remain inside!"

It is a moment before her words catch up with me, my blood a racing tumble of sparks. *We have been taken for guests already.*

With a humble bow, Ben answers her. "We're terribly sorry. We must have gotten turned around while looking for the courtyard, and wandered out here by mistake. If you could—"

"How can one miss the central courtyard?" the woman demands, becoming somehow even more upset. "And we were told that the young men would be on hand to guide guests away from the back of the villa. Has one of them left his post? We have over two dozen dishes to prepare, and we cannot do our work with people tramping about—"

"My lady," Ben begins deferentially, but he makes no headway.

"How did you end up out here? What part of the house were you in that there was no one to mind you?" The woman wipes her forehead. "Lord Capulet will need to know—"

"Dorothea!" An urgent voice interrupts her, coming from somewhere behind us, and the woman spins around with a jolt. Paolo stands in an open doorway, steam billowing around him, lit by the pulsing orange glow of a fire. "One of the kettles is boiling over."

"Oh, for heaven's sake, the broth!" The woman presses a hand to her temple and gives an agitated groan. "I need to tend to that, but these young men—"

"I'll see that they find their way back to the party," Paolo promises, his face unreadable in the half-light. Dorothea hesitates, giving us one last unhappy look, but then nods. Tossing the contents of her bucket into the midst of the tomato plants, she then gathers her skirts and stalks for the kitchen door. Before she disappears, however, she glances back. "See that his lordship is made aware that his guests are being left to wander freely through the house. Someone should lose his position for this!"

And then she is gone, and a silence falls over the garden, disturbed only by the culinary symphony of two dozen dishes being prepared in the bowels of the villa. Lifting his mask, Ben stares at Paolo in delight. "Well done, my friend! If it weren't for you, we'd be the ones fertilizing those tomatoes right now."

"You said you would be here more than ten minutes ago!" Paolo hisses in return, his cheeks pink. "If his lordship starts looking around, *I* am the only one missing from his post!"

"Then we've wasted all the time we have to spare." Ben doesn't even break a sweat. Tucking his mask back into place, he gestures ahead. "Lead the way, young sir."

"I am being serious." As he herds us toward the laundry, I notice how tense and pale Paolo looks. His hands are twitchy, and it takes him two tries to get the door unlatched. "My mother is counting on the money that Lord Capulet pays me! I cannot afford to be dismissed from this household."

"There is nothing to fear, Paolino. Dorothea has her hands too full to raise a stink, and we would never betray your trust." Benvolio puts on his most disarmingly charismatic tone, and I watch the boy fall under its power. "Besides, it's not as if we came to rob the place; we're only here to add life to what would otherwise be another boring society ball!"

"Do not make me wish it had stayed boring," Paolo retorts promptly, but the fire has gone out of his frustration. He is putty in Ben's hands, and my cousin knows it.

We creep through a maze of hallways, the air in the basement so humid from the kitchens and laundry that it is practically a membrane against my skin, and then up a cobwebbed staircase to another floor. Peeking around corners, Paolo hurries us into a salon that smells of dust and disuse, and then heaves a shaky sigh. There are two doors on the far wall, and through them I can already hear strains of music.

True to Dorothea's word, there are servants roaming the

back hallways, guiding people away from the rooms that are not open to the attending guests—including this salon; and so it is only when Paolo is convinced the coast is clear that we are led through one of the doors, down a short gallery, and into a truly grand ballroom at last.

My fears of being recognized and expelled diminish as I take a look around, my jaw slack behind my mask. This is no intimate gathering; there might be sixty people in this room alone, pressing flesh and comparing their lavish costumes. Candles backed by mirrors spill their light throughout the room, lending a tawny luster to marble and wood, and swags of emerald silk shimmer like oil where they hang from the balustrades. It is decadent and romantic, and we will be but two small fish in this great sea of revelers.

The party ranges from one room to the next, down hallways and galleries, the musicians fighting to be heard over the aggressive chatter of wealthy Veronese. In short order, I remember why I've always loved breaking the rules. Benvolio turns our anonymity into a game, devising a new accent and a new backstory for each person we encounter, and we improvise banter, conflicts, and détentes on the spot. Almost everyone here is known to me, some of their identities barely concealed behind masks made of lace or ribbon, and to keep them guessing is an unexpected thrill.

Here and there, I have to lift my mask in order to partake of the food and drink that circulates on trays borne by countless servants, but if anyone recognizes me, they pay me the favor of silence. Once or twice I even catch a surprised look from a familiar face—followed by a wink, or a knowing smile, and then a pointed glance away.

This is a masquerade, after all; for once, I am expected to be deceitful.

As the wine flows, the tightness around my heart dwindles and the warmth of the candlelight seeps into my blood, and perhaps I grow more confident than I should. I'm somewhere that "Romeo Montague" is not allowed—but for once I don't have to be a person called Romeo Montague at all. I am whoever I wish to be, whoever I say I am when the mood strikes, and I am indulging in the fantasy.

At least, that is, until someone at my back seizes my elbow, digging strong fingers into tender flesh. Pain darts clear up to my shoulder, fear turning my insides to water as a low voice growls into my ear, "You know Montague scum isn't welcome in San Zeno!"

My head spinning with all the terrible fates that are about to befall me, I turn to face my captor . . . and my terror transforms as I recognize the young man who has me in his grasp.

"M-Mercutio?" My lips are numb, and my veins are filled with ice crystals, but my skin tingles pleasantly where he grips my arm. Even behind the half mask he wears, I would recognize him anywhere; his dark, wavy hair, the square jaw and broad shoulders, the ears that stick out in an endearing way . . . I have his features memorized by now.

He lifts his mask, his dark eyes twinkling, and a charmingly gap-toothed grin lights his handsome face. Just like that, I've forgiven him for scaring me—I even forgive him for laughing as he says, "You should see the way you looked just now, Montague! I really had you going, didn't I?"

As I'm struggling for a response, Ben appears over Mercutio's shoulder, grinning just as wide. "Do not deny it, Cousin—you were clearly about to wet yourself!"

Shrugging against Mercutio's grip, I fight to regain my dignity. I wish like hell I'd governed my reaction better, because I hate giving them the satisfaction.

"You definitely got me," I concede at last, mustering my cool with an arched brow. "Now if only you could manage to get a girl, I might be impressed."

Ben hoots with laughter while Mercutio's eyes widen in shock; and then he begins to laugh as well. Yanking me close, he thumps a happy fist on my chest. "I'm glad you decided to come, old friend! And not only because the ladies here will find me twice as attractive in comparison."

"Oh, so you plan to keep your mask on, then?" Benvolio interjects gleefully, and Mercutio gives him a thump as well.

Leveling a finger in my cousin's face, Mercutio continues, "You know, Ben, everyone says you're nothing but a lazy, insincere drunk who thinks only with his groin, but they're wrong. You haven't thought once in years!"

"Not if I could help it," Benvolio rejoins. "But I resent that characterization just the same." Scooping a goblet of wine off the tray of a passing servant, he raises it to us in a mock salute. "There is nothing I am more energetic and sincere about than getting drunk."

With that, he downs the entire cup in a few lusty swallows—and then chokes a little as some of it goes down the wrong way. We trade jabs a while longer, and I remember how much I love their company; I miss these two foolish boys, and however uneasy I am about the evening's task, I hope it allows for more nights like this in the future.

As if reading my mind, Mercutio turns my way with a sly grin. "So, Montague, Benvolio tells me you intend to test Rosaline Morosini's resolve tonight! Finally got tired of keeping your own company?"

He makes a rather crude gesture meant to imitate just how he imagines I keep myself company, and a flush spreads across my face. *Yours is the company I long for*, I think, and the words are so close to the surface that I bite my lips together for an instant to keep them from spilling out.

"My company is very enjoyable, thank you," I finally manage, after clearing my throat. "Now I just need to convince her of it."

"Well, don't expect any testimonials from us." Ben cranes his neck around, scanning the crowd. We have been moving from room to room throughout the villa, seeking new company and avoiding any familiar Capulets. "You know how much I hate lying to girls."

"Ignore him," Mercutio advises me. "He is only in a foul mood because having to wear a mask all night robs him of his only redeeming feature."

"Piss off!" Ben's indignation is feigned. "Or are you finally admitting that my rugged handsomeness is the reason you two follow me about like lost ducklings?"

"We follow you about because you only move if it is in the direction of free ale!"

"Speak for yourself," I say to Mercutio. "I follow him because when he drinks, he tends to steal things, unless properly supervised."

Ben makes vigorously rude gestures at both of us.

Mercutio doubles over with laughter, clinging to my shoulder for support, and I am aware of nothing other than the heat that gathers beneath his touch. When he regains his composure, he wipes tears from his eyes. "Well done, lads. I really am relieved you decided to show up tonight—I have had my fill of listening to boring snobs make excuses for why my family has been excluded from their guest lists ever since we became poor."

His bluntness causes me to wince a bit, as my own parents are as guilty of this oversight as any of the other highborn Veronese in the room; but Ben scarcely blinks. Snagging yet another goblet off a passing tray, he says, "As a matter of fact, I was wondering what made Lord Capulet remember your name again when planning this little jubilee."

"It was no sense of nostalgic fondness for me, I can assure you. The man hasn't spared me so much as a glance all evening." Deftly, Mercutio snatches the goblet out of Ben's hand, just as my cousin raises it to drink. "But a relation of ours—a nobleman, no less—happens to be a guest of honor tonight, and I believe I am here as a gesture of goodwill." Rolling his eyes, he downs the wine, his mouth puckering. "So many painfully polite conversations . . . this party has been offensively dull until now."

"Speaking of 'offensively dull,' we still have to discuss Romeo's love life," Ben interjects, and I punch him in the arm before he's even finished his sentence.

I'm only half-kidding. Broadening my range of womanly acquaintances is our whole mission this evening, I know, but I still hold out a slender hope that if we have enough fun together—or enough wine—it will be forgotten.

"Are you certain you wish to pursue a girl who's taken a vow of chastity?" Mercutio asks me with a doubtful look. "You might be better off starting with one of Benvolio's former paramours, as you are less likely to disappoint a lady whose standards are already that low."

"I am quite certain." Nervous heat prickles beneath my arms.

"Quiet, the both of you louts," Benvolio orders peevishly, waving us into silence. "The fair lady of Romeo's dreams has entered the room, and you would do well to behave respect-fully!"

The flesh between my shoulder blades goes tight as I turn around, following my cousin's gesture; and there, sure enough, is Rosaline Morosini. She is as striking as ever, dressed in elabo-rate Moorish robes, with a velvet mask serving as a blot to hide her delicate features; but she is still recognizable. The solemnity with which she carries herself, her slender hands, the line of her neck . . . they all give her away.

Not for the first time, I wish her beauty stirred something more in me than just a sense of admiration.

"You might as well get on with it while there's still ample time to be consoled after she turns you down." Ben slaps me on the back. "Remember: Women cannot resist a man who is confident, witty, and handsome. So pick someone who has those traits and pretend to be him."

"You can pretend to be me," Mercutio chimes in. "I won't mind."

Ben nods. "Yes—pretend to be Mercutio, but if he was witty and handsome."

"Piss off!"

And, with that, I'm on my way across the room, my stomach shrinking. I have no fear of what might come from this encounter with Rosaline—neither of us desires any intimacy, and we have always been friendly in the past—but the sooner it begins, the sooner it ends, and the sooner I must indulge my cousin's whims of finding a girl who *will* have me.

Rosaline bows graciously when I approach, but what ensues is less of a conversation than a performance. The mask she wears is a moretta—it has no laces, but rather is held in place by a button that she keeps between her teeth, meaning she cannot speak unless she removes it. And, of course, she chooses not to.

"Good evening, my lady," I begin, with all the charm I can muster. "I hope you are enjoying the party?"

Rosaline bobs her head in silent assent, her eyes indifferent through the dark field of the mask.

"It is rather a spectacle, is it not?" I venture next. "I was told there were peacocks wandering the property, although I've yet to see one."

Her shoulders rise in a delicate shrug, and then she goes still again, looking past me.

"I . . ." My face heats. I am terrible at this sort of thing under even ordinary circumstances, and these are almost farcical. "The music is truly invigorating, don't you think? Would you . . . would you care to dance?"

When I first envisioned this scenario, I imagined my invitation coming last—the logical conclusion to a standard encounter at such an event as this. But the pressure I feel is enormous, and I have outsmarted myself by blundering ahead too quickly. And, of course, Rosaline mutely but unambiguously declines.

"Oh," I say. It is an insipid reply, and nervous sweat sticks my shepherd costume to my skin. I feel eyes on my back, Ben and Mercutio watching me like circling vultures, waiting for the inevitable. Meekly, I ask, "Are you . . . enjoying the food?"

Rosaline blinks.

When I finally run out of polite topics to monologue about, and our exchange is quite definitely finished, a ball of dread forms in the base of my throat. Those eyes bore deeper into my back, and I resist the urge to turn around.

Five girls. I can dance with five girls. What's the worst that could happen? They attempt to flirt, and I evade; they make an overture, I make an excuse; they ask to see me again beyond the limits of this party, and I . . . *do what*? Rudely decline? Agree for formality's sake, and then unchivalrously spurn them later? Say yes, and then act out some elaborate charade of courtship and hope it eventually gets easier?

What's left of my stomach turns over, and without thinking,

I hazard a glance at an arched doorway set back in the nearby wall. From here, all I can see beyond it are shadows, but right now that's good enough for me. When the music changes a few moments later, and a shifting throng of dancers temporarily blocks me from the view of Ben and Mercutio, I make a break for it.

Maybe it's cowardly to run away, to choose the illusion of escape over a promise I regret having made in the first place. But right now, as the darkness swallows me up and the distance between me and my obligations grows wider, I feel nothing but relief.

7

A LOW-CEILINGED PASSAGEWAY, LIT BY FLICKERING SCONCES, LEADS me to another salon and then another gallery, and then a loggia—and then I'm stepping into a leafy, open-air space that I don't expect. It's another courtyard, though much smaller than the central one—from which I can still hear voices ringing over the tiled rooftops—with little room for more than a few benches, and a lemon tree that arches over an ornately carved well.

The air is sweet here, and I remove my mask, sweat cooling on my overheated face. The tree is in full blossom, and its perfume fills my lungs, mixed with the rich green scent of moss; a lantern sways from the roofline above the loggia behind me, and some imperfections in its protective shade send pinpoint constellations of light across the ground at my feet. For the first time all night, I am alone.

Or so I think at first.

It isn't until I've walked all the way up to the well, peeking over the edge to see if I can tell how far down the water is, that I feel eyes on my back again—and when I turn slowly around, I finally see the figure leaning in the shadow of the lemon tree.

Startled, I nearly drop my mask. "I-I'm sorry, I thought . . . I didn't know anyone was here."

He tilts his head. "It's okay. I mean . . . I'm not one of them." With this, he gestures vaguely at the villa, sprawling every which way around us—and I take it to mean he's not a Capulet. What I don't know is if it also means he's recognized me as a Montague, or if he's simply saying he has no private claim on the courtyard. "You're as welcome here as I am."

I'm struggling to think up a reply when he finally steps forward—out of the shadows and into the moonlight . . . and my mind goes utterly blank.

He. Is. *Magnificent.*

Dressed as a faun for the masquerade, he must be about my age, but he looks eternal and otherworldly and terrifyingly elemental. His hair is an unruly tumble of blond curls, his torso is bare but for a leather vest that hangs off his lanky frame, and his skin gleams with some kind of shimmering powder. He wears fur breeches, a pair of false horns bursting through his tousled mane, and his eyes are bronze—the color of dark honey, or tarnished gold—where the light catches them through the openings in his half mask.

His mouth is even more appealing than Mercutio's. I didn't know that was possible.

"I just needed a minute away from everything," he continues, when I fail to produce any words of my own. With a melancholy sigh, he leans over the rim of the well, staring down into the shadows. "There are so many people here, all trying to talk at once, and I don't really know any of them. It's a little overwhelming."

I watch him watch the darkness, his skin practically glowing under the moon. He looks like a sorrowful dryad, a lonely nature spirit that time has cruelly forgotten, and my heart actually aches. Coughing, I manage, "Parties like these are overwhelming no matter how many people you know. My best friends are in there now, probably wondering where I am, but I just . . ."

"Couldn't breathe?" he supplies, that exquisite mouth pulling up on one side—and I find myself nodding by accident. I do agree with what he's saying, but it's a little scary to realize I would have nodded anyway, even if I hadn't. "It shouldn't be so hard to meet people, and make friends, and talk about nothing, and yet . . . sometimes it is."

"Talking about nothing is only easy with your closest and most intimate acquaintances." I try not to stare at him, but it's a battle I keep losing. "If you want to have a meaningful conversation, you need a stranger."

He smiles. "Like me?"

"I didn't know there *were* strangers like you." Too late, I realize I've said it aloud, and feel the blood drain from my face. After a slight hesitation, though, the faun only smiles wider—amused, or maybe even pleased. Nervously, I rush ahead. "H-have you ever noticed that? How much easier it is to say important things when you don't know the person you're saying them to? My cousin and I talk almost exclusively about nothing, b-but—"

"I do know what you mean," he interrupts softly, saving me from drowning in my own mortification. "There's only one person here tonight who really knows me, and when I tried to tell him that I wasn't sure I was prepared for . . . all of this, he wouldn't hear it. Or maybe he *couldn't* hear it. In the end, it hardly matters; here I am, just the same."

I am the most selfish boy in the universe, because all I can think about is how grateful I am to the insensitive soul who ignored his concerns and compelled him to be here.

"If you pretend you're an assassin, it helps." I only realize how this sounds when he glances up at me, his bronze eyes going wide. "W-what I mean is that you make a game of it! Whenever my parents have forced me to play the dutiful son at one of their social events, I've tried to imagine myself an impostor who has replaced the true Romeo in order to get closer to one of the guests for some nefarious objective. It just . . . makes it easier, somehow." He continues to stare at me in silence, his mouth drawn into a thoughtful moue, and my nervous laughter squeaks a little. "You are looking at me as though I might actually be in the habit of murdering people at banquets, but I assure you I am not!"

"Romeo," he repeats in a quiet way—and a shiver runs up my spine when I hear my name spoken in his voice. "Is that . . . who you are?"

"Yes? Um, yes." My hands are sweaty around my mask, and the way he watches me makes me feel terribly exposed.

"You don't sound very convincing." He straightens his back, folding his arms across his chest. "Can you prove it?"

I blink a little. "Prove . . . that I am Romeo?"

"Yes," he answers with a sly look. "I have heard from a very reliable source that assassins are known to impersonate the sons of prominent Veronese households, in order to commit terrible crimes against unsuspecting party guests."

For a moment, I'm too startled to realize that he's teasing me; but then his mouth quirks into a smile, and I can't help laughing. "I suppose I have put myself in this position. How am I to prove my identity, though, when we've never met before?"

For another moment, he's quiet—as if I've said something significant—and then he prompts, "Tell me something only the real Romeo would know."

"I, um . . ." *I am terribly attracted to you.* "I have a cat—named Hecate!" It is the second thing that comes to mind, and infinitely safer than the first. "Well, she isn't *mine*, exactly. And she may not be a cat, either. I have not ruled out the possibility that she is a demon sent from hell to torment me."

"A cat that isn't a cat, and that doesn't belong to you?" He shakes his head. "That means nothing, and anyone might say it. I shall need more."

"I am"—*wondering if your hair is truly as soft as it looks*—"v-very fond of . . . art?" He says nothing, but cocks his head in confusion, so I add, "My secret dream is to one day become a master of frescoes, like the great Giotto di Bondone, but . . . my parents would never stand for it. I am to be a silk merchant or a soldier or . . . nothing else."

"Have you ever painted a fresco?" Out of Benvolio's mouth, this same question would have sounded patronizing; but the faun is merely curious, and it warms me.

"No," I admit, letting out a sigh. "I hope to, someday, but my parents . . ." Stopping, I shake my head, trying to figure out the simplest way to explain. "They don't believe it's an appropriate pursuit for me. To their way of thinking, those that produce art

71

are of an inferior class—and yet, it is only the superior classes who are capable of *appreciating* art."

The sarcasm in my tone is enough to wither the lemon blossoms that hang above us, and this boy—this beautiful boy, with shimmering skin and elegant fingers—tousles his already tousled hair. "That sounds somewhat hypocritical."

"It is infuriating." I have never been able to say this to someone who actually agreed with me, and I am drunk on the satisfaction. "They say they want what is best for me, but somehow what's 'best for me' only ever looks exactly like what's best for *them*. And even my dearest friends don't—" Emotion chokes my voice, and I struggle to calm myself. "Sometimes I feel as though I am being crushed alive, but it's happening so slowly, no one believes me when I tell them. Sometimes it feels like the most important parts of me are the ones I can't share with the *people* who are the most important to me. Does that make any sense?"

"Yes." His voice is barely a whisper, but it echoes in the depth of the well. "When someone has decided who you are, and they won't let you change their mind, what are you meant to do? Where is left to go?"

We look at each other, and something passes between us that I cannot quite understand; only, for the first time in ages, I feel as though someone *sees* me. His eyes are soft and intimate . . . and lonely, in a way that speaks right to my heart. Maybe the courtyard is expanding around us, because even though we are standing still, it feels as if we're moving closer together.

"I believe that you are Romeo after all," he finally says, and when he sees my confusion, another smile twitches at his lips.

"All of that sounds too honest to be an assassin's trick, and I doubt even the cleverest impostor could imagine a truth your closest friends choose not to recognize."

"Ah. Well." I shrug, focusing on the stones of the well, tracing a tiny crack with my fingernail. "There are many things my friends don't know about me." Glancing up, I realize that he's been examining my features. "You are taking a chance, trusting me."

"Perhaps, but I think the risk is worth it. You have . . . an honest face."

"But I am far from honest." Unable to help myself, I smile. "I have, in fact, only just finished telling you precisely how deceitful I am."

"The hallmark of an honest man," he replies. "A deceiver always pretends he is telling the truth—it is only the virtuous who lie."

I grin, charmed and confused, wishing this interlude could last the rest of the night. It frightens me, the way I feel inside when he smiles while looking into my eyes—like water just before it boils—but it also excites me. No one has ever looked at me that way before.

"Perhaps I assumed you would think that." Two can play this game. "And so, in order to convince you of my virtuousness, I claimed to have concealed things from my friends—when in fact I've been honest with them all along."

"You can drop this charade—the more you try to convince me how untrustworthy you are, the more honest I believe you to be." He moves closer, thoroughly delighted, and my gaze is tempted

73

by the glimmer of moonlight on his bare chest. "Besides, a true assassin would certainly have tried to attack me by now, but you have only studied me when you thought I wouldn't notice. Therefore, I can only conclude that you are the true Romeo."

My eyes snap back up to his face in an instant, my neck going hot enough for blacksmithing. "I was not . . . *studying* you, I was . . . admiring your costume! It's very"—*enchanting, ethereal, beguiling, handsome, handsome*, handsome—"um . . . well made?"

Finally, he looks perplexed. "It is just a lambskin vest and some powdered mica—there is hardly anything to it. I came up with the idea this morning over breakfast."

"It was a very good idea, though!" I seem to have lost all control over what I'm saying, and if the lemon tree were to topple and crush me to death just now, I wouldn't mind. "You wear it well. It suits you."

He hesitates, reappraising his own ensemble, and then makes a thoughtful shape with his mouth. Slowly, he asks, "What do you like about it?"

My airways constrict, and pressure starts to build in my head. There are too many ways to answer this question, and none of them are prudent choices. He looks elemental, almost feral, like a creature who escaped from a canvas depicting a bacchanal. His bared skin, brushed with that sparkling dust, is both resplendent and inviting; and his mournful lonesomeness makes it . . . poetic.

Weakly, I finally manage to say, "You look like a painting."

"A painting." He repeats me in a curious tone, and then he frowns. "Hm."

"Are you . . . does that displease you?" I rub one sweaty hand down my shirtfront, cursing my clumsy choice of words. "I'm sorry; I didn't mean—"

"My only displeasure is self-directed, I assure you." He leans against the well, his hand coming to rest only a few inches from my own, and I try not to think about how close I am to touching him. "What I had hoped to look like tonight was 'nothing much at all.' I thought the less effort I put into dressing myself, the more likely I was to go unnoticed; but the way you've been looking at me makes it clear I have regrettably achieved the opposite effect."

It was a silly goal to begin with, I wish I could tell him, for he is far too beautiful to be ignored, even at a crowded ball. "If it consoles you any, I expect there are very few people here tonight who are quite as passionate about paintings as I am. Perhaps they won't see what I see."

I've chosen my words carefully, and yet when I hear them out loud, I fear that I'm revealing too much of myself anyway. But the faun merely smiles, and there is that strange sensation again of the walls retreating, of us drawing together. He glances down at his hand, and his finger nudges just a little closer to my thumb. "Do you make any paintings of your own, Romeo?"

Another shiver runs up my spine at the sound of my name. "I'm afraid I've no one to teach me proper techniques, so I mostly do sketches with chalk. It's not as impressive, but it can still be challenging."

"If you were to do a sketch of me, what would it look like?"

"Like this." I don't even have to consider my answer. "Exactly like this. A melancholy faun, alone with the moonlight, a flowering tree, and a well into which he can whisper all his secrets." The lantern above the loggia sways on its hook, making the little pinpricks of light dance at our feet. "Only . . . I would draw you without your face so hidden."

He hesitates, but then reaches up, carefully undoing the laces of his mask. "Like this, then?" His voice is sweeter and more resonant than the string music filtering through the villa, gentler than the fading warmth still baked into the courtyard's flagstones from the long, hot day. "Is this better?"

Incapable of speech for a moment, I can only muster a jerking nod. For the first time, I see him for who he really is—more boy than faun, more man than myth—and I cannot drink him in deeply enough. He has freckles and a high forehead, his brows incongruously dark against his blond hair; there is a scar close to his left temple, a birthmark under his right eye, and his eyelashes are much longer than I thought they were at first. There is something familiar about him, a quality that makes me feel as though he belongs in my memory. And yet, how could I have ever seen someone this startlingly unreal and not know him instantly? He is splendid and imperfect, and I wish . . . I don't know what I wish.

I'm not even sure what it is I'm supposed to wish *for*.

"It is . . . much better," I manage at long last, trying not to think about how he's still looking me in the eye; not to think about how, when he sets his mask down and returns his hand to the edge of the well, his fingers are now even closer to mine than before.

"I almost didn't realize I was still wearing it," he remarks. "I guess that's the thing about masks . . . you wear one long enough, you eventually forget it isn't your real face."

"Perhaps." The cumbersome bit of porcelain I'm holding is so heavy, my ears still hurt from where its ribbons have been digging into them. I'll probably have bruises in the morning. "In my experience, a mask seems to fit worse the longer you have it on."

He hesitates, and then murmurs, "I'm . . . glad you're not wearing yours."

His fingertips close the tiny gap between us, and for the first time I feel his touch—soft and tentative, a delicate question—and it awakes something monumental inside me. My arm comes alive with a sensation like sparks erupting from a jostled campfire, and goose bumps spread clear to the base of my skull. I've never felt anything like this; it's like the first time I drank too much wine, the first time I lost my footing on a patch of ice, and the first time I was so excited I couldn't sleep, all rolled into one overwhelming moment.

My instinct is to pull away, but instead, my blood hot and racing, I choose the contact. And when I see his gaze flick from my face to our joined hands, I realize that he's choosing it, too. He leans a little closer, his fingers pressing with more confidence, and his lips part.

A gate opens inside me, releasing a flood of emotions I don't know how to handle or quantify: anticipation, fear, desire, joy, and something else I can't even name, because I've never experienced it before. But the way he looks at me . . . I am seized with the urge to kiss him the way Benvolio kisses girls at the tavern

when they've both had too much ale. And I don't even know . . .
Can boys do that?

"You're trembling," he remarks quietly—and it's true. This, this shared awareness, this mutual . . . *whatever this is*, is more than I've ever been prepared for. I don't know what's going to happen, but I want it more than anything.

I want it so much it scares me to death.

And then—

"*Romeo!*" My name comes barreling suddenly out of the shadows beneath the loggia, a singsong call echoing in the dark, accompanied by the scrape of approaching footsteps. The faun jolts back, breaking the tenuous spell between us, and the voice sounds again—closer, more musical, and awfully familiar. "Where are you, Romeo? You're missing all the fun!"

I spin around, only a second before Benvolio lurches out of the gloom and into the courtyard, sending my heart into my throat. When he sees me, he lets out an exasperated breath. "*There* you are. How did I know I would find you hiding all alone in the dark, trying to avoid fun at any cost?"

"I'm . . . I'm not hiding," I lie, basting in a cold sweat beneath my shepherd costume. "And I'm not alone, either. I met—"

But when I turn back, the faun has vanished—gone without a trace, as though he was never there to begin with.

8

BEN STEERS ME BACK TO THE BALLROOM IN THE MANNER OF A guardsman escorting a prisoner to his doom. We're barely through the arched columns and into the candlelit chamber, string music rising and falling over us like waves, before he's introducing me to the first young lady I'm meant to dance with this evening. The daughter of a commander in the prince's army, she's someone I've met before only in passing.

With Benvolio's gimlet eye carving a hole in my spine, I lead her out to join a group of dancers already doing a Black Almain, and then struggle mightily to remember the order of the steps while she attempts to engage me in conversation. The experience is, it must be said, not any worse than I'd imagined—but no better, either. I do my best to flatter her without crossing the line into genuine flirtation, but all the while, my mind can focus on nothing but what just happened between me and that mysterious boy in the courtyard.

The most frustrating thing of all is that I can't even be certain what *did* happen. What *would* have happened, had Benvolio not blundered in at just that moment? I keep picturing his face—the wide, golden eyes, the charming birthmark, the softness of his mouth—and my heart throbs. I am homesick for a stranger, for that fleeting moment when his hand touched mine and I realized he was doing it on purpose.

That one gentle touch was louder than any of the words we spoke, and more exciting, nerve-racking, and memorable than any prolonged flirtation I've muddled through at one of these parties. I cannot forgive myself for failing to ask the faun his name before it was too late, as I have no idea how I could begin to find him again.

When the song finally comes to its overdue conclusion, my partner hints that she would be very glad to receive a formal visit from me at her home someday soon in order to continue our acquaintance. With a courteous bow, I deliberately misunderstand what she's suggesting, and bid her farewell—one dance removed from my list of debts.

Benvolio does not wait for me to clear the dance floor before he grabs me by the elbow again, and then I'm being herded toward another lady he'd like me to woo. And if anything, this next encounter is worse than the first: The music is slower and more intimate, the conversation is slower and less interesting, and the young woman's romantic overtures are blunt and difficult to sidestep.

She's offended by the time the song is over, my evasions not artful enough to suit her, and nerves cramp my stomach. Once again, Benvolio barely lets me leave the lady behind before he's handed me over to another potential match, another stilted conversation where I try to be friendly without inviting any notions of romance.

When my third obligatory dance is over, I'm depressed, over-worked nerves leaving me damp under my tunic. Ben and Mercutio have been watching me the whole time, hovering on the periphery with the scrutinizing, analytical aspect of horse traders evaluating an animal's potential; when they grab me as I'm trying to slip away, back to the courtyard where I met the faun, I have to stifle a pathetic mewl of frustration.

This time, they want a detailed report of what passed between me and my dance partner, and then proceed to debate my choices as though I weren't in the room with them. They argue over whose mercies to throw me at next—and as I don't have much to add to the conversation, I tune them out, gazing back across the room at the swirling extravagance of the ball and its guests.

And that's when I see him again.

The musicians have gone temporarily quiet, taking a moment to retune their instruments; and as the dancers begin to clear the floor, a head of tumbled blond curls comes into view. Conversing with a girl dressed as a barbarian princess, the faun stands below a swag of emerald silk, a cup of wine in his hand. The ballroom's cleverly reinforced candlelight dances in the shimmering powder he wears, making his skin sparkle, and I feel something twinge in my chest as I drink in the sight of him.

"Who is that?" I blurt before I can think better of the question, and Benvolio makes a strange expression when he sees what direction I'm looking.

"Are you being serious?" His brows furrow a bit, a thread of suspicion in his tone, and I bite my tongue. I should never have opened my mouth. "Romeo, that's—"

"Why are you asking?" Mercutio interrupts my cousin, deliberately but smoothly. His expression is unreadable, but I feel caught nevertheless. When you are secretly carrying gold, everyone looks like a thief.

"Because I—I . . ." *Think, Romeo, you* clod. "I assumed I would know most everyone here, and I am just . . . curious about an unfamiliar face. That's all."

As answers go, it is pathetic and unconvincing, even to my own ears. Lightly, Mercutio returns, "Most everyone here is wearing a mask. You are positively surrounded by faces that are either unfamiliar or invisible altogether. So it's somewhat interesting that your curiosity awakens only now—don't you agree, Benvolio?"

"I agree, certainly." My cousin's tone is crisp, and again he won't look at me. "But I can't say I didn't see something like this coming. I put all this work into finding him a nice girl, and it was all wasted effort in the end."

"Clearly, his attentions were elsewhere," Mercutio agrees, and I almost lose control of my bladder, my worst fears finally materializing with the force of a lightning strike. Time slows as my truth is exposed, dragged into the light by two of the people I'd been most desperate to hide it from.

And yet.

They haven't actually said the words out loud, and until they do, I still have an opportunity to bluff my way out. Whatever girl they choose for me next, I will play the perfect suitor—I'll repeat every bit of rote flattery I've ever heard come from my cousin's mouth. But first, I have to divert them, and by any means necessary.

Scratching at my neck, I splutter, "I should have known better than to ask a simple question of you two clowns. Please go back to discussing how low our expectations ought to be, and whether it is inappropriate to arrange a liaison between me and a girl who shares a name with my mother."

"Look at him," Ben says to Mercutio. "He's gone absolutely crimson."

"Redder than the strawberries they're serving with the dessert!"

There's no point denying it, because my face indeed boils over with anxious heat. "I just need some fresh air, that's all. So if you don't mind, I'll—"

Before I can move an inch, Mercutio claps a firm hand on my shoulder, and I feel the impact of it all the way down into the balls of my feet. "You know what I just realized, Ben? This is the first time all night that our dear Romeo has shown any interest in a single person at this party who isn't you or me."

"You are both being ridiculous," I squeak out, but they ignore me.

"Well, what shall we do about it?" Ben asks. "We cannot simply *allow him* to indulge in—"

"Are you not tired of trying and failing to match him with

83

a girl?" Mercutio counters, his grip growing stronger, and the bottom of my stomach drops away. "Do you think we are gods, that we can control either his heart or his loins?"

Ben frowns. "I am not interested in controlling my cousin's loins, Mercutio."

"Then it's settled. We let him sate his curiosity—star crossed as it may be."

And with that, I am being whisked through the thinning crowd, straight across the polished dance floor and toward the glimmering, golden faun. Fear streaks up my spine, cold as the Adige in December, and terrified sweat drips into my eyes. *What is happening? What are they going to* do?

We come to an abrupt stop in front of him and the barbarian girl by his side, and when he glances up and sees me, his eyes go wide behind his mask. His mouth parts, but it is Mercutio who speaks first. "Valentine! I hate to interrupt, but it looks as though the musicians are about to start playing again, and this is somewhat urgent."

"*Valentine?*" I repeat the name on a gasped breath, my own eyes popping open.

"Yes," Mercutio says jovially. "My long-lost brother is back from Vicenza! Val, I'm sure you remember . . . well, our dear friend here, who really requires no introduction." There's a sort of warning in his tone that I don't comprehend, and Valentine closes his mouth again. "Anyway, the four of us will all have to celebrate our reunion someday this coming week, but for now, there's a serious matter that needs to be addressed."

"I . . . I don't . . ." Everything is moving too fast, and my thoughts can't catch up. The faun is *Valentine?* As in, *Mercutio's brother*, Valentine? *I was swooning over Mercutio's long-absent brother Valentine?*

Relatedly, but not quite as important in this exact moment: What is it with me and those brothers, and their confounded, incurable handsomeness?

Any second now, I am expecting my secret to be revealed, for Mercutio to announce that I have been ogling Valentine—*his brother*—from across the ballroom. I don't know what will happen after that; I don't know how these people, *my* people, will react.

But then, to my further shock, Mercutio turns to the barbarian girl—her auburn hair gathered into an elaborate crown of braids at the top of her head—and says deferentially, "My lady. I hope it is not impertinent of me to insinuate myself in this manner, but my friend here"—he swivels me by the shoulders until I am facing her, my eyes still wide, my fingers still jumping with nerves—"noticed you from across the room, and was quite struck by your beauty. He was hoping for a dance."

A thick moment passes, during which my heart counts the seconds in painful beats, and I realize that my friends have made the most fortunate of unfortunate mistakes: They assumed it was *this girl* whose beauty had caught my eye. Of course they did. And now they are seizing the opportunity to hand me over to her, and I've got no choice but to play along.

Jittery with the aftermath of unadulterated panic, I perform a shaky bow, my mind blank. Ben and Mercutio stand behind me, gloating with anticipation. But it's Valentine's gaze I feel the strongest, like sunlight through a window. I have no idea what he expects, or what might have happened had we not been interrupted in the courtyard. But I know exactly what I have to do right now to keep my life from coming open at the seams.

"If you would be so inclined," I begin, keeping my head bowed low, "I beg the honor of a dance."

"Very well." She says it just like that: brisk and polite—friendly, but with none of the coquettish ceremony I've come to expect and dread from aristocratic girls of a marriageable age. "Any friend of Mercutio's is . . . well, probably trouble. But most likely entertaining trouble, at the very least."

Silently, still trembling with misplaced excitement, I force myself to smile and extend my hand. We find some space among the other couples on the floor, the new music calling for a saltarello—a lively dance that never fails to make me feel ridiculous. As I stumble through the ordered and prancing steps, my mind is a hot stone that turns coherent thoughts to vapor the instant they make contact.

"I'm surprised I don't know you," the princess finally states in a contemplative manner, after the silence between us has grown unignorable. "I'd long since given up expecting to encounter anyone new at these tiresome soirees. It's always the same guest list every time, and I was certain I'd met everyone there was to meet by now."

"It's an evening full of surprises," I mumble, reluctant to share just yet that I was not actually *on* the guest list. Tossing a glance at my friends, *at Valentine*, I muster an embarrassed smile.

"I fear I must apologize for interrupting your conversation. It was not my intention to be rude—"

"Oh, please!" She laughs, husky and musical. "If anything, you saved poor Valentine from having to listen to more of my endless complaints about nights such as these. As much as I enjoy good food and good music, I truly hate all of the exhibition. Don't these people have anything better to do than play dress-up and show off their gaudiest jewelry?"

"Maybe they don't." I give her a knowing little smile. "Some of them may have nothing to do at all, besides arranging their social calendars and trying to keep from falling out of favor with the prince. At least a masquerade allows them to be a little creative. Did you see the man dressed as Jason of the Argonauts? He even fashioned a Golden Fleece!"

"Oh, yes—that's Antonio Caresini. He's an adviser to Prince Escalus."

I lift my brows in surprise, recognizing the name. "Not the one with the vendetta against the taverns?"

"You've heard of him, I see." Her tone is so dry there is practically dust in the air.

Caresini, a determined enemy of public drunkenness, has been trying for years to get the prince to force Verona's taverns to shut their doors on Sundays, if not to close them altogether for good. It has made him rather notoriously hated by the circle of roustabouts and wastrels my cousin has lately fallen in with.

"Judging by how unsteady on his feet he was when I spoke

with him earlier," the princess continues, "I predict he'll be retching up a gallon or so of wine into the flowerbeds tonight."

"Caresini is a *drunk*?" I whisper it, genuinely scandalized.

"Caresini is a *hypocrite*," she returns. "And in that, he is surrounded by his peers tonight."

My eyes widen a fraction. "That's quite the pronouncement."

"It is merely the truth." She makes a sweeping gesture. "Look around you, my noble shepherd—you are in a very den of hypocrisy. Lift up any mask in this room, and you will find at least two faces lurking underneath."

Her scorn is palpable, and I scratch my head. "You are quite the cynic."

"Perhaps. Or perhaps I have simply grown tired of masks and the people who wear them." With a restless sigh, she adds, "Did you know that the refacing of San Zeno's campanile last year was funded almost entirely by the Capulet family?"

"That was generous of them." I keep my tone neutral.

"Was it?" she challenges. "What if I told you the abbey and its cloisters are falling apart—that they've *been* falling apart for years, and the church has barely been able to afford critical repairs. The monks sleep three to a cell when it rains, because so much of the roof is compromised! But when a donation finally comes, it is with the stipulation that it be used for the bell tower, and *only* the bell tower. Do you know why?"

It isn't hard to solve this mystery, though it brings me no pleasure. "Because everyone sees the bell tower."

"Very good." She smiles without mirth. "The extremely visible campanile is freshened up, and Alboino Capulet gets praised for his munificence and devotion to the Church—while a dozen or so poor, miserable monks shiver in their damp cells. And to reward himself for his piety, the great benefactor of San Zeno throws a decadent ball for Verona's wealthiest citizens to indulge in their luxuries."

There is something invigorating about how brazenly she gossips. Cautiously, I venture, "You are not an admirer of the Capulets, I see."

Here, she hesitates, finally seeming to consider her words. "Let us say that I know them a little too well to be impressed by their grand and empty gestures." Belatedly, she adds, "I'm sorry if that offends you. You are probably a friend of the family, somehow?"

"Not exactly." We execute a turn in our saltarello, and I make a decision. "Can you keep a secret?"

"I keep many." She adjusts her mask. "What's one more?"

Murmuring, I tell her, "I am not on this evening's guest list."

"Oh." She straightens up, and then a delighted smile spreads across her face. "My, my. You just became the most interesting person in the villa—an uninvited rogue!" We do another turning step, and she cocks her head. "But how did you get past the door? There's a gentleman the size of a draft horse in the front hall, looking over everyone who enters."

"I should probably keep that little trick to myself. If word gets out, it might spoil future chances for other uninvited rogues." I can't resist giving her a little wink.

We spin and hop a few more times, and her mouth pulls into a thoughtful twist. "It seems so odd to me that our paths have never crossed before—you are exactly the sort of boy I expect to see at these parties. How could you have been excluded from the guest list?"

"That's rather a question for our hosts, is it not?" I demur, suddenly feeling cautious again. "Anyway, I might be a farmer or a bricklayer . . . or even an impostor, for all you know."

"You're not." She says it with conviction. "Clearly, you have been educated, and you know how to dance—"

"That might be a matter of perspective."

"You are no stranger to courtly dances," she amends, "and although you are wearing a shepherd's costume, I can tell by the fabric and tailoring that it was not cheaply made—so you are a young man of some means."

I let out an uncomfortable laugh. "And you are analytical enough to be a coroner."

"You also appear to be unmarried, but you are of an age to seek a bride, and the Capulets have an eligible daughter they are nearly desperate to give away."

"So I've heard," I acknowledge.

For the first time, it occurs to me that the Capulets' daughter—Juliet—is probably at the ball tonight, though I would not recognize her. Despite our families' constant, rancorous entanglements, she and I have scarcely met. Where Tybalt has always made a point of seeking conflict with the Montagues, the Capulets have made an equal point of keeping their teenage daughter removed from the fray.

"You also keep the right company," she continues. "And you are certainly Verona born, as Mercutio described you as an old friend when reintroducing you to his brother . . . but that hardly makes sense."

"Why not?"

"Because *I* am an old friend of Mercutio's!" She blurts this just as the song ends, and a few heads turn our way. "Verona's social spheres are simply not large enough for us to have avoided each other's acquaintance for this long by chance alone, and there are very few aristocratic names my—that our hosts would intentionally snub."

We stare at each other, gone still all over, as realization comes down on us like ash. I dare another glance at Ben and Mercutio, who are all but doubled over with laughter, their plot to maneuver the barbarian princess and me together bearing the exact fruit they'd hoped for.

Cold fingers poke their way up my spine. "You . . . you are Juliet Capulet."

Her shoulders droop. "And you can be none other than Romeo—"

"Montague!"

When my surname explodes throughout the room—coming not from her but from behind me, and snarled in a deep, menacing voice—I nearly jump out of my skin. Turning abruptly on my heel, I find myself face-to-face with the one Capulet I'd hoped to avoid most this evening.

Tybalt.

9

"Unhand my cousin, you filthy mongrel!" Spittle flies from his lips, and his eyes flash behind an incongruously whimsical half mask. It has a feline aspect, with whiskers and two pointed ears—not the sort of choice I'd expect from the swaggering, ill-tempered brute who is busy waging war on all Montagues.

Only a fool would dare laugh, though. Tybalt is taller than me by about six inches, broader across the shoulders by another six, and his hand already rests on the hilt of a dagger at his hip. Lord Capulet has almost certainly forbidden weapons at this celebration—but no rules apply to his favorite nephew.

"I'll not have you *molesting* Juliet—and in her father's house, no less!" He steps forward, and just as I am considering how cowardly it might look to turn and flee, Juliet speaks.

"You are overreacting, Cousin," she says sharply, her teeth gritted. I've never heard anyone take that tone with him, and I brace myself. "We were only dancing. No one has been molested here—he has scarcely even touched me."

"Then I arrived in the very nick of time." He takes another step forward.

"Stop this!" she orders—not quite coming between us, but at least not leaving Tybalt to skin me alive. "This boy has done nothing but make polite conversation—"

"And drink your father's wine, and eat his food, and mock his hospitality by cavorting with his only daughter in front of all Verona," he shouts. Heads swivel our way in a mix of curiosity and alarm. "I am sickened, and I cannot fathom why you are so complacent about this . . . this *insult* against our family!"

"You are creating a spectacle, Tybalt." Juliet's voice is ice in contrast to his heat, and her hands tighten into fists. "There is no need for any of this."

"Oh, but there is. I'll not have my uncle's generosity abused, his Christian virtue disrespected before his peers, without demanding satisfaction!" His hand closes on the hilt of his dagger, and I reach instinctively for the empty space at my own hip where my sword belongs. "Juliet, go fetch your father, as he will surely want to be here when I teach this Montague brat some manners. You should find him in the east salon with Count Paris."

There is apparently some hidden meaning in this, because Juliet goes rigid when she hears it. But I am still a little too preoccupied to care what secrets pass between them.

"How now, Tybalt?" Appearing suddenly at my side, clapping a protective hand on my shoulder that nearly melts me into my boots, Mercutio is all bright smiles and wide-eyed ignorance. "You're looking quite debonair this evening, I must say. What's your costume meant to be—are you the Prince of Cats?"

"Mercutio, please escort my cousin to the east salon," Tybalt orders smoothly, ignoring the attempted distraction. "There is to be some violence here, and I won't have her exposed to it."

"I am going nowhere, and I will not permit you to turn my father's ballroom into a battleground," Juliet states. "Have some dignity, for heaven's sake!"

"*Me?* You tell *me* to have dignity?" Tybalt sputters, knuckles white on his dagger.

The golden boy of the Capulet family is built for fighting; and although his technique with a sword is notoriously sloppy, too governed by rage to be precise when it counts, he has yet to lose a single duel. According to an untested rumor, he has his blades coated with a remarkably deadly poison, so that even a shallow strike could prove fatal.

"You prance about with a Montague, dressed like this, and yet you would tell me that *I* lack dignity?" Tybalt's face is red under his half mask. "Mercutio, take her to my uncle!"

"'*Mercutio, do this, Mercutio, do that*,'" my friend mimics, frowning. "I am not one of your feline subjects, Tybalt. A 'please' and a 'thank you' would be appreciated."

"*I do not have time for your childish clowning*," Tybalt roars, drawing an inch of his dagger free from its scabbard, sending my heart up into my throat. Unarmed, and in hostile territory, my chances to escape will dwindle fast once that blade is swinging at me. Even if I can dodge a thrust or two, even if I can outrun him at full bore, I'm not sure I even know the way out of the villa. "Either do as I say, or step aside while I put this mongrel down!"

But at that moment, a flutter of bright green catches my attention from the crowd of onlookers. Benvolio leaps into view, tossing one of those swags of emerald silk over Tybalt's head. At the same instant, Valentine appears on his other side, slinging a thickly braided curtain cord around the Capulet boy's shoulders, pinning his arms down.

"Watch your step, Your Highness!" Benvolio trills, shoving Tybalt at Mercutio, just as the latter boy sticks out one of his booted feet. My hapless would-be murderer stumbles forward, trips, and crashes straight to the floor with no way to break his fall. Before he even lands, I'm already moving—two pairs of hands at my back, propelling me forward at a reckless gallop while Mercutio leads the way.

I manage one glance back over my shoulder, and the last I see of the Capulet ballroom before we plunge into the shadows of a candlelit gallery is Tybalt, writhing around like a trout caught in a green bag, while Juliet stands over him and watches us go.

We get lost only once in the villa's labyrinth of dim corridors, but it costs us our narrow lead time. When we finally burst into the great hall, the front door heaving into view, Tybalt is on our heels once more—and he has managed to marshal reinforcements.

True to Juliet's word, there is a man of some formidable size guarding the entrance; but his edict is to keep people out, not in, and he is scarcely prepared when we hurtle past him and into the night. Wind whips the trees, the air gauzy with damp rising off the Adige, and freedom beckons from the narrow lane leading back into the city.

"We must split up," Mercutio declares breathlessly, barely slowing down as we sprint across the forecourt. "It was an honor to serve at your sides in this worthy campaign—I shall see you in Valhalla!" He veers abruptly to the right, heading not for the lane but a darkened hillside covered in grapevines.

Shouts come from behind us as our pursuers gain ground, and I barrel heedlessly away from the glowing lanterns of the Capulet villa and down the pathway in the shadow of the garden wall. I barely even notice when Benvolio breaks free, ducking into a separate part of the vineyard. My thoughts are scattering fast, fragmented by visions of what will happen if Tybalt and his lackeys catch up with me.

If anything, I am only in more danger out here, where there are no distinguished witnesses to check Tybalt's desire for blood-shed; and when the lane bends sharply, and I stumble into a wedge of total blackness that pools in the lee of the garden wall, I have the brilliant notion to escape the same way Benvolio and I made our way in.

The stone of the wall is rough, but I'm too panicked to feel any pain as I scramble my way to the top. I am so dizzy with nerves that I don't even realize I'm not alone until I hear a small, frantic voice whispering behind me, "Wait, Romeo!"

When I look back, Valentine is struggling to climb in my wake, his amber eyes so wide with fright the whites are visible all the way around. The clatter of Tybalt's men stampeding down the lane draws closer by the second. Without pausing to think twice, I reach down, grasping the boy's hand and heaving him up with all my strength.

For the second time tonight, I tumble to the loamy floor of the Capulet orchard. The wind is knocked from my lungs, but there is no time to recover. Shoving Valentine ahead of me, I guide us aimlessly into the darkness. When we reach the first adequate hiding place—a gnarled fig tree with a wide trunk—I pull him down behind it. My heart pounds so loudly I am certain it can be heard all the way over in San Pietro.

Tybalt's crew thunders past on the road, a muffled riot of pounding feet and angry voices; a few minutes later, they make a slower return. After several more agonizing heartbeats, there is movement at the top of the wall, and a head rises into view, a dark cap of hair silvered by the moonlight. Beside me, Valentine takes a sharp breath.

The head retreats, then reappears, and a long-limbed man vaults over the top of the wall to join us in the orchard. When Valentine flinches, I tighten my grip on his waist, willing him to remain still. I can't see much from our vantage point, but I hear the snick of metal as a blade is drawn, and then a harsh voice calls, "You might as well come out—we know you're hiding here, and we will find you."

Footsteps—first one way and then another, prowling through the trees . . . and then silence. Too much silence.

When the voice comes again, it is startlingly close by, only a few yards off to our left. "Show yourselves, you cowards!"

Sweat rolls under my shepherd's tunic, sticking it to my chest and the small of my back. Valentine vibrates beneath me, breathing hard, squeezing my hand until it hurts.

"Matteo!" Another head rises into view atop the wall, and I hear the man near us pivot on his boot heel, looking back. "Give it up, mate—we've lost them."

"No, they could not have simply vanished!" Matteo insists, thrashing at some leaves with what must be his sword. "They must be in here, somewhere."

"Then they might as well be in Padua," comes the sarcastic reply. "Do you have any idea how vast these gardens are? Come—I don't fancy wasting my night on a wild goose chase. Not when there are pretty girls inside, and all the wine we can drink."

Matteo grumbles doubtfully. "Tybalt will be unhappy if we come back empty handed."

"So what? He's always unhappy." The second man's head disappears behind the wall again, but his voice floats back over it. "Do what pleases you, but the rest of us are returning to the party."

Matteo continues thrashing the shrubs for a few minutes more, drifting slowly away from us, until he at last seems to concede defeat. But even after he has clambered back over the wall, and the orchard is silent once more, I wait a good long while before I feel it's safe to leave our hiding place.

"Well." Valentine hugs himself tightly, shivering a little in the cool, damp air. "I can honestly say that this evening did not end quite the way I imagined."

It finally occurs to me that he's shirtless, and probably freezing now that we are no longer moving at a sprint. I wish I could warm him but have nothing to accomplish the task; all I wear, other than my decorative tunic, is a flimsy linen shirt.

Come to that, I'm cold as well. But despite my clamoring nerves, my limbs still shaky with residual fear, I begin to laugh—and continue at it until Valentine joins me, and I find myself gasping for air. "Do you know what is truly deranged? I knew the night would end in *precisely* such a disaster as this, and yet I let myself be coaxed into it nonetheless!"

"I suppose Mercutio did promise me excitement, and has proven me wrong for doubting him."

"Welcome back to Verona," I quip, with a smirk. And then I shake my head. "I cannot believe you are *Valentine.*"

"Why? Because when last you saw me, I was a spindly runt with a high-pitched voice, chasing after my brother and his dazzling cadre of important friends?"

"Well, there is that." I grin, wondering if my teeth shine the way his do. "Although I might have said 'sophisticated and handsome' instead of 'dazzling.'"

"Sophisticated, handsome, important, and egomaniacal," he appends, smiling wider.

"Even more accurate!"

"I suppose I have changed." He looks down at his body, his bare torso and long limbs—lanky, perhaps, but not spindly anymore. "To a greater extent than the people I left behind, at any rate. Although it feels quite the opposite to me. Mercutio has turned fully into a man, and our sister, Agnese, is *with child* now!"

I hesitate to ask my next question. "Have I changed? I mean, from your memories of Verona in the years before you left."

"You . . ." He gives me an appraising look that sends color into my cheeks, and I'm grateful again for the shadows around us. "You have grown taller, and broader in the shoulders—and your voice is deeper. But I recognized you almost immediately."

"And yet you said nothing," I manage after a slight cough. "Why did you not reintroduce yourself?"

"I was curious to see if you would remember me." He glances away, scratches nervously at his shoulder. "I suppose that I meant what I said, about wanting to be unseen. Tonight was so exhausting—even before we tackled a man to the ground and fled for our lives." Valentine spares a wry smile for me that is so startlingly attractive, something flips over in the pit of my stomach. "Mercutio kept wanting to show me off, to add fanfare to my homecoming, and it meant constantly encountering people whom I could scarcely recall. I was answering the same questions over and over, and then . . . with you I had the chance to just be myself. Not 'Valentine the Returned,' just . . . me."

"That is all understandable," I say softly. After all, I'd have given anything to have remained a little more anonymous at the masquerade myself.

"There was also my curiosity about what the renowned Romeo Montague might say to a stranger." He smiles again, coyly, and that feeling in my stomach turns dangerously pleasurable.

It takes me a moment to find my voice. "Sophisticated, handsome, important, egomaniacal, and *renowned*. I am getting better all the time."

Valentine laughs at this, and the sound of it tickles me in places I didn't know about, like warm water surging through unseen cracks in a stone panel.

"We should be on our way," I say at last, reluctant to break this spell, this delicate curtain of happy wonder that seems to have fallen upon us. "There are only so many ways back to San Pietro for me, and Tybalt knows it well. If we give him long enough, he'll harangue his minions into preparing an ambush. And for safety's sake, we ought to avoid the lane—we can cross the orchard and exit on the other side."

"I don't suppose you have a map." He hugs himself tighter, squinting into the trees. "This is a veritable forest, and we could wander for days before ever finding a way out."

"Fortunately, there is plenty to eat," I volley back. "But it won't come to that. Whichever direction we walk, we'll come eventually to a wall that we can climb back over."

It is one promise I feel I can make without reservation. In Verona, there is always another wall just waiting for you to run up against it.

10

We wander in a companionable silence for a while, the air perfumed by blossoming trees—fig giving way to pear, to apple, and then to quince. It's surprisingly pleasant, and I keep stealing glances at Valentine, his chest sparkling in the moonlight. If he looked in his element by the well, a woodland spirit seeking his purpose, he looks only more so now.

"You are studying me again, when you think I am not looking," he says quite suddenly, in a sly way.

"I . . . I am only making sure that you are keeping pace with me!" I am backfooted, flustered by his perceptiveness. "How am I to do that unobtrusively when you are apparently *always* looking?"

A complicated expression ripples across his face. Softly, he says, "I don't really mind if you wish to study me, you know."

"Well . . ." Heat makes porridge of my insides. "I shall have to bear that in mind the next time you tell me you long to be unseen."

"You should." He seems quite proud of himself. "I knew you'd learn my name eventually, but I did choose to show you my face when I didn't have to. Perhaps you ought to bear that in mind as well."

The way he says it pulls at me, taunts me, makes promises that I want so badly to be true that I am frightened half to death. "But . . . why?"

"If I tell you directly, it takes away all the magic." He frowns. Then, in a nearly undecipherable undertone, he mutters, "But I think you know the answer already."

I think I do, as well. Or, at least, I know what I *wish* to be the answer—even if I've never dared to imagine it as something possible, something more than a fantasy. What I wish to be true is something I'm not even sure I know the language to express, and the fear of misunderstanding knots my tongue.

"The truth is, I cannot seem to help but keep checking to make certain you are real." I divert to a lesser truth, my face and throat aflame as a deeper honesty threatens to surface. "You . . . you are somewhat fascinating to me, Valentine."

"Me?" He glances up, genuinely shocked. "I've not been fascinating a day in my life."

His reaction makes me laugh, in spite of my inner turmoil. "It is a compliment, not an accusation!"

"Just the same, it is untrue." He hunches his shoulders, hiding from the praise. "I am an ordinary boy with a boring life . . . it is only because I am not what you remembered that you find me interesting."

"That is not so! When we first encountered each other by that well, you said so many things that I had thought myself but never spoken aloud," I reply. "Even before I knew that I knew you—before I knew enough to have any expectation of you—you had intrigued me."

"That is . . . that's . . ." But he cannot seem to complete the thought. He tucks his chin, shoulders hunching even more, and I realize I have made him *bashful*. For some reason, it delights me, an even more rewarding sensation than escaping from Tybalt and his dagger.

"You are fascinating for having gone away and come back, though," I persist. "The longest I've been outside of Verona was twenty days, and that was on a trip to Venice with my parents. Sometimes . . ." Letting out a weary breath, I look back, the Capulet villa somewhere behind us in the vast and spreading dark. "Sometimes I hate this place. I wish I could know what it's like to be invisible, because all too often this city is a bear pit—where I am the bear, and everyone is watching and waiting to see how long I'll survive."

"You might not like being anonymous as much as you think." Valentine tugs at his leather vest, pulling it closed. "You're lucky to have your name, in a city where having a name like Montague makes a difference. Anywhere else, without that distinction, you'd *still* be in a bear pit—only in that scenario, you'd be one of the dogs."

I consider what he's said before I reply, aware that he is not incorrect . . . even if the point he's making somewhat misses the point *I'm* making. "It's true that I'm very lucky. I want for nothing material, my family is respected even by Prince Escalus himself, and—so long as I remain in San Pietro, at least—I am rarely in any danger. But . . ." And here is where I struggle to articulate something I've had precious few occasions to address aloud before. "There are parts of me that need more than just the security of this containment. I have problems that even my name cannot solve; problems that my name makes worse, because of the expectations it brings and the scrutiny it puts me under."

The evening washes back over me, a deluge of awkward introductions and forced conversation with hopeful girls, all part of an endless, wearying performance I'm not sure I'll ever be able to retire from. Anonymity would rob me of my creature comforts—but even Valentine understands the value of not being always noticed.

"'The harvest is always richer in another man's field.'" Valentine gives me a half-cocked smile. "That's from Ovid's *Ars Amatoria*. My uncle Ostasio had it in his library, although I'm fairly certain he would not have wanted it in my hands, if he'd known I could read. It contained the sort of information a good Catholic boy isn't supposed to look for."

"There are worse vices than seeking knowledge."

"Tell that to Adam and Eve," he quips without hesitation, and I laugh again.

"Was this Ostasio the relation you were staying with all this time?" I ask, and he nods, pushing those long fingers through his hair. "What was it like, living in Vicenza?"

He shrugs. "It wasn't so bad. My uncle was well-to-do, but he already had eight children of his own, so there was little in the way of luxury to go around. They expected me to earn my keep, and so I essentially became another of their servants. But they fed me, clothed me, and put a roof over my head, and they allowed me to sit in on my cousins' daily lessons." His tone remains impartial. "They weren't particularly warm, but they were generous, and I was lucky enough for that."

"Did you miss Verona?" I don't mean to pry, exactly, but I meant what I said when I told him I was fascinated by his temporary absence. "Surely you must have made friends while living there."

"I did. After a while." Just when I think he isn't going to offer any more on the subject, he sighs. "When I first arrived at my uncle's, I was bitterly unhappy. I didn't understand why I had to be sent away, and I cried every night, wishing I could still be with my brother and sisters. Verona wasn't even that far away, I realize now, but at the time it felt like I'd been dispatched to the edge of the world." Valentine makes a loose gesture with his hand. "And yet . . . coming back has been almost as difficult. Everything that was familiar to me has changed since I saw it last, even if just slightly, and it feels as though I have lost something important."

"Your brother is quite overjoyed about your return. That must make it easier."

"Yes. Mercutio has been amazing," he agrees readily. "But I think we are still getting to know each other again. He remembers me as a boy of thirteen years, and I remember him as . . . well, the brother to a boy of thirteen years. It used to be that we knew each other so well we could each predict the other's moods. But now everything is a bit of a mystery."

106

For a moment, I let this settle. Everything in my life has been so fixed, so constant, that I can hardly imagine the kind of adjustments he's had to make—to life in a new city, with a new family and no friends. Having to spend years pining for what he left behind, only to return at last and discover that everything he left behind had shifted out of alignment with his memories.

"But you've only been back just over a fortnight. Surely it will get easier, in time," I suggest, desperate to provide some sort of comfort. Then, with a gesture at myself, I add, "And, look: You are already making new friends out of old friends!"

Valentine smiles, and I feel it under my skin. "Yes, that's true. I suppose I am sulking a bit too much. I cannot be who I once was, and who wishes to relive their thirteenth year?"

"Did you . . . do you really have memories of me? From back then, I mean." My face burns as I ask the question, because I am aware on some level that what I'm seeking is not answers but intimacy. I remember Valentine-of-thirteen-years, but I want to be closer to *this* Valentine—the one who is older, and so startlingly handsome. What I really want is something I don't know how to ask for.

"I remember . . ." He looks at me, and then away. "I remember that you were different from Mercutio's other friends."

"Was I?"

"Of course you were." He laughs a little, as though I am being absurd. "My brother is . . . well, he has a contagious point of view. If he feels a certain way, it's not long before all his friends feel the same, whether they agree with him or not." A crooked smile lights his face. "I remember a day when we all went into the countryside, because Mercutio wished to hunt rabbits, and I brought a net to capture butterflies. I meant to bring them home in a jar and keep them as pets—because I was precisely that naive—but of course the ones I managed to catch quickly grew sluggish and immobile under the glass.

"That's when Mercutio finally explained to me that they were suffocating, that the whole point of catching insects was for them to die, so they could be pinned to a canvas and studied or admired." He shudders all over, but laughs ruefully at the same time. "I became utterly distraught, and immediately let all the butterflies go—which embarrassed my brother, who thought I was being foolish and feminine." His tone becomes more somber. "He mocked me, and all his friends laughed along with him . . . except for you."

"I didn't?"

Vaguely, I do recall that afternoon, but only in fragments. The sun burning lazily over myrtle and pine trees on the hillside, Ben trying to use a good luck charm to coax a rabbit out of some shrubbery, and Valentine crying as he shook half-dead butterflies out of a jar. Mercutio was ill-tempered, for reasons of his own, and each animal that escaped his arrow only soured his mood further. The rest of us spent most of the afternoon trying and failing to cheer him, and when he erupted at Valentine, it was because he had finally found a convenient outlet for his restless anger.

I remember the others laughing at his mean-spirited taunts, hoping it would somehow encourage him into a better humor; but I do not remember that I refrained from joining in. It shames me a little, how surprised I am to think I was capable of doing something as simple as disagreeing with Mercutio—even when he was clearly wrong—because agreeing with Mercutio was necessary if you wished for him to like you.

And I did wish for that, fervently.

"You offered to walk me back into the city, since I was not supposed to be outside the walls on my own, and on the way we stopped by a stream to look at frogs." There is warmth in his voice, and fondness, and long-forgotten memories turn up suddenly in my mind. I can just see a tiny gray-green creature, cupped in the palm of my hand, its delicate body thrumming. Over my shoulder, a boy demands I give it a name before I let it go again.

"Stella Nera," I blurt, the words coming to me out of the past.

"For the black star on her throat." Valentine grins from ear to ear, but there's a timidity to his gaze when he looks at me; that sensation of something turning over in my stomach grows almost deadly. "I . . . I never forgot how kind you were to me that day."

"Don't be too quick with your praise. I was almost certainly doing it to curry favor with Mercutio." The admission brings me no pride, but it is at least honest.

"Probably." He doesn't sound bothered in the least. "But you were generous when you might have been impatient, and you comforted me when my brother tried to make me feel ashamed. The way you acted matters more to me than *why* you acted."

"Perhaps that makes you the generous one," I mumble awkwardly, not sure how to respond to his kind words. They make my insides turbulent—my limbs jittering, my blood running hot in my face and chest while it runs cold in my feet and hands.

Fortunately, I am spared further comment when we push through a cluster of tall bushes and find ourselves faced with another section of the garden wall at last. There is no gate in sight, but ivy blankets the rough stone, its roots robust enough to serve as footholds. Gripping one of the sturdier vines, I say, "This, I suppose, is where we make our exit."

"Wait." Valentine steps forward, and the moonlight reflects in his eyes as he searches my face. His sudden closeness causes my stomach to go tight in a way I've seldom experienced, and I am terrifyingly aware of his shimmering skin, his artistically crafted mouth. "I needed to say that . . . even though I concealed my identity when we first saw each other tonight, I meant everything I said. I meant everything I did."

He reaches out then, his hand finding mine where it still rests among the vines, his fingers slipping gently over my own in an echo of our final shared moments in that hidden courtyard. My heart races, and I can only stare and want and hope. The longer I fail to resist, the more confident his touch becomes.

Cautiously, he teases my grip free from the vine and turns my hand over, his fingers threading through mine. He keeps looking at me, fearful, seeking permission, and I don't know what to do. I'm afraid to say yes, but I refuse to say no, and I'm not sure what options lie in between. My hand is shaking—*I* am shaking, everywhere—and he finally whispers, "Do you wish me to let go?"

"No." I barely manage to produce the word. "No." Then, "What is happening?" It feels as if lightning has struck me, is striking me. I can't breathe, and I can't stop breathing, and I can't stop thinking about how close he is. "What happens now?"

"I don't know." Valentine is shaking, too, I realize, and he stutters a laugh. "I've never gone further than this before." Staring at me, the moon dancing in his eyes, he says, "I think . . . I want to know what it feels like to kiss you. I want you to—"

He doesn't finish, because in the next moment, I've pulled him all the way into me. I've wrapped my free arm around his waist, and pressed my mouth against his. This is a moment I've never known how to imagine, never known was even possible for someone like me, and it feels . . . it feels like I am floating and sinking and turning inside out.

His lips are soft, but his grip is strong at the base of my neck, and the sound he makes—this feral grunt in his throat—causes my flesh to pebble. I don't know what I'm doing, but I can't get enough; I can't taste him enough, feel him enough. The breeze swirls, redolent of black earth and blossoms on the cusp of fruiting, and I'm lost in a rich sensation of *living* in a way I've never known before. He's more intoxicating than the Capulets' wine, more decadent than their honeyed dates and drunken figs.

When he pulls back, his mouth swollen, his eyes dazed and glittering, he gasps, "Is this . . . is this what it's meant to feel like?"

"I don't know." I am unable to catch my breath. "I've no idea what it's meant to feel like—but if it's always like this, how does anyone ever stop?"

He kisses me again, his hands grasping tighter, his lips pulling at mine with even more hunger. Leaves shake around us, the night air alive, heavy with the green of the river and the pink of the orchard. I have nowhere to put the feelings that burst under my skin, no way to understand them; it's as though every part of my body is recognizing itself for the first time.

We draw apart at last, our eyes still wide and searching. I know he feels it, too—this breathless, scratchy awareness of the world, this new realization of its vibrancy and sharp edges— because I see it in his face. It's like being thrown from a horse, having the wind knocked out of you and realizing you're still alive.

"What do we do now?" he whispers, searching my face over and over.

"We have to go home." I'm not answering the question he's truly asking, because I have no comprehensible answer to give. "Your brother will be waiting for you, and Benvolio might well be waiting for me, to see if I successfully escaped from Tybalt."

"But—"

"We will meet like this again." It's the second promise I've made to him tonight with neither doubt nor hesitation. "I don't know how, or when, but I cannot go another week without . . . *this*. I could get drunk on kissing you, and will, as frequently as I can see to it." Reaching reluctantly for the vines that cover the garden wall, I add, "But only if we make it out of San Zeno before our enemies can rethink their strategy for catching us."

"I will hold you to that." Valentine watches me hoist myself up, preparing to follow. Then, softly, his voice carrying up on the silky air, "And I hope you will hold me."

This final sentiment keeps me warm all the way back to San Pietro.

ACT TWO

LOVE'S SWEET BAIT

11

BEYOND VERONA'S FORMIDABLE WALLS, THE WORLD SPREADS OUT for miles of bucolic landscapes in gold and blue and green. The Dolomites rise to the north, cutting their teeth against the sky, and the snow-covered Apennines lie somewhere to the south. But throughout the valley that encompasses the Adige, what hills exist are gentle, and glazed with sunlight from dawn to dusk at this time of year.

I've wandered this stretch of countryside countless times, its dusty lanes and evergreen sentinels as familiar to me as the patterns in my bedchamber floor, but today, everything under the sun is strange and new. The world is scented with resin and rosemary, the day slowly gathering heat, and I drink it in with lustful abandon.

For the first time in as long as I can remember, I am actually looking forward to returning to the city when my day is done.

The road winds past a grove of wild olive trees, and then a meadow, where brilliant flowers host the bees and butterflies. Then it slopes again, where a rushing stream curls beside a church of tawny stone, its size almost startling in the midst of all this nothing.

The day is well begun, so I don't even bother checking the cloisters. Instead, I head straight for the gardens behind them, a collection of thriving plants that surpasses even the Capulets' own—in variety, at least, if not in size and scope. And here, as expected, is where I find the man I'm looking for, grimy to the elbows as he teases weeds up from a bed of damp soil.

"Good day, Friar Laurence," I call out the second I recognize him, his lanky form unmistakable.

"Ah, Romeo!" He squints up at me, the light finding his face beneath the wide brim of his straw hat—a necessary precaution to protect his freckled skin. He is originally from someplace in France that I have never heard of, although I understand it is very far north. "I was beginning to think I wouldn't see you today—you usually make your appearances around here before the sun does."

"I . . . I somewhat overslept this morning." I glance away as I admit this, somehow afraid of what my expression will betray. After crawling back into my room last night—to find Benvolio waiting for me after all—I was awake for hours. Even after my cousin left, I could not sleep, my imagination replaying that kiss in the orchard over and over until I gave in to sheer exhaustion sometime before dawn.

"Well, I'm always glad of your company, no matter the hour." The long-limbed monk sits back on his haunches, wiping sweat from his brow and absentmindedly leaving a streak of dirt across his forehead. "I must apologize, though. I have quite a bit to get done, and I'm not sure how much time in which I have to do it."

It is maybe a little embarrassing to confess that when first we met, I was a trifle smitten with Laurence. He is still young, not ten years my senior, and although he is somewhat awkwardly built, there is an appealing warmth to him. It became soon apparent, however, that he did not see me the same way—that he does not, I think, see anyone that way. He is content with his vow of chastity, and I am grateful to have his friendship.

"Have you somewhere you're meant to be?" I ask.

"Old Guillaume woke with a stiff hip and insists that rain is coming." He gestures at the bright blue sky that stretches overhead, the only clouds in sight mere shreds of foam on the eastern horizon. I cock a questioning brow at this, and Laurence shrugs. "I know, but Guillaume has surprised us all before. These weeds need to come up, and there are cuttings I must make, and . . . well, if the weather takes a poor turn, I will miss my chance."

"If there is anything you need my help with . . ."

"There *is* a task that I would gladly use your hands to accomplish, if you don't mind." Getting to his feet, he wipes his fingers on an old rag, and then leads me to a row of some flowering plants I cannot identify—low and leafy, with white buds just beginning to spread open. "These blossoms need to be plucked, and without much more delay. They've been left too long already, and if it really does rain today, I'm afraid it will be too late."

"Why?" I ask, as he passes me a basket to collect my bounty. "They're only just beginning to bloom."

"Precisely." Laurence says this as though I have just proven his point. "The flowers are pretty enough, but it is the leaves that matter most to me. I use them in poultices and for a salve to treat skin irritations, and the bigger they are, the better. If the flowers continue to grow, they will draw nutrients away from the rest of the plant, as they will eventually bear the fruit that begins the cycle of its life anew."

"So if we pluck them now," I conclude, "it is the leaves that will continue to grow?"

"Precisely!" he says, beaming at me. "Still, we ought to keep . . . let's say every third plant with its blooms intact. That way there will also be plenty of seeds to harvest at the end of the season. Now, be quick, but be careful, and find me when the deed is done."

With that, he returns to his own task, and leaves me to mine— and although I did come all this way to seek his counsel, I actually rather enjoy the silence and the work. I understand why this life appeals to him, even if it cannot be an easy one, and I like to think that I am absorbing some of his wholesome tranquility when I toil in his beloved gardens.

Back home in France, he grew up as the son of an apothecarist, and spent most of his life training to join his father's profession. He left that future behind, of course, when he was called to join the Franciscan order; but he retains a staggering amount of knowledge about plants and medicine, and he is forever mixing up strange unguents and potions that always seem to work exactly the way he claims they will.

I lose track of the time after a while; when the sun stops tin-

120

gling against the back of my neck and the light turns milky, I don't even notice. It's not until I realize that Friar Laurence is standing beside me again that I look up and realize the blue sky has vanished behind a ceiling of heavy clouds.

"Well. Old Guillaume was right again!" Laurence clucks his tongue. He is even grimier than when I first saw him, and the basket he carries is full to the brim with his cuttings. "We'd better hurry if we don't wish to be caught in the deluge."

It's shocking how quickly the clouds go from a dingy white to an angry gray. We hurry for the cloisters, but we don't quite make it before the first drops of rain begin to speckle my shoulders. The downpour begins shortly thereafter, and when Friar Laurence ushers me into his cell, I am grateful to see that the Franciscans are faring better than their Benedictine counterparts at the San Zeno abbey: The roof of the friary does not leak.

The rain is pleasant enough, but its drumming and burbling make me only more aware of the silence I've brought into the room with me. I've been here many times before, of course, eager to gain Laurence's advice or simply bend his ear. Out in the garden, the quietude is its own form of communication—a conversation about the importance of *just being*. But here, indoors, it is another empty space that demands to be filled.

"Have you come to make confession, Romeo?" Laurence prompts gently, when I go too long without speaking—when it's clear enough that I have something to say.

"Um. I suppose." It's a reasonable guess; he's been my chosen confessor for some time now, but where do I even begin? "I . . . told a lie to my friends. Well, several lies."

"I see." Friar Laurence waits patiently, and when I don't continue, he says, "Did you lie to hurt someone?"

"No, no." I give him a sharp look, almost surprised he would ask me that. "I lied to, to . . . make things easier. For me *and* for my friends—though mostly for me, if I'm to be honest." A nervous laugh overtakes me. "If I am to be honest about being dishonest."

"People lie for many reasons." Laurence shifts on the edge of his bed. "One of the most common reasons is kindness. We tell people what they want to hear, or what we think they need to hear in order to be happy. Sometimes it works. Sometimes allowing someone to believe a harmless falsehood can feel like an act of charity." He watches me try and fail to meet his eyes for more than a second. "What is it that you lied about?"

"The same thing I am always lying about." My voice has grown small and thin, and I scratch at an insect bite on my hand just to give myself something to do. "There was a party last night, and my . . . my cousin was determined to embroil me in a romantic liaison with a young lady. Any young lady."

Laurence makes a noise of understanding, and when I hazard another glance in his direction, I see the same patient, open expression on his face. I've talked to him of this matter before, to a greater or lesser degree, and he has never offered the sort of opprobrium I always fear, and yet I always fear it anyway.

"I agreed to let him play Cupid for me, and then I suppose I lied to some very nice girls—by omission, really, but it amounts to the same thing—and all the while I was perfectly miserable."

"So it did not, in the end, make things easier for you," the monk points out in a careful way, and eventually I nod. "And your cousin? Did your lie make him happy?"

I give this some genuine thought for perhaps the first time, and frown at my own conclusion. "Perhaps. Really, though, it was more like he was . . . relieved. And he will be very frustrated when he learns his plan did not work, and that I am the same as I ever was. He is . . . he is beginning to become suspicious, I think, of the reason behind my recalcitrance."

"So, then, the lie did not result in happiness for any of you. And instead of making things easier, as you had hoped, it may in fact have made things more difficult?"

"Yes." Now I am the frustrated one. "But the truth would only make things harder still. How could I explain a thing like . . . like that?" With agitated hands, I gesture at myself. "Like *this*? How do I explain something I barely understand myself?"

Laurence fingers the cuff of his robe, the coarse fabric made soft by countless washings, his gentle eyes turning sad. "It can be much harder to live with a lie than you might think, Romeo. Even one that feels safer than the truth."

"Even if I tell the truth and am forced to live the lie, all the same?" I challenge. Surely, he cannot be naive enough to think this is so simple a proposition. Would anyone even understand? It would certainly not stop my father from choosing me a bride anyway—and as for my friends, it's hard to even imagine how they would react. What would Benvolio think? What would *Mercutio* think? *What if he barred me from seeing Valentine again?* "Even if the truth costs me more than the lie ever could?"

"What is lost in the short term may be regained over time,"

123

he replies, and the sheer banality of his statement makes it clear that he does not comprehend the seriousness of my situation. "You do not yet know what lies on the other side of the truth, Romeo. Some leaps require faith—and, sometimes, achieving your purpose in life, your happiness, requires sacrifice." When he can see that his platitudes are having no effect, he sighs. "You know, my parents expected me to marry as well. Certainly, they never imagined their eldest son casting aside his responsibilities to become a mendicant priest, living in poverty. They could not understand that I had no desire to take a wife, and that the simplicity of this existence was the happy answer to every disheartening question I'd ever asked myself.

"In fact . . ." He leans forward until he catches my eye at last. "The monastic life is home to many who are just like you, Romeo—who are like us both: young men who needed an environment of love and oneness with the world, where they could be free of societal expectations and not pressured to live a lie."

"If you are suggesting I might consider life as a monk, it is probably not the path for me," I tell him, my face going hot as I remember Valentine's lips on my own—as I remember how my body responded, from the roots of my hair to the tips of my toes. "I don't think I'm suited to a vow of chastity. Among other things."

He smiles a bit at my discomfort, but there is affection in it. "You would not be the first to balk at the priesthood on those grounds. And you are also not the first to have this plight—you are not even the first I have personally counseled, in my few short years."

"Is that true?" I can't say why this comes as such a relief to hear, but it does. Friar Laurence is not some stranger, or a noble whose private business is shared in markets and taverns through whispered rumors; he is a friend, someone close and tangible, and it makes his other acquaintances somehow more *real* to me. That he actually knows others in my position, has even befriended them, makes me feel less alone.

"Of course!" He laughs, his voice echoing against the close, barren walls. "I hope you don't take this the wrong way, but you are not nearly as unique as you suspect."

I open my mouth to make some sort of joke; but instead, to my surprise, I blurt, "At this party, I met someone—someone who finally made me feel all the things my cousin so often describes when he speaks of being with girls. And I think the experience was mutual."

"Really?" Friar Laurence tilts his head, pleased but obviously somewhat confused. "Well, I . . . this is good news, is it not? If there is a young lady who—"

"There isn't." My voice is now small enough to fit on the head of a pin, and I have to take several deep breaths before I can continue. "It wasn't . . . it wasn't a girl. We met in a funny little courtyard and had the most important conversation I believe I've ever had with anyone. And then, later . . ."

Only, how do you explain a kiss? It's like waking up—or maybe it's even more like falling asleep. Plunging into a dream world, where the impossible is not only possible, but it's suddenly at your fingertips, and better than you could ever imagine.

"I have never felt this way," I tell Laurence hoarsely, and

then shake my head, because this doesn't express what I mean. The attraction is not new to me, but there is more to it than that. "I have never felt this way *with* someone. I have never had it shared like this—never had anyone feel this way about me *in return*."

"And what was it like?" Friar Laurence asks. "How did it make you feel?"

The question makes me laugh, because I have spent all night failing to answer it. Looking into Valentine's eyes and recognizing myself in them was . . . apocalyptic, in the original sense of the word: *a revelation*. Holding his hand, kissing him, made some dormant part of me leap to urgent, full-throated life. A part of me I knew existed, but had no idea was capable of such sound and fury. I discovered myself in the Capulets' orchard.

Whispering, I manage, "It made me feel like I was in the right place, the right skin, for the first time in my life."

Friar Laurence takes this in, his expression contemplative. "Something I have learned, both through observation and personal experience, is that happiness is not guaranteed to anyone. If it finds you, if it seeks you out, it is best to revel in it for as long as you can. It is perhaps the greatest gift fate has to offer."

"And when fate takes it away again?" I demand, growing surly. "When a world that has no room for us together inevitably forces us apart?"

"It is true that cities like Verona do not allow much space for those of us who walk a different path." Friar Laurence gazes out the window, where the rain has retreated from a torrent to a shower. "But there is far more out there than just those walls and the people within them, Romeo. There is more space in this world than you could ever dream of."

"But I am here," I remind him, "and here I am destined to remain—stuck within those walls, among those people, living whatever life my father permits me." Because I am annoyed that he will not indulge my pessimism, I insist, "And aren't you supposed to tell me about my sacred duty to take a bride and have a great swarm of babies?"

"Is that what you wish to hear from me?" He grins, cockeyed and terribly amused. "It would make me something of a hypocrite if I suggested that might be anyone's sacred duty, given that I have forsworn it myself." With a self-conscious flush to his cheeks that is very endearing, he adds, "And given how easy it was to forswear in the first place. As you may recall from some of the things I've said to you in the past, making a formal commitment to celibacy was perhaps the least challenging step for me in becoming a mendicant friar."

"I . . . I do recall." My own cheeks warm a little, embarrassed to be thinking about Laurence and his celibacy right in front of him.

"I feel guilty, on occasion, when my brethren struggle with the weight of their vows, as it required no great sacrifice on my part. Where, in quite the opposite sense, it was one aspect of worldly life and worldly considerations that was a relief to leave behind."

"Do you never feel . . . temptation?" I ask, my face burning. Until just recently, merely being in Mercutio's presence was enough for me to feel consumed by temptation. Even just thinking of him was enough. Even someone *else* thinking of him was enough!

"Oh, I experience the occasional urge." Laurence gives a cheerful shrug. "But it's rare, and somewhat like church bells being rung across the hills: loud enough to hear, though quiet enough not to distract."

"But what about me?" I try not to sound urgent, but my knuckles are white in my lap. "The things that I feel . . . I cannot seem to relinquish them, no matter how hard I try."

"That sacrifice is not asked or expected of everyone," he points out with care. "You know, I have found that no matter how well or how poorly I tend my plants, I have little control over when they blossom, or how high they grow, or how much fruit they bear. For all our planning, some things are always unexpected. Tiny miracles, happening everywhere.

"The natural world is our truest vision of the Divine, in all its splendor and curiosity and unexplained phenomena." He leans forward again, tucking his hands beneath his chin. "There are far stranger things on this earth by heaven's design than a Montague desiring a romantic liaison with someone who is not a girl. Romeo . . . have you never considered that perhaps you are *meant* to have this happiness?"

The simplicity of this question, with its manifold kindness and generosity, is more than I can bear. My chin quivers, heat builds behind my eyes, and tears rush out before I can act to quell them. In seconds, I am sobbing openly, my face buried in my hands, my shoulders shaking. No one has ever told me I might deserve to be happy on my own terms, rather than just happy with what I've been given. No one has ever told me I might simply deserve to be *happy*.

I cannot remember the last time I cried. My parents consider it low behavior, and my friends have gradually developed a similar opinion, losing their patience with any emotions other than joy and anger; but Friar Laurence neither shames me nor tells me to stop. Instead, he waits quietly until my tears are all shed and my breathing has evened out.

Wordlessly, he passes me a handkerchief, and I mumble a polite thank-you as I dry my face and blow my nose. The rain has stopped, I notice, the skies ceasing their downpour just as I have concluded my own.

"If you like," the monk suggests, after another thought-filled silence has passed between us, "we can go outside and hunt for rainbows."

With a crooked smile, I nod. Maybe it's time for me to seek the Divine.

12

WE FIND OUR RAINBOW ALMOST IMMEDIATELY, BENDING ACROSS the sky in the direction of Lago di Garda, its tones brilliant against a dark backdrop of defeated storm clouds. But then Laurence wants to explain an important lesson about a flock of martins that swirl through the air overhead, and after that, we stumble across a cluster of wild mint that he needs to take cuttings from for his medicines.

When at last I manage my goodbyes, the sky is clear again, the humidity regrouping as the sun sidles its way into heaven's western vault. My shirt sticks almost instantly to my flesh when I set off along the rocky path that leads away from the friary grounds, beginning my journey back to Verona.

I am so preoccupied by my thoughts that I almost fail to notice when another person rounds the bend in the road just ahead of me, appearing as though out of nowhere. When I see that it's someone I recognize, and perhaps the last person I expected to encounter—not just here, but anywhere—I stop in my tracks.

"Well." She arches a brow. "Once may be an accident and twice a coincidence, but if we meet again tomorrow, I shall begin to suspect a conspiracy." Lifting her chin appraisingly, Juliet adds, "If I didn't know better, I'd think you were following me."

"I was here first," I riposte, but mostly out of reflex. Although I am on my guard, there is nothing in her manner that suggests hostility, and she does appear to be alone. For the first time, in daylight and without a mask to obscure her features, I take her in—Juliet, my counterpart, the only child of my father's greatest enemy.

"Tybalt would say you were lying in wait for me."

"Tybalt is not known for his wisdom."

"But he is infamous for his paranoia, which is fueled by the belief that everyone else is as unscrupulously conniving as himself." She smiles wryly. "He would suspect an ambush, because his first thought would be to *set* an ambush, were he in your position."

It's much the same thing as what I said to Valentine the night before, when we were debating which way to leave the orchard, and I automatically crane my neck to peer down the lane behind her.

"You needn't worry," she says, seeming to have heard my thoughts aloud. "He has little use for me outside my father's orbit, and I would sooner spend an hour inside a trunk full of scorpions than partake of his company when I did not have to." Stepping aside, she allows me a clear view around the sycamores, to a small carriage waiting at the roadside. "I have brought only my nurse along today, and I assure you she is no more favorably inclined toward Tybalt than I am."

"I am glad to hear it. Outrunning Tybalt wasn't easy, and your nurse has a horse." I grin, and Juliet grins back, and then we are giggling together. It feels almost like friendship. "I am sorry, by the way, for last night. It was never my intention to cause such calamity."

"Please, you caused nothing." Juliet waves my apology aside. "We'd have carried on having our very awkward and civilized conversation and parted ways peaceably, if Tybalt hadn't decided to grandstand on my father's behalf. He is the one to blame."

"Somehow I doubt your father agrees."

"Perhaps not. Tybalt is certainly the apple of his eye, and he has never once failed to defend my cousin's many outrageous provocations, even when he is so often clearly in the wrong," she acknowledges glumly. "But there isn't a soul in San Zeno who does not know exactly what a petty, backbiting little snake Tybalt really is—even Alboino Capulet."

"Well. I am sorry, just the same." I do not know what to make of how boldly she still articulates her disdain for her family, even when she has no mask to hide behind. "Thank you, also, for coming to my defense against Tybalt's accusations."

"There is no need to thank me for speaking the truth when I had nothing to lose. He is displeased with me—but that is hardly new, so it is but one more wave against the beach." She squints into the sunlight. "I ought to be thanking you, really. I never thought I would see my cousin so roundly humiliated in front of every person whose respect he craves, but you and your friends managed the job nicely. It was easily worth his anger."

"I am glad to have been of service." I turn my hands up. "Though, truly, the only thing more satisfying than besting Tybalt would be having nothing to do with him whatsoever."

A silence falls, a lull in the conversation, and probably my cue to leave—but again, I find myself loath to depart. For my whole life, it has been impossible to escape talk of the endless feud between the Capulets and the Montagues, our well-seasoned mutual distrust. But today, for the first time, I am able to conspire about it with *one of them*—one who is just as sick of the inherited enmity as I am.

Looking for a new topic to explore, I ask, "What brings you to the friary?"

"I told you already: my carriage," she answers promptly, and then grins from ear to ear when she sees my expression. "I'm jesting, Montague—I know what you meant! I am come to a building full of priests . . . what do you think I am here for?"

"Oh, of course." My face warms. Confession, counsel, prayer, patronage . . . they are the only likely options for her visit, and none of them are my business. "I apologize for the impertinent question, it is just . . . I am here often, and I have never encountered you before. I thought the Capulets preferred the abbey church of San Zeno?"

"And I thought the Montagues preferred the church of San Pietro." Her rejoinder is delivered without ill will. "It seems neither of us falls quite in step with our expectations."

"Aptly put." *If she only knew.* Emboldened by her candor, I offer, "My parents do prefer the church of San Pietro, but the reason is far more social than spiritual. The beau monde of our

133

district finds it the perfect place to see and be seen, and that is all Lord and Lady Montague need to know." My face burns with the terrifying exhilaration of betraying them this way. "You might say that I come here for confession and counsel because it is the one place I can go where I do not feel San Pietro breathing down my neck."

"*Yes.*" She exhales the word, an entire conversation embedded in one syllable. "My parents march me to services at San Zeno, because they built the bell tower—which makes the church part of the family image. They have paid handsomely for their reputation as Verona's most pious citizens, and I am to help them reap the benefits." With a disgusted snort, she continues, "I come here because these monks, in their poverty and humility, represent everything my parents fear and cannot understand. And sometimes I need to feel justified in my resentments. I know that sounds terrible, but it's the plain truth."

"It sounds reasonable to me." Saying so, finally having someone to share these sentiments with, casts a weight from my soul. Benvolio thinks my fascination with Franciscans is part of an ordinary rebellion—that I am spoiled, and seeking the poorest company I can find to horrify my parents. Juliet, however, seems to truly understand just how far I have to travel to escape the circumference of my father's thumb.

"I am fascinated by the Friars Minor and their way of life." She looks around us at the wild growth of plants, and the birds spiraling around the church tower, its crevices bristling with their nests. "It is humbling to see how self-sufficient they are."

"Truly." I think of all the things Laurence does, wholly apart from growing and harvesting his own vegetables, from crafting his medicines. The monks also sew garments and make furniture, do their own washing and make their own wine—the daily chores they must perform alone are staggering. "I would love to feel so free, though. To know I could go anywhere at any time, and be . . . all right."

Juliet opens her mouth, and then closes it again, before finally offering an awkward, "One day, you will replace your father as the head of the Montague clan, and then you'll at least have some freedom to make your own decisions."

My life, of course, is a little more complicated than she knows, but I can hardly point it out. Besides, what has gone unspoken here is that her own future offers no such promises. Her parents will give her hand to someone, and she will become the lady of another house—almost certainly a distinguished one, but not one of her choosing—and then her decisions will have to be made with her husband's priorities in mind.

Also unspoken is the fact that when I am the Montagues' patriarch, the Capulets will be led by Tybalt.

As if reading my mind, Juliet wrings her hands. "Romeo . . . I hope it is not untoward of me to offer advice, but I hope you meant it when you said you prefer to avoid my cousin."

With a vigorous nod, I reply, "Quarreling with him brings me no pleasure, and to meet him is to invite a quarrel. What I said about besting him being less enjoyable than missing his company entirely was sincere, I promise you."

"Good. I am glad of it." She relaxes her hands, but with some effort. "He does not forget his grudges, and his fury does not subside with time. He is incensed about what a fool he was made of last night, and he will not relinquish his anger until it has been sated. He will be looking for you, and so you must look out for him in return."

"I understand. Believe me, I am familiar with the endurance of Tybalt's grievances."

"Good." She sucks in a breath. "You wounded his pride, which is what he values most in the world; and, worse, you set him back in my father's estimation. Or, at least, that is how he sees it. I believe he will make a mission out of recovering his pound of flesh from you."

Heat swells in the muggy afternoon air, sweat creeping down my back on tiny insect feet, and I fight the urge to squirm. Tybalt's bellicose posturing is notorious, and he has never needed any special excuse to provoke me. But now he *has* an excuse . . . as well as plenty of opportunities. There are only so many places to go in Verona—only so many places I can manage to *not* go—and it bears repeating that he does love an ambush.

"I will be careful," I promise her, darting a look out at the open countryside—at the long road and the bright sun and the lack of hiding places between here and the city. "Thank you for the warning."

"Again, I hope you don't think it inappropriate for me to say this, but . . . you seem to me a gentle soul, Romeo. Tybalt is not. Whatever fears and doubts you have, if your paths cross again? You must swallow them and do what needs doing." Forcing a smile onto her face, she then steps back. "I have taken up enough of your time. Needless to say, if asked, it's probably best that we tell no one we had this encounter."

"Agreed," I say. As I make my way down the lane, past Juliet's carriage and onto the road, I can only marvel at the strange turn of events that has led me to having an ally within the Capulets' stronghold.

13

ON THE JOURNEY BACK TO VERONA, I GRADUALLY STOP EXPECTING Tybalt to leap out from every ditch or shrub that I pass. In truth, I am not sure just how to evaluate the danger he poses me. It is true that the prince has taken a harsh stance against any bloodshed within the city walls, but then Tybalt has already found ways to do violence out in the open and get away with it.

Soberly, I vow to myself that I will live a quiet and careful life for the weeks ahead—no more clandestine trips to San Zeno, fewer parties where Tybalt might expect to find me, and more time spent with my friends. Now that I have fulfilled my deal with Benvolio, I should not need to worry about having to sidestep his intrusive questions—and of course I always look forward to seeing more of Mercutio.

And then there is Valentine.

Just thinking his name makes my feet lighter, as if I could step right off the ground and float the rest of the way home. Those eyes, like dark brandy; that tousled hair that was so pleasing to the touch; his quiet voice, his careful gestures. Heat blooms in the pit of my stomach, and then floods everywhere as I relive those kisses in the orchard.

I've watched Ben and Mercutio kiss many girls before—sometimes more than one in the same evening—and it always seemed such an odd thing to me. A clumsy mashing together of wet lips and slimy tongues, breathing in someone else's hot, damp exhalations . . . I could never comprehend the appeal, or why they were so eager for more.

Now, though, I finally understand, because I do not believe I could ever have enough of Valentine's kisses. The first one left me as breathless and exhilarated as if I had just run a footrace, and still I immediately wanted a second. I will never roll my eyes at my cousin's wolfish behavior and unbridled libido again, I realize.

If kissing all those girls feels for him anything like kissing Valentine feels for me, then I wish him as much as he can ever get.

I am still lost in thought as I reenter the city, choosing a circuitous route home—hugging the inner walls, and keeping my eyes peeled for any sign of Tybalt's minions. Perhaps I cannot avoid him forever, but I can at least avoid him for now.

Whether it be providence, or the possibility my feet have been listening to my heart, I soon look up and find myself near the alley on which Mercutio lives. It's long and narrow, a ribbon of dusty earth strewn with refuse, and two enormous rats are in a fight to the death right at its opening—and yet I am drawn down it nonetheless.

When their father was still alive, Mercutio and his siblings lived in a much nicer part of the city. But after his death there were debts to settle, expenses to be paid, and too many living off too little. Two of Mercutio's sisters were married early, Valentine was sent away, and Mercutio had to cease his education and find work. Having become the man of the house overnight, he suddenly had new and urgent responsibilities to see to.

Originally, his parents had plotted a cerebral future for him: a formal education; a distinguished career as a barrister, like his father before him; and then, hopefully, a ceremonial appointment to some position in the prince's cabinet of advisers. It wasn't even an unrealistic possibility; with friends and influence throughout Veronese society, their family has always been highly respected among the nobility—enough so that they managed to remain neutral in the never-ending feud between the Montagues and Capulets, and thus friendly with both sides.

But with the sudden reversal of fortune, all Mercutio's plans had to be rewritten.

He spent two years working for one of his father's barrister colleagues, with diminishing enthusiasm for a future of legal arbitration, and then, quite by chance, became a carpenter's apprentice. It turned out to be a vocation he excelled at—work that demanded precision, attention, and occasionally brute strength. And the pay was good enough that, when his sister Agnese convinced her husband to take their mother in, Mercutio was able to use his earnings to bring Valentine home from Vicenza.

The arrangement can't last forever, of course—the two brothers sharing their lodgings in a gloomy, cramped house on this filthy byway. Someday, Mercutio shall take a wife; and some-day, probably soon, Valentine will need an income of his own. It is strange to imagine. Although I could picture him as something quiet and thoughtful, like a bookbinder or a scribe, he already told me he was more or less a servant in Vicenza.

Could that be the future he has in store? With his partial education, and his family's lingering good name, he could take a position in one of the city's most respectable households. For a fleeting moment, I could just see that precise future: Valentine as an assistant to an important man, his cultured manner and refined speech making him someone his employer would be pleased to show off in front of aristocratic guests.

For a fleeting moment, I could see myself in that same future, as the man my parents intend me to be: a great merchant of fine silks, the head of the family line. A man in need of an assistant with cultured manners, refined speech . . . and lips that are as plush and supple as the flesh of ripe cherries. It's a ridiculous fantasy, I know, but it slips into my mind as if it has always belonged there: the possibility of having someone like Valentine at my side, for as long as we want it, without ever having to explain ourselves to anyone.

It's with a start that I realize this lost-and-found boy has made me do something I once thought impossible: envision a future in Verona that I do not unilaterally dread.

The closer I get to the house that Valentine shares with his brother, the less I know what I'm doing here. Am I really going to knock on their door? I keep thinking of what I might say, ways I could initiate an amusing conversation after the evening we had—and I cringe in violent embarrassment at each one in turn.

How are you? Too boring, too impersonal.

I wanted to be certain you made it home safely last night. Potentially suspicious, if anyone overheard . . . would Ben worry about the safety of another boy? Would Mercutio?

I thought you might like to . . . Only, there seems to be no reasonable way to end this prelude. *Have someone reacquaint you with the city?* As if his brother hasn't already done this. *Go for a walk?* I can't even think of a way to say *hello* without humiliating myself, I certainly can't hope to sustain an afternoon's worth of dialogue! *Kiss some more?* Oh yes, that will definitely impress him—well done, Romeo, you silver-tongued devil.

Just as I am passing their house, just as I am thinking that I shall break into a sprint and make for San Pietro before I can do something even more ill-advised than listen to Benvolio when he says he has a brilliant idea, their front door opens. And although they share this house with several other families, it comes as no surprise—given how much fate seems to enjoy punting me about lately—that it is Valentine who emerges.

"Romeo!" He blinks, startled, and my mind becomes a snowy wasteland, his impossibly thick eyelashes stirring a wind that whooshes through the emptiness. There is a pail of food scraps in his hands, and he moves it behind him. "What are you doing here?"

"I was . . ." *Coming to see if you got home safely.* The words almost emerge . . . but the truth beats them to the punch. "I was thinking of you. And I suppose my feet brought me here on their own."

He blushes slightly, and a smile plays at the corner of his mouth. It's the first time I've seen him in daylight, I realize. There are angles to his face I never noticed, and where the moon made his eyes shine, the sun makes them sparkle with a sea of golden flecks. *It is impossible, how well constructed he is.* "I am glad. I've been thinking of you as well."

"Have you?"

"In truth, I have struggled to think of anything else."

Inexplicably, my head spins, delight and fear swirling suddenly together. How do I contend with this absolute unknown? This realm of feelings I have no experience with, needs I don't know how to name, futures I can't predict. I do not know how I am to negotiate my next days with Valentine, let alone our next hours, our next few *moments*.

"Last night . . . ," he begins, and then falters, his gaze dropping down to his feet. "I never thought something like that might happen. Not for me. Not with you."

"With me?" I feel a fool, repeating him, but my mind is still terrifyingly empty.

"I told you I remembered you fondly, Romeo." His ears turn pink, and he darts a nervous glance along the alley. A cart rolls by somewhere to our left, and a woman leans out a window two houses down, shaking dust from a cloth, and he whispers, "I have kissed you over and over in my imagination, long before we ever held hands in that orchard."

With my pulse thudding in my temples, I swallow, and drop my gaze to his mouth. I have spent the afternoon reliving those passionate moments under the garden wall, experiencing them again with all my senses as though they were really happening. Now they seem achingly far away, impossible to conjure up in adequate detail. I need more.

"Is your brother at home?" I ask, scarcely above a growl, and I see Valentine's breath catch—but he nods.

"He is. We can't . . . I mean, if you were thinking . . ."

"I was." With a frustrated sigh, I attempt a smile . . . but I am *still* thinking about it, longing for it, staring at his mouth. "I would like to be alone with you again, Valentine."

"I would like that, too."

"Soon. As soon as possible." I am surprising myself with this talk, with how forward I'm being, how brazen. My whole life, I *have* been spoiled, able to get anything I've ever wanted . . . except for this. In this, I am not nearly spoiled enough, and it makes me greedy.

"I am in Verona to stay," he points out with a coy smile. "There will be opportunities. I will make certain of it."

"So shall I." Sun slides past the crooked rooftops, painting the sides of the alley in fingers of irregular light. It reminds me of the cypress trees that line the road away from my home. Impulsively, I ask, "Do you have any interest in . . . in artistic pursuits?"

"I do love the frescoes at the church," he answers, recalling what I'd said about the great Giotto at the masquerade. "My uncle had his portrait done while I lived with him, and the process was fascinating. I watched it done with eyes like saucers." Affecting a self-deprecating smirk, he adds, "Sadly, I have no knack for it. I had an idea once that I might draw a horse on the gallop, only everyone thought it was a beer barrel on stilts."

Laughing, I reassure him, "We all draw that way when we are children—you just need to work at it!"

"This was four months ago!" he exclaims, but he is laughing as well. "I'm afraid that when it comes to preserving beautiful things for posterity, I will have to stick with more mundane techniques, such as pressing flowers or pickling vegetables."

Poking him in the shoulder, I tease, "You find vegetables beautiful, do you?"

"I once saw a radish that was downright lovely." His eyes twinkle. "Ravishing, even! A ravishing radish."

"Still in its salad days, I imagine." I keep as straight a face as I can. He laughs, and it warms me all the way through—and all I can hear in my head is Friar Laurence saying that *maybe this happiness is meant for me.* Maybe this moment, his leaving the house just as I passed by, is no coincidence.

Some irresistible gravity pulls me closer to him, heedless of the people who share this alley with us; I hardly even notice the cats and chickens that scurry past, a society of frenetic beasts chasing one another under our feet. Again, I picture that future where we have all the time alone we want, the time we need to explore this happiness to its fullest.

"It is too bad that you do not enjoy sketching," I murmur, eyeing a coil of his blond hair and remembering what it felt like twined in my fingers. "There is a meadow just outside the city that I've come to love, and I often go there to gather inspiration.

It is quiet and beautiful, just the flowers and the sunshine . . . and I am most often quite alone . . ."

He looks up at me, and I notice his gaze moves first to my mouth as well, his eyes drowsy in a way that only quickens my pulse. "I may be a terrible artist, but I do love the countryside. Perhaps I could keep you company sometime?"

"I would like that." My skin tingles all over, as if it might leap from my body at any moment. He is so close to me now that I can count the freckles spilling across his cheeks—a charming constellation I long to memorize. "Will . . . would your brother be suspicious? If you left the city alone with me?"

"It is hard to say." Valentine's face clouds. "Mercutio . . . I think he is aware that I am . . . not like him. That is to say, he asked me once if there were any girls I had my eye on, and when I could not answer him, he dropped the subject and has not brought it up again." Restlessly, he fidgets with the pail he holds, shifting it from hand to hand. "I don't think it has changed how he treats me, but he is either unable to speak of it or unwilling to know more about it. Would he be suspicious on your account?"

"I don't think so," I tell him, giving it some consideration. "Mercutio . . . he thinks my lack of feminine companionship is owed to my being too shy to pursue girls properly. Otherwise, I don't believe he thinks much about my interests in that arena at all." *If he ever did*, I choose not to add, *he might have noticed how much of my attentions have been focused on* him. "Ben, on the other hand . . . I believe he has an idea about me. He hasn't said so, but he has lately made a habit of pushing me into the arms of this girl or that, and pressing me to behave in the ways expected of men."

Valentine is quiet for a moment. "You think he would not understand."

It isn't a question, but I answer him anyway. "No. I think he would not."

He is quiet for a longer moment, and when he looks back up at me, the sunlight that bounces off the painted houses marbles his eyes with gold and pink and blue—two dreamy summer storms that make me yearn for that open meadow. "And if spending time alone with me were to rouse Mercutio's suspicions after all? And perhaps stoke Ben's even more than they are already?"

"It would be worth it." The words come out of me on a hoarse breath, and I realize that I mean them. In this moment, I cannot imagine anything that would not be worth a few more kisses from Valentine, a few more hours to just gaze into his eyes like this and let it mean what it means—without having to pretend it's less than what it is. I've never had this, and didn't know how much I needed it. "Valentine—"

But in that instant, as I am reaching for him, the door to the house bursts open and Mercutio stumbles into the alley. I jolt back, just as he glances over, his gaze darting from me to his brother and back again. The look that flickers in his eyes makes my mouth go dry. Did we separate fast enough? *Does he see the guilt on me?*

Just like that, I realize that I am a liar and a coward, because I am undeniably terrified of arousing Mercutio's suspicions.

And then my friend's face splits into one of his brightest grins. "Romeo? What luck! What on earth are you doing here?"

My tongue won't catch up to me, and I struggle to formulate a reply. "I . . . I happened to be nearby—"

"He ran into me as I was taking out the scraps," Valentine interjects, hoisting the pail, his face scarlet, but his brother hardly seems to notice.

"This is about as fortuitous as a coincidence can get!" Mercutio claps me on the shoulders, beaming, and a swarm of butterflies tumble through my blood.

Not long ago—twenty-four hours, even—this closeness with him would have weakened my knees. His dark eyes turned into half-moons by his smile, the dimples in his cheeks, the square shape of his jaw . . . it all used to leave me envious and jittery inside, in a way I couldn't reconcile. I was angry at him for how much I wanted to be him; I was angry at myself for *not* being him; and, most of all, I wanted him to choose me somehow—to desire my company in a way I couldn't explain to myself.

But now, even with his hands on my shoulders, it is Valentine whose presence is the most significant. Everywhere Mercutio is rough and loud and cocky, Valentine is pensive and quiet and calm, and it is a sensibility I didn't know I found appealing until now.

"What coincidence?" I manage, straining to appear normal. "What are you on about?"

"We are to meet Benvolio in the piazza within the half hour!" Mercutio exclaims, as though I ought to have known this already. Tossing an exasperated gesture in the general direction of San Pietro, he continues, "He said he would fetch you from your home—where I imagine he still is now, most likely furious that you are not there to be fetched."

"I had errands to run." I make excuses when no excuses are called for. "It's only by chance I came across Valentine on my way back home. I hope Ben isn't too put out. If I'd—"

"Please, he could do with a little frustration." Mercutio draws me into a quick, manly embrace, and I enjoy it enough that I find it hard to meet Valentine's gaze over his shoulder. "I am only glad that you survived our harrowing escape last night, and that we all live to tell the tale. I cannot wait to hear you describe what happened after we parted ways, because my brother's account was excruciatingly dull." Releasing me, he turns to Valentine, whose face has gone a dusty pink. "Empty those scraps already, so that we may be on our way. We are reunited—the Four Horsemen, together again—and our adventures await!"

Valentine does as he is commanded, tossing the contents of the pail into the gutter and then tucking it back inside the door of the house; and then we're off down the alley, with Mercutio placing himself conspicuously in the middle of our little trio, his arms cast around our shoulders.

But although that charged, private moment between me and Valentine may be over, the air is still thick with its memory— sweet and heavy, like the scent that lingers after it rains.

14

WHILE THERE IS A LIMITLESS SUPPLY OF TROUBLE TO BE FOUND AND had in Verona, the city offers only a handful of respectable ways to entertain oneself that don't become boring after the third or fourth repetition. From horseshoes to hunting, from backgammon to knucklebones, we've exhausted all of them; and now that we're old enough to drink in the taverns, trouble is about the only pastime that's left for us to explore.

Mercutio leads us on a roundabout journey, treading cobbles worn smooth by years of our own footsteps, ebulliently greeting all the familiar faces we pass. There's not an avenue in this city that we haven't walked—outside San Zeno, of course—but this route is the one we've traveled most. At this point, it is a pilgrimage where, in the place of shrines, there stand our fondest friends.

For all my life, I've been someone known to the people of Verona, even to those I had never met. Strangers knew me before I knew myself—because anything Bernabó Montague did was worth talking about, and having an heir certainly qualified. It is his name that people see when they look at me, his name to which they pay their courtesy when they treat me well.

In too many ways, I have never been seen for who I am *without* my name, except for the occasions when I am with Mercutio and Ben.

"Francesca, my angel!" Leaning against the doorframe of the bakery on Vicolo al Forno, Mercutio greets the woman who has been running the place for as long as I can remember—the Widow Grissoni, raw boned and weathered with age. "Have you anything to offer a poor, half-starved urchin such as myself?"

"Yes." The old woman gives him an exaggerated scowl, her nostrils flaring. "The business end of my broom! Now get out of here before you and your pack of mangy whelps scare away my respectable clientele."

"Impossible." Mercutio is at his most flirtatious, his most debonair. "I am so lovable, not even the rats are scared of me."

"Hard to be scared of your own kind," she retorts, but she is fighting to contain a smile. "Get along, already—I've no handouts today!"

"You wound me, Francesca." Mercutio claps his hands over his bosom and pouts. "I come to bid you good morning, and you cast aspersions on my honor!"

"Your hide is thick enough to weather the blow." She finally takes the bait, though, walking up to him, hands on her hips. "It is your purse that's always too thin."

"I have my younger brother to take care of now, don't I?" His eyes widen innocently. "He was a rich man's servant in Vicenza for three long years, and it took every penny I could save to bring him back to Verona where he belongs. Perhaps that means I haven't much money to spare, but no one who is truly respectable would hold it against me. You remember my brother, Valentine, do you not?"

He gestures back at us, and on cue, Valentine bows his head with a humble, "Good morning, my lady."

In an instant, his limbs go from graceful to angular, his eyes doe-like and pitiful. He might as well be an orphan in sackcloth, and the effect he has on the baker is unmistakable. Francesca is used to battling Mercutio, with his quicksilver charm and rugged handsomeness; but now he has a new weapon, and she is clearly powerless against it.

With an aggrieved sigh, the woman mutters a few curses under her breath, all while snatching up a small loaf of bread and some rolls. "I know I am being swindled, but I cannot help it. Take these—and if you actually pay for some of it, *any* of it, I shall toss in a few extra crusts that I cannot sell because they burned in the oven. Take it or leave it."

"I shall take it," Mercutio says graciously, bowing low, and they negotiate the rest of their exchange in a similar manner: him teasing, and her pretending to be irritated. In the end, the "crusts" she adds are substantial, and not really burned at all.

No one brings up the fact that I could have paid, had I been asked. The Widow Grissoni knows who I am, but for once, that is not the point. Here, I am allowed to be disreputable, I am allowed to be part of the "pack of mangy whelps" she has unofficially adopted. She and Mercutio have done this dance before, countless times—him wheedling and her scolding until she finally gives in. It is a ritual, and each step of it is important.

After leaving the bakery, we continue toward the heart of

town, following Mercutio's lead. We exchange a few friendly jibes with Abramo, the rat catcher; I give some coins to the beggar who is always seated in the piazzetta outside the old baths, and Mercutio tosses him some of our bread; and then we stop to serenade the old woman who used to sell flowers by the shrine to Saint Justina. She is too frail to leave her second-story rooms now, but we sing up to her while she looks down and smiles.

Whether he realizes it or not, Mercutio has led us all the way around the Via de Mezzo, where Tybalt has staked his outrageous territorial claim; but the closer we get to the piazza— where all lives in Verona eventually and inevitably intersect—the more I find myself looking over my shoulder and worrying that I have not been cautious enough.

This pilgrimage, as much as I love it—even though it makes me feel more like *Romeo* and less like *Montague*—is possibly too familiar. If a list were made of places to seek me out in town, this warren of crumbling and colorful alleys would be at the top. Even Tybalt would know that. And as the sun moves farther west, the streets grow busier, and it is becoming harder and harder to distinguish friend from foe among the faces we pass.

I am relieved when we encounter Benvolio outside the Palazzo del Podestà—the official residence of the prince, only a stone's throw from the piazza. People stream in from every direction, coming and going from the marketplace just outside our view, and I am dizzy from trying to recognize them all. Fortunately, my cousin has us moving again before we've even come to a full stop, heatedly lecturing me for the time he wasted climbing up to my empty bedchamber in San Pietro.

"Honestly, Cousin, you could be more considerate," he huffs, driving us ahead of him like a herd of cattle, away from the piazza. "I am covered in bruises from the ascent up your wall, and that demonic beast you call a cat even *scratched* me when I made it through the window! The least you could have done was actually be there to receive me."

"First, as you are well aware, Hecate neither belongs to me nor listens to my admonitions regarding her poor etiquette," I point out, pleased that she has finally turned her vicious little claws on someone else. "And second, how was I supposed to know you'd come by?"

"That is a pitiful excuse." He sniffs, turning up his nose. "You know an unannounced visit is my favorite sort to make, and you ought to have had the foresight and courtesy to have at least left a note behind explaining your absence, just in case."

"I'm sorry, Ben." I cannot actually tell if he is being serious, and I struggle to contain a laugh. "You're right. When it comes to you, I should expect only what is not expectable."

"Or *re*spectable," Mercutio interjects, netting a dirty look from my cousin.

"Thank you, Romeo." Ben adjusts his doublet, somewhat mollified. "I shall allow you to make it up to me by paying for my ale today."

The tavern Ben forces us into is grotesque—worse even than the one near the Arena—but with lower prices. It takes only one tankard of foul-tasting beer before Mercutio and Ben have the clientele captivated by their usual repartee, taking command of the room with confidence and charm. Valentine is right, I realize: They are practically men now, and have stepped easily into the roles that have been written for them.

I join the performance when the occasion calls for it, but Valentine has little to add, as most of the stories they tell come from the years while he was gone. He glances over at me from time to time, his eyes dancing in a way that makes me shiver, a way that makes me wish we were alone. I've finally found something new to explore in Verona, and yet I must wait until a more favorable time. The delay is sweet agony.

For this next hour, my senses grown warm and gauzy with ale, my heart swollen with love for these young men, I feel . . . almost whole. Like there is nothing to be afraid of about the future after all. What if happiness *is* meant for me? Ben really does care about our friendship, and Mercutio clearly adores Valentine . . . might there not be a chance that they could accept the truth? Perhaps I can be both who I am and who I am expected to be.

I savor this fantasy for the remainder of the afternoon, until we have finally had enough of the tavern, and make our woozy progress back out to the sun-washed street. My senses are just dulled enough that my earlier worries fall off me like autumn leaves, and I am lighter without their weight to hold me down.

We laugh and sing together as we walk, Mercutio shepherding our curious little flock, apologizing to passersby for our condition. When we tumble into the piazza, its vastness glazed by the thickened light of late day, we exhale in pleasure. Spread out over the remnants of a forum that dates from Roman times, and bordered by towers, palaces, and guildhalls built of sumptuous ocher stone, this is the true center of Veronese life.

We collapse at the edge of a grand fountain, watching life go by, trying and failing not to doze off. It is just when I am beginning to think that I have had one good day in the midst of endless difficulty that disaster inevitably strikes.

"Montague!"

I am on my feet in an instant, fear clearing my head, just like that. Storming toward us with murder in his eyes, Tybalt Capulet is flanked by a couple of his usual hangers-on—Duccio and Galvano, a pair of toadies with plenty of muscle and not one wit between them.

"You and I have unfinished business," he snarls at me as he draws close. Instantly, I have Ben and Mercutio at my sides, poised but ready for trouble. Stopping a few measured feet away, his face contorted with fury, Tybalt continues, "Will you answer at last for your disreputable acts against my family, or are you coward enough to run from me twice?"

"Good evening, Your Majesty!" Mercutio greets Tybalt with an exaggerated bow, disrupting the intensity of the moment with his playful tone. "I almost didn't recognize you without your adorable little ears on." To the people who have stopped to watch our confrontation unfold, he then calls, "Bow down and show some respect, you sad lot—we have the Prince of Cats among us!"

"You would do well to stand back and keep your foolish

mouth shut, Mercutio." Red blotches appear in Tybalt's cheeks, and behind him, Duccio and Galvano almost perfectly duplicate his threatening, narrow-eyed glare. "You are pitiful, you know— still behaving like a child, living in a filthy hovel in the worst part of town. Were it not for your late father's good name, you would be just as unwelcome in respectable society as a beggar off the street."

"At least beggars say 'please' and 'thank you,'" Benvolio puts in. "More manners than you've ever demonstrated, Tybalt."

"And I clean my hovel once a week, thank you very much." Mercutio pretends to be affronted. Then, with a guilty look at Valentine, adds, "Well, every other week. Normally."

"It is no surprise that this is all some great joke to the two of you—sneaking into my uncle's home, taking advantage of his kindness, and luring his daughter into humiliation." Tybalt gives the pair of them a contemptuous look. "Neither of you has any honor to protect, not an ounce of dignity. There is no act that could bring shame upon you, because you have nothing to take pride in to begin with!"

"I take quite a bit of pride in how much restraint I have shown by not knocking your teeth down your throat," Mercutio answers reasonably.

"I am filled with pride." Ben thrusts out his chest. "Who would not be proud to be born such a perfect specimen of manhood? I did not ask for the burden of my devastating handsomeness, and I have risen to the challenge admirably."

"Yes, a 'burden,'" Mercutio interjects drolly. "That's the word I was thinking of when the subject of you came up."

"You mock me, but the ladies cannot resist my ginger hair." Ben turns a cheeky grin on Tybalt. "Just ask your mother, if you don't believe me."

"*That is enough!*" Tybalt goes purple with rage. "I will not tolerate your impudence for a single second longer, Benvolio— begone from here before I beat a lesson into you!"

Ben doesn't move an inch, but after a moment of silence in which the hazy air simmers with tension, he smiles. "There. You have just tolerated my impudence for another second— and you thought you could not do it! Congratu—"

He does not finish, because with a feral shout, Tybalt lunges at him, taking a wild swing with his fist. Ben counters by grabbing him around the torso, and together they go tumbling headlong into a cluster of men standing by an empty market stall. Three of them are knocked to the ground—and when they rise again, they, too, are spoiling for a fight.

Within seconds, the entire piazza has descended into an all-out brawl.

15

It happens so fast it's hard to take in, anger jumping from person to person like sparks whirling off a wildfire, fresh blazes beginning everywhere they land. And before I can think, Duccio and Galvano charge Mercutio and me, and we are swept into the melee.

Although I've been trained to handle blade and bow, I've little experience in hand-to-hand combat—and a real fight is nothing like it appears onstage, where everything is choreographed and cleanly performed. When Galvano dives at me, there is no time to plan, only to react. I find myself on the ground in seconds, his fists hammering at my ribs while I drive my knee into any tender flesh it can reach.

It's brutal and exhausting, my mouth soon full with the taste of blood, and everything becomes pain, breathlessness, and survival. We thrash at each other, and the din gets louder around us, makeshift weapons hurtling overhead. I'm not afraid for Ben or Mercutio, both of whom have been in situations at least this absurd before, but in the back of my mind, even as I'm being pummeled by Galvano, I worry about Valentine.

I lost track of him in the scrum, have no idea where he is now, and cannot reconcile his gentle demeanor with the sort of blood-and-guts battle that's unfolding. It panics me, to imagine him being hurt—and it panics me that I am being *literally attacked* and yet I cannot seem to stop thinking of him. Mercutio will protect him if I can't . . . but, selfishly, *I want to be the one to protect him*.

Galvano ends up behind me, catching my throat in the crook of his arm. As he begins to squeeze, I throw myself backward as hard as I can, slamming his body against the unforgiving stone of the fountain. The air leaves his lungs in a great whoosh, and his hold breaks.

Just as I am about to whirl on him, however, a shockingly loud blast of horns fills the piazza, freezing us in our tracks. When I turn, I see two trumpeters bearing the insignia of Prince Escalus—and standing just behind them, clad head to toe in the royal purple silks my father has regularly prepared specifically for him, is our sovereign himself.

"What on earth is the meaning of all this?" He shouts it into the dazed crowd, his voice ringing imperiously off stone and tile. Flanked by his armed guards, and accompanied by two other men in noble dress, he cuts an imposing image. As he is recognized, people scramble into positions of respect, humbling themselves as quickly as they can. "Have you all taken leave of your senses? Knocking one another about like drunks at a country revel, wrecking the public peace—is there not one man among you with any civility?"

He is answered with silence, the crowd shifting uneasily, and

I drop to one knee—pain flaring up as I discover that I have scraped it badly enough to rip open my hose.

After a moment of his question hanging in the air, Escalus thunders, "*Well?* I demand an explanation for this shocking behavior!"

The first person to take the bait, of course, is Tybalt. "It was Romeo Montague who started this clash, my lord."

"That's a lie!" Even as I snap the words out, I hear them echoed from my left and right—Ben and Mercutio backing me up—and I lift my chin the way my father taught me. "Tybalt Capulet was the instigator here. He attacked my cousin Benvolio."

"That's the truth, and I was witness to it," Mercutio adds, his voice rumbling.

"Mercutio." Escalus redirects his focus, his expression pulling into a paternal frown. "I must say I am disappointed to see you here, and in front of your kinsman, no less." He gestures to the fancy-looking man at his left, someone I do not recognize, but who is dressed as if he intends to maybe buy Verona outright. "What brought you into this display of debauched violence? Surely your father raised you with better judgment than this."

"It is as Romeo said, my lord." Mercutio keeps his tone deferential, despite a hint of color stealing into his cheeks at this reprimand. "We were here—Romeo and his cousin, and I and my brother—to take in the evening, when Tybalt advanced upon us. It was he who initiated a confrontation, and he who delivered the first blow."

"Young Capulet?" Escalus arches a thick brow. "You have

accused Romeo, and he has accused you—with witnesses supporting his claim. What have you to say for yourself?"

His face scarlet, Tybalt states, "I cannot help what lies a scoundrel and his low-life companions are willing to tell someone of your stature. All I can say is that I am an honest man. Romeo Montague entered my uncle's home without an invitation this past night, took advantage of his hospitality, and attempted to compromise the virtue of my cousin Juliet—"

"I did nothing of the sort!" I exclaim, my face burning as eyes everywhere turn on me with disdain and suspicion. "We shared a dance, and that was all we shared!"

"He violated my uncle's household, violated my uncle's trust, and—I put it to you, my lord—he would just as comfortably have violated my uncle's only daughter had I not denounced him before the assembled guests." Tybalt bows his head in a simulation of humility. "I came here to seek the satisfaction that any man would, whose honor had been challenged by so base a ruffian as Romeo Montague."

My shoulders are up around my ears, my thoughts cooked all the way through with anger, by the time Prince Escalus's troubled gaze returns to me. "Is all of this true?"

I want to argue, to call Tybalt the liar he is . . . but at least half of his claims *are* true, even if none are presented in an honest way. How can I explain something like that without sounding preposterous? And if the only wholehearted denial I can manage is one against a charge of "nefarious seduction," then there hardly seems any point. Bitterly, I manage, "I wish I could spin a tale as imaginative as all of that."

"It was I who persuaded Romeo to ask the young lady for a dance." Mercutio shoots a venomous look at Tybalt. "His motives were pure, and there is not one person who was at Lord Capulet's masquerade who could honestly say he acted in any inappropriate manner!"

"I saw what I saw." Tybalt speaks through gritted teeth, refusing to back down.

To the fancy man at Escalus's side, Mercutio then calls out, "Cousin Paris—you were there, at Capulet's ball, and you know we share the blood of honest men. Am I lying?"

The man shuffles his feet, glances between his cousin, the prince, and my mortal enemy, and in that moment I can already tell he is no ally to us. Wherever Mercutio gets his honesty, it is not from the blood they share.

Clearing his throat, Paris states, "I was not in the ballroom when any of this took place, so I cannot vouch for either account. However, I . . . I know Tybalt to be an honest man as well."

He won't look at Mercutio, whose face has gone ashen with humiliation at being effectively called a liar in front of the prince, and by someone from his own family. Escalus simmers quietly for a moment himself, looking angrier than I think any of us have ever seen him before, until he finally snaps.

"I am pushed beyond the limits of my patience with the endless, childish squabbling of your families!" Turning to the still-gathered mob of erstwhile combatants, none of whom dare to budge an inch while he holds the floor, he booms, "All these men have insisted that witnesses will support their conflicting accounts, and so apparently we must find one. Was anyone else here present at Lord Capulet's party this past night? Anyone who can tell us which of these rogues is being truthful—if any of them are?"

There is a heavy, damning silence . . . and then: "I was there, my lord."

The voice comes from the periphery of the crowd, and everyone turns in its direction, where a lone figure holds a deep curtsy at the edge of the impromptu battle zone. Escalus gestures impatiently, urging, "Come forward, then, if you believe you have something to add to this sordid affair."

"Oh, I am certain that I do." As she rises, the hood of her cloak falls back to reveal none other than Juliet Capulet herself.

"Juliet—I mean, my lady?" Paris splutters, eyes bulging comically.

The prince only frowns. "I am surprised to see you here."

"Half of Verona is here," she points out, casting an innocent glance at the scattered brawlers and the thickening pack of spectators beyond them. "I came in search of my cousin, at my father's behest, only to hear my name being tossed about—and with no particular restraint. Am I less welcome here than my reputation?"

To his credit, our sovereign is shrewd enough not to fall into the jaws of her sharp question. Instead he asks, "What have you to add to these proceedings? What is the truth about that which occurred last night?"

"The first truth, and the one that matters most to me, is that I am a virtuous woman, and I am slandered by any conversation that impugns my character or my moral resolve." Her words are nominally directed at Tybalt, but they serve as a denunciation of anyone who would willingly entertain his account—the prince included. "As I am sure you are aware, the good Count Paris has come to Verona for the purpose of meeting with my parents, regarding our potential suitability for marriage. All this talk of my supposed 'dishonoring' is not just an insult to my person, but a threat against my good name."

Escalus evens his voice. "I am certain that no one here has intended to cast any doubt upon your moral integrity, my dear Juliet. This is not a question of your virtue, but of the actions performed by these men present."

"Then let me put those questions to rest," she counters coolly. "Romeo Montague did not, in fact, enter my home without invitation. I bade him come myself."

At this, a chorus of startled murmuring ripples through the gathered audience. Paris flinches, Tybalt's jaw drops—*my* jaw drops—and I dare a glance at Benvolio, who looks as stunned as I am.

"That's not possible!" Tybalt fights the urge to leap to his feet. "I . . . your mother and father review your correspondence, and they would absolutely have stopped you from inviting this . . . this *filth* to attend. And I would certainly have heard about it if you'd tried."

"I did not invite him by letter." Juliet remains unruffled. "I sent the request by way of a servant, whom I tasked with committing the message to his memory."

"Subterfuge and treachery!" Tybalt's hands clench into fists so tight his knuckles blanch. "Which servant was it? I'll see that they are cast from the household."

"You shall not." Juliet glares at him. "It is not your household to command—and no servant of mine shall be dismissed for doing just as I have asked."

"But, my sweet girl . . . ," Escalus interrupts, clearly at something of a loss for words. Beside him, Count Paris is pink in the face, whether from rage or embarrassment or both. "Why would you do such a thing?"

"Should I not have?" She turns a look on him that is the very picture of guilelessness. "I have spent my whole life hearing of Romeo, who shall someday succeed his father; but until last night, we had not once set our eyes upon each other. Can you blame me for being curious? How are we to be proper enemies, to hate each other with the appropriate zeal, without ever meeting face-to-face?"

Silence follows this, and a change comes over the prince's expression. Her argument is a weapon tailored perfectly to its target, and she has struck him in just the right spot.

"You are a wise young woman, Juliet Capulet," the prince intones, his brows furrowing as he turns a distasteful glance at first Tybalt and then me. "Wiser in almost every regard than the men present here today, who still insist on waging bloody war against ghosts and rumors of the past. Where you chose to break bread with your supposed adversary, these boys have chosen instead to break the promise of peace and safety that Verona offers to its precious citizens." His voice turning sharp,

Escalus states, "It would seem, Tybalt, that young Romeo did not, in fact, dishonor your uncle's household with his presence—although you have both dishonored *my* household with yours."

"Please, my lord!" I gasp out, unsure what it is that I mean to say here—unsure how to handle a situation in which I am personally disfavored by the sovereign of Verona. My family has always been held in high esteem by those who rule the city, and although I certainly now regret attending the Capulets' masquerade, it was not I who had an agenda of violence. It was not I who wanted to see bloodshed in the piazza.

"I am neither my brother nor my father," the prince says, "both of whom held some inexplicable reverence for your families' undying feud. But I *am* Verona's prince, and I will not tolerate vendettas that put the supposed glory of two bloodlines above the welfare of an entire city." He takes Juliet's hand, giving her a sad smile. "It is shameful that this young lady had to resort to subterfuge to finally meet a young man from a house equal to her own, and brave of that young man to answer her entreaty with a spirit of openness and due decorum. It is an example that I believe everyone present could learn from."

"He tried to make a fool of me in front of every person of high standing in this city!" Tybalt exclaims, his face so flushed it is almost burgundy. "He answered my cousin's invitation only because he knew that to do so would be a finger in the eye of my uncle! Juliet has been shielded from them for a reason, and her naivete does not excuse his deviousness."

"*Enough!*" Escalus roars, a flock of pigeons lurching into the dusky air. "Out of admiration for the lady Juliet's willingness to invite amity over enmity—and as it would seem that no real crime lies at the heart of this evening's ignoble outburst—I shall allow your breach of the public peace to pass. But this is the last time." He fixes us with a gimlet eye. "I hope you boys will consider how fortunate you are to have tested me on a day when I am feeling merciful, and how fortunate you are to be on this side of Verona's walls—a privilege that can be revoked at any time, no matter what name you bear.

"If I must ever intervene between your families again, I shall see to it that examples are made." His lip curling, he barks, "Now begone from my sight, and do not anger me again."

16

ESCALUS HOLDS HIS GROUND AS WE ALL BOW AND SCRAPE OUR WAY out of his presence—making certain that Tybalt is not behind us. As foolhardy as it would be to launch a fresh attack so swiftly after that dire warning, I would put nothing past him. Twice now he has been publicly disgraced in an attempt to get the better of me, and the shame of it will fester in his heart like a bedsore. He will not let bygones be bygones.

Benvolio, of course, has never been in higher spirits. "Did you see Tybalt's face? I thought he would bleed from the eyes!"

"I've never seen anyone turn that color." Valentine laughs. "He looked like a pomegranate!"

Mercutio flexes his hand, his knuckles already swelling from their use during the fight. "I could not believe my ears when Juliet lied for us—for you, Romeo. She saved your skin, sure as we're all standing here."

"You do not have to remind me." My head is filled with a dozen or more explosive scenarios in which she did no such thing; in which I am punished by the prince, raged at by my father, and left with a stain on my own good name—when it has been made quite clear to me that the only thing I possess of any real, tangible value *is* my name.

"Believe it or not, when Escalus reached the peak of his fury, this entire wretched spectacle finally had me regretting that we'd hoodwinked you into that dance with Juliet in the first place." Ben leaps into the air, hooting with joy. "Whatever lies you told her about your anatomy were worth it, Romeo, my boy. One dance, and the daughter of your father's worst enemy is lying to the prince—*the prince*—in front of *your* worst enemy!"

"Why would she do such a thing?" Valentine turns to me, and although I do want to tell him about my meeting with Juliet at the friary, she bade me not to.

"Why, indeed!" Walking backward, his eyes still feverish with victory, Ben gives me a knowing leer. "What *did* you tell her? And remember that I have seen your anatomy, Cousin; we are at least comparable, and while I have certainly had no complaints, I have also never had a girl betray her family in my name before!"

"I think we came to an understanding" is what I find myself saying. How can I explain what connects us—how stifled we both feel, despite our comfortable lives? How our futures have been decided for us: rich in goods, and poor in satisfaction. "It turns out that we have quite a lot in common, and I believe she feels some sympathy for me."

"Oh, sympathy, of course." Benvolio rolls his eyes knowingly, as if this is a clear euphemism for something more salacious. "Well, what luck that you finally discovered one girl in all Verona whose heart melts for you, despite your sorrowful lack of ginger hair."

170

"For a rather terrible moment, I thought Tybalt was going to succeed in turning the prince against Romeo's case," Valentine murmurs. He is not walking at my side, where I'd like him, but his eyes won't leave me. "I cannot believe how confident he is that he can do violence and make others answer for it."

"It is because he does violence often, and others *do* answer for it." Mercutio kicks a stone with unnecessary force, narrowly missing a clay pot sitting outside someone's door. "Even now he escapes the justice he is owed for his actions—a cat who insists it's the mouse's fault for tempting him, and so both are scolded and set free again."

"If it comes down to us both being flogged and exiled, or us both being reprimanded and dismissed, I shall gladly take the latter," I say, but for some reason an expression of gladness eludes me. "I live to avoid him another day."

"Avoid him?" Mercutio scoffs, giving an unkind laugh. "He has claimed San Zeno and the Via de Mezzo, and now we must give him the piazza as well? What will you do when he comes marching into San Pietro—hand him the keys to your family home?"

The sharpness in his tone takes me by surprise, and Valentine frowns. "Mercutio . . ."

"No, I mean it!" Mercutio steps in front of me, something rancorous lurking behind his eyes. "How much of your territory, your *dignity*, are you willing to concede to Tybalt Capulet? Are you content to be nothing but the mouse he bats around when the prince isn't looking, or are you man enough to contend with him, measure for measure?"

"I want no war with Tybalt." It is my turn to scowl; this is something Mercutio already knows. "If I cannot be rid of him altogether, then I would prefer to keep him at arm's length. And you heard what Escalus said: If we let him goad us into another confrontation, we will all pay the price!"

What I do not add, because I'm too weary to discuss it, is that what Tybalt wants so badly to fight us for—power and prestige in Verona—isn't even something that I care about. If we could just each avoid the other, I would live happily; but his happiness seems to depend on belittling me, somehow proving his family is superior to mine.

"What is it that you do not understand here?" Mercutio tosses his hands. "He will not need to goad us into another conflict, because this one is not yet over! He isn't going to just crawl away and lick his wounds and hope you cross him again in a more convenient place—he's just going to think of some devious way he can strike at you without incurring the prince's wrath."

Blinking up at him, I step back. "Are you actually angry with me over this?"

"I think my good friend Mercutio here is annoyed because his big important cousin told everyone in the piazza that he can't be taken at his word," Ben chimes in, still unbothered, "and he's exercising his resentment on you."

"Piss off!" Mercutio snaps at him—but he turns away from me at last and begins stalking down the road again, allowing our progress to continue.

"Don't let it get to you, mate." Ben slaps a hanging sign as we pass, making it swing. "Everyone could see what a spineless little worm he was."

"Is he a close relation—this Paris?" I ask the question of Valentine, who, thanks to Mercutio's breaking of our ranks, is now beside me at last.

"He was, at one time." Valentine runs his fingers through his wild hair, and just the sight of them makes me want to kiss them. "When we were small, and he was barely older than Mercutio is now, we admired him a great deal. He would answer any question we could think of about all the subjects our parents considered inappropriate."

"I suspect he is talking about 'connubial relations.'" Ben wiggles his brows, and Valentine laughs.

"I am, of course, although that was not the only topic he seemed to know everything about. There wasn't a scandal under the sun that he couldn't explain in vivid detail."

"Most of what he told us was just nonsense he made up on the spot." Mercutio remains churlish, although his temper has lost some of its energy. "We were too young to know the difference, so any answer was as good as another—as he well knew. He just wanted to look impressive." Grumbling, he adds, "Once a charlatan, always a charlatan."

"He was never meant to inherit that title," Valentine supplies next, almost secretively. "There were two older brothers, but the pestilence took them both, and their father died of a broken heart. Or so the story goes. Anyway, he wasn't prepared."

"He is a joke, a laughingstock." Mercutio shoots a look back at us—and this time, in the gathering blue of the evening, I finally recognize pain in his expression. He is silent for a moment longer, before saying, "He was . . . he was the first person I wrote to, after our father died. When his debts were unearthed, and it became clear that we were all in trouble."

Valentine startles, his hands going still. "I never knew that."

"There was no reason for you to know it." Mercutio speaks to his feet. "I was grief stricken. I told him you'd be sent away if we could not devise some solution. I thought—I *believed*—that if anyone would be sympathetic toward us and our poor, dead father, it would be a close relation who had been through something very much the same." He won't look at us, and suddenly it is quite hard to look at him as well. "And in no time at all, Paris wrote me back, saying that he was 'very sorry for our lamentable situation,' but that if he gifted his money to everyone who asked, he would have none left for himself."

These last words hang in the air, turning it acrid with disdain. Ben coughs, his face pink. "He certainly seemed comfortable enough in the piazza, your 'very sorry' cousin."

"His doublet was silk brocade," I remark. "My father would have salivated."

"Oh, believe me, he has more money than he knows what to do with. He could be robbed of half, and never even notice it was gone." Mercutio's anger has abated, and in its place is a deep sadness. "Now he seeks to further pad his wealth with a Capulet dowry—and the most he can summon for his 'poor relations' is a public remark about how their honesty cannot be vouched for."

It is shortly thereafter that we stumble onto the embankment along the Adige, stars just beginning to appear in the indigo sky above the cypress trees. San Pietro lies on the other side of the river, across the Ponte Pietra, and this is where I am supposed to leave my friends. Valentine meets my gaze, and through it, I try to communicate everything I've not had the chance to say aloud since we were alone in the alley outside his house.

I wish we did not have to part just yet—that we could leave here together, head our own way, and continue our conversation. To wrap ourselves in a private cocoon and indulge the magic that fizzes around us when we look into each other's eyes.

"Good night, Montague." Mercutio is somewhat abashed when he salutes me, and I can tell this is him expressing contrition for the friction between us. "What do you suppose the odds are of us all having a nice, boring day tomorrow?"

"I would not count on it," I retort, saluting back. "Fortune may favor us, but catastrophe likes us even more."

Ben sighs. "Damn my irresistible appeal."

We say our farewells, and then they turn and start up the embankment. But just as I reach the torches that mark the point of the river crossing, I glance back to see that Valentine is doing the same. Furtively, I blow him a kiss—and the smile that lights his face warms me all the way home.

17

Two hours later, lying in bed with my eyes wide open—and Hecate resting indulgently on my stomach as if we are friends—I dwell on that parting smile. I dwell on all the moments from this afternoon in which I was denied a chance to hold him, to breathe him into me. The moon glares through my window, and I glare back, more awake than I've ever been, despite the exhausting rigors of the long day.

Over and over again, I relive that moment in the alley, where I very nearly threw caution to the wind and claimed his lips. The desire I'd felt was overpowering—perhaps because, for once, I knew he felt it, too. In the privacy of my rooms, with only the moon and a cat as my witnesses, I can live it the way it should have happened: his hair threaded between my fingers, his breath caught in a gasp as we press together, his mouth soft and ripe . . .

A sudden noise at the window jolts me out of my reverie, sending my heart into my throat. There is a sharp clatter, like something striking against the half-closed shutter from the outside . . . and then silence. A few long seconds pass, my head whirling with images of a dagger-wielding Tybalt trying to scale the walls of our home. Just as I am telling myself it was nothing, the sound comes again.

Clack.

The shutter rattles with impact, and Hecate wakes at last, her nasty little claws digging through my nightshirt as she scrambles upright.

Clack.

A third strike, this one glancing off the edge of the shutter, a tiny stone hurtling into view through a shaft of moonlight and skittering to the floor. Hecate abandons me, dashing for the shadows, and my head spins. It could not be Tybalt, really . . . could it? Surely my canniest and most bloodthirsty foe would have a more wicked vengeance in mind for me than tossing pebbles at my window in the hopes of disturbing my slumber.

Cautiously, I ease out of bed, creeping along the wall to the edge of the sill. I wait for one more rock to bounce off my poor, abused shutter before I toss it aside and hazard a glance at the grounds below.

To my shock, I see Valentine on the pathway that runs behind our villa, stooped over as he searches out more missiles to fire into my bedchamber. Relieved, my pulse still throbbing in my temples, I lean through the window. "What are you doing here?"

"Good morning!" he calls up to me in a rough whisper, his eyes shining with both guilt and pleasure. "I hope I didn't disturb you."

"You were throwing rocks at my window," I point out drily. "And it is not yet gone midnight, so you can hardly call this morning."

"Good night, then." He grins, the moon kissing his mouth the way I was dreaming of doing myself, moments ago. "I . . . I remembered that I had something I meant to tell you earlier, but never got the chance."

"Oh?" I wait, but he says nothing, still just staring up at me with night-gilded features. Laughing, I say, "You came all this way to tell me something . . . so, what is it?"

He merely shakes his head, maintaining that coy little grin. It is frustrating and intriguing, and some curious charge begins to build in the air—a swarm of buzzing secrets just waiting to be caught and learned. I think perhaps we are flirting, and it makes me twitch with delight.

"All right, then, keep it to yourself!" I try to feign nonchalance, although I am quite close to leaping through the window so I might land on him. "Won't your brother wonder where you are?"

"He is nearly impossible to wake," Valentine answers. "I doubt he will even notice I was ever gone, and I did not want to wait until tomorrow to see you again. What I wish to say requires . . . privacy."

This last is spoken in a soft undertone, his voice a ribbon of silk twisting in the air, and it coils around my desire for him, tugging at me.

"I'm coming down!" I answer hoarsely. Struggling into my hose, trying not to tear them in my haste, I clamber over the sill and scale the ivy to the ground.

Valentine beams at me, and when we are side by side, his nearness makes the hair on my neck rise to attention. I am again seized with the urge to take hold of him, to draw him even closer.

"Well?" I demand. "What is it?"

"I will tell you . . . ," he begins playfully, backing away, stepping toward the dark shape of the orchard that covers the hill behind our estate. "But only if you catch me first!"

And with that, he takes off running, vanishing into the trees and leaving me to scurry after him. The moon is bright, but the branches are dense with leaves, and their shadows make for uncertain footing. Ahead of me, I catch glimpses of Valentine as he darts through patches of light, his golden curls flashing, his laughter trailing on the air.

He is not truly trying to escape, and seems to have no destination in mind; but he runs and I give chase, my blood still hot with want and wonder. I have no idea what I'm doing, or what will happen when he lets me capture him, but I am desperate to find out. The breeze rippling my nightshirt, the charge in the air grows stronger the faster we go.

It is in a grove of pear trees, the perfume of their blossoms falling upon us like a veil, that Valentine turns the tables. He disappears into a pocket of shadow—and then, as I pass by, he leaps at me from behind. We collide, wrestling and yelping, stumbling over grass that will soon be moist with dew. And then, without any words passing between us, our mouths connect, and I am living all the daydreams I have had over the past several hours.

It is no gentle connection. We turn quickly ferocious, growling hungrily, hands tangling in each other's garments, pulling at each other's hair. Swaying under the moon, fighting to kiss deeper, we stagger against tree trunks and trip over fallen boughs. All of this is new to me. I have no idea if I'm doing it the way it's meant to be done; all I know is that every touch is a thrilling discovery that leaves me greedy for another. There is nothing I try, nothing he tries in return, that does not bring me more pleasure.

We kiss until we are drunk on the feel and taste of it, breathless from the effort it takes to resist immolation. I have no idea how much time has passed when we finally drag ourselves apart— possibly minutes, possibly hours—gasping and weak. My lips are swollen, and they still remember the shape of his teeth.

Woozy, his eyes filled with dreams, Valentine collapses to the ground and sprawls at my feet. "Lie down with me."

"Ants thrive in this orchard," I warn him, surprised to find that I have been sweating, the scented breeze chill against my back. "And you will stain your clothes with the grass."

"Not if I remove them." He says it teasingly, but then turns a gaze on me that I feel from the pit of my stomach to the tips of my ears. "Lie with me, Romeo. Please."

It is a request I can hardly deny, and my hose are already quite ruined from my shoeless flight through the orchard; so I stretch out beside him and look up. "*Oh.*"

The moon above us is full and emphatic, but delicate clouds feather the sky at its edges, making a frame of partially illumi- nated lace that contains the stars. Wind shakes the pear trees, their scent swirling around us, and peace spills over the hillside. For a moment, I am speechless.

"It's lovely, isn't it?" Valentine whispers.

"I wish I could paint this well." My hand finds his, our fingers knitting together, and I nestle into him. After a while, I finally ask, "What was it that you came to tell me?"

Valentine begins to laugh, his leg brushing against mine in a way that leaves me flustered. "I had nothing to say—I only wanted you to kiss me some more, and I could not stand to wait and hope there would be time for it tomorrow."

I begin to laugh as well, because I had been feeling the same way all afternoon, all day. "You risked walking all the way out to San Pietro in the middle of the night for this?"

"Of course I did." His voice is drowsy, but his eyes dance. "It's all I've been able to think about since last night. And when could be safer to brave the streets of Verona than when its cats are all asleep, and the mice are left to rule the city?"

The moonlight frosts his cheeks, makes them shine, and for a moment it is as if the ground is giving way beneath me. Some unseen force pulls and twists my insides, shaping them into a knot that I suspect only Valentine will be able to untangle.

My memory finds its way back to that alley again, where all my little daydreams really began—to when there seemed no fantasy too outlandish to consider, no wish too absurd to hope for. But now, after enjoying this taste of the sublime, we've stepped closer to the future, and somehow I am afraid it makes that future harder to reach.

"What is it that you desire?" I blurt, and then go hot when his gaze lingers on my mouth. "Other than kisses, I mean. I shall need to rest for at least a few minutes before I have regained my stamina." He laughs, a beautiful, drunken sound, and I press,

"What I want to know is what sort of life you want to have. Mercutio has his carpentry apprenticeship, Ben will almost certainly become a soldier—if he does not end up in jail first—and I will one day take on my father's affairs . . . but what is it that *you* wish to do?"

Valentine is quiet for a time, before saying, "I will probably end up working for the Widow Grissoni—the baker. She is getting older and will need some assistance."

"But is that what you *want?*" I squeeze his hand. "If you could do anything at all, have any future you desire, what would you wish for yourself?" He looks blankly at the sky, his brow furrowed, and I wonder if he has ever given himself permission to think this broadly. Prompting him, I add, "One day, I will know everything there is to know about importing fine silks—and the thought of it bores me to tears. It is what will happen, but not what I want."

Valentine contemplates this, and then shifts closer. "I think I would like to be a gardener."

"A gardener?" I repeat, not quite keeping the surprise from my tone. "You know that would require shoveling rather a lot of manure, don't you?"

"I know. But my uncle had a gardener, and he was the most fascinatingly knowledgeable man—there was nothing he could not tell me about nature. He spent each winter planning how he would revive the dead ground of the estate, and then . . . he did it." Awe coats his voice, a honeyed whisper that mingles with the sweetness of the pear blossoms. "Watching the beds turn green, the flowers open, the branches turn heavy with fruit . . . all of

182

it exactly as he planned, as he predicted. It was impressive and beautiful and magical."

He continues to watch the stars, their light caught in the thick ends of his lashes, and I cannot take my eyes off him. "You are somewhat impressive and beautiful and magical as well, I think."

"And you have revived me." He touches my face, and I shiver, my flesh solidifying under his fingertips. "But if you want to know what I'd *really* like, if I were as rich as Escalus or even Paris, and never had to worry about feeding myself or keeping a roof above my head? I would like to travel."

I go still. "You wish to . . . to leave Verona?"

"For a time, at least." He sighs. "My uncle had an old friend, Marsiglio, who had been a sailor in his youth. He would spin tales about the places he had been, the great cities he had visited—in France, Byzantium, Catalonia—and his encounters there. Listening to him describe the food, the land, the people, how *different* everything was from home . . . it made me yearn to see it for myself."

"A trip like that would take years," I point out, unaccountably worried. "And it would be very expensive."

"I know." He laughs wistfully. "It is only a dream—unless I become a sailor myself, I suppose. I'm not sure I'm built for a life at sea, but if the baker won't take me on . . ."

He trails off, and I am cold through to the soles of my ruined hose. It is irrational, I know; Valentine and I have only just renewed our acquaintance, but I am gutted at the thought of him leaving again. The future I truly desire, even more than being an artist like Giotto, is a nightly feast of *this*. Of lying close with someone who makes me feel reckless, of hands and legs intertwined, of warm lips and hot breath and fingers in my hair.

If Valentine leaves, will I ever find something like it again? Or will I simply end up married to a stranger, an aristocratic girl of my father's choosing, and spend the rest of my life living out one of his passionless, strategic alliances while he rots in his grave?

"But what about"—I choke on the words I want to say, embarrassing ones that don't even make sense yet—"your brother? You would leave him behind?"

"I . . ." Valentine trails off. When he looks over at me, his eyes are so deep, I am afraid I could fall into them and tumble forever. "You cannot know what it was like for me, being sent away. My father was dead, and my uncle refused to acknowledge it. He would rage if I brought the matter up, and punish me if I cried. He was ashamed of the weakness of grief, and so I was forced to hide it." He reaches out, his fingers playing with the starlight. "My brother, my mother, my sisters . . . they could rely on one another. They lived and grew for three years without me, and now I am practically a stranger to them."

"I am certain that is not true." Propping myself up on an elbow, I say, "Since the day you left, Mercutio has talked of nothing but bringing you back."

"Yes. He wrote to me steadily while I was in Vicenza, and told me all the news of home, and shared every joke he could remember to brighten my spirits." A smile turns his features into poetry. "But even so . . . we have both changed enough that, some days, it feels as if we are still getting to know each other.

And, in any case, it won't be long before he takes a wife and can spare the room for me no longer."

This last sentiment precisely echoes my own thoughts from earlier in the day, and the panic that comes with it breathes new life into my unlikely dreams. "What if I appointed you to be the gardener here? When my father leaves me in charge of his empire, when I hold the keys to the villa, I could put these grounds in your care!"

He pulls me down again, tucking in closer, pressing his forehead to mine. "But I have no actual experience, Romeo. And how long will it be until you have the power to make that decision?"

"I don't know." A gust of wind shakes the trees, leaves and petals coming loose from their branches. "But I . . . I don't want you to go anywhere."

The honesty is difficult, leaving me open and uncertain. I've never felt this way with another person, never been this vulnerable, and I have no clue how to navigate the storm that's brewing in my heart. But Valentine sighs, his breath soft and warm against my cheek, and I melt inside as he murmurs, "You don't?"

"I want more of this," I tell him plainly. "Days of it—weeks, months."

"Only months?"

He is being coy, but I am not. "Years, then. Forever, if you can spare it."

"No one gets forever." He says it with sad finality, shifting subtly away. "I know it better than most. Fates can change, just like that." Valentine flings a careless hand into the wind, leaves flying as they are shredded from the trees. "You might even grow weary of me, one day. And we do not live in a world that will allow us to make such fanciful plans."

"I . . ." My voice sticks in my throat, because of course he is right. Time and again, I've seen Benvolio become smitten with a new girl, enraptured to the exclusion of all others—only to lose interest within a week, and start the cycle over with another.

But Ben has never had to look far for his companionship. He may have exaggerated his appeal a little in the piazza, but there are ladies all over Verona who are eager to fall into his arms, and he has grown spoiled by abundance.

Meanwhile, it has taken seventeen years for me to find Valentine—seventeen years to at last know what it means to desire someone who desires me back; to find how much pleasure can be extracted from a touch, a smile, a word. What Ben takes for granted, I have scarcely had time to appreciate, and already we speak of the day I will be without it again.

Whatever is happening between us, I want to savor it—if not forever, then for as long as I possibly can.

"You speak of planning and growing." I am still holding his hand, and I rub my thumb over his skin, magnetism building in the air. "Why can we not plan and grow our happiness? We are not promised forever, that much is true; but this has been the most wonderful day of my entire life." Softly, I urge, "Why should we not hope for more, plan for more? Why should we not seek as many days like this as we can get?"

"I would like that," he whispers. Reaching up, his hand finding my chest through the fabric of my nightshirt, his fingers exploring the muscle underneath. "The truth is, I have never felt this strong and this helpless before at the same time, and it frightens me."

"I am frightened, too." A sense of freedom washes over me with this confession. "You are the first thing to happen to me that I never expected, and it has me questioning everything I once believed was certain about my life. Two days ago, I could not think of one thing to look forward to, and now I am dreaming in weeks and months and years." I lean over him, planting my hands on either side of his shoulders. "However many days we are given together, Valentine, please let us strive to make each of them as fulfilling as this."

"Yes," he says, his voice captured by the wind, stolen into the treetops. His other hand moves up my hip and finds its way under my nightshirt, touching the bare skin at my waist. My blood lights up, my skin contracting, every part of me coming alive. "Yes. Kiss me, Romeo. Please."

I lower myself, pressing my body to his, and greedily honor his request. And there, under the starlight and the dancing limbs of the pear trees, we make more discoveries—new and wonderful and utterly unexpected.

18

WHEN MORNING BREAKS, I AM IN MY BED AGAIN, AND RELUCTANT to leave it. For the second day in a row, I roll away from the light and bury my face in the sheets, trying to return to the satisfaction of my dreams. If I keep my eyes closed, my mind suspended just a while longer, I can keep experiencing Valentine—his touch, his words, his taste—as many times as I like.

But the cock crows incessantly, and Hecate, who continues to sense that her affections are even more of a nuisance than her antipathy ever was, kneads my shoulder with her dainty paws. She demands attention, putting more gusto into pummeling my flesh than the Widow Grissoni has ever employed against one of her bread doughs.

At last I am forced to rise, groggy with contentment and a lack of sleep. My nightshirt is covered in grass stains, my hose completely ruined, and I will have to find a way to dispose of them before they are found and explanations are demanded.

I am in such a lighthearted mood that I even agree to break-fast with my parents, bearing their unfriendly scrutiny with as much patience as I have ever been able to muster. My mother is horrified by what she has heard about the spectacle in the piazza, and how my public shaming at the hands of the prince will reflect on our family. My father is enraged that I would attend a Capulet soiree for any reason, and accuses me of disloyalty.

"Those *people*," he fumes, "are neither our friends nor our equals. To their very marrow they are conniving and duplicitous! I have raised you with more sense than to allow some sloe-eyed trollop like their Juliet to turn your head." Leaning across the table, he slams his fist down in front of me, making my cup and plate jump. "Do you have any idea how much you have weakened our image? My only son, an easy mark for the Capulets! A foolish little lamb, obediently led to the slaughter."

There is no point in telling him that Juliet's story was counterfeit, and that I infiltrated the masquerade at Benvolio's instruction; he would simply widen the framework of his anger to make room for the new facts.

"I could almost respect your willingness to fight with that coxcomb Tybalt," he continues, "had the result not been so humiliating. Had your willing treachery against your own blood not been announced to one and all before the prince himself!" His glare pins me to my seat. It's almost shocking how swiftly he can reduce me to a cowering mouse with so few words. "I have been too lenient with you. This is my fault."

"It is not your fault, my love," my mother assures him, looking wounded on his behalf. "Do not blame yourself."

"But I must. It is clear that I have not acquitted myself properly as a father." He leans back in his chair—and the way he gathers himself makes the hairs on my neck rise. "Romeo, I was content to leave you this summer to at last shuffle off your childish interests and dedicate yourself to becoming a man, to becoming a *Montague*. But I can see that my faith in your developing maturity was misplaced."

Steepling his fingers, he assumes a stern air that chills my blood. "The time has long since passed for you to make a choice. Either you will seek to become an officer in the prince's army, or you will finally take a position as my apprentice and begin to learn the trade of importing silks. You have two weeks to make up your mind." Then, reaching casually for one of the rolls stacked in a tower by his plate, he adds, "Also, we will commence the search for your bride immediately, with a goal of having you married by the season's end. I'll not have all Verona thinking you are the same sort of degenerate satyr as your cousin—easily manipulated by any young lady with a full bosom."

"*F-Father*," I splutter . . . and then peter out to a cold, terrified silence, my mind too blank to conjure up any further defense. This is the horizon I had hoped never to reach, the future I have tried variously to ignore, delay, or deny. I believed I had the summer—the whole summer—to wait and hope for a miracle, but my time has been cut short.

Valentine was right after all: Fates can change, just like that.

"Do not bother to argue; my decision is made, and it is final." My father waves his hand, done with me. "Two weeks. And in the meantime, your mother and I shall begin to make an assessment of your marital prospects."

These are the statements that ring in my ears as I stumble

from the house with birds singing and the sun casting its cheerful and careless light into my eyes, my gut writhing like a nest of eels. I am cold to the core, realizing that all the tomorrows I was counting on have suddenly begun to run out. To have this cataclysm dropped into my lap now—the morning after I have only just discovered what companionship truly means—is horrifying.

When I didn't know what passion felt like, it wasn't hard to imagine living the rest of my life without it. But now that I know what I will spend my whole future missing—now that I know what sort of deceptions will be required to pass myself off as some poor girl's devoted husband—I am no longer certain I can do it.

For once, I managed to grab hold of happiness. And now my father has hold of its other end, and he is starting to pull.

Yesterday, when I was lost in thought, my feet led me to Valentine's door; this morning, however, dazed as I am, I know exactly where I am headed as I cross the green expanse that leads to our stables. There is only one person I can turn to with this terrible news—one person who might understand the depth of my distress, and offer me guidance. And today, I cannot risk making that journey on foot.

In addition to this fresh devastation, in addition to all the terrible inevitabilities that are just creaking into motion, there remains the matter of Tybalt and his vengefulness to consider. He has made it clear that there are no lines he will not cross to seek a bloody recompense for all the slights he imagines me responsible for; and no matter what Mercutio says, I have to take the threat seriously.

It doesn't take long before I am saddled up and on my way. But even as I gallop through the San Pietro gate and into the countryside—a passage that has always given my lungs more room to breathe—my chest is tight under my doublet. I am still shivering as the sun bears down on me, still flinching away from the Sword of Damocles that dangles overhead, threatening to sever my dreams from my future.

I was never fool enough to believe there might be some version of the world where I could choose my own fate, or even the person I would share my heart with. Even my most unrestrained fantasy of a romance with Valentine was one where I assumed my father's responsibilities against my personal desires, and carved out some secret space for what I truly wanted on the side. With nothing between me and the clear blue sky, I still could not imagine myself beyond the hard borders that my parents have built around my life.

But my fate was always somewhere in the distance; so long as it was out of sight, I could pretend it was always far enough away not to pose an immediate threat. Now, though, I realize that destiny itself is an ambush.

I drive my horse ahead, his hooves pounding the road, and in record time, we leave Verona well behind us. But my bleak thoughts cling to me, a swarm of hornets that are not so easily escaped. No matter how far I go, and no matter how fast I get there, I will still have to return. My doom will still be lying in wait.

For a wild, giddy moment, I borrow Valentine's fantasy of leaving for good—heading to the docks along the Adige and offering myself to the first merchant vessel I encounter as a sailor or a deckhand. It could be as simple as that: one crew short of a man, and then a swift departure down the river, out into the open water, and gone forever.

The only problem with this scenario is that I am almost certainly not suited for a life at sea. And while abandoning Verona would rescue me from my father's plans, it would mean leaving behind everything else as well—my friends, my home . . . and my Valentine. That revelatory encounter at the Capulets' came when I was just beginning to think I would never find another boy who felt the same things I do; I do not want to wait seventeen more years to see if I can come across another one who makes me laugh, who makes me feel warm inside, who kisses me as sweetly as he does.

We may not have forever, but how can I sacrifice our *now* as well?

When the bell tower of the friary first comes into view, I slow my horse to a trot and then a walk, my stomach churning as I think about what I will have to say. At the turn of the lane, I am surprised to find a familiar carriage parked at the roadside— Juliet's nurse peers worriedly out at me as I pass by and head for the front of the church.

I tie my horse to a post, and am just starting for the doors when they fly suddenly open and Juliet herself comes stumbling into the daylight. Before I can offer a greeting, I catch sight of her expression, and words fail me. Ashen faced, her eyes red rimmed and swollen, she looks as though she has not slept since I saw her last.

"Juliet?"

"Romeo." She stares at me for a moment, uncomprehending, and then her face crumples and she begins to cry. At first, I am so startled that I cannot think what to do; but when she begins to wipe her eyes with her sleeve, I finally remember my manners.

"Here," I say, pressing my handkerchief into her hand. Then, taking her by the elbow, I guide her to a bench under a nearby tree, and wait with her until her tears subside again.

"Thank you." Her voice is thick and miserable when she finally speaks. "I am ashamed of myself. This is very unbecoming of me."

"I assure you there is no need to be ashamed—not on my account."

"Still." She wipes her face and takes a deep breath. "I hate to cry in front of people. It is always used against me."

"I hate to cry at all," I return, that swarm of hornets still hovering close, still casting their shadows. "And when I do, I try to keep it secret for the same reason. But if it is any comfort, I can think of no convenient method to turn your sadness into a weapon, so you are at least safe from me for now."

This draws a weak laugh out of her. "I have shown vulnerability in front of my mortal enemy, and he tells me not to worry. What a world."

My eyebrows go up. "Are we enemies now?"

"We are certainly supposed to be." Juliet slumps back against the bench, letting out a defeated sigh. "My father heard about what took place in the piazza last night. Of course he heard—*all*

Verona has heard, and all Verona is evidently unwilling to talk of anything else! And he was . . ."

"Angry?" I can only think of my own father, and his tantrum at the breakfast table, my most sublime night turned into my most wretched morning.

"Irate," she amends. "Apoplectic. I have never seen him so furious, and . . . well, believe me, I have seen him in every available size and color of fury. He believes Tybalt's account, naturally, because he refuses to see any fault in my cousin whatsoever." Juliet wrings my handkerchief with such determination that I am afraid it will split in half. "Well, I should say that, in a sense, he believes us both: He is convinced that I smuggled you into our house for the masquerade, but he also believes that you had nefarious designs on my virtue—a humiliating conversation I cannot seem to stop having. There is not one man from here to Bohemia who isn't obsessed with my moral purity these days."

She reports this last with a biting sarcasm, but it only makes my stomach twist further until it resembles the mangled handkerchief in Juliet's hands. The last thing I need now is another powerful Capulet—the *most* powerful Capulet—putting a target on my back. "But that's absurd! Escalus publicly accepted your testimony. Even your father cannot contradict the prince."

"Escalus rules Verona, but Alboino Capulet decides what is true and what is not," she declares acerbically. "I am to blame for the scene at the party, because I brought you into our home and flaunted you in front of his guests. I am to blame for our disgrace in the piazza, because I defended you against Tybalt's false accusations."

195

"But none of that is fair." I don't know why I even bother to point it out; the main principle that governs life in our social stratum is eternally consistent, and never fair: Blame always belongs to the most defenseless person available.

"Of course it's not." She gives a lethargic shrug, staring off into the haze of the afternoon. "I told him that, thanks to my intervention, Tybalt escaped an official punishment by the crown. All he did was become even angrier at me for back talk. There is no winning with him, because he decides the case before he hears the arguments."

"That is a very familiar story," I murmur, again recalling the purple tint of my father's complexion at breakfast as he called me a "foolish little lamb."

"It's easy for him to believe I am the one causing trouble, because all I am to him is an expensive and uncompliant bargaining chip." Her tone is frosty enough to kill Friar Laurence's entire garden. "He intends to marry me off, to use me as collateral in an attempt to forge ties with a powerful man, and he expects me to be sanguine about it. I made the mistake of voicing my objections once, and he has not had a kind word to spare for me since that day."

I can offer little more than heartfelt empathy. "I'm sorry."

"Men I have never met, some of them three times my age or more, come to our home and examine me like a hunting dog— asking me to speak and smile and do tricks—so they may decide if I am fit for their home! It is . . . it is . . ." Juliet's face turns scarlet; but then, just as quickly, she deflates again. "It is no use being outraged over, because it is how things are. It is not for a girl to determine her own fate."

This is true, I realize—although I had never really considered the matter from a girl's perspective before. Come to that, I do not think I've ever encountered a girl who didn't seem enthusiastic about marrying into status . . . although it may be that, as an eligible bachelor with status to spare, I've just never met one willing to tell me she resented the arrangement.

Juliet's words remind me again of my conversation with Valentine, about all the things we would do if only our world were a fairer place. Hesitantly, I ask, "What if it were? What fate *would* you determine for yourself?"

"I would leave Verona," she answers flatly, immediately, "without a husband. Without anything that might connect me to this place or the people in it. If I could do as I pleased, I would go somewhere else and, and . . ." Juliet trails off, shaking her head, slapping the bench in a sudden burst of frustration. "And then I do not know. I do not *know* what I would do if I could decide such things for myself, and it makes me . . . *furious!*"

"But there must be something you have never done that you have always—"

She cuts me off, heat making her voice rough. "I have never gone anywhere outside of San Zeno without some form of an escort, and I very much long to do so. I have never had a future of my own to think of, dream of, hope for, and I should like to do all of that as well!" For a moment, she broods silently. And then, quieter, she says, "If the world were no obstacle to me, I think I could be a merchant. Not, perhaps, on the same scale as my father—although he has taken a great many of my notions about our family's business and later pretended they were his own—but I think I would be skilled at the trading and selling of wares."

"What sort of wares would you choose?"

"I do not know that, either," she huffs, tossing up her hands. "Where would I start? *How* would I start? And what is the point of fantasizing, when the die is already cast?"

"Fates can change in the blink of an eye." That blissful night in the orchard spins through my thoughts. "Perhaps one of these rich old men will take you for his bride and quickly leave you a happy, young widow?"

"That is a very optimistic way to phrase what might be the most cynical thing I have ever heard." Juliet laughs in spite of herself. "That would, though, be the best I could realistically hope for . . . Isn't that terrible? And yet, I'm still not certain what I would do, should I be lucky enough to gain such independence. The only interests I have been permitted to cultivate are wifely ones: music, at which I am terrible; art, at which I am worse; embroidery, which hurts my eyes *and* my fingers; and poetry, which I find to be an excruciating bore."

"Everyone finds poetry excruciating," I point out.

"Good poems are unbearable," she agrees. "But the very bad ones can be terribly amusing."

After a moment, I take a breath. "I am glad we encountered each other this morning, because there's something I've meant to tell you. I was very grateful for what you said on my behalf before the prince yesterday. I *am* grateful. You showed a tremendous amount of courage, and most certainly saved me from a dreadful punishment. It was very brave, and I wish there was something I could do to help you in return. I wish your fate was in my power to alter, as you altered mine."

"My father is going to promise my hand to Count Paris." She says it quickly, and her eyes swim anew. "He told me that after what I did in the piazza, it was clear that he needed to commit me to a marriage before my 'obstreperousness' could 'cost him everything.'" Juliet presses my handkerchief to her face and sobs without making a sound. Then, in a strangled tone, she adds, "So, you see, all I am good for—all I have been raised for—is to act as a bridge between my father and some other man with something he wants.

"Paris is practically a stranger, and I am being given over to him, for the rest of my life, or at least for the rest of his. And it is not because he desires me, but because he desires my father's influence." My handkerchief trembles in her hands. "The reason I came here was to seek counsel from Friar Laurence . . . but of course there is nothing he can offer *besides* counsel. There is no solution to my problem." She meets my eyes, her expression utterly abject. "Romeo . . . I am not certain that I wish to wed *anyone*, but I am terrified and distraught to be married away to someone I feel nothing for. My mother keeps telling me that love will develop between us 'in time,' but . . . what if it does not?"

Her question rings in my ears, a knell so dismally familiar that it takes my breath away. And again, it's hard to answer without exposing my secrets. "I do not know. It's something I've had to ask myself before. Have you ever considered taking a vow of celibacy, as Rosaline Morosini did? She is unlikely to leave her father's house, but her commitment is respected and even admired in Verona."

"I have gone so far as to consider entering a convent," Juliet answers with a brittle laugh, "but I cannot without my father's permission. I told him once that I wished to remain celibate, and he said my tune would change after he found me a husband. It was the end of our conversation on the matter." Her jaw flexes. "It is ironic, is it not? Chastity is the one virtue I should like to retain, and yet I shall be subject to public speculation about it until the moment I am married—at which point I shall be expected to give it up, whether I want to or not."

With a bleak feeling, I lean back against the bench. "I suppose that neither of us is permitted to make our own choices. And the people who make them for us are interested in us only as possessions, rather than people."

Juliet touches my arm, giving me a look full of understanding. "I think that perhaps you and I have even more in common than I had previously believed."

"My father is furious with me over the scene in the piazza as well, and for much the same reason as yours. He has also decided that it's time for me to marry, and will hear no arguments against his agenda." Saying it aloud makes my stomach rebel again. "But I am no more ready than you are, and no more interested. And to complicate matters . . . ," I begin, and then swallow reflexively, my head feeling light. "Recently . . . I have met someone. Someone I have grown very fond of, very quickly. I do not know if it is love, exactly, but it is beginning to feel very much like it. And when my parents arrange for me a bride of their choosing, I may lose this precious thing altogether from my life."

Her hand finds mine, and she holds it tightly. "How can we be two of the most and least fortunate souls in Verona at once?"

"I do not know, but I have grown weary of the honor." The bells in the church tower begin to chime, and I realize how much time has passed. "Come . . . let me escort you back to your coach. Your nurse has been waiting, and I have held you up."

"Not at all. I feel . . ." She stops, and then laughs a little. "Well, not better, exactly. But I feel as if I have been screaming at the top of my lungs for weeks, and someone has finally heard me." Looping her arm through mine, Juliet gives me a kind look. "Thank you, Romeo. You have been a friend to me when I needed one, and I won't forget that."

When we reach the foot of the lane, we stop in front of her coach to say our goodbyes. Another carriage comes into view on the road, headed toward the city.

"I wish . . . I wish we lived in a less cruel place—a place that would permit us to be friends even where others could see us," Juliet says. "But I will take comfort in knowing that, no matter what or how many petty grievances our families wish to dote on, you and I will not be enemies."

"Never," I assure her.

Leaning up, she presses a kiss to my cheek, and I embrace her warmly, gratefully . . . and that is exactly the tableau we present as the rattling carriage finally trundles past.

A shocked and terribly familiar face stares out at us from inside.

It is Galvano—one of Tybalt's lackeys.

19

My ride back to San Pietro is even more frantic than the journey out, speed being very much of the essence. I overtake Galvano's carriage, and although I briefly consider stopping to confront him, in the end I only spur my horse on, galloping faster.

"Galvano will make trouble," Juliet said, her face pale again as she broke away from me. "You should try to reach the city before he does. We must tell the truth—that we encountered each other by chance—and hope we are believed."

My mouth dry, I asked, "Is Galvano dim enough to think we would select a church for a romantic assignation?"

"Yes." She started for her carriage. "He is. But what should worry you more is that Tybalt will decide to believe him." Lunging up into the cab, Juliet ordered the driver to go. As the wheels began rolling, she called, "I hope my alarm is unwarranted, but . . . if you own a blade, I suggest you carry it with you from now on. And you might advise your friends to do the same."

And then she was gone in a cloud of dust, hurrying up the road and leaving me behind in a state of escalating dread.

There is not a doubt in my mind that Tybalt will use my

embrace with Juliet as further proof of my devious intentions, as justification for his vengeance. He made a line in the sand at the Via de Mezzo; he drew on me in the middle of a crowded ballroom; he attacked my friends and me in the middle of the piazza, slandered me to the prince, and got away with it all. At this point, I would be a fool to doubt that he might cross the Adige into San Pietro—with his steel and his confederates—to assuage his wounded ego.

When I make it back to the villa, my horse in a lather and both of us breathing hard, I am prepared to lie low, but my father has other ideas. I am scarcely in the safety of my rooms for three quarters of an hour before he is pounding at my door.

"There you are!" he growls, as if he has been summoning me all afternoon and I have ignored him just to be vexing. "Of course I would find you in your chambers, indulging your ungrateful laziness, as though there were not a dozen urgent matters at hand." All I can do is stare up at him and blink in surprise as he thrusts a leather folio at me. "I need you to bear these papers to the guildhall, and make sure they are delivered into the hands of my associate Piramo. You remember him, yes?"

It is only a question in the sense that he expects an answer; he knows I am familiar with the elderly and eccentric Piramo. What I am not familiar with is being ordered to run simple errands that are generally performed by the servants. Still dazed, still thinking of Tybalt, I venture, "Isn't this something one of our pages should do?"

"No, Romeo!" His voice thunders, his eyes full of fury in an instant. "If it were an appropriate task for a page, I'd have sent one hours ago. I am sending you because, lest you forget, you are to be my apprentice." Drawing himself up, my father growls, "You will do what I say, and without complaint! Whether you like it or not, you have responsibilities to uphold—and your first is to take those papers to the guildhall. Am I understood?"

All I can manage is a meek nod. If I tell him that I am reluctant to leave San Pietro because of Tybalt, he will call me a coward. If I explain what I have done that has provoked Capulet anger this time, he will become only more enraged, and he will invent some terrible new punishment for me as a lesson in obedience.

Nervously, I dress to leave, fastening my scabbard to my hip with Juliet's warning ringing in my ears. Before I go, however, I dash off two brief letters and hand them to my page. "Deliver these as fast as you can. One is for my cousin Benvolio, and the other is for my friend Mercutio and his brother. Advise them that the contents are urgent."

With a serious nod, he scampers out of the villa, kicking up dust as he races toward the Adige, and then I duck out behind him, heading the opposite way. The guildhall is located right on the piazza, its distinguished arches holding pride of place nearly smack in the center of the elongated market square—my page will probably cross it to bring Mercutio his letter. But I cannot risk taking so direct a route.

Galvano has had more than enough time by now to make it back to Verona, locate Tybalt, and stoke his rage. It has been at least enough time for the ill-tempered Capulet to begin planning his next moves, if he was not planning them already.

205

In truth, he is probably not quite arrogant enough to storm San Pietro, which is flush with Montagues and those loyal to our family. He may be erratic and governed by his temper, but he is at least clever enough to assess the odds. He's also clever enough to know that I cannot stay in protected territory forever—that I will have to enter the old city sooner or later—and that if he waits me out, his patience will eventually be rewarded. After all, there are only so many places I can reasonably cross the river from here.

Were I in his position, the first thing I would do is post a sentinel at the far end of the Ponte Pietra. As the only truly convenient bridge for those of us who live north of the Adige, it is an obvious choice for a trap. There are plenty of ferries, of course—oarsmen who row passengers across the water for a penny or two—and I could pick any one of them. But all it might take is the promise of a generous reward from Tybalt, and they would become a network of his spies, eager to report on my movements.

I could walk south to Campo Marzio and try the bridge there, but that would only leave me at the mouth of the Via de Mezzo—where Tybalt already has a crew of faithful soldiers watching for anyone named Montague. One way or the other, he will be expecting me from the north or east, which means my best strategy is to come from the other direction: crossing the river from the west, and approaching the guildhall from behind.

The journey takes longer than I'd like—long enough to second-guess all my choices, anyway—and I am nervous as a hunted cat when I make it across the Adige at last. I enter the twisting warren of alleyways on Mercutio's side of the city, cleaving to what few shadows the midday sun permits, my hand on the hilt of my sword the whole time.

As the crowd thickens, the noise of the market growing closer, I finally catch my first glimpse of the guildhall—and of a familiar figure, standing at attention where the alley breaks open onto the piazza. Flooded with relief, I call out, "Mercutio!"

He hails me in reply, but his expression is as grim as I've ever seen it. Drawing closer, I see that there are others with him: Ben and Valentine, of course, but also some of my more distant cousins, and a handful of the men who work for my father. Each of them carries a blade—and while I am relieved to see that my warnings were received and taken seriously, the sight of all those weapons, all those militant faces, only puts me more on edge.

"There you are." Mercutio may be repeating my father, but his attitude is far more welcoming. "Come. We ought to get inside, and it would be best to do so quickly."

"I thought you were exaggerating when I first read your letter," Ben tells me, gripping my right elbow, guiding me through the colonnade and into the guildhall. "But then I noticed one of Tybalt's boys in a doorway across from my house. He followed me halfway to the piazza before I managed to shake him off."

"There was one in our alley as well." Mercutio squares his shoulders as he takes up a corresponding position on my left. "I suspect he was watching for you."

I breathe easier inside the guildhall, where the threat of violence is minimized—owing to general decorum if nothing else. A frontal assault here, within a meetinghouse for the city's wealthiest merchants, would be difficult for the prince to dismiss as another folly of youth. Even for someone with as many second chances as Tybalt.

"There are Capulet informants stationed in the piazza, too," Valentine reports gravely, somewhere just behind me. "At the very least, I recognized the man who followed us over the garden wall when we fled the masquerade. He was watching the north end of the market—and Mercutio identified two others."

"Three others," Mercutio amends, "but the point remains."

"It would appear that our friend Tybalt has decided to make a project of locating you." Ben affects a jovial tone, in defiance of the prevailing mood. "And I doubt there is any chance we all trooped into the guildhall without his spies knowing you were with us."

My gut rumbling, my fingers sweaty where they grip the folio my father sent me here to deliver, I glance around. "Should I leave before they can gather reinforcements?"

"There would hardly be any point," Ben says decisively.

"You're assuming the reinforcements are all back in San Zeno." Mercutio makes a fist, his knuckles cracking. "But it's more likely they're scattered at this end of town, waiting for word. I'd be surprised if any of them are more than five or ten minutes away."

"Tybalt will be close as well," Ben continues, "and the stooges he already has watching the piazza would surely intercept you if you tried to make it back to San Pietro."

"Then . . . what am I supposed to do?" My voice echoes in

the guildhall, throwing my own nervousness back at me. "Should we send a page to notify the prince?"

"Of what?" Mercutio retorts. "Capulets in the marketplace? He will not ride to the rescue—he would only be annoyed that the antagonism between you two has not been quashed, and that we would trouble him anew with the same old business."

"He's right." Ben meets my eyes, nodding brusquely. "If you want my advice, what you must do is call for reinforcements of your own. Your best chance at leaving the piazza and returning home with your skin intact is to make Tybalt think twice about a confrontation. Intimidate him—make him realize that you are prepared to put up a fight, and that things will not go his way if you do."

"Intimidation is the key word. We need to raise the greatest numbers we can." Mercutio speaks as though the plan is already decided—and perhaps it is. "We're lucky you already have plenty of allies on this side of Verona, and San Pietro is much closer to the piazza than San Zeno. I already have a dozen or more men in mind."

Swiftly, he and Ben round up every page they can find and start giving orders, Mercutio marking cards with his sigil to authenticate the call to arms. My head spins as I watch this all play out—my friends swiftly raising an army on my behalf. It is difficult to believe this is still the same day I woke with a smile on my face, and the imprint of Valentine's teeth in the skin of my shoulder.

"You're nervous." Valentine's voice is pitched low, but the suddenness of it in my ear still causes me to jump.

Forcing a weak smile, I ask, "Is it so obvious?"

"To me, it is," he replies, his mouth turning up a bit on one side. "But I have made a hobby of studying you when you think no one is looking, and I am familiar with your private moods by now."

"This is not . . ." I struggle to express a thought I wish I did not have. "This will be no simple confrontation. It will be unlike any of the perilous encounters I've had with Tybalt in the past— even the ones that ended in split lips and bruised egos." At the core of me, just beneath my heart, there is a fretful vibration that makes my limbs restless. "What if I am not enough to face this challenge?"

"You are." Valentine all but whispers; and even though we are surrounded here, enjoying none of the privacy of my family's orchard and its generous pear trees, he slips his hand into mine and holds it tight, the gesture barely hidden by the fold of his cloak. "You are more than enough, Romeo. There is little I know as well as I know that."

Even if only for that moment, it calms the vibration in my chest, and I feel the sun on my face.

It takes less than an hour for the men to start answering the summons, first in a trickle and then in a flood, stout bodies crowding the guildhall until Mercutio begins ordering some into loose positions outside. All the new arrivals report that the Capulet presence in the piazza is also expanding, and that our numbers are roughly equal. As the last of my erstwhile soldiers finally straggle in, Ben takes me aside.

"I believe it must be now or never, Cousin." His eyes are

hooded, and a muscle jumps in the curve of his jaw. "It does not look as though we will have him outmanned after all, but we can show him that to get to you, he will have to truly wage war."

My tongue sticks to the roof of my mouth. "You think that will dissuade him?"

Ben is quiet for a moment, and then he sighs. "What I think is that there is no sense putting off the inevitable. It will either be a stalemate or a bloodbath, and that won't change with waiting." Smiling grimly, he checks himself. "Well, there is a third possibility. We are also within shouting distance of the palazzo, and if this standoff continues long enough, the prince will probably step in. And Mercutio is right—if Escalus has to intervene again, it will likely be to everyone's detriment . . . but particularly yours."

"If I go out there and confront Tybalt with a battalion of angry Montagues, and blood is shed in the piazza, the prince is going to have something to say about it no matter what," I point out bleakly.

Ben doesn't even bother to argue. "You will either have to ensure there is no bloodshed, so he may praise your levelheaded pacifism . . . or you will have to provoke Tybalt into striking first—without appearing to do so—so that the blame can be his. All that will be required is laughing at his threats." It is a joke, but it is also precisely how our last altercation began. "Now, we might as well enter the battlefield."

20

WE MAKE A TENSE PROCESSION OUT OF THE GUILDHALL AND BACK into the piazza, my volunteer soldiers eager for this clash with the enemy. Valentine stays close, schooling the worry from his expression as we file back out into daylight. Ben and Mercutio have stepped comfortably into their roles as my lieutenants, flanking me, issuing confident orders.

Their composure mystifies me. I want no archnemesis to plan my every movement around, no brewing hostilities to constantly fret over, no perpetually looming danger of violence or death. As we fan out over the square, confronting the Capulet forces at last, it hits me for the first time that some of us might actually lose our lives over this.

"*Romeo Montague!*" Tybalt breaks through the front line of his gathered militia, his face shining with anger, and he thrusts a finger at me. "You are a liar and a mountebank, the vilest scum of Verona, and you will finally answer for your violation of my cousin!"

Gasps and murmurs spread through the gathered onlookers— another audience to yet another ugly encounter between the

Montagues and Capulets—and I try to ignore them. With a calm I don't feel, I say, "Good morrow to you as well, Tybalt."

"You have been meeting in secret with Juliet—do not attempt to deny it. You were witnessed this very morning, embracing each other during a secret assignation in the countryside!" He waits for his words to settle, for me to refute them. When I hold my tongue, he lurches closer. "Do you admit it, then? That you have lured my sweet cousin into immoral liaisons, spiriting her beyond the city so as to not be discovered?"

"If Galvano described what he witnessed as an 'immoral liaison,' then he is lying to you," I counter, my tone collected, even as my scalp prickles with nerves. "And you might ask him precisely where it was that he saw us."

"It was at a lonely spot, some four miles along the post road south of the city." Galvano shoves his way forward, as puffed up as Tybalt. "You were kissing—I saw you!"

"You did," I confirm. "And from your coach, yes?"

"Aye." He says it immediately, and only after the word is out do his eyes cloud with the realization that I may have just entrapped him somehow. "I was escorting my mother home from the Shrine of Saint Agatha, where she makes a regular pilgrimage."

"So you saw us standing beside the road, in full view of anyone who happened to pass by." I wait, but he has no answer for this. "Does that sound like two people trying to have a 'secret' assignation?"

"You are twisting my words!" Galvano accuses.

At the same time, Tybalt declares, "He is playing games of rhetoric, but he has confirmed meeting with Juliet!"

"I never said we did not encounter each other this morning—I said that Galvano has misrepresented what he saw." Sweat makes a cold path down the middle of my back, and my eyes keep flicking to the sword at Tybalt's hip. "I'm assuming you never bothered asking Juliet's nurse for her own account of this same meeting, for if you had, you would not be embarrassing us all and slandering my name *again*."

"That woman is untrustworthy. She tells falsehoods without an ounce of shame." Tybalt dismisses my witness with a toss of his hand. "As do you! Sneaking into my uncle's house, turning my cousin against her kin, luring her out of Verona in order to—"

Cutting him off, I turn to Galvano again. "The place where you saw us—four miles south along the post road—that also describes the location of the Franciscan friary, does it not?"

This time, he blinks, shooting an uncomfortable glance at Tybalt. "I worship at the Benedictine church in San Zeno. I neither know nor care where the Franciscans keep themselves."

"It is at a friary roughly four miles south of here along the post road," I supply patiently. "In fact, Juliet and I were only thirty yards or less from the front door of their church. Seems a curious place to conduct the sort of activities you are implying, Tybalt."

There are more murmurs from the crowd, and more befuddled silence from Galvano. But in Tybalt's eyes, I can see that he's exploring my statement for weaknesses. And when his expression shifts, I realize he's found one. "You took Juliet to a church?"

There is a change in the air, the murmurs falling silent for a moment, and then rippling faster as the inference is passed around the piazza. Aggression is a pot with a rattling lid as each side watches the other, waiting for an excuse—and Tybalt is intent on giving them one. Heat creeps into my face. "I took Juliet nowhere. We happened to meet—"

"You 'happened' to meet," he repeats with savage contempt. "What a marvelous coincidence! And on the very day her father has decided upon her future husband." He advances, and immediately Ben and Mercutio flank me. "My fair cousin may be too naive, too trusting, to recognize you for the rake you are, to see that you mean to corrupt her. But she is also too penitent a woman to let you or any man have her outside of a marriage bed, and you know it well!"

"That is absurd." I cast a look around for support, but suddenly there are men who will not meet my eyes. "It was a chance meeting, and nothing more—a fact to which her nurse and the friars will openly attest!"

Tybalt ignores me, a glint in his eye betraying his enjoyment of this turn in the tide. "Did you *consummate* your fraudulent union and despoil my poor cousin? Or is there still time to preserve her honor for the noble Count Paris?"

"You have never once cared about anyone's honor," Mercutio interjects scathingly. "Least of all Juliet's. Clearly you have no care for your own, either, or you would not be making such baseless accusations in a venue where you know they will be remembered. The truth will inevitably out, Tybalt—and you will be cast out with it."

"Then I suppose you have no objections to our getting to the truth of matters here and now." The unctuous Capulet boy

215

is finally in his element. "This degenerate coward has seduced my cousin, and now meets with her in secret at a church outside the city—where he knows her family would neither worship nor think to search for her." He takes another step forward, and the crowd shifts again, ready to boil over at any moment. "I ask you again, sir: Have you defiled Juliet, or is she still pure?"

The murmurs jump to full-voice exclamations, deadly rumors forming and taking flight at breakneck speeds. This implication— that I may have wed Juliet in a clandestine ceremony with the sole aim of wrecking her future and reputation—is just grandiose and sordid enough to be believed.

My blood chills as I finally begin to accept that there will be no peaceful conclusion here after all, no reasoned exchange ending in a ceasefire; Tybalt will simply not allow cooler heads to prevail. By hook or by crook, he will have his revenge on me, and there is no pathway out of the piazza that is not painted with blood.

What is left is for me to ensure that, when the dust settles, I remain standing—and that for once the blame is his alone to bear. *All that will be required is laughing at his threats.*

"Not every man in Verona is as keen to lie with your cousin as you are, Tybalt," I retort, drawing abrupt and nervous laughter from the crowd.

His face twists, knuckles white on the hilt of his blade. "You bite your tongue, villain."

"You speak of her as if she were a spoon or a serving tray—an object to be scrubbed and put to use by men. But she certainly scrubbed the piazza with your dignity yesterday!" I laugh at him, and though it is forced, the imitation of levity is enough to break the thick crust of tension in the air, humor quickly spreading through the mob. "Fair she may be, as well as trusting and penitent, but she is no naïf. And before you suggest she is easily fooled, you should consider how easily she made a fool of you before Prince Escalus!"

The laughter builds, and Tybalt's lip curls, saliva bubbling between his teeth. "My cousin's virtue and reputation are at stake, and you make jokes. You delight in your attempted sabotage of Juliet's integrity, in your relentless attack on my family's respectability, because you will never be anything more than the issue of dishonorable scum!"

He draws his blade at last—and I respond in kind, and the gesture is repeated over and over through the clustered ranks, the piazza ringing with the sound of greedy metal.

"You will confess willingly to your sins," Tybalt announces, brandishing his sword, "or I will thrash the confession out of you!"

And then he charges.

I do not like to fight. Despite being trained in the weapons preferred by Verona's aristocratic class, I much prefer peace; and there has never been a time when I truly feared for my life before, when I knew that if I did not win, I might not walk away. Tybalt, however, has made it his own point to seek that experience out and learn from it.

Unfortunately for Tybalt, though, while I do not enjoy a sword fight, it is something I am quite good at.

Handling a blade well requires dexterity, precision, and control—all essential skills, as it happens, for the creation of fine art. And although I have never drawn my rapier with the intent to kill, I have also not lost a single training match since I turned fifteen. Tybalt has more mass than I do—broader shoulders, thicker arms, longer legs—but his moves are all predictable, and his reliance on brute strength is a flaw I can use against him.

His sword slashes at me, and I counter instinctively, deflecting the strike with a flick of my wrist that encourages his momentum and throws him off balance. Almost instantly, Mercutio is upon him, driving him back with a series of thrusts and parries that give me just enough time to breathe before Galvano leaps in to take his de facto leader's position.

Galvano is defter than Tybalt, but he underestimates me— or perhaps he overestimates himself. I let him take momentary control, so I can see what he will do with it . . . and watch as he repeatedly leaves his midsection exposed when he lunges forward. The next time he does so, I jab the point of my sword in between his ribs. The wound I leave should not be fatal, but it is deep enough to make him retreat in a panic.

After Galvano, there are other challengers, and I quickly learn that not all the Capulet loyalists can be fended off with simple flesh wounds—that some will only back down if I injure them gravely enough that they have no other choice. I begin targeting shoulder joints and upper arms, casting aside my mercy as I tear the flesh they need to wield their weapons. Around me, chaos swells, blood painting the stones at our feet.

Through the melee, I catch glimpses of my friends: Mercutio brandishing two swords at once; Ben with a bloodied face and a triumphal grin; Valentine sticking close to his brother, holding his own. The skirmish has gotten louder, and I look toward the palazzo. The prince will be upon us in no time, and maybe this battle will come to a close before any unimaginable loss.

I have scarcely thought the words when Tybalt finds me again.

His face bruised and sweaty, his teeth stained with blood, he growls, "No more hiding behind your companions, Montague. This matter comes down to you and me, and we will settle it like men!"

"If you have finally become one, I am proud of you." I carve a few loops from the air so he can see how much fight I have left. My breath comes hard, but the moves come easy.

"I hope you are still talking when my blade sinks through your heart." Tybalt does not mince his words. "I shall be glad to shut your mouth for good!"

He is not taunting me, or trying to shake my confidence; he honestly means to kill me. The truth of it burns in his eyes, and there will be only one way this confrontation can end.

Tybalt swings and thrusts in a wild frenzy, having gained desperation but no new skills since our previous encounter. With gritted teeth, he hammers one blow at me after another, and my arm begins to ache with the strength it takes to counter his maneuvers.

I take a forced step back, and then a second, and Tybalt's mouth pulls into a vicious grin as he realizes that he is gaining the upper hand. To my right, through the mayhem, I catch sight of Mercutio and Valentine. Thinking fast, I retreat a little farther still, curving my path their way, fearing I might soon need their help.

It is funny to think how fixed I once imagined my destiny—how in every direction I looked, it seemed there was only one future that waited for me. For when the moment comes that my fate suddenly does change, when everything I once thought inevitable is tossed out of reach, it happens so fast I can barely see it coming.

Tybalt lunges, off balance, and as he pulls back again, he leaves his shoulder exposed just long enough for me to run the point of my sword through it. Roaring in pain, he tries to maintain a grip on the hilt of his rapier, but his hand quakes as he turns it my way again. Disarming him is only a formality, a matter of a few simple moves.

Victory surges through my chest, certain as I am that this is the moment where I prevail. I am watching his rapier hit the ground, blood already streaming from his coat sleeve, and it is not until I hear someone shout my name that I remember:

Tybalt also carries a dagger.

Too late, I understand that he baited me with that last, helpless gesture of his blade, that he tempted me to step closer in order to disarm him—to move within reach of his knife. Time slows as its point comes at my right flank, angled up to find its way between my ribs.

And then a sword flashes between us.

Colliding against me, Valentine knocks the dagger upward in the last possible instant with the tip of his blade, sending it off course. The knifepoint rips the thick fabric of my coat, missing the flesh of my torso by a mere hair's breadth, and continues on its way . . . right toward Valentine himself.

Tybalt lets the dagger claim this new path, his vengeance hot in the air, and stabs the boy I am learning to love just beneath his collarbone.

Something breaks open inside me, my veins going hot, the roar of blood drowning out my reason.

Valentine staggers back—his flesh torn, his eyes wide with panic—as Tybalt spins in my direction . . .

And meets the tip of my blade.

Steel plunges through his throat, deep enough to scrape bone, and when I yank it out it drips a hot, slick red.

I am breathing so hard my vision sparkles as Tybalt stumbles backward, clutching his ruined neck with one hand. Silky ribbons of blood slip through his fingers and trail down his arm. The crowd shifts, but I am rooted in place, listening to the gurgle he makes as he drops to his knees and then crumples to the crimson-streaked stones.

His legs twitch, a hideous rattle coming from deep in his chest, when Mercutio howls his brother's name and I finally come back to myself.

Valentine lies on the ground, his face waxy and pale, his lips turning blue as his coat turns red. My knees give out, and I would drop beside him if Ben didn't catch me under the arms. Mercutio, his face ravaged with horror, cradles his brother's head in his lap.

Choking on grief, he looks up at us. "I don't . . . I don't think he's breathing!"

To Lose a Winning Match

21

I AM STRUGGLING TO FREE MYSELF FROM BENVOLIO'S GRIP WHEN
the blast of horns splits the air, finally announcing the arrival
of Prince Escalus. He is too late, though. By one minute—sixty
merciless seconds—he is too late to save my heart from breaking.

"Romeo, we must flee!" Ben grunts fiercely, wrestling me
away from Valentine. He still lies on his back in the piazza, Mercutio cradling his head and weeping openly. Absurdly, all I can
think is, *That should be me.* I don't even know which of the two
boys I mean.

"*No.*" With what strength I have left, I fight against my cousin,
writhing in his grip. Ben is bigger than I am, but my despair
could crush an army, it could level a mountain. He has no idea
what he is dealing with. "Let me go—*let me go, damn you!*"

"You cannot help him, Romeo." Ben has to shout to be heard
when the trumpets call again, closer this time. "Do you understand me? *You cannot help him!* He needs a surgeon, and you need
to run as far and as fast as you can. *Now.*"

He heaves me back, my heels scraping the stone, and the

crowd spills into the gap we leave. They block my view, and I begin to panic, thrashing wildly. "I will . . . not . . . *leave him*—"

"He is not alone, he has his brother, and—*Romeo, look at me.*" Ben shakes me hard until I comply, dazed. His face is ashen and bloodied, his eyes round with urgency. "You killed Tybalt! Do you realize what will happen if you fall into the prince's hands? Do you?" He shakes me again, and to my surprise, tears spill down his cheeks. "You will be exiled, Romeo, *if you are lucky*. More likely you will be hanged for taking a life within Verona's walls, when you were commanded to drop your enmity in the name of peace—and I will not let that happen!"

"But Valentine . . ." My voice breaks, the crowd growing thicker and more disturbed.

"We cannot help him," he insists again, desperately, "and if you do not flee, you will be cast out, or you will die! What good will that make you to Valentine? Or Mercutio, or me?" He shakes me again, and the weight of what he's saying nearly pushes me to the ground. "If you ever wish to see us again, you must get to some place the prince cannot find you. Come with me, Cousin—let me take you from here while there is still time!"

He nearly lifts me off my feet this time, dragging me away from the approaching guards, and I finally give up. The piazza no longer rings with the clash of swords, and around us, men are growing subdued as they realize the battle is ended. In a matter of moments, we will have no chaos to cover our escape. Like a sleepwalker, I let Benvolio drag me from the piazza and into the maze of alleys that splinter away from the heart of Verona— pulling me farther and farther from Valentine.

The next two days are lost to me in a fog of shock and sorrow. There is, of course, only one place I can think of that is safely outside Verona—that I believe will welcome me in—and somehow Ben gets me there. At least, he must; because it is where I find myself, two mornings later, waking up in a barren cell with nothing but the clothes on my back.

"You are awake," Friar Laurence observes as he pushes through the door, his expression showing relief and surprise. He bears a tray of fresh bread and water, which he places on a small table beside me.

"Am I?" My body is heavy and my heart hurts, the room swaying like one of those lanterns in the Capulets' secret courtyard—the ones that made Valentine's chest glimmer that night at the masquerade.

Just thinking his name causes something to twist painfully in my chest.

"You have slept for most of the past thirty-six hours." The monk takes a seat across from me on the lone chair in the room, light spilling across him from the window. "I am not certain it was a healthy sleep, but I had the sense that you needed it."

As my head begins to clear, the scent of cut grass and fresh air swirling into the room, I look around. "I am at the friary. You took me in, after all—even though I . . ."

I cannot quite finish the statement, and Laurence musters a worried little smile. "We did. In truth, not all the brothers were in agreement on the matter—it is rather against our creed to shed

227

blood in anger, as you know—but my testimony as to the nature of your character swayed them in your favor." He tugs unhappily at the folds of his robe. "I do know you after all, Romeo, and I listened to your cousin's account of what took place in the piazza. You acted in defense when he attacked someone important to you. The scriptures are filled with tales of honorable men performing similar acts."

It is a sympathetic way to acknowledge that I took a life; despite knowing how much danger Tybalt posed in that moment, I am still struggling to make peace with it.

"Valentine saved me from Tybalt's blade." I still recall the flash of metal against metal, the dagger deflected in the nick of time. "And he was paid in vengeance. I did not think when I ran Tybalt through; it all happened so fast, and I only knew that if he was not stopped, we would both be dead." Tears splash onto the sheet that is drawn up to my waist. "Do you . . . have you heard any news from Verona? Do you know if . . ."

Laurence spares me from finishing the thought. "I've not heard much of anything—just that the prince is in a state of fury over the clash in the piazza, as you could no doubt surmise. He sent riders out on the roads leading from the city in search of your trail, but so far that is all his search has amounted to where we are concerned." He hesitates, scratching his beard. "Otherwise, the talk is mainly of Tybalt's death. I sent for the names of any other fallen yesterday afternoon, and as of that time, your Valentine was not mentioned."

"He . . . he was not?" I straighten up, confused and alert. Engraved in my thoughts is that last image of him that I saw:

pallid, bleeding, insensate . . . could he have possibly recovered? "Does that mean—"

"All it means is that his condition was not known." Friar Laurence measures his words, keeping to the facts. "Let us not speculate too much until we have more information. What we learn today and tomorrow will be more reliable than what we've heard thus far."

"I understand," I tell him. And I do . . . I think. But my heart coils protectively around the hope I feel that Valentine is alive. "Is there news of my mother and father?"

Laurence squirms a little. "Any number of wild rumors. As I said, it would be best if we waited another day or two before we begin counting any of them as reliable."

This time I understand him perfectly: The news is bad, and he wishes not to say. Letting out a breath, I turn to the window and stare into the wedge of blue sky it presents to me . . . and realize for the first time that I will likely never return to Verona. Are my parents grieving? Are they angry? Have I left them in peril of a Capulet vendetta?

There comes a knock at the door of my cell, which Laurence answers. I am expecting it to be another of the friars, and so I am nonplussed when it turns out to be Benvolio.

"Cousin?" I scramble from the bed, throwing myself at him in an embrace, and he squeezes me so tightly that I eventually struggle to breathe. "What are you doing here? What is the news of home? Is Valentine . . . did he—"

"There is much to tell," Benvolio says, his voice weary, and for the first time I realize how drawn he looks. "But I have come a terribly long way. I am now being watched not just by Capulets who think I will lead them to you, but by spies in the employ of the prince who are likewise hopeful. I had to ride all the way to San Bonifacio before it felt safe to double back to the friary." He drops heavily onto the edge of my bed. "I had to leave home before daybreak, change horses three times, and have had no food or drink for hours!"

"You are welcome to my bread and water," I tell him, indicating the repast Friar Laurence brought in for me. "I've not had much of an appetite, myself."

Benvolio glances at the tray and its humble offerings, and then gives me a mistreated look. "Bread and water? I have come to *visit* the monks—not join their order!"

"They are well known for their baking, Ben."

"They are also quite well known for their brewing," he points out peevishly. "Have I come all this way, sweating through my underclothes and catching gnats in my teeth, to not even be offered a measly dram of ale?"

His pouting is so ridiculous, so perfectly *him*, that I cannot help but laugh. "This is not an inn, Ben—we cannot place orders on the friars' hospitality!"

"Nevertheless, we are quite well known for our brewing, at that." Friar Laurence grins brightly. "But, please, we are as famished for knowledge as you are for food and drink. Have your fill of what is here, and I shall fetch a round of ale when you are done."

Grumbling a bit, Ben acquiesces—eating half the bread and

downing the pitcher of water in nothing flat. Wiping his mouth on his sleeve, he announces, "Valentine is alive."

My relief is so intense my body goes limp with it. "So he—"

"—but barely," Ben appends, the words grim, and one look at his expression sends my hope back into hiding. "The wound he received from Tybalt was mercifully shallow, and although it bled ferociously, a surgeon was successful in closing it again. But still he has not woken up, and the physician who attends him says his condition is slowly worsening."

Unable to trust my voice, I remain silent, and Friar Laurence sighs. "He has developed an infection, then?"

It's the obvious answer, and a bleak diagnosis; scores of men die every year from wounds that fester. But Ben surprises us both. "No—or, at least, the physician swears that the site of his injury shows all the signs of healing, and yet his temperature climbs and then plummets, he sweats and seizes, and seems to be in terrible pain."

"He cannot die," I whisper, speaking to the window, to the blue sky and whatever lies beyond it. "It will be my fault if he does."

"It will not, Romeo." Ben squeezes my shoulder. "Tybalt is the one who stabbed him. Do not blame yourself because Valentine caught the dagger meant for your heart."

"What is being said of Romeo's actions?" Friar Laurence leans forward. "We know the prince seeks him, but what is it that he seeks him *for*?"

Ben plucks at a loose bit of string in his hose. "A determination has not yet been made . . . Tybalt is dead, and the Capulets are baying for blood. But he was no innocent victim, and enough honest men have testified that it was he who started the battle." A mirthless smile creasing his lips, he adds, "And you'll be happy to know that Juliet's nurse does indeed corroborate your account of all that transpired here that day."

"So they . . . seek him for the formality of sending him into exile?" Friar Laurence twists his eyebrows into a question.

"They seek him for punishment," Ben says uncomfortably. "Only the prince is still deciding what shape that punishment shall take. Romeo was warned against continuing the feud, and then slew Tybalt the very next day, and in the very same place— the circumstances, at least as far as Escalus is concerned, are essentially irrelevant." Bitterness soaks his tone. "He wants to make an example."

"I only slew him because he attempted to kill Valentine!" I exclaim, finding my voice at last. "He attempted to kill us *both*!"

"The prince cares not what your reasons were—he cares only that his grand speech before the public was ignored." Ben rubs the back of his neck. "But as loud as the Capulets have been in condemning you, the Montagues have been even louder in your defense. They have put at least as much pressure on the prince to recognize Tybalt's long history of troublemaking, and to recognize that he died in the act of trying to take a life himself."

"They have to ask for this?" It is only because I am a fugitive, my ruined future *still* hanging in the balance, that I can muster the will to be incredulous about Verona's perpetual indifference to justice.

"It is a reasonable point." Friar Laurence frowns. "Tybalt was not assassinated; he drew his blade on another man, and fell. And if Valentine's condition does not improve . . ." He darts a concerned look my way. "Well, he may turn out to have been guilty of taking a life within Verona's walls as well."

"Yes," Ben agrees. "And therein lies the reason the prince has not determined Romeo's sentence." Outside, wind shakes the trees, and a cluster of birds fly from their branches. "If Valentine dies, then Tybalt will be guilty of murder, and his sentence would have been death anyway. Romeo will have simply meted out the penalty a little early."

He stops there, and the silence is unbearable. "But what does that mean?" I press. "Will he take the circumstances into account, or won't he?"

Somberly, Ben meets my eyes. "It means that, if Valentine dies, the prince will merely banish you for the part you played in that wretched skirmish. But if Valentine survives . . . Romeo, you will then be considered guilty of murder, and an official sentence of death will be issued upon you."

22

THE ROOM ABRUPTLY EMPTIES ITSELF OF THE AIR I NEED TO BREATHE, and for a moment, all I can do is cling to the edge of the bed and swallow bile. *If Valentine dies, I will live . . . But if Valentine lives, I will die.* How could the prince be so cruel? How could fate?

We have only just rediscovered each other; we have only just learned what sort of happiness we are capable of sharing. I have only just begun to recognize the shape of love, and now our destinies are pinned together—but back-to-back, so that only one of us may face the light.

Friar Laurence comes to my defense again. "How can Escalus justify so preposterous a decision? Tybalt laid a net to ensnare Romeo and seek vengeance. He was struck down in the act of trying to take a life. Either our young friend's retaliation was just or it was not, but it should hardly matter in the aftermath whether Tybalt's aim was true."

"The situation in Verona is extremely precarious right now." Ben rubs his face miserably. "The Capulets are demanding Montague blood—and your father has decided he will not rest until Alboino has learned his lesson once and for all. Everyone is enraged, the families and their supporters clamor outside the palazzo from sunrise to sunset, and more fighting threatens to break out every hour." He shakes his head. "This equivocating decision from the prince was his attempt to appease both sides, and force a détente."

"Like King Solomon," Friar Laurence remarks. "Only this time there will be no one spared thanks to a mother's love."

"I have heard from a . . . a lady who I sometimes visit"—Ben shoots a guilty look at the monk in the room—"whose husband is an adviser to Escalus, that the prince is frankly glad Romeo fled Verona and has no desire to track him down. Your flight, Cousin, effectively settles a thorny matter he'd rather not handle." With a sweeping gesture, he adds, "Besides, arresting you and bringing you back to face his judges would only exacerbate the mounting tensions even more."

"But did you not just tell us that they chased you hither and yon this morning, hoping you would lead them his way?" Laurence furrows his brow.

"The prince may not want for Romeo to be found, but he is still obliged to search for him." Ben sighs. "The Capulets are looking over Escalus's shoulder—and it was not necessarily *his* spies who dogged me all the way to San Bonifacio. Alboino has plenty of loyalists to do his bidding, and the money to hire mercenaries for a manhunt of his own."

The room spins, blood draining from my face. Somehow, even when I believe I have reached the absolute bottom of my despair, the floor drops away and I sink deeper still. A week ago, what I dreaded most was a future soaked in falsehoods, frustration, and dreams deferred. Today I am a fugitive, worried not only about Valentine's fate and a punishment of either death or exile—but now about hired assassins who will share none of Escalus's ambivalence regarding my escape.

Laurence's expression turns grave. "We will have to move you. Your association with our humble friary has been made too well known. Eventually someone will surmise that we have offered you sanctuary—if they've not done so already."

"He's right." Ben watches me. "And it won't be long before patrols are stationed along this road—either by the Capulets or the prince—to see if you can be caught trying to make your way back into the city. You could end up trapped here."

I stare at the walls, danger slowly twisting itself into a noose around my neck.

Laurence clears his throat. "For a while before I came here, I was in Mantua. I still have friends among the mendicant friars there, and I can ask if they will take in a refugee." He tries to smile, but it does not meet his eyes. "There is no guarantee, but I can write to them, and see that the message goes out today."

"There is no time to waste," Ben agrees—and no sooner does he say these words than there comes another frantic knocking at the door of my cell.

Already on edge, I am nearly separated from my skin by the unexpected noise, and the three of us exchange worried looks. Laurence answers the summons cautiously, revealing a wild-eyed novice on the other side.

"Men," the boy gasps out, gesturing along the sheltered portico of the cloisters. "Armed men . . . from the city. They're here to find . . ." He does not finish this statement, but his eyes seek me over Laurence's shoulder, and the back of my neck goes cold. "They are searching the grounds, and even the church itself! I think . . . I think they intend violence. Guillaume has waylaid them, but it won't be long before they come this way!"

"Thank you for telling me, Tommaso." Somehow, Friar Laurence manages to sound calm—and gains an expression I recognize from watching him evaluate the plants in his garden, considering their potential applications. "I need you to fetch some things for me from the storehouse and bring them back as quickly as possible. Before Guillaume can run out of ways to distract our unwanted visitors."

Once Laurence has explained what he needs, the novice scampers away, his footsteps like the patter of hard rain. Around a lump in my throat, I whisper, "What are we to do?"

"Do not leave this room. Remain quiet, and pray that your bad luck has run its course." As advice goes, it's far from heartening—my bad luck has more stamina than Pheidippides, the Greek messenger who ran clear from Marathon to Athens. But I nod anyway, for even a bad plan is better than no plan at all.

"What if they force the door?" Reflexively, Ben reaches to his belt, his fingers closing around the hilt of his rapier. "There is nowhere to hide in here."

"If my plan succeeds, it will not come to that." Friar Laurence hesitates, and then solemnly adds, "If it fails, if they dare search our residences without our permission, you must not draw your weapon."

"But they will take Romeo!"

"They will take him either way," Laurence says softly, and my empty stomach turns over. "You would have to kill them to prevent it from happening, and that would only make matters worse for both of you."

"He's right, Ben." I shake my head, frightened but resolute. "You have done so much for me already. I will not permit you to take any more foolish risks on my behalf."

"But—"

"Please." I school myself to appear brave. "You have always been more like a brother to me than a cousin. What I need from you most is not to put your life in peril for my sake—I could not bear it if the consequences of my actions hurt you as well."

Ben opens his mouth . . . and then shuts it again. His chin wobbles, and his eyes turn glossy for a moment before he blinks the moisture away. He finally manages a reluctant nod.

A moment later, there is another round of frantic knocking at the door, heralding the return of Tommaso. "It's me—I have done what you asked, but Guillaume has lost his audience, and the men are headed this way!"

"Remember what I said," Friar Laurence admonishes, picking up the now empty food tray and striding for the door. "Do not make a sound!"

He slips outside, and only a few scant heartbeats later, we hear a deep voice from along the portico bellow, "You there! What rooms are these?"

In my bones, I know this man is looking for me—possibly sent by the Capulets, happier to take me dead than alive—and his closeness makes my skin prickle.

But Friar Laurence remains as calm as ever. "These?" he replies mildly. "They are cells, messieurs—lodging for the friars who reside here. But who permitted you onto the grounds? There—"

"We do not seek *permission*." This is a second man, his retort laced with contempt. "We seek a coward—a murderous runagate from Verona—and we have been told there is reason to believe he may have sought refuge in this church. If he is here, we will not be held off by a bunch of barefoot men in dirty sackcloth!"

"There is a bounty on his head that we mean to collect," the first man declares, "and if you know what is good for you, you will begin unlocking these doors for us, so we may see who hides within. We are prepared to insist."

"There is no one hidden here, messieurs—and no locks to turn, either, so you needn't bother with threats."

"No locks?" After this incredulous response, a door slams open—so close by it might be the next one over—and Ben and I exchange a damp, panicky glance. "You mean to tell us that you just go to sleep at night hoping you will not be murdered in your beds by thieves?"

"The Friars Minor keep no personal possessions, so there is nothing here to steal," Laurence says, his tone turning cold. "If you mean to invade our private quarters, I will not stand in your way—as unwelcome as you are—but I would strongly advise you against it."

"Oh? And why is that, monk? Afraid of what we may find?"

"Only of what you may take back to Verona with you when you depart."

"First he says he has no possessions to steal, and now he accuses us of thievery!" The second man laughs. "Which is it to be, you patchy hypocrite?"

"I speak not of theft, my lord," Friar Laurence says patiently, "but of the pestilence."

The silence that follows is profound—a great, echoing blast of it—and my back sweats. I know this to be a ruse, but the mere mention of the catastrophic disease that decimated the country only a handful of years before my birth still makes my skin crawl.

In a rough whisper, the man repeats, "*Pestilence?*"

"Yes." Grit scrapes under Friar Laurence's bare feet. "Did you not mind the notice posted on the door to the church?"

"What notice?" the second man inquires, his voice suddenly shrill. "I saw no notice!"

"We posted a warning. One of our novices took ill the night before last, and by the morning there were two more cases among the friars. By the evening it was three, and so we isolated the men in this wing of the cloisters and posted a notice on the church door."

"I saw no notice!" The second man's hysteria is even more pronounced—and for good reason. "Why were we not warned upon our arrival? Why were we permitted to go about the church and its grounds if there is . . . *Black Death* here?"

"As I understand it, you neither sought nor cared for our permission, my lord," Laurence reminds him.

"How do we know this is true?" The first man is cagier than his partner. "If there is pestilence in this wing, what are you doing here? You emerged from one of those rooms as we came along this passage."

"The sick and dying still need sustenance, my lord, and one of us must bring it to them." The rattle of my own food tray carries back along the outside corridor, and I realize that Laurence took it with him as a prop. "Ministering to the afflicted is part of our purpose, and I am not afraid of what awaits me beyond the veil. Are you?"

The second man makes a strange sound in the back of his throat. "I will go check to see if he is telling the truth about the notice on the door."

"As you wish. In any event, I certainly cannot stop you from searching the cells along this wing, if you insist." Laurence takes on an almost bored air as the second man's hasty retreat echoes beneath the portico. "But if you bring the pestilence back to Verona with you, may God and Prince Escalus both have mercy on your souls."

"Why did you not send word to Verona when you first discovered the plague among your household?" The first man's voice is suddenly muffled, as though by a wad of fabric. "You are only four miles away—the city ought to have been warned. Had we known, we never would have planned to stop here!"

"We did send a messenger—yesterday at first light—but it seems that the entire populace is in a state of disarray owing to a disturbance in the piazza. Perhaps the warning was ignored or forgotten in the turmoil?"

The man seems uninterested in sustaining an argument.

Without a word of farewell, his booted feet scrape urgently along the open corridor until they fade from earshot. There is another long silence, almost as heavy as the first . . . and then there is a rapping at the door of the cell.

"You can come out now," Friar Laurence announces with both triumph and relief. "Our visitors have gone."

23

"Masterfully played!" Benvolio is practically floating, his white-faced nervousness already a distant memory. "No doubt they'll spread the word as soon as they return to Verona. Romeo will be safe here for at least a week hence!"

But where Ben crows, Laurence broods. "I would not count on that. We have been lucky—there were only two of them, and neither was watching when Tommaso tacked up the notice. We may not be as lucky a second time." Looking at me, he adds, "We have likely bought ourselves two more days, three at the most. But those who suspect Romeo of being hidden here may find this timely outbreak a bit too convenient to be trusted, and they will find ways to spy upon us. They may even send a doctor in from the city."

"What will you do then?" I ask. *Is it my lot to bring trouble to everyone I know?*

"The sick will have a miraculous recovery." The monk tilts his head with a cheeky grin. "From time to time, it is known to happen. But if matters come to that, we must ensure that you are no longer here to be found."

My family has extensive connections throughout the region—blood relations, friends and associates, nobles who might extend their generosity to the scion of a wealthy mercantile dynasty. But I can take advantage of none of them, for they will be where Escalus and the Capulets seek me first. In the end, I have no other choice but the friary in Mantua . . . and the understanding leaves me somewhat hollow.

Morosely, I wonder if this is how Valentine felt when he was bundled off to Vicenza—deprived of his home, given no say over his destination, separated from everything and everyone he knew. And I wonder if he'd not have been better off had he never returned . . . had he never met me again.

Just the same, my heart aches to see him. The memory of his body, limp and bleeding in his brother's lap, is a whirlpool from which my mind cannot escape, and it tortures me. He is somewhere in Verona, getting worse or getting better, and I cannot even keep vigil at his side. Part of me wishes to sneak back into the city, to find his sickbed and at least set my eyes upon him one last time, the consequences be damned.

But I would surely be caught, and the consequences would see us separated forever—one way or another. It is a price I cannot face paying. Not yet.

After indulging Ben's request for ale, Friar Laurence insists that I must get some air that has not been strained through my window, and he herds us outside. There, as the sun begins to sink into the western rim of the sky, we are ordered to take in the waning daylight—and to maybe also check some of the garden beds for signs of hungry insects. I try to resist it, but eventually the caress of cool air against my face and the scent of the green-ing shoots underfoot work to improve my mood.

In fact, I get so involved in the simple work that I do not hear the sound of fresh company arriving on the lane. I am to the side of the church, crouched among a flourishing copse of thyme, when there are footsteps behind me and an urgent voice says, "Excuse me, I am looking for Friar Laurence."

When I turn around, I find myself face-to-face with Juliet Capulet.

For a moment, we can only stare. It occurs to me that I have not thought of her once since I came back to myself in the cell this morning, that I have given no consideration to her own tumult. In front of a grand audience, Tybalt implied that she was a liar and a fool, cavorting with me behind her father's back. He attacked me on the premise of avenging her honor . . . and then I killed him—her own flesh and blood—and she has been left to bear the aftermath of both grief and false allegations all by herself.

"Romeo!" she exclaims, clearly unprepared to find me here.

"Juliet." My face goes hot, and I fight the urge to step back. "I am . . . terribly sorry about Tybalt. I am sorry for your loss, and for the role I played in it. You may doubt that, I would not blame you, but it is the truth. And if you are angry with me, I understand."

Now that Juliet has seen me with her own eyes, there is no hiding me any longer; and while her relationship with her cousin was obviously fraught, death has a way of reframing memory. If she is feeling at all vengeful on Tybalt's behalf, at all remorseful about harsh words she may have spoken to him or wistful over happier times they may have shared, she could easily denounce me to the prince—or her parents.

"I will never be able to undo what I've done," I press on, forcing myself to look her in the eye, "no matter how badly I wish I could for your sake—and for mine, and for Tybalt's."

And for Valentine's, I think, but do not say aloud, uncertain I can trust myself to speak his name just now without betraying the depth of my feeling for him.

"I am sorry, too." She sighs heavily, closing her eyes. "For all of it. For Tybalt's death, for your having dealt the blow that slew him, for his juvenile belligerence—and the wretched mischance his impetuousness has driven us to. I cannot even find the words for how sorry I am." Juliet's shoulders sag, and when she turns to face the retreating sun, I see how tired she looks. "There is nothing I wouldn't give to unweave time, to put that day back together a different way."

"Juliet!" Friar Laurence, appearing around the corner of the church, hurries toward us with his bare feet slipping in the grass. "Whatever are you doing here?"

His voice is thin with alarm, and it takes me a moment to realize that if Escalus or Capulet are appointing men to follow anyone they think might lead them to me, Juliet would be high on the list, thanks to Tybalt. Instinctively, I dart a glance over her shoulder, and Laurence echoes my motion at the same time.

"There is no one with me but my nurse," she declares, having apparently read our minds. "And we were not followed—at least not this far. My parents believe I am in seclusion at the Convent of the Poor Clares, mourning the death of my cousin. We were escorted that far earlier this afternoon by some extremely quarrelsome men hired by my father, but the sisters would not allow them past the front gate. The moment we were out of their sight, my nurse and I fled through the back and hired a new coach to take us here."

"But . . . why?" A breeze stirs the folds of Friar Laurence's robe.

"I needed to see you," Juliet answers simply, "and I knew I would not be allowed out of the home if I said this was my destination." Her features go stormy. "Following Tybalt's death and Romeo's flight, my parents' fury was unmatched—they raged at me for the terrible things my cousin said I had done, they locked me in my chambers, and my father pledged to see me married to Count Paris by the week's end." She, too, casts a glance over her shoulder. "I am afraid I somewhat manipulated Escalus into persuading my parents that I should be allowed to pray for my cousin without distraction, for more than just a sad handful of hours."

Friar Laurence lifts his brows. "So you are . . . hiding at the convent?"

"In a manner of speaking, I suppose I am," Juliet acknowledges. "And I am grateful for the opportunity. Otherwise, I would be a prisoner in San Zeno for what few days remain before my father tosses me upon the marriage altar like a sacrificial lamb."

It is as she concludes this embittered statement that Benvolio finally makes his own appearance, coming across the lawn at a sprint. Before my cousin has even reached us, he calls, "Whatever you are thinking, my lady, you are wrong! That is not Romeo Montague!"

"It is not?" She cocks her head, and then looks at me. "You are not?"

I shrug. "This is the first I am hearing of it."

"This is an impostor I hired to throw the prince's men off the track of the real Montague heir," Ben declares, panting, doing his best to appear masterful. "So it will do you no good to inform on his whereabouts!"

She squints at him. "But . . . is that not the point of an impostor? To fuel false reports as to the whereabouts of the individual being doubled?"

His eyes go blank. "Um . . ."

"I believe the young lady is teasing you." Friar Laurence smiles, his relief palpable. "Unless I am much mistaken, Juliet is not interested in seeing any doom befall our Romeo."

"That was a very clever gambit, though," I tell Ben. "Albeit a shade too late."

"My cousin and I had a difficult kinship," Juliet says, addressing Friar Laurence. "He was always argumentative, always ready to believe he'd been insulted. But as a child he had a gentle side, too. He saved me, once, when I fell into a quarry—climbed down and carried me back up, and then carried me all the way home as I cried." She looks down at her hands, studying a scar on the back of her thumb. "At some point, though, his affection turned to envy . . . and his envy allowed him to be as cruel and manipulative as his ambition required.

"I do mourn my cousin," Juliet insists, a thread of guilt in her tone. "But the Tybalt I grieve for has been gone much longer than the boy who died in the piazza. No matter how much a fool he made me sound that day, I have no illusions as to his character. He had long courted death at the point of a blade, and it was his own hubris that led to his downfall."

Friar Laurence gestures back toward the church, its stone face turned rosy by the setting sun. "If counsel on that matter is what you came all this way for, my lady—"

"It isn't. I am always grateful for your counsel, of course, but . . . the matter I have come to you about is not my cousin's death, but the boy whose life might still be saved—the one Tybalt struck down."

"Valentine?" My attention is caught so quickly that I take an involuntary step forward, and from the corner of my eye, I see Benvolio watching me. "Is there anything new to report of his condition?"

"Not exactly." Juliet hesitates. "The physician who attends him seems to think that the reason he will not recover is due to some hidden infection, or an imbalance of his humors. But I believe there is a more likely and more nefarious cause." She turns to Laurence. "And you are the only person I can think of who might be able to help."

"I will admit I am intrigued," the monk says, cocking his head. "But I am no doctor . . . the ailments I treat for the friars here are all simple matters—aches and rashes. My remedies are not up to the task of undoing a knife wound."

"But you saved Friar Aiolfo's life last summer, did you not?" she presses. "He was gravely ill, on the very edge of death, and you brought him back to health!"

"That was quite a different situation," Laurence demurs. "Poor Aiolfo ate some poisonous roots by mistake, and I was able to save him with a tincture known to counter their effects." Shrugging apologetically, he continues, "My knowledge of deadly herbs and their antidotes will be of no help to a boy who has been pierced by a dagger."

It is as he says this that I finally understand Juliet's request, and why Valentine's body continues to fail even as his wound heals. "But what if the trouble was never the wound, but rather the blade itself?"

"Exactly." Juliet keeps her eyes fixed on Friar Laurence. "My cousin hated to lose, but he lacked the discipline to master a sword. He was better with a knife, but that is a short-range weapon—and when pitted against a rapier, it does not allow any room for error or shallow strikes. Unless—"

"Unless he coated the metal with a poison so deadly that even a simple laceration could prove lethal." I can barely hear my own voice above the roar in my ears, a cacophony of rumors remembered—of my own apprehensiveness when Tybalt first confronted me in the middle of the Capulets' ballroom.

Friar Laurence goes still. "Do you believe that to be the case?"

"I *know* it to be the case, because I have spied upon him while he was doing it!" Juliet exclaims. "Poor Valentine is dying, and all his physician does is bleed him and hope for the best. He needs someone who understands poisons and antidotes—he needs you!"

"I . . ." Laurence looks startled by the request. "Naturally, I am willing to help any way I can, my lady, but . . . without knowing the exact nature of the poison, I would only be able to guess at potential solutions." Gazing fretfully in the direction of Verona, he adds, "Furthermore, all my texts and materials are here at the friary, and they are all too inconvenient for transport; Valentine would need to be brought to me."

Juliet nods. "As to the latter point, Mercutio would gladly make the necessary arrangements if we could convince him that you might be able to—"

"Leave that to me," Ben cuts in. "He will need little persuasion just now."

"As to the former point . . ." Juliet wrings her hands. "I do not know the source of Tybalt's poison—but I do know that he kept it in a glass vial, which he secreted somewhere in the rooms he used on his frequent stays at our villa." Above us, the church bell begins to toll. "If I can procure it for you, would that aid you in your work?"

"Possibly." Friar Laurence gives a frustrated little shrug. "There are tests that can be done to explore its composition, which might give me somewhere to begin . . . but I'm afraid I can make no promises."

"A slim chance is better than none at all," Juliet replies with a wan smile. "Once the sun has set and it is fully dark, I will return home and attempt to retrieve the poison."

"What if you are seen?" I ask worriedly. "What will happen if your father or one of his men catch you and realize that you are not with the Poor Clares after all?"

"I . . ." Juliet swallows. "I suppose I would not make it back here, in that event."

"Then I will go with you."

"*What?*" Laurence looks at me as though I have taken leave of my senses.

"Romeo." Ben puts his hands on my shoulders. "Think about what you are saying. You are a wanted man in Verona—and nowhere are you *less* wanted than inside Alboino Capulet's home! If Juliet is caught, her father will be displeased; but if *you* are caught, you could easily be killed!"

"If Valentine must face death as a consequence of saving my life, then surely I can face it to repay the favor." I hope I sound much braver than I feel. "To succeed at this, Juliet will need someone to stand guard or create necessary diversions. And, besides, who better to help her infiltrate the villa than one who has already gotten away with it once before?"

"You will have to convince young Paolo to unlock the laundry door from the inside again," Ben reminds me, his jaw tight. "How do you plan on getting word to him when he cannot read? The message will have to be recited. Do you think a breathless monk demanding private audience with one of Alboino's pages will not raise suspicion?"

It takes me a moment of struggle to think my way around this. "What about a visit from his mother? Surely they would allow her a private moment with her son."

He stares. "You are suggesting we inveigle a poor washer-woman into—"

"Into a scheme to save the life of a young man from one of

Verona's most respected families?" I finish for him. "Tell her she will be rewarded handsomely."

"Very well, then, it seems the issue is settled." Juliet steps in before Ben can argue. "Romeo and I shall wait until sunset, and then make our way into Verona under cover of darkness. We will search Tybalt's rooms, and if all goes well, we will be back here again in no time, bearing the vial of poison."

"And if all does not go well?" Ben counters, his voice thick with reluctance.

Juliet swallows again. "Well, should that be the case, at least Friar Laurence is in the proper location to pray for us."

24

A FEW SCANT HOURS LATER, JULIET AND I BEGIN OUR FURTIVE JOURNEY. Tension thickens the air inside the rattling coach until it is nearly unbreathable, the both of us privately contemplating the fates we will face if our plan fails. There are numerous ways we might be caught, numerous challenges we might not surmount, and I manage to envision all of them in explicit detail before the city even heaves into view against the night sky.

To make matters worse, I must picture myself falling prey to each deadly scenario while clad in the mourning dress of a middle-aged woman.

"You are sitting like a boy again," Juliet points out, kicking at my right foot, which has drifted apart from my left in an unladylike fashion. "And stop playing with your veil—every time you lift it, your face becomes visible!"

"When I leave it down, everything becomes *in*visible!" I am annoyed—and very hot. I had no idea women's clothing was so heavy. "And who cares how I sit? No one can see me inside this coach but you."

"You would be shocked to learn how many men will openly

leer into a passing coach, if there are young ladies within." Juliet sniffs. "Regardless, if you are to pass yourself off as my nurse, you need to start practicing. If you cannot manage it now when there is no danger, how am I to trust that you will manage it once we are in the city?"

She has a point, of course, but I still let out a grumbling sigh as I bring my ankles together. This bit of subterfuge, it must be said, was not my idea; but it was simple and convenient, and hard to argue against. Juliet's nurse was more than happy to trade her cumbersome vestments for one of the friars' roomy habits, and to rest in an empty cell while awaiting our return. And, in truth, the shapeless garments disguise my angular figure, and the mourning veil hides my face—we should be able to ride right into San Zeno without anyone recognizing me.

"If we are stopped for any reason, let me do the talking," Juliet repeats for what might be the hundredth time. The coach hits a rut, and we both slide sideways on our seats. "I have no idea how many of my father's men know I am supposed to be in seclusion, but I will tell them that we have returned on some trivial errand and will be headed back to the Poor Clares at first light."

"And if we are caught inside the villa?"

"Then I hope you know how to run and fight in skirts."

Fortunately, we pass no patrols on the road, and when we reach the city walls, the watchmen on duty ignore me, offering Juliet some perfunctory condolences on Tybalt's death. And then they wave us through the gate, and just like that, we are back in Verona.

Once again, I find myself on the same side of the walls as Valentine—and the knowledge of it makes my throat go tight. That desire to see him again, to cast all caution aside for one more chance to take his hand in mine, stirs to restless life in my breast. I can imagine it so easily, the nurse's veil keeping my name and face a secret as I find his bedside, as I say the things I am terrified he'll never get the chance to hear from me.

But the dream evaporates in an instant as the wheels grind to a bumpy halt beneath us, and the familiar landscape outside reminds me what we've come for. Our errand is urgent; there is no time to waste—not even on such a precious visit as the one I long to make—and if we are caught, then Valentine's life may be forfeit. I will not risk it.

The coach drops us at an empty crossroads in San Zeno, near the rambling garden wall that encloses the Capulet orchard, and we creep to it on foot. Climbing proves nearly impossible in the nurse's voluminous gown, which keeps getting caught under my feet. But Juliet shows me how to tuck the skirts up between my legs and tie them at the waist to form makeshift breeches—and then scampers up and over the rough stones ahead of me.

She permits me to remove my veil only until we have cleared the fruit trees and come into view of the villa's back side, the air revived with the scents of juniper and rosemary, and then I must lower it back into place. My disguise will fool no one for long at this stage, but any protection is better than none.

"Those are my rooms," Juliet whispers, indicating a balcony overlooking the flowering herbs. "I cannot count the hours I've spent there—sleeping, reading, avoiding my parents. And now . . ." She is quiet for a breath. "If my father has his way, I will become Paris's bride the minute I return from my seclusion. This has been my home all my life, but now I will exchange one gilded cage for another . . . and I am coming to find that I wish for neither."

"Losing one's sense of place is a strange thing." For the first time in my own life, I realize, I do not have to answer to my father—and it is an inestimable weight off my shoulders. I may no longer have access to all the privileges that came with my station, but I will be able to plan my own future now. Provided I still have one at all.

We are both preoccupied as we dart across the more open expanse of the gardens, heading for the shadows along the back of the villa. When we reach the laundry door, the dutiful Paolo is waiting for us, jittery with nerves.

Upon recognizing my companion, he gawps. "M-my lady?"

"Thank you for letting us in, my young friend," she says graciously. "And thank you for your discretion."

He gives a quick, jerking nod. And when she sweeps past, he tugs my arm, his eyes wide and his voice a hungry whisper. "Does this mean . . . it is true what people are saying? That you two have—"

"Hush!" I place my hand over his mouth, trying to contain his excitement for him. "You cannot believe everything you hear, lad."

"That doesn't mean he has to doubt it, either," Juliet calls back musically, and Paolo nearly faints.

Lord and Lady Capulet are in bed, but the entire household does not slumber, and our progress across the villa is made in fits and starts as we dodge servants already laying the groundwork for tomorrow's early breakfast. When we finally reach our destination, my heart has spent so much time in my throat I have nearly strangled on it.

Once inside Tybalt's rooms, I shed the nurse's dress and stop the door with it in the dark, not anxious to learn what sort of antics might arise if a sleepless maid wandered by and saw evidence of a candle flickering in a dead man's chambers. We risk only a single lantern, and move as silently as we can, checking every crack in the wall and every loose stone in the floor, leaving no cabinet unopened, no shadow unexplored.

The room smells of Tybalt, the air remembering him, and my stomach sinks. In my mind, I see him again as he fell, his legs twitching and his blood at my feet. Guilt makes me shudder. On a table next to his bed sits a strange collection of objects—a set of dice, a stone bird seemingly carved by the hands of a child, a frayed ribbon, a seashell—and I realize they are keepsakes. Tokens to remind him of precious memories.

Pressure builds behind my eyes, and I squeeze them shut, but a tear escapes anyway. It may sound foolish, but it never occurred to me that Tybalt might be a person capable of sentimentality. He was always so cutthroat, so vindictive, it was easy to see him as a calculating monster—the minotaur in my own personal labyrinth. Facing evidence that there were things he cared about beyond power, beyond pride, I am swamped with unexpected grief.

"I have found it," Juliet whispers excitedly, and I turn to find her holding up a small enamel box, the lid open. Her eyes shining in the glow of our lantern, she turns it to show me a glass vial nestled within. "Romeo, we have done it—we may yet save Valentine!"

"You are certain?" I ask, too hopeful to trust our luck. "There could not be a second vial somewhere, perhaps?"

"No, this is the one. I recognize it." She indicates the box. "And I recognize this, too—he carried it with him whenever he moved between his house and ours, never wanting it too far from his side. I had to force the lock to open it."

The hair on my neck begins to rise. "Does it bear a label?"

"'*Dragon's Tears*,'" she reads aloud, and then makes a face. "Hopefully that will mean something to Friar Laurence."

She passes the vial to me, and I hold it up against the wavering light, the liquid inside moving sluggishly as I turn it over in my hands. The temporary affection I felt for Tybalt's cluster of childish mementos dissolves as I remember that *this* is what the Capulet boy truly cherished: death, and being its deliverer. "Dragon's Tears . . . who knew poisoners were so whimsical?"

"Come, we haven't any time to waste. The longer we're here . . ." Juliet snuffs the lantern, and into the darkness she concludes, "Well, there is even more at stake now."

My free hand drops to my hip, where a knife I borrowed from

Ben is tucked into the folds of the nurse's robe. "If this is what is killing Valentine, and having it will help Friar Laurence to save him, I will cut down any man who tries to stop us."

It is a grand statement—and sincerely enough made—but I am still more than grateful when our exit from the Capulet villa goes unchallenged. Paolo guides us back through the maze of the servants' quarters and out through the laundry, clearly relieved to see us go and taking the danger to his livelihood along with us.

The coach is waiting where we left it, and as we pass back through the gates, the watchman—a new one this time—tips his hat, but makes no move to stop or question us. And then we are out in the open again, nothing between us and the friary but a starlit landscape and four miles of anxious anticipation.

Juliet stares fixedly out the window, checking the road behind us and listening for riders in our wake. She has barely uttered a word since we left Tybalt's chambers, and his presence in the cab with us is palpable—a ghost at the banquet. Uneasily, I wonder if being around so many of his private things, touching his clothes and breathing in his air, has changed her feelings about his death.

But when she finally rouses, speaking without quite looking my way, she says, "I cannot stay in seclusion for very long. My hope was to buy myself at least a week, but my father told me he would allow no more than five days. Five days to be alone— the first five such days in my entire life—and the instant I return from them I am to be washed, painted, and presented to my future husband for immediate acquisition."

My own thoughts are clogged with Valentine, and what Friar Laurence may make of the vial we procured, so my response is slow. "What do you think you will do?"

"I think I shall be forced to marry him," she answers, with a blunt and mirthless laugh. "He does not actually like me, you know, let alone yearn for me. Tybalt's constant aspersions on my virtue and moral character—combined with my own 'obstreperousness,' it must be acknowledged—have convinced him that I am not a good woman."

"And yet he has no objection to the marriage your father wishes to arrange?"

"Objection?" She finally looks directly at me, her expression incredulous. "He has all but insisted on it! At this point, my reputation is in tatters, and now that my father's heir apparent is dead, Count Paris feels emboldened to place any number of conditions on his willingness to accept me." Absentmindedly, she tugs at a lock of hair that came unpinned as we scaled the garden wall. "I am frankly terrified by how he may treat me when I am no longer an asset he must win away from another man—when I am his by law, and we are behind closed doors . . . when he no longer has to feign his courtesy."

Once again, I am flummoxed in the face of Juliet's reality: a lack of control that so far surpasses my own it's hard for me to comprehend. Even with my father commanding me like a puppeteer with his marionette—even with my choice of companion in his hands, my future occupation—I still had more freedom promised to me than she does.

"Is there anything that might dissuade him from the marriage at this point?" I hate that she would suffer such a fate, particularly when she has been so selfless on my behalf, so eager to help Valentine. "Maybe you could encourage the rumors . . . let him think you are even more disreputable than Tybalt made you out to be?"

"Then my father would be stuck with me, and I with him; and given the nature of his escalating fury, my situation would be quite substantially the same." She inhales sharply. "No, I fear that there are only two scenarios under which I could successfully escape marriage to the count—the first of which would be if my father refused to pay my dowry. At this point, it is the only reason Paris wants me, and the only aspect of my appeal as a bride that has not been compromised by scurrilous rumors."

"On what grounds might he refuse? Perhaps there is some way—"

"There isn't. Believe me. Unless I could turn up some evidence that Paris is a traitor or an assassin or a bigamist, my father will pay to see our dynasties connected." She slumps, listless and weary, staring back out at the moon. "It's funny, isn't it? That dowry is all I'm worth—the only money that will follow me wherever I go—and yet none of it is mine. It will only ever belong to my future husband, and I am but the useless chest in which it travels."

These words do not sit well with me, my limbs turning restless. We have only been acquainted a short time, but already I know her to be brave and clever, and certainly worth more than just access to a dowry. "You said there were two conditions under which you might circumvent your marriage to Count Paris. What is the second?"

"Right. The second." Juliet draws herself up, giving me a look that could almost be described as timid. "It is quite simple. My father could not give me to Count Paris, under any circumstances, if I marry someone else first. A man highborn enough that an annulment would be hard to arrange, but also someone with nothing left to lose—no business for my father to sabotage, no reputation left to destroy. Someone Verona already believes me to be secretly in love with, perhaps."

By the time she is done, I can hardly trust myself to speak. "Juliet—"

"Romeo." She gives me a beseeching look. "Will you marry me? Please?"

25

"I . . ." Desperately, I search for words, but the shock of this proposal seems to have cast them all out of reach. "You . . . are not being serious."

"No?" The fingerprint of a smile presses into the corner of her mouth. "Why not?"

I blink at her. "To begin with, we are still nearly strangers!"

"That's not so unusual. I barely know Count Paris, after all, and my parents had only met once before their own wedding." Gesturing, she states, "At least I enjoy being in your company, which is more than I can say for any of the men my father has considered suitable for me—and I daresay you enjoy mine."

"I do, of—of course I do," I stammer, "but—but I am a fugitive, in case you have forgotten! Wholly aside from the fact that your parents would be enraged—that *our* parents would be enraged—what sort of future could you possibly hope to have with me?"

"One as far from Verona as we can reasonably travel." Her answer is too firm not to be one she anticipated giving. "My dowry is substantial, Romeo. In addition to gold and other goods, it includes land in Brescia—a vineyard, with an old Roman villa that is still in quite decent shape. I've not been there myself, but I have heard it described, and it sounds . . . peaceful."

"Juliet." I take a breath, finally able to gather my thoughts now that the initial surprise is fading. "Your father would never pay that dowry. Not to me. We might succeed in freeing you from a life with Count Paris—if your father truly could not wield his considerable influence at the Church of San Zeno to demand that our marriage be annulled. But he would still refuse to relinquish so much as a florin to me." Appealing to reason, I point out, "We would be destitute, with nowhere to live and nothing to our names."

"If we are properly married, in a church before witnesses, and by a man of God—a friar, for example, who knows us well and can testify against grounds for annulment—even Alboino Capulet may struggle to buy what he wants from San Zeno." She sits back, folding her hands in her lap. "You are right that my father would refuse to pay the dowry at first. But I believe he could be compelled to deliver it eventually."

"Never." I blurt it reflexively. "*How?*"

"There is one man in Verona who has more influence than either of our families put together, and I have a feeling he will gladly champion our cause and pressure my father."

"Surely you're not referring to the prince?" I wait for her to deny it, but she merely shrugs, and I give an unsteady laugh. "You do remember that the entire reason I am in hiding just now is because Escalus wishes to make an example of me for Tybalt's death, yes? An impoverished life in exile for us would be an *optimistic* prediction."

"The prince has never had any patience for the war between our families, and the conflict has only grown more volatile since the tragedy in the piazza." There's a spark in her eye as she talks, this debate reinvigorating her. "He seeks you as part of a weak compromise meant to pacify two hostile camps—which he already knows will refuse to be pacified by any compromise at all. No matter what punishment he metes out in the end, the Capulets and Montagues will continue in their strife until it tears Verona apart."

I raise a skeptical brow. "And this is where our marriage becomes useful to him?"

"Of course!" She tosses her hands. "You will no doubt recall that what finally soothed the prince's furious disposition the other day was my pretty speech about being frustrated by the antipathy that has kept us apart our whole lives. He said that our families should learn by our example. If we give him another such example, an even grander one in the face of all this mounting vitriol, how could he resist supporting us?" Leaning forward, she exclaims, "Our marriage would symbolize unity between our bloodlines, proof that our ancient conflicts are surmountable. It is something Escalus has openly yearned for."

"All of that may be true," I allow, still filled with trepidation. "But I nevertheless remain a fugitive. You speak of a future that can only be if Valentine succumbs to Tybalt's poison, and I am officially banished. Otherwise . . ." My throat closes, and it takes me a moment to continue. "If this vial of 'Dragon's Tears' helps Friar Laurence devise an antidote, which I very much hope it will . . . there is a good chance that I will be hanged, Juliet. Long before the matter of your dowry would come to the prince's attention."

Hearing it out loud is no better than thinking it in silence. In the best of all possible worlds, Valentine will recover . . . and I will never see him again anyway, forced to run as far as possible to escape the deadly reach of Verona and Lord Capulet.

"Perhaps." Juliet nods, undaunted. "And if you are, what you stand to lose is identical to what you would lose anyway if you did not marry me first." Her tone is so candid, so unapologetic, that it almost draws a laugh out of me. "If we wed and my father refuses to pay my dowry, and the prince cannot or does not intervene, you would still have lost nothing in the arrangement that you would not have before."

"You make it all sound so simple." I rub my temples, fatigue and self-pity catching up with me at last. "But it will change the shape of our lives forever."

"Your life has already been reshaped," she counters. "But I am offering us both a chance to decide what happens next. All you can do is run or hide, and all I can do is split the minutes into seconds, pretending it lengthens the dwindling hours I have left before I must marry a man who despises me." Juliet reaches across and grips my hands in hers, her expression pleading. "I know this is sudden. I know it feels rushed, but my time is slipping away, and this is our best chance to start over when the dust from this terrible moment in our lives has settled."

I open my mouth, but no answer comes to me. Only a matter of days earlier, I was despairing because my father had decided to choose a bride for me—because the destiny I always feared, and yet always knew to expect, had finally fallen in my path. And now, for the first time in my life, I have no idea what lies ahead of me at all.

There are no more silks at the guildhall, no more important banquets to attend, no pressing expectation that I will be married and then measured for my father's life . . . but neither is there any sense of what my future *will* be. Where am I to go after Mantua? The friars cannot hide me forever, unless I am to join their order—and that is already a possibility I have considered and dismissed.

On the other hand, marrying Juliet is a far more complicated matter for me than it might be for some other young man in my position. She speaks of this covenant in practical terms—and that is, of course, the example our parents have set for us. A tactical match, where affection is second to pragmatism, and must be cultivated over time. But . . . I already know it will not happen between us, no matter what fate befalls Valentine.

My stomach cramps with nerves, and it takes more courage to give Juliet this answer than it took to do battle with Tybalt. "I am not what you may think I am, Juliet. Some days ago, when we encountered each other at the friary, I told you I had recently met someone with whom I believed I was falling in love."

"Yes, I recall," she says quietly. "But I assure you, Romeo, I am asking only for your hand—not your heart. That shall be yours to do with as you please."

"I am afraid you do not understand." Without warning, I begin to tremble, and tears spill from my eyes. I have never said this to anyone but Friar Laurence, and now my voice shakes so badly I can hardly get the words out. "The one . . . the one who has my heart already . . . is Valentine."

More tears slide down my face, and I have to use the nurse's handkerchief to wipe them away.

Juliet watches me with a thoughtful expression, then says, "I think I *do* understand."

"Do you?" I am shaking all over, waiting for her confusion. "I am in love—or I am falling in love—with someone I am not meant to have. And whatever that might mean for a man like Ben, who falls in love once or twice a week with girls his father would never approve of; or all the men in Verona who parade their mistresses around behind their wives' backs; it means something wholly different for me."

Juliet touches her chin thoughtfully. "Does he feel the same?"

"I . . . I think he does." That night under the pear trees comes back to me on a rush of warm emotions. "Yes."

"You know, Romeo," she begins, a philosophical look in her eye. "Half the men who came to Verona to inquire after my hand had mistresses back home—women they desired, but could not wed. Women they most certainly had no intention of giving up, no matter what arrangements were made for the disbursement of my body and dowry." Slowly, she adds, "For the likes of us, love and marriage must often be kept separate, even in the best of circumstances."

"This is . . . I speak of something far different from that." My neck is unbearably warm.

"Yes, that's true," she agrees. "But I meant what I said about having no designs on your heart, Romeo. I ask for your hand without any aim of coming between you and the love you may share with Valentine—or anyone else."

"It does not perturb you, to know how I feel?" I cannot govern the incredulousness from my tone. "You are not shocked, or dismayed?"

"What does it matter to me how you feel for someone else?" she counters. "I do not mean to diminish the importance of what you have told me, but so long as I am being done no harm, and you are bringing happiness to a dear friend, there is nothing else to it that concerns me."

Sitting back, utterly perplexed, I hazard, "Whatever concessions you are willing to make in this desperate moment . . . I am trying to make you understand that I could never be a true husband to you, Juliet. Ever. Even if the worst comes to pass and I lose Valentine."

"Then be a false one!" she retorts, tossing her hands up in exasperation. "If I may be frank, I am not interested in having you fall in love with me—in fact, I cannot tell you how relieved I am to know that such an eventuality is one I would never have to negotiate!"

I am bewildered, my body still trembling from the rush of nerves that came with my confession, and I try to take in what she is saying. "You truly mean that?"

"Love, at least the way it is described by the bards—that

270

sudden thunderstorm of passion, urgent and fiery—has always eluded me." She says it simply, without regret. "When my childhood friends began to speak of their first infatuations, their first feelings of desire, I thought . . . well, in the beginning, I thought it was all a game they were playing. You pick a boy, speak in exaggerated terms about his characteristics, and invent some fantasy in which he kisses your hand or brings you a jewel or slays a dragon." Juliet laughs. "As pastimes go, it was somewhat amusing for an afternoon, but then it lasted for *weeks*. When I finally grew bored of it enough to complain, to ask that we play something else for once . . . that's when I finally realized it was not a game at all. Not to them."

"Oh." It is my turn for a quiet revelation—because of course I can relate to this story as well. Ben's gradual discovery of girls, Mercutio's lurid tales of his romantic exploits, the way they could speak of little else . . . it was a language they were learning under my nose, but which I could neither speak nor quite comprehend.

"I tried very hard to understand what my friends were talking about. I reached down deep and struggled to pull those feelings out from within me, to look at a boy—or anyone, really—and foster some romantic inclinations . . . but they wouldn't come." She shrugs again, her mouth pulling to one side. "And I'm not certain they ever will. Whatever fuel causes that particular fire to burn inside others, it does not seem to burn inside me."

"Not at all?" I do not mean to appear dubious, for certainly it sounds similar to the way Friar Laurence has described his own experiences. But it surprises me to know how many of us there seem to be who do not feel things we've been told are conventional and innate—that perhaps what is innate is much more complex than I ever dreamed.

"Not so far." Again, she seems untroubled about the matter. "It frightened me when I was younger. I was terrified that there was something wrong with me, because everyone else seemed to experience this . . . this *intensity* that I couldn't quite understand— everyone! And I didn't know why." She fingers the edge of the curtain swaying by the window, moonlight curving over her cheek. "It was the loneliest I have ever been, and that is saying something."

I can only manage a nod. Loneliness has been no stranger to me, either, of course, and neither has that dreadful sense of being out of step with everyone else, of being the only one who can't quite find the rhythm to which the rest of the world moves.

"It wasn't until I met Friar Laurence, until I gathered the courage to express my fears, that I finally began to realize I'm not alone after all. He made me see that I *am* whole, just like this, and that I do not need that particular intensity in order to have joy in my life." She smiles, her eyes glossy, and I remember again how Laurence's counsel changed something inside me as well. *Have you never considered that perhaps you are* meant *to have this happiness?* "What it all amounts to, though, is that I do not wish to marry Count Paris, nor any of the men my father has considered. I frankly do not think I wish to be married at all, but that is simply not a choice I get to make, any more than you can marry Valentine." Juliet shifts, giving me a probing look. "If I have to become someone's wife, I cannot think of a better match than someone who understands me—someone who will place no expectations upon me."

"I see." The full weight of her proposal is finally settling in now that all the pieces of it are out in the open, and I am beginning to examine them.

"You need to give Escalus a reason to drop his pursuit of you," she summarizes. "And you will require both a place and the means to live. Meanwhile, I must free myself from this obligation to Count Paris, without losing my own means to live in the process."

The carriage begins to slow, the sycamores that mark the approach to the friary black shapes against the starry sky. "My dowry offers us both a chance to escape certain doom and to land on our feet—and I think, now more than ever, that we are each exactly what the other needs. We would be freed from the pressures that have dogged us both, and while I would encourage your happiness, I trust that you would respect mine."

"Of course." I say it reflexively, amazed to find myself considering the notion. It is rash and impulsive, an eleventh-hour grasp at some narrow salvation in the midst of numerous unfolding disasters—but nothing she has said is incorrect. And it may indeed be our last, best chance at a solution to our problems. "I will . . . I will have to think about it."

"I expected as much. It is a lot that I ask, and I know you will need some time to evaluate my points." As the coach rounds the turn of the lane, however, the bell tower soaring into view, she adds, "But, Romeo? Do not take too *much* time, or else all will be lost. For both of us."

26

As it happens, the name *Dragon's Tears* does in fact mean something to Friar Laurence. After Juliet and her nurse depart for the convent, and he and I are alone again by the light of the brazier he has lit in the rectory, he turns the vial over in his hands. "Of course. I was expecting something crude and simplistic, but I ought to have guessed that someone with Tybalt's character and hard-hearted imagination might seek out a poison like this instead."

"What is it?" My nerves worn to the quick, I want nothing more than to crawl back into my uncomfortable bed and hope I can fall asleep—but I'll never manage it without some reassurances first. "Is it something you can cure?"

"One does not 'cure' a poison, exactly," he murmurs, choosing tonight of all nights to be pedantic. "Dragon's Tears is a mixture of several ingredients, all known to be quite deadly, and has been rather popular among assassins—only a very little bit of it added to food or drink can kill a man in a matter of hours. It is widely outlawed, of course, and I am fascinated to know where Tybalt might have gotten his hands on it."

"But what does that mean for Valentine?" I demand, grabbing his arm and forcing him to focus on me. "Can he still be saved from this?"

Laurence puts his free hand over top of my own, his expression turning kind. "There is a chance, I think."

The relief that sweeps over me is so strong my knees buckle, and he must guide me onto a bench so I do not collapse to the floor. "H-how great of a chance? What must be done, and how quickly?"

"Well, speed is always of the essence. As for treatment, I will begin preparing the antidote tomorrow, just as soon as I can gather the materials. Some research will be necessary, as well. I am accustomed to nursing my brethren here through fits of illness brought on by picking the wrong berries, but this"—he turns the vial over again—"is a more sophisticated problem, and it will require a more sophisticated remedy. With regard to how successful I might hope to be . . . I am afraid I can have no answer to that until he is moved here and I have been able to assess his condition myself."

"I want to help." Setting my jaw, I dare him to refuse me this. "Whatever assistance you need, I will provide it—I will wash and carry equipment, I will fetch whatever books are required . . . anything."

"You may leave the research to me," he answers with a faint smile. "I doubt I will be able to fall asleep until I have done some reading on the subject, anyway, and the texts are all in French. But I will compile a list of plants to be harvested and equipment to be cleaned and carried—and for the accomplishing of those tasks, I will gladly take advantage of your apprenticeship, beginning tomorrow."

And so, at first light the next day, I find myself tottering behind Friar Laurence as he marches through the friary's garden, the both of us carrying baskets, knives, and partial lists of items to be gathered. There are so many plants to be culled that my back and shoulders begin to ache in short order, but I make no complaints. To help save Valentine, I will bear any discomfort.

We work diligently for hours, side by side, collecting a variety of berries, roots, leaves, and seeds—setting some aside to be dried, and others to be rendered for their juices. When that is done, and we have sorted our bounty in the room near the friary's kitchen that Laurence intends to use as his workspace, he produces a second list.

"All of this, I am afraid, was the easy labor." He says it as though he is making an apology, yet I have not seen him so energized in ages. "There are a few more necessary ingredients to be acquired—possibly the most important ones—and to fetch them we will have to go on a foraging expedition in the hills."

It takes most of the afternoon—scraping bark from trees and pulling up fistfuls of lichen the color of blood. Evening is beginning its approach when we are at last done, the shadows lengthening as we return to the friary. When we get there, sweat in my eyes and hope in my heart, we find some commotion at the entrance to the cloisters.

Tommaso, the young novice who tacked up the plague notice, darts immediately to Friar Laurence's side. "Your patient arrived while you were gone on your errands. We have placed him in the cell closest to yours, as you asked, but his brother—"

I do not hear the rest of it, because I immediately drop my basket of cuttings, shoving my way past the gathered monks and all but breaking into a run as I reach the portico. The door adjacent to Friar Laurence's stands ajar, and I shoulder it the rest of the way open, coming to an abrupt halt on the threshold when I burst inside. My breath catches fast, and my hands tremble.

Valentine lies on the narrow cot against the wall, his body slack, his skin so pale it is almost translucent. There are circles under his eyes, purple enough to pass for bruises, and a layer of moisture on his face shines in the light from the window. It feels as if something is being pulled out of my chest, and I have to bite down hard to keep from whimpering in despair.

All I can think of is that night under the pear trees, how warm he was, how alive. His smile, his desire, his kisses . . . I've been to the sea only once, when I was very young, but it brought back the same sense of being caught at the crest of a great wave—a force of nature so strong and unpredictable that you can only hope you won't be pulled under. Stepping forward, I reach for him, prepared to wash his hands in my desperate tears.

"Romeo?"

At the sound of my name, I jerk back and reel around, blinking in surprise. My attention was so fixed on Valentine I had not realized we weren't alone. But there, leaning against the wall opposite his brother's sickbed, looking haggard and unshaven, is Mercutio. His eyes are bloodshot and his cheeks sunken, but he breaks into a lopsided grin just the same when he sees me, and reaches out, dragging me into a fierce embrace.

He begins to speak, but the words dissolve immediately into sobs. Clinging to me, hanging off me, Mercutio begins to weep—and it is all I can do to keep him upright. It is all I can do to think of how I might possibly comfort him, when I am on the precipice of collapse myself. In all the years we've known each other, I cannot recall a single instance in which he has been in need of my solace.

"What will I do?" he asks plaintively, his voice hoarse and raw. "If he dies, Romeo, it will be my fault. I could not simply leave him in Vicenza, where he lived in peace with our uncle—I had to bring him back here, because *I* needed him. Because *I* could not let him go." His tears begin to soak through my shirt, hot against my skin. "All I wanted was to make things right. All I wanted was for him to have the life he has always deserved."

"You are a good brother, Mercutio." My throat is so tight the words resist me. "And I am not going to let him die. Friar Laurence thinks he may be able to devise an antidote to the poison that Tybalt used, and I have promised to help him. And I believe he can do it—you have no idea how clever he is."

"*Tybalt.*" Mercutio rasps the name as though it were a curse. "I hope the devil has that bastard!" The muscles in his back bunch beneath my hands. "The only thing I shall truly regret to the end of my days is that I am not the one who delivered his death blow—but I shall name my first child in your honor to show my appreciation for driving your blade through his worthless neck."

"Mercutio . . ." Guilt is a thunderhead above me, darkening the air, and I swallow. "I am sorry. I am sorry for Valentine, I am sorry I could not prevent Tybalt from injuring him . . . and I am most of all sorry that it was my family's relentless feud with the Capulets that caused all of this. That *I* caused this."

He screws up his face in confusion. "What are you talking about? It was I who insisted that Tybalt had to be dealt with directly—you wished to avoid him, and I gave you grief for it. Had I listened to you, had I cared more about safety than pride, none of this would have happened!"

"The Capulets laid a trap that I had no choice but to fall into," I remind him. "There was no avoiding Tybalt that day— and even if I'd somehow managed, he'd have laid a different trap elsewhere and caught me anyway. But I am the one who sent for you, because I was afraid to face him alone. Because I knew he wanted blood on his hands, and I feared it would be mine." Tears make my vision blur. "It was my actions that sparked his rage, and my call to arms that brought Valentine within range of his dagger."

"Had you not called for us, you know very well I'd have been furious with your corpse," he replies, an ironic lilt to his words that finally reminds me of the brash, joyful Mercutio I have always known. "You are our friend, Romeo. We chose to answer your summons because your fight is ours, and we'd never leave you to face Tybalt on your own."

"I am just . . ." But my breath hitches, and finally I begin to weep as well.

We stand together, a pitiful mess of tears and guilt—and that is how Friar Laurence finds us when he enters the room a few minutes later. Softly, he says, "Good evening, Mercutio. I trust your journey here from the city was safe?"

"Yes, thank you." My friend clears his throat, mustering his composure. "Verona knows about the warning of pestilence here, and it was somewhat difficult finding a cart and driver willing to come this far, but I managed it. I cannot express how grateful I am for your help. If you can save my brother's life, I shall pay you any sum—no matter how high."

"There is no need for that, I assure you." Friar Laurence holds his hands out in a quieting gesture. "I seek this antidote because I have been blessed with the knowledge to do so, and because I believe in helping people—not for any recompense. I will do everything I can for Valentine, and pray that I am successful, but . . . I cannot promise you results. At least, not yet."

"I understand," Mercutio says, clearing his throat again. "Romeo tells me he intends to assist you. If there is anything I can do, you must put me to work as well."

"I shall happily accept your offer." Laurence smiles, and then puts a hand on my shoulder, nudging me toward the door. "Just now, however, I must ask for a little peace and quiet so that I may examine my patient. And, Mercutio, I suggest you get some rest—"

"I will stay with Valentine," my friend declares, lifting his chin. "Bring a bedroll in here, if you like, but if I take any rest, it will be by his side."

"Which will put you underfoot and make it harder for me to

do what needs to be done for him." Friar Laurence is firm, but not unfriendly. "You will not help Valentine by making yourself ill, you know, and your own suffering does nothing to alleviate his."

"Perhaps I deserve to be sleepless," Mercutio counters, daring the monk to contradict him. "Perhaps I deserve worse."

"And perhaps you have punished yourself enough already," Friar Laurence suggests.

"If he dies from this, I will never be able to atone for my part in it."

"And if he lives, he will need you healthy and strong." Ushering us back to the door, Friar Laurence adds, "You may make use of my room while I am with your brother. I have already taken the liberty of asking one of the novices to bring you something to eat, as well as a drink of brewed herbs that will clear your head. I believe you need it."

"I am not hungry," Mercutio insists sourly, even though his stomach rumbles as he says it. The fight has gone out of him, though, and he allows me to guide him into the adjacent cell. Tommaso appears moments later with fresh bread, water, and a steaming mug of some murky liquid that smells like a wet dog.

"Friar Laurence says that he will bring you both some ale, provided that you"—he gives a pointed look to Mercutio— "finish everything on your plate."

"Can you believe his nerve?" my friend complains indignantly, the instant Tommaso is gone again. "'Finish your meal, or you shall receive no treat afterward!' How infuriating—it is like being an infant again." He stuffs some bread in his mouth, and swallows it almost without bothering to chew. "He's lucky I happen to be in dire need of ale just now, or I'd have thrown all of this in his face."

He shovels some more bread into his mouth, and I watch him eat in a kind of horrified fascination. It is like seeing a wild animal take down a fresh kill. As the last of the bread vanishes down his maw, I nudge the steaming liquid a little closer to him. "Do not forget your, uh . . ."

"Ugh." Mercutio grimaces, then plugs his nose and gulps it down as fast as he can. When the mug is empty, he shudders all over, letting out a belch. "Abominable. But my head does feel somewhat better. I think." Turning, he gives a worried look at the wall that separates us from Valentine. "Do you . . . do you really believe that Friar Laurence can reverse whatever that poison is doing to him?"

"If anyone can, it will be Laurence." The afternoon spent in the gardens and hills returns to my mind, the sensible way he talked about each different plant we gathered. I think about Valentine touching my face, and smiling with his eyes. "In truth, I am afraid to hope for too much, but . . . I am choosing to have faith that he can. That he will."

"Me too," Mercutio whispers. He turns back to me, and then shakes his head, his eyes drooping and unfocused. "Or maybe not. That foul drink was supposed to revive me, but it definitely did not work! I feel all woozy . . . and why is the room moving about like this?"

"Perhaps you ought to lie down?" I push him toward the bed, and although he puts up a token resistance, he is not at all difficult to maneuver. "By your own account, you've not rested well these past days. Could be it's catching up with you."

"I will not lie down, but I suppose I am willing to sit," he declares, flopping onto Friar Laurence's cot and sprawling immediately onto his back. His eyes are glassy as he stares up at the ceiling. "But only until the ale arrives and the room stops this infernal spinning."

"How long *has* it been since you last slept, Mercutio?" I ask with concern, glancing at the empty mug and its residue of soggy herbs clotted at the bottom.

"I do not remember." He makes a lethargic gesture, and then follows my gaze. "Your monk has tricked me, hasn't he? That horrible potion was meant to make me sleep."

"I suspect so."

"That wily bastard." He almost sounds impressed. Rubbing his face, he sucks in a breath. And then he looks at me, and something serious creeps into his expression. "Before I go . . . Romeo, there is something I need to understand. I may not have the courage to ask about it later, once I have slept and regained my wits, so I will have to ask it now."

"Yes?" The way he says it, the way he watches me, makes my skin wrap tight around my shoulders. "What . . . what is it?"

"Why does Valentine call your name whenever he rouses from his stupor?"

My heart stops. "I . . ."

"I would prefer you did not lie to me." He says it sternly, although the words are soft at the edges. "The one thing I cannot tolerate is being lied to about my brother. Romeo . . . when did the two of you become so close that yours is the name that always hovers closest to his lips when he wakes?"

"We . . . I . . ." It is like falling through darkness, not certain how far away the ground is—but knowing that the longer it takes to land, the worse the impact will be. "We talked in the Capulets' orchard, after fleeing from the masquerade. He told me about Vicenza, and . . . and I suppose we grew closer then."

It is an inadequate reply, my squawky pitch only making it sound worse, and Mercutio frowns impatiently.

"My brother told me more or less the same, but he is terrible at deception. I know there is something more that neither of you has said." He narrows his eyes—and adds something that makes my stomach drop. "Valentine was absent from his bed a few nights ago, and did not return home again until just before dawn. He tried to convince me I'd dreamed it, as if I cannot tell the difference between being asleep and being alone. Was he with you that night? And do not lie to me, Romeo. You are no better at it than he is."

Even in this state, laid out on his back and half-drunk on Friar Laurence's herbal brew, he is intimidating. And I am too shaky, too overwhelmed, to attempt a bluff. My mouth so dry it clicks, I say, "He . . . he came to San Pietro that night, yes. He said he could not sleep and wanted to . . . continue the conversation we'd had at the Capulets' villa." This much is all true, even though it tastes false. "We spent most of the night in the orchard behind my home. But whatever you are sugg—"

"Valentine is not like I am." Mercutio cuts me off decisively, staring back at the wall, pressing his fingertips to it as though he might be able to reach through. "It used to irritate me—how quiet he was, how sensitive . . . how reluctant to follow my example. I could always tell that there was something different about him." He swallows, and to my shock, his eyes well with tears. "For a while, I thought maybe he would grow out of it. Then I thought maybe I could change that part of him, if only I encouraged him to the right interests, showed him how he was meant to act."

The tears break from his eyes, and Mercutio makes a clumsy attempt at scrubbing them away. "I had so little patience. I was so ready with my anger, so quick to pounce when he displeased me. And then our father died, and Valentine was sent to Vicenza, and . . . it took the disintegration of my whole family for me to realize what a fool I'd been." His face turns pink, and he squeezes his lids shut. "So much time wasted on punishing my brother for something he never did wrong in the first place—and then not knowing if he would ever be able to return, if he would even *want* to. I was a terrible brother, Romeo. It would have served me right if he'd never wanted a thing to do with me ever again."

"You are not a terrible brother." It is all I can think to say. "I have seen you with him. I see you with him now."

"I am but a poor sinner, gambling for my forgiveness as Judgment Day begins to dawn." He looks back at me, and all the strength has been drained from him. "But I promised. I made a promise to God, Romeo, that if He let Valentine come back to Verona, I would be the brother he deserved—that I would do things right, and cherish him, and not try to make him into someone he's not meant to be." Mercutio's lip quivers, and his voice is slurred. "All I want is for him to be well. All I wanted was to put things back together in their right place, and not take what I have for granted this time."

"He is not going to die." It is my turn to make brash promises, ones I am not yet certain I can even keep, but I do know that I will move heaven and earth to make this one true. "I will not let that happen. You will have more time with him, Mercutio."

"Just tell me . . ." His eyes don't open, and I can see he's fighting to stay awake. "Is he . . . is he happy when he's with you, Romeo? Are you happy together?"

"I . . ." The room blurs, and it takes a moment for me to speak. "Yes. And I have never counted myself so lucky."

"Good." He sighs, his shoulders relaxing, the worried lines in his face smoothing out. "I am glad. That's all I wanted."

And with that, he falls asleep.

27

It is only a few seconds later, as I am still standing there in a state of bewilderment—overcome by emotions I cannot name or enumerate—that Friar Laurence eases open the door. Mercutio's chest rises and falls in the rhythm of sleep, a soft rattle escaping in his throat. The crafty monk smiles. "I see my little tisane has worked. I am glad—he needs the rest."

"What did you give him?" I indicate the mug, surreptitiously dabbing the tears from my eyes. "Will he be all right?"

"It's just a blend of some calming herbs and soporifics." He shrugs amiably. "Nothing too powerful. His fatigue and distress had him at the point of collapse already, and he required only a gentle push toward sleep. With luck, he will not rouse again until the morning—at which time I trust he will be more clear-headed."

"You are rather devious," I remark, unable to contain a smirk of admiration. "You told him that drink would clear his head, but you were very misleading as to how."

"He did not ask." Laurence is the very picture of innocence. Then he says, "I have finished my examination. Valentine is lucky that he did not ingest the poison, and likewise fortunate that his wound bled so profusely—for it certainly flushed some of the Dragon's Tears from his veins before it could reach his heart."

"What does that mean?" I implore. "Will you be able to help him?"

"Although his condition is deteriorating," Friar Laurence begins, "I think . . . I believe he has not yet reached a point where it is too late to reverse the poison's effects." It is so precisely what I have wished to hear that for a moment I must doubt that I *have* heard it, and he reiterates, "I think we can save him, Romeo— but only if we act quickly."

Words fail me. My chest swells, heat pressing behind my eyes, and I throw myself at Friar Laurence. "Th-thank you," I whisper into the rough fabric of his robe, embracing him as tightly as I can. "*Thank you.*"

"Do not thank me yet." He rubs my back with friendly affection. "There will be no remedy at all without much hard work, and . . . Romeo, there is still the chance that it will not be enough."

"But there is a chance it will." I wipe fresh tears away with my sleeve, shocked my body still has any moisture left in it to shed. "And I will do whatever is asked of me, anything. Say the word, and I will start right now."

"In good time." He gathers the tray and starts for the door. "For now, Mercutio needs to sleep, and I thought perhaps you'd like a few minutes alone with Valentine."

"Yes." The thought makes my heart jump. "Yes, very much."

"Just take care not to wake him," he admonishes. And then he leaves, gliding off along the portico, the fading light casting long shadows over the central garth.

Valentine looks just as he did before—inert, ashen, and sickly, the air in the room already taking on the sour taste of illness. My throat bobs, dry now as I finally have the time and the privacy to take in what has become of a boy who once made me feel invincible.

His skin is cold to the touch when I weave my fingers with his, longing to feel the pressure of his response, and his soft hair is matted and dull. But I breathe him in, the familiar scent unlocking emotions I've been trying to suppress—memories too happy to bear. The taste of him beneath the pear trees, our hands meeting for the first time, when I did not yet know if it could possibly mean to him what it meant to me, the private smiles we exchanged when no one else was watching during that one perfect afternoon.

I remember the way his voice sounded—giddy and breathless—when he lay beside me in my family's orchard. "*I had nothing to say—I only wanted you to kiss me some more, and I could not stand to wait and hope there would be time for it tomorrow.*"

My heart wrenches as I sit there beside him, just the two of us—alone at last, for the first time since that same night—and I must face what has become of him as a result of my quarrel with Tybalt. This feeling is not *like* love, I realize; it *is* love. My heart would not be breaking this way if it were not.

I love him. And even if he cannot love me back, even if he should blame me for what has happened to him and curse my

289

name, I will do whatever it takes to see Valentine whole and healthy again.

When Friar Laurence returns to collect me, he does not intrude on my thoughts or press me to speak. Instead, he leads me to the kitchen and shows me a list of chores that will have to be accomplished before the antidote can be assembled. After explaining which ones are mine to execute, he leaves me to them.

For the next few hours—by scraps of starlight, and the glow of lanterns and braziers—we engage in the science of alchemy. Under Laurence's direction, I hang herbs to dry, boil roots and bark so we may distill their essence, and separate berries into flesh and skin and seeds. We label flasks and pour clear brandy into a bottle packed with handfuls of bloodred lichen, the liquid turning an angry hue. We are halfway through the list when he says we have done enough.

The next morning, after a dreamless sleep, I am back in the kitchen again. Mercutio is at my side this time, working diligently and looking all the better for a good night's sleep. What unfolds before me over the course of the day is fascinating: familiar matter reduced to salts, liquids, and vapors, the disparate parts combined again in specific orders, specific quantities. Drop by drop, the antidote to Dragon's Tears slowly coalesces, a murky fluid smelling sharply and strongly of the earth.

"This is it." Friar Laurence looks somehow worn and revived at the same time, holding the tincture up to the light. "This is what will counteract Tybalt's poison."

"So we can give it to him now?" Mercutio stares intently.

"How long does it take to work? How will we know if it *has* worked?"

The question he does not ask, but which is etched plainly in his worried expression, is, *What will we do if it does* not *work?*

"It is ready to be used," Friar Laurence allows cautiously, "but we cannot rush the treatment. We are not throwing water on a fire, but sending one animal to fight another." To Mercutio, he elaborates, "If too much of this elixir is consumed at once, it can have dreadful effects of its own; so it must be given sparingly—no more than five drops, at three-hour intervals. I will show you how, but then it will be up to you."

"Of course. Yes."

"If it works, it should not take long for us to know it." Laurence gets to his feet.

"And if . . . if it does not work?" Mercutio barely manages the question.

"Well." A grim look crosses the monk's face. "That will not take long to know, either."

It is an awkward business, holding Valentine's mouth open and dripping the strange medicine past his lips. His throat moves as he swallows, and his mouth puckers, his brow flexing. And then his face goes slack again, and he . . . simply lies there.

"Did it not work?" Mercutio drags his hands through his hair, causing it to stand on end. "He is the same as before; nothing has changed!"

"Give it time," Friar Laurence soothes. "The poison has had several days to do its work, and our remedy has had mere seconds.

You may sit with him between doses, to keep watch on his condition, but only one at a time. Crowding will do him no good."

"I will take the first watch," Mercutio declares, brooking no argument. I consider my position, and then give a reluctant nod, wondering what I will do with myself until it is time to hold Valentine's mouth open again.

"If there is some marked change in him, send for me," Laurence says. "Otherwise, I shall be by now and again to appraise his condition. Remember: No more than five drops."

"I understand," Mercutio and I say in unison. And when the door shuts again with me on the wrong side of it, night pouring through the colonnade and filling the portico, I cannot tell if the air I breathe tastes of hope . . . or fear.

The second dose goes down exactly as the first, and although Valentine appears perhaps a bit more flushed, he shows no measurable reaction. His throat moves, his mouth puckers, and then he subsides again, insensate. Mercutio refuses to budge from his vigil, and so I grudgingly return to my cell.

The hour is long after Compline, the monks all asleep, and the garth frosted in silvery moonlight. It is beautiful, and for the first time in days my hands itch for my book of sketches. It is the sort of scene I wish I could share with Valentine, and for all the faith I profess to have in Friar Laurence, I am suddenly terrified that the antidote will fail.

When I come back for the third dose, it is finally apparent that the medicine is having an effect. Valentine's hair is damp at the temples, his face taut with discomfort, and he breathes harder than he did before. Mercutio, once again weary from lack of sleep, swabs his brother's face with a damp cloth. "Does this mean it's working? Should we fetch Friar Laurence?"

"I don't know what it means," I tell him honestly—although it seems to me that there are only two possibilities: Either Valentine is getting better . . . or he is getting worse.

This time, he is feverish, and he resists me as I pry his mouth open. Mercutio counts out the drops, and then we step back, watching him squirm fitfully before he settles. His brow is pinched, and more sweat beads up like small blisters at his hairline.

"You may stay or go, but I will not be leaving him," Mercutio announces, placing himself on the floor beside the bed. Even though Friar Laurence admonished us to take our watch one at a time, I cannot bear the thought of going back to my cell for more sleepless anticipation. So I sit as well, leaning against the wall, waiting for either good news or bad.

Whatever is happening to Valentine, he will not go through it without me.

———

Before the hour is up, matters take a sharp turn. I am half-asleep when a soft moan comes from Valentine, the first sound he's made since arriving, and Mercutio and I startle instantly awake. His hands gripping the tangled sheets, he arches his back, the cords in his neck standing out in high relief. He moans again, shuddering in pain.

"Valentine? *Valentine!*" Mercutio grips his brother's sweaty face, quickly overtaken by panic. "Wh-what is it? What's wrong?"

"I don't think that he's awake," I say, sensing the heat that rolls off his bare skin. "Mercutio, his fever has gotten worse——"

Valentine collapses onto the bed and then arches again, and another pitiful sound comes from his throat—a moan that crests into a whimper. His face turns red, and he kicks his legs against the sheet, pulling it low enough to reveal the puckered wound on his chest. With a jerking motion, he then twists to the side, wrenching his arm away from me.

"*Valentine!*" Mercutio shouts, wrestling him onto his back again with difficulty. "Romeo, go for the monk! *Now.*"

Racing to the adjacent room, all notions of sleep are shaken from my mind, my blood filled with cold sparks. If Valentine does not recover, if that mixture we've poured down his throat has only made him worse . . . I cannot permit myself to complete the thought, my head spinning with fear.

Friar Laurence wakes easily, and when we scurry back to Valentine's cell, the boy still writhes in his brother's grip, clutching at the sheets and mewling in agony. Mercutio turns a tear-streaked face to us, his voice breaking. "Help him—please!"

Laurence moves swiftly to the bed, examining Valentine with a calm and organized methodology—gauging his fever, taking his pulse, peeling back his eyelids—and then gives a brisk nod. "I told you we were sending one animal to fight another. This is the hour where we will learn which one is to be victorious."

"What does that *mean*?" Mercutio demands through gritted

teeth. "He is in agony—he might be dying! Can you do nothing?"

"I will bring more cold water and fresh cloths, but he must do the rest." Friar Laurence speaks with patience and sympathy. "Dragon's Tears is a formidable poison, and the antidote had to be equally potent in order to counter it. Your brother's pain is surely distressing to witness, but this is the treatment taking its course. Hold him steady so that he does no harm to himself, and eventually this terrible moment will pass."

He makes no promises as to what will come afterward, and we are far too frightened to ask. So, instead, I sponge Valentine's forehead while Mercutio holds him down, his arms shaking and both our faces wet with silent tears.

Gradually, Valentine's thrashing becomes less frenzied, his cries tapering off—and, sometime after Matins, he goes limp again. The bedding is soaked in sweat, and blood leaks from his reopened wound . . . but his breathing slows and deepens, the muscles in his face relax, and the flush begins to fade from his skin.

Mercutio and I are exhausted, wrung dry by hours of a panicked vigil, but eventually we realize that Valentine's fever has finally broken.

28

I DO NOT KNOW HOW LATE IT IS WHEN I AT LAST SUCCUMB TO SLEEP, but when I wake again, it feels as though mere seconds have passed—and I am in excruciating pain. Slumped against the wall, I am more twisted out of shape than an ancient grape-vine, and sunlight pours into my eyes through the open window of the cell. The bones in my neck make a crackling sound as I struggle upright.

And then I freeze, my heart in my throat when I see the tableau before me: Valentine, awake in bed, watching me with that same mischievous smile he had when throwing pebbles at my bedchamber window. He is pale and gaunt, the dark circles under his eyes even more pronounced than before . . . *but he is alive.*

"Valentine?" I practically croak his name out. "You are . . . am I dreaming?"

"I truly hope not," he returns, his voice weak. He grins, and it is a sight I have missed for days. "It would rather hurt my feel-ings if this is how you see me in your dreams."

"But you are beautiful." My eyes fill with tears, smearing the room in bright color, my body aching as I limp to his side. "You are . . . you are well again."

"I seem to be." He looks down at his body, his arms slender and pale, his wound already healing again from the torment his convulsions put it through. "It would be nice to say that I've never felt better, but . . . at least I can say that I am feeling better than yesterday."

"Yesterday you were unconscious," I point out, tasting salt when I laugh.

"That's true—I am feeling much worse than yesterday." He laughs, too, and then coughs a little. "It is as if I have been trampled by horses. With very large riders."

"I . . . I cannot quite believe that you are all right." Easing onto the edge of the bed, I place my hand close to his, afraid to touch him—afraid of how fragile he still seems. "You have no idea how many times I have grieved for you, how many times I have wept, thinking your fate was sealed by Tybalt's dagger."

"I have some idea. Before you woke just now, my brother told me that you have been in quite a state over me." He almost looks smug, and my face warms.

"Where *is* your brother?" I ask, flustered.

"Asleep in one of the cells, I hope." Valentine pushes a hand through his tangled hair. "We had a long conversation while you were crumpled up in the corner over there. He was in genuinely abysmal shape, and although it took some time, I made him promise that he would get some rest." He hesitates, and then reaches out, finding my hand with his own. "I also told him that I desired some time alone with you. And he agreed."

"You did?" I can think of nothing more eloquent to say, my blood humming at his touch, his fingers cool and dry and implausibly alive. "He . . . he did?"

"I do not know how to account for it." His eyes widen. "Not only have I survived a brush with death, but my brother knows what I feared his knowing most of all . . . and he loves me just the same."

"He does. I have witnessed it."

"Moreover, Romeo, I think he loves you, too." Valentine looks down at where our hands are connected. "Though perhaps not quite in the same way that I do."

"You . . ." I cannot finish, my throat too tight to speak. Pressing his hand to my lips, I kiss him until I can breathe again. "You love me?"

A rosy flush spreads across Valentine's cheeks, heating the freckles that dot his perfect nose. "I think I have always been a bit in love with you, Romeo. But I was too afraid to say it before. A person can only lose so many good things before he begins to expect all good things to be taken from him, sooner or later."

"And yet you were the one nearly taken from me." I cannot let go of his hand, cannot stop reveling in the way he squeezes mine back.

"I almost missed my chance to tell you when I could." Reaching for me with his other hand, he touches my face, the sunlight picking out little flecks of gold in his eyes. "I might have died and never said I loved you. How could I have ever been so foolhardy?"

"Valentine . . . you almost died on my account. That dagger

was meant for my breast, and you put yourself in its way for me, because I was too careless to see it coming."

"And I would do it again."

"I would not let you." I shake my head vehemently. "I will never let you put yourself in danger on my account, not again, not ever."

"But I already have," he answers, his expression open and unguarded. "I have told you that I love you—I have set my heart into your hands, and now . . ."

He trails off, waiting to see what I will say, his eyebrows turned subtly upward with worry. My vision swims, my own heart expanding in my chest. "I love you, too, Valentine. Of course I do. You had me beguiled from the moment I encountered you at the Capulets' villa—but by the night we spent in my family's orchard, I knew that what I felt for you was something deeper than that . . . something extraordinary."

Drawing a shaky breath, I lean into his touch, grateful beyond words to feel it again. "But it was not until I thought I was going to lose you forever that I understood the true nature of that feeling."

"Romeo . . ."

"I love you, Valentine." I repeat it, because the words taste so sweet on my tongue. "I love you, and I do not know what I am meant to do about it."

"You could start by kissing me," he suggests in a whisper— and I leap to fulfill his request.

His lips are dry from his days-long ordeal, but when they yield to mine, the sensation is no less magical. They welcome me, opening softly—and the heat of him spills into my body. Warmth shoots through me to the pit of my stomach, to the soles of my feet, skin tingling at the small of my back. His fingers curl at the nape of my neck, and a hungry noise comes out of me, an unbidden growl that excites him.

I pull at his bottom lip, pressing my hand against his chest, feeling his heart race beneath his smooth, warm skin. The more I kiss him, the more I need him—the more I need *of* him—and the less I ever want to stop. This could last for days, for months, and I would not tire of it.

But we do not have months.

After a while, we break apart, breathless and dizzy. Valentine closes his eyes, raking a hand through his hair, his face flushed in a way that makes me suddenly worry I have pushed him too far. With a sigh, though, he says, "That was . . . wonderful. But I fear I shall have to rest for some time before we can attempt it again."

I smile, but now the question of time hovers in the air, a dark cloud I cannot ignore, and it dims the light that had been burning in my blood.

Before I can address it, there comes a knock at the door, and Friar Laurence enters with a tray bearing far more appetizing food than anything I've been served since I arrived. "Oh, good, you are both awake! I wanted to see how my patient was doing, now that he has returned to us—and, Romeo, I am glad I shall not have to step back and forth across your sad little body as I do it."

"Oh, ha ha." I roll my eyes, but Valentine grins in earnest. "I shall have the both of you know that my neck might be permanently bent after that dreadful night's sleep."

"We shall put you to work illuminating manuscripts, then." Friar Laurence loses none of his cheer. "It will twist your neck the other way in no time."

"I hope you did not bring all of that for me." Valentine's brows go up as he takes in the spread on Laurence's tray—steaming broth, fresh bread, fruit, cheese, dried figs, and even eggs cooked with some fragrant herbs. "I'm afraid I haven't much of an appetite."

"I do," I say, reaching immediately for one of the figs.

Friar Laurence smacks my hand away. "You will need to eat in order to recover your strength," the monk tells Valentine gently. "Start with something simple—the bread, or the broth—and see how it sits."

My stomach growls. "While he is enjoying something simple, perhaps I ought to remove the more complicated dishes from temptation's path."

"You may eat whatever Valentine does not, but he must choose first, and put down as much as he can." Laurence places the tray beside the bed and puts his hands on his hips. "He has gone days on an empty stomach, and I will not see him succumb to a simple fever after we have just freed him from the deadly grip of Dragon's Tears."

He watches carefully while Valentine pieces together a modest breakfast, eating until he insists he can consume no more. All the while, that dark cloud expands, forcing the air from the room. By the time Friar Laurence is offering me the generous scraps of the meal, I haven't much appetite left myself.

"How long will it be until Valentine is well enough to . . . to return home?" I ask, my voice as hollow as my stomach, and I watch as both of their faces fall.

"Well." Friar Laurence pauses, looking down at the tray. "There is no way of telling exactly. We will have to assess his progress day by day, and see—"

"But it will not be weeks." I cut him off, supplying what he won't say—what he has surely realized is the point of my question. "And as his condition is of particular interest to Verona, they will come to want reports in time."

Laurence hesitates, darting a worried glance at Valentine, who swallows hard and whispers, "Mercutio has explained the nature of the prince's unjust compromise. It is . . . I cannot believe the unfairness of it."

"It is needlessly cruel," the monk agrees with a heavy sigh. "And, yes, I imagine they will demand a report before long."

"What will you tell them?" I cannot look at him as I ask.

"I . . . I do not know." He lowers himself to the edge of the bed, rubbing his brow. "We are quickly running out of time to deceive them. If I say he has recovered from the poison, they might issue a sentence of death upon you then and there. But I can only claim his condition is not improving for so long before they will expect me to send them his body."

"But people can be sick for ages, with no seeming change," Valentine protests. "In Vicenza, there was a woman who took to her bed for months. Every time they thought she was improving, she would get worse; and when they thought she was at death's door, her symptoms would suddenly abate."

"Lingering illness is certainly not unknown, but it will not satisfy the prince—and nor will it satisfy either the Capulets or the Montagues." Laurence shakes his head. "As it stands, our false claim of pestilence only leaves us a few more days of protection from the scrutiny of unwanted visitors. I doubt I can hold them off with conflicting answers for any longer than that; at their first opportunity, they will surely send someone here to see for themselves the true nature of your condition."

"And my fate will be sealed." The bread I tried to eat sticks in my throat. "Which means I must leave for Mantua as soon as possible, and hope there is no patrol on the road between here and there to capture me."

"No!" Valentine stares at me, stricken. "You cannot just *leave*! It is not necessary, not yet. Friar Laurence said that we have entire days before someone could be sent here to examine me—and even then, I could easily pretend to still be dying from the poison."

"The Capulets will only grow more impatient and more organized," I tell him morosely. "Already they have paid men to seek me out. Soon they will be offering rewards for anyone who can provide them information as to my whereabouts. The longer I stay within arm's reach of their gold, the more danger I am in."

"He's right." Friar Laurence sounds no happier about it than I am. "The truth of the matter is that even Mantua may prove to be too close. The Capulets have influence throughout the region, and Romeo cannot hide in a friary forever."

In the back of my mind lurks Juliet's desperate proposal, a plan that also demands timely action, however slim its chances of success. If her predictions are accurate, it could mean an end to fearing retribution, but it would keep me no closer to the boy I love.

"But . . ." A tear rolls down Valentine's cheek, and my heart aches as though it has been kicked. "Our time together has only just begun. How can it be wrenched away so soon again? How can one more precious thing be taken from me when I have so little left?"

My voice breaks. "Valentine—"

"Why can you not simply tell them I have died?" he demands, turning on Friar Laurence, his face flushed again. "If that is what they need to hear in order to spare Romeo's life, then that is the report you must send! It will settle matters once and for all."

I am almost too startled to think of a reasonable reply. "It would settle nothing. We cannot simply claim you have died and let that be the end of it."

"Unfortunately, he is right." Friar Laurence sighs. "Given the nature of the prince's decision, he might very well expect your body to be returned to Verona for proof—and the Montagues would almost certainly wish to make a spectacle of your inter-ment, a grand reminder to all and sundry of Tybalt's crime in the face of Romeo's official banishment."

"Tell them I have died of the pestilence, then!" The desper-ation in Valentine's face is painful to look upon. "They already believe the friary to be under quarantine, so it should be no trouble to convince them. They would not be able to deny the logic of a hasty burial, and thus no body to return."

"True though that may be, it would not necessarily be enough to save Romeo's neck." Laurence worries his hands together. "The decision Escalus made depends upon your succumbing to the wound you received from the dagger. If we claim you fell to disease instead, the Capulets will insist it makes Tybalt innocent of your death on practical grounds, and Romeo therefore guilty of murder."

"And it is no petty deception, Valentine." I reach for his hand again, but this time he pulls away from me. "It would not be the sort of falsehood that is easy to maintain, or which people could ignore if it were ever found out. If Friar Laurence tells the prince that you have died, it would mean you could never go home again!"

"Verona has not been my home for some three years," he fires back, anger heating his tone. "What do I care if I cannot go back? Do you think I would rest easy at night, asleep on my brother's floor in our rat-infested house, knowing that you were hanged at the end of a rope because I continue to breathe?"

"But . . . it is your life. It is where you belong—"

"You do not know where I belong!" he exclaims. "*I* do not know where I belong, and I will not trade my life for yours—I refuse! It is . . . monstrous, and if you love me as you say you do, you would not ask me to make so barbaric and selfish a choice."

Friar Laurence places a comforting hand on Valentine's knee. "Please try to remain calm. I know this issue is fraught, but you are still weak, and it will do you no—"

"Do not tell me how I am to feel about Romeo meeting his death as punishment for my recovery." Valentine fixes the monk with a resentful glare, his eyes shimmering. "Do not tell me to make a simple peace with his leaving Verona for good, when I have only just managed to express to him how much he means to me."

"Your sorrow is justified, and I do not argue against it." Friar Laurence maintains his quiet optimism. "But all is not yet lost. We have cheated Death once already; perhaps we can find a way to do so again. Even if Romeo must flee for now, it may be that in time the Capulets' hearts will soften, and they will set aside their vendetta."

"Never." Of this I have no doubts. He has not known the Capulets as long as I have, nor has he an intimate understanding of how old and deep the acrimony between our bloodlines truly is.

"The only solution would be for me to die and then somehow be resurrected." Valentine sniffles despondently. "The prince would commute Romeo's sentence, the Montagues would have their public spectacle . . . and then I could be free to go where I pleased." He looks at me with a sad dream in his eyes. "Maybe even to Mantua."

"You could not follow me." Even though I wish it more than anything, it would be wrong of me to allow it. "What about your brother? Your mother and sisters?"

"I would miss them, of course—Mercutio most of all—but I am accustomed to missing them by now." He seems far older than his years as he leans back against the wall, his cheeks hollow. "My sisters rarely wrote to me in Vicenza, and our mother has not been the same since our father died . . . I doubt they would even notice I was gone again."

It takes a moment for me to realize that he is not merely fantasizing aloud, that there is both sincerity and resignation in his face. "You . . . you mean this. You are being serious."

"I told you once that I would gladly leave Verona if I could see the world." He manages a smile, wiping the tears from his face. "Why not start now, with Mantua?"

"What if our love should not last?" I counter, my own eyes beginning to film. "What if you grew tired of me?"

"Then I should make my way to the nearest boat, and from there to the open sea," he returns with a serene little shrug. "But if we build our love so that it *does* last, think how many adventures we could share together! If only we could rob Peter to pay Paul."

"If we could, I would. I want as many tomorrows with you as time will permit me." I reach for him again, and this time he lets me take his hands in mine. A breeze stirs the air, carrying a few soft petals through the window from the friary's orchard. Our time is already running out, but for now the sun shines, and I still have more chances to kiss him before it is too late—before we are forced apart forever.

Then Friar Laurence shifts, giving us both a tentative look that is touched with only a shade of misgiving. "If you really do mean what you say, Valentine . . . I may have in my library the very solution that you seek."

29

"Among the many arcane secrets I learned in my father's workshop was the recipe for an elixir that can induce a state that simulates death." Friar Laurence folds his hands together, pensive. "Its effects last for roughly two-and-forty hours—adequate time for the body to be interred, at which point the one who drinks it can be made to wake again, as though from a very deep sleep."

"Wake again?" I repeat, the blood draining from my face. "What . . . in the *earth*?"

"Or a crypt." Laurence nods carefully at Valentine. "Much like the one belonging to his family on the grounds of the old cemetery, southeast of the city walls."

"It is damp and frigid, even in summer—but it is sealed by a locked door, rather than six feet of soil and turf," Valentine says, watching the monk with keen interest. "It is where we laid my father to rest three years ago. If . . . if I were trapped inside for some reason, it would only require a key to let me out again."

"And the sun would rise on a new day, with none the wiser for your absence," Friar Laurence finishes in a low and careful voice. "It would not be without great risk—and if it worked, you would need to live with the consequences of its success—but . . . it could give you precisely what you ask for."

"What do you mean when you say 'great risk'?" My stomach revolts at the notion of more danger. All of this is happening too quickly, our fortunes changing like the playing cards in a gambler's hands. "Valentine has almost died once. I could not bear to see him in such peril again."

"The tonic is necessarily potent, of course, and to invoke the appearance of death it requires components that can be unsafe if balanced incorrectly." He says it as one might speak of salting a meal. "But most importantly, to wake him again, to undo the dram's effects, a second elixir is required. And it must be administered before the two-and-forty hours have elapsed . . . or else it will be too late, and the feint of death will become quite real."

My blood runs cold. "No. It is too uncertain, too hazardous."

But at the same time that I say this, Valentine announces, "I shall do it."

"No!" I give him a horrified look. "You have only just recovered from being poisoned once—and barely, at that! What if something goes wrong? What if you cannot be woken?"

"I was not meant to wake this time, was I? And yet here I am." He lifts his chin. "You helped Friar Laurence save me, despite the threat you knew it would pose to your own life; and now I wish to save you, despite the threat it could pose to mine. You cannot argue against that."

"Of course I can!" Frustration heats my face. "Especially if you say you wish to do it for my sake. What was the point of all this fretting, of stealing the Dragon's Tears and forging an antidote, of nursing you back to health, if you will turn around and toss yourself back into Death's arms in the hopes he does not catch you?" With a decisive gesture I announce, "I . . . I forbid it!"

"You can do no such thing." Valentine remains infuriatingly calm. "Had I been able to cast a vote, I'd have told you to leave Verona and not look back after Tybalt's death. Certainly, I would not have approved your foolhardy adventure with Juliet—for my sake—but the decision was yours to make, as this one is mine."

"And what of your brother?" I try next, gesturing wildly in the direction of the garth. "You cannot possibly think that argument will persuade him—that he will be content to stand by and watch you tempt the same fate you have only just barely escaped."

"Mercutio does not have to stand by; he may sit, if he likes." Valentine folds his arms across his chest. "My mind is made up."

"But . . ." I struggle against the panic in my chest. As often as I have dreamed of a perfect future where I could somehow keep Valentine at my side, the thought of losing him is even worse than the thought of having to leave him. To Friar Laurence, I say, "Surely he is in no condition to be drinking death potions just now!"

"We shall measure Valentine's recovery day by day, and see how quickly he regains his strength." Friar Laurence gets to his feet. "In truth, we will not be able to wait long—I expect we will be forced to make a decision before the week is out. If he is not ready to meet the challenges of the tonic by then, the matter will be out of our hands."

"Thank you," Valentine says earnestly, even as trepidation needles my heart.

"The antidote to Dragon's Tears helped correct a terrible injustice, and I believe this plan can do the same." Laurence gives us an affectionate look. "I told Romeo once to allow for the chance that he was meant to be happy . . . and I have faith that it is still his destiny."

With that, he excuses himself from the room, leaving us to ourselves.

The next few days pass in a sort of forced peace as we strenuously avoid raising the issue again, our silence on the matter louder than the thunderclaps that intermittently shake the springtime sky. Mercutio flew into a rather theatrical rage when he learned of the suggested plot, of course, but even his most emphatic rantings failed to dent his brother's resolve. By degrees, Valentine's health improves, until Friar Laurence permits me to escort him on short walks around the friary's garden.

On one such occasion, with the sun warming my back and the boy I love holding on to my arm for support, I gather the courage to address a different subject that has been weighing on me. "Valentine, what do you think of marriage?"

"I am . . . quite uncertain how to respond to that." A surprised laugh punctuates his statement. "It is not an institution that has ever particularly interested me—for obvious reasons— and the only wedded couples I have been able to observe up close were married not for love but political advantage. For better or

311

worse." He shrugs. "Some are successful, some are not, and few have ever struck me as truly happy."

"What if it were marriage for the sake of survival?" I ask, unaccountable nerves twisting my tongue a bit. Easing him onto a bench near a row of flowering shrubs, I explain Juliet's scheme—a nuptial arrangement that could free me from the threat of Capulet vengeance and her from becoming Count Paris's trophy. "I do not know precisely what it is that I'm asking you to understand, but . . . I need to hear your thoughts, Valentine." My face is boiling hot. "Marriage has been something I've spent years dreading, for all the reasons you describe, and now I find that it may be difficult to refuse. And yet . . ."

He waits, but when I do not continue, he prompts gently, "And yet?"

"And yet, if I could choose to spend my future with anyone, it . . . it would be you." I compel myself to meet his soft brown eyes, despite how vulnerable it makes me feel. "I know it is not possible to live the way I wish we could, but I feel disloyal just the same, somehow, for even considering this. I do not know what the future holds, and every moment we've shared since you woke from your stupor has felt snatched from fate itself. What am I to do?"

"I do not know how to answer that, either," he says quietly, after a long pause. "In this future—where you are still alive, and free to make choices of your own—I would only want you to be happy." Tilting his head, smiling in a far-off way that reminds me of that first night under the lemon tree, when I saw such a poetic melancholy in him, he adds, "We do not always get to choose the future—sometimes the future simply happens, and we may only choose how we will live with it. All our wildest dreams must be tempered by strategy, Romeo."

"I . . ." Squirming a little, I clear my throat. "That is somewhat cryptic, is it not? I cannot tell which direction that advice is meant to guide me."

"Well, it seems a rather uncertain plan. Perhaps even hazardous," he muses, his tone abstracted. "There are a good many risks to face, rushing into marriage with Juliet Capulet, not knowing how it will end. What if the dowry isn't paid? Are you prepared to live in poverty together forever after?"

Heat courses up my neck, and I go still. "Well, I—"

"What if you are not the least bit compatible?" he presses. "Juliet can be quite stubborn, you know. Imagine being destitute *and* fighting every day, over matters both great and small. Does she know that you bite your fingernails when you are nervous?"

Pulling my thumb from between my teeth, I splutter, "Surely, she is not so unreasonable—"

"And what if a devastatingly handsome youth from Verona, once presumed dead, should mysteriously return and catch your eye? Would temptation lead you to be unfaithful to your bride?"

I glance up at him, just in time to catch the smirk that flickers across his devastatingly handsome face, and I huff out a breath. "Aha. I see what you are doing."

"I have no idea what you mean." Sitting back with an innocent smile, he says, "I am merely pointing out that the plan you describe comes with risks as great as its rewards, and that you will have to live with the consequences of its success. That's all."

313

"You are trying to make me feel like a hypocrite for not wishing to see you poisoned a second time, and it won't work," I inform him, narrowing my eyes.

"No?" He turns to me, the breeze ruffling his curls, kissing the freckles that are sprayed across his nose. "It seems to me that everything we want is within arm's reach—if only we are willing to take a chance on it. The alternative is that I shall be returned to Verona, and you shall become a beggared fugitive, and we might never see each other again."

Reaching up, he brushes his thumb across my cheek, his touch making me catch my breath. "What I want is for our wildest dreams to come true. And if you support mine, I shall support yours. Always."

Later the following day, a lone figure appears in the fields behind the friary, spotted by Tommaso as he rings the bell for Vespers. Trudging through the high grasses, dressed in a heavy cloak with the hood up, their identity is impossible to discern. A tense conversation ensues, worries arising over who might seek the friary by such inconvenient means; and in the end, Laurence, Guillaume, and Aiolfo go forth to intercept the new arrival.

It turns out to be Juliet.

"My father grows ever more impatient," she reports when she is seated in the chapel, breathless and sweaty from her journey. "Already he seeks to break my seclusion, ordering me back to Verona so that I may be married to Count Paris. He has hired more men to search the countryside for Romeo, and to patrol the road that passes by here."

Friar Laurence's mouth presses into a flat line. "I feared as much."

"I had to leave my nurse with the horses some three miles away, and hike across the meadow to avoid being seen. I do not know if he suspects Romeo to be hiding here, but I have word that he is raising doubts about your quarantine."

"He has sent a daily emissary to beg news of Valentine's condition—and to inquire about the progress of our supposed outbreak." Friar Laurence lights a sconce, the shadows in the church deepening as the sun sinks. "I am running out of ways to put him off, and my brethren are becoming restless over the interruption to our regular services. We will have to report deaths or recoveries soon, and reopen our doors to the public."

My stomach aches, now perpetually unsettled. The past days have allowed me nearly as much time as I like to sit with Valentine, to read to him, to walk with him in the gardens—but every minute we spend together is one less grain of sand left in the hourglass, and we both tiptoe around what will happen when it has all run through.

"How *is* Valentine?" Juliet asks, and behind me, I hear Mercutio stir. True to his word, he has not left the friary once since arriving with his brother—and he is more reluctant than any of us to entertain talk of the inevitable.

"Ask your father's emissary," he counters churlishly. "Friar Laurence has already shared with him what is relevant information for Capulet ears."

"We can trust her, Mercutio." I put a hand on his arm, urging him to settle. "She is not our enemy."

"I ask only as Valentine's childhood friend." Juliet gives him a wounded look. "If I were in a mood to be sharing news with my father, I would already be wife to Count Paris by now. And it is as to that point that I have made the troublesome journey here again."

Her eye lands on me, and I realize that the time to make another difficult choice has come. Gathering myself, I rise to my feet. "There is something the lady and I must speak about privately." Offering her my arm, I ask, "May I escort you to the garden?"

"Please." She smiles, but it does not chase the weariness from her eyes.

"I will not ask after what came of our searching Tybalt's rooms," she says as we exit the church into the cloisters, birds hunting for insects in the garth. "Even if I think I am some-what entitled to know it." Her tone is light but pointed—like my rapier—bearing no particular ill will. "I cannot fault Mercutio for doubting my motives, however, given what my family has put him through."

"He likes to pretend he is too rough and rowdy for any-thing as delicate as emotions, but he has a generous heart." I think back to some of the things he said while under the influ-ence of despair and drowsy-making herbs. "He feels things very deeply. And twice as much so where his brother is con-cerned."

The truth is that Valentine has improved by leaps and bounds since that harrowing night when we plied him with the anti-dote. His appetite is back, and although he sleeps frequently, his stamina increases all the time. He has even begun to joke that he is almost well enough to fake his own demise.

Juliet says nothing more until we have entered the walled garden, where we can speak without being seen. With the sun turning the sky a brilliant orange above us, she says, "As you have guessed, I am here to see about your answer to my proposition. I wish that I could give you more time to consider it, but . . ."

"Time and luck are luxuries of which we are both in short supply." I give her a meager smile, and then steel my nerves. "It is true that, between us, we have precious few hours left in which to ignore the future and do as we please. But enough have already passed for me to come to a decision."

"Oh?" She goes still, and I think she holds her breath.

"You were right about what awaits us if we do not act to take control of our own destinies," I begin, suddenly nervous despite having rehearsed these words several times. "And . . . I am persuaded. A strategic marriage would offer us the best possible chance of creating a life the world will not grant to us. And if the ploy does not succeed, well . . . we will be no worse off for trying."

Juliet exhales heavily, swaying on her feet, and drops onto the closest bench. Staring back up at me, relief plain on her face, she says, "You're saying you accept, then?"

I scratch my neck, the moment of truth at hand. "I do . . . on one condition."

"Name it. If you will save me from Count Paris, I will give you whatever you ask for."

"You told me you had no intention of obstructing the happiness I share with Valentine, that you were glad for us to have found each other," I remind her nervously. "I need to know if you still feel that way."

She shrugs, baffled. "Of course I do."

"Then my condition is this: I will marry you, and wait as long as it takes for your dowry to be paid. And then we may go to Brescia, or any other place that fortune permits . . . but only if Valentine goes with us."

Juliet blinks, opens her mouth, and then shuts her mouth again. After a moment of thought, she says, "Out of respect for Mercutio, I shall not ask too many of the very obvious questions that statement demands; but it would be remiss of me not to point out that if Valentine lives, you will officially become a murderer on the run—at least as far as Verona is concerned. My father could not be compelled to pay the dowry."

"If Verona could be persuaded to its satisfaction that Valentine was dead, when in fact he was not," I begin carefully, not sure how much to divulge—not sure how much culpability is too much to share, should our plans go awry—"would you object to his fleeing with us? To his joining us wherever we might go, and living off whatever fortunes the three of us might scrape together?"

Juliet stands again, her expression intrigued but unconflicted. "If Valentine could live, and I could still escape a marriage to Count Paris, there is very little I would not agree to. He is a dear friend and always has been. I would be overjoyed to have him with us."

I take my deepest breath in days, a weight lifted from my chest. "Thank you."

"I will not ask how you intend to manage it, but I am grateful if you have found a way." Juliet offers her arm, but as we start for the church again, she hesitates. "As to our nuptials, I had a thought—and I do hope you won't take this the wrong way." When I cock my brow, she continues, "Once we are married, and after some respectable time has passed, I . . . I was thinking it might be nice if you died."

With a startled blink, I say, "I'm sorry. Is there a proper way to take that?"

"I don't mean really, of course," she adds hastily, her face turning pink. "I only meant that . . . well, if Verona could be persuaded to its satisfaction that *you* were dead as well, it could solve a great many problems. If you were to be lost at the bottom of Lago di Garda, for example, there wouldn't even need to be a corpse. And you would no longer need to worry about retribution from Escalus or Alboino Capulet, or anyone else; I would become a happy young widow in command of her own fortune, just as you once suggested." Juliet gives a wistful sigh. "I would reward you handsomely for your death, of course."

"Of course." I cannot help but laugh at how she says it . . . but I also cannot help considering her points. Freed of the Montague name, I could become anyone I wished, *go* anywhere I wished—I could even fulfill Valentine's daydreams of seeing France and Byzantium and Catalonia.

And, after all, if he can die and live again for my sake, doesn't one good turn deserve another?

To Juliet, I give a courtly nod. "I can think of no reason not to honor such a request. It is thanks to you that I shall have the thing I want most—a new beginning—and you certainly deserve the same."

"A man willing to die for me. My mother would swoon," she remarks with a snort. As we reach the portico again, however, she turns to me, worry lines etching her forehead. "And, Romeo? I think . . . we should not wait any longer to share the glad news with our friends."

There being no time like the present, Juliet and I are married in the chapel of the friary that same evening. It is a strange and unpretentious ceremony, officiated by Friar Laurence, and witnessed by Guillaume, Mercutio, and Valentine—who insists upon revealing himself when he learns that Juliet has accepted my terms.

The ground does not shake, and there is no change in the air, no change in my soul; I am merely unmarried one moment, and married the next—my life altered again in the blink of an eye. And as the church bells ring for Compline, a trio of doves roosting in the ceiling take flight, swooping around us and spiraling for the open doors in the atrium.

"A good omen," Friar Laurence pronounces optimistically.

"Let us hope so." Juliet ties her cloak beneath her chin again, raising her hood. "I must return to the convent, but I will wait for further word."

And then she leaves as she came, disappearing across the fields behind the friary, her figure a smudge against the gathering darkness until she is gone altogether.

30

THE FOLLOWING DAY, AS FRIAR LAURENCE IS DASHING OFF A LETTER to his friends in Mantua, another group of men turn up at the door to the church, demanding admittance so they may search for a fugitive. This time, however, they are accompanied by a physician in the employ of Lord Capulet, who is not intimidated by the alleged outbreak.

"If you will show me to their rooms, I will examine your patients myself," he announces, pushing his way past the monk in the doorway. Caught off guard by the intrusion, I dive into an empty niche between two columns, just barely hidden from sight, pulling Valentine along with me. "All of them, I mean. I am certain you have done your best, but this is a poor excuse for an infirmary, and they will need a man with knowledge of medicines."

"There is little you can do for victims of pestilence other than wait for the disease to run its course." Friar Laurence keeps his voice unworried. "As I am certain you are aware. And one of our patients had to be removed from the inadequate care of a

Veronese doctor once already . . . I am afraid his brother will not permit you to examine him."

"Do we look to you as though we wait on the assent of some common guttersnipe to do as we have been commissioned?" A second voice—not one of the men who visited here initially, but clearly learned in the same tactics.

Pressed up against each other, trying not to breathe too loudly lest we give ourselves away, Valentine and I have a silent and desperate conversation with our eyes. What will we do if these men decide to force their way in? There is nowhere else to hide, and I have nowhere left to run.

"I only mean to say that he is quite deft with a sword—and although the four of you working together could most likely cut him down, I do not think Prince Escalus would approve." Friar Laurence is still calm, but frost coats his tone. "Killing an innocent man in a house of worship, merely because he is in your way, is not a crime he'd likely forgive."

There is an awkward silence, and then the first man tries again, twice the bluster in his voice as before. "No matter how noble your intentions are in treating this young man, you are not a physician, and not qualified to render his care. But I am—and neither you nor any hotheaded brother shall prevent me from seeing to my business!"

Beads of sweat prick the skin at my temples and begin to roll, my eyes flicking to the south transept, where a door leads to the sacristy. There's a window there—small, but just large enough for me to fit through—if I could make it there in time. I stare into Valentine's honeyed eyes, willing him to understand my plan, and he does. With a fretful gaze, he shakes his head an emphatic *no*. Instead, he laces his fingers with mine, squeezing tight, holding me there with him. I can feel his heartbeat in the palm of his hand, in the palm of my own, and I go still.

How strange it is that only a short time ago, this same gesture nearly shook me apart, and now it seems to be all that can hold me together.

"And if you had any business here, I would gladly leave you to it," Laurence rejoins. "Our quarantine will be lifted in only a few days' time, at which point you are welcome to return for services. As for young Valentine, we will send word to the prince as soon as there is a significant change in his condition. But until then, although your offer of assistance is appreciated, it is not necessary. Good day to you, gentlemen."

There are more weak threats, and spluttering protests—but soon the doors bang shut again, and the men are gone.

Valentine and I are still clinging to our niche, still taking shallow breaths and staring into each other's eyes, when Friar Laurence rounds the column with a grave expression. "We are out of time."

One more full day passes, and then, in the morning just before Lauds, when the sky is gradually turning from black to gray, I am summoned to Valentine's bedside. I am dressed to ride, in boots and a borrowed habit that itches against my skin—and there is a lump in my throat I cannot seem to swallow down.

"You look very handsome," he says, his face lighting up as I shuffle into the room. Propped up on a stack of pillows, he is shirtless again—the way he was when he arrived, the way he shall be when he leaves here—and I flush at the sight of him.

"You are the handsome one," I return, unaccountably shy. But it's true; his skin has regained its healthy color, his face is no longer gaunt, and his eyes are practically twinkling. "How can you be so unafraid? I am a nervous wreck, and I am not the one about to wander through the valley of the shadow of death for a second time! Do you harbor no doubts at all?"

He shrugs, as though somewhat baffled himself. "I do not know why exactly, but I feel mostly . . . excitement. Perhaps it is just that, for the first time, I am deciding the life I wish to live. I am choosing where I go next, and why—and with whom—instead of simply being told." He pulls me down onto the bed beside him. "I am excited about more days spent loving you, Romeo. More days spent being honest about who I am, about living for myself, and not fearing an empty future."

"That is beautiful," I murmur, more aware than ever how lucky I am to know someone as good as Valentine, to be loved by him. "It will be my honor to cherish you as long as I am able . . . but in the meantime, I wish I had a tenth of your courage."

"I have seen you in combat—twice, in fact; you cannot tell me you have no courage." Caressing my face, he coaxes me to smile. "We are about to manage the impossible, to fool the world and have our happy ending. You cannot tell me you feel no excitement at all!"

"I am saving my excitement for later, when it will seem less like tempting the devil. But the more you tell me about the future, the easier my stomach rests." Running my thumb along the back of his hand, his flesh warm again where so recently it was terrifyingly cool, I add, "I cannot stand to think of you lying in a tomb somewhere, waiting for me."

"A crypt," he corrects with a teasing smirk. "For all its chill and gloom, it is surprisingly spacious inside. Although, in truth, it is not something I care to dwell on, either. I am only glad that I will not be conscious to endure it."

A thousand or more nightmares clamor at me, reminding me of all the disasters that might befall us, but I shut my ears to them. For Valentine's sake, I must focus on what we stand to gain if this wild and fiendishly daring scheme we've laid out should work.

"It may be the longest two-and-forty hours I shall ever spend, but . . . each minute of it will bring me closer to the day when I will hold you again in my arms," I tell him, breathing in his scent, picturing what I imagine a vineyard in Brescia to look like. "No secrets to be kept, no double lives, no public expectations or dynasties to uphold . . . just us. And the sunlight on the hills, and as many kisses as a lifetime contains."

"Just us and the kisses, and a life of our own design." Valentine moves his hand to my heart, which thumps faster at his touch. "But that life only starts with a little death. And for me, who nearly died once already, it is hard to be intimidated by such a petty challenge."

"Just us, the kisses . . . and Juliet," I remind him.

"Well." He grins. "At least we won't be lonely."

And I kiss him, because his mouth is begging for it—and because the sky is growing lighter outside his window, and candlelight licks at the walls, and the stars revolve slowly overhead . . . gradually uncrossing themselves, or so we hope.

A knock at the door provides just enough warning for us to separate before Friar Laurence enters, a self-conscious Mercutio in his wake. "I apologize for interrupting. It is not my wish to cut your time short, but Romeo still has a long journey ahead of him, and . . . well, so do you."

"I know." Valentine leans back against his pillows, untroubled, confident that there is still plenty of time to share ahead of us.

"Once the deed is done, we will notify Verona of his death—and at the same time, we will convey the details of your marriage to Juliet." Friar Laurence gives me a serious look. "It would be best if you are already in Mantua by the time that news finds its way beyond the ears of the palazzo."

"You have my word." I rarely look forward to predawn rides, dangerous as they are, and this one will be particularly harrowing. The landscape crawls with Capulet spies, and I will have to change horses at least once to make good time. "I will head straight for the lodgings you procured, and will be quite content to remain out of sight until it is time to . . . to administer the second elixir."

He hears the tension in my voice and gives me a comforting squeeze. "Juliet has already been moved into the cottage that was arranged for you. It is on land belonging to a farmer who is happy to do a good deed for the Friars Minor, and who does not ask questions." Then he hesitates. "Once Verona learns you are man and wife, there will be no small amount of uproar, and I imagine both your fathers will be aggressive in seeking answers. But two days from now, when your sentence has been officially reduced to banishment, it will no longer matter. You will be rid of your families' endless feuding, and free to live the lives you were always meant to."

"Thank you." It is so simple and weak a phrase, so inadequate to express the fullness of my gratitude. "Thank you for everything you've done for me, for us. I do not know how I would have managed without you."

"For good or ill, you will never have to wonder." Humor flickers in his eyes. "My faith demands that I help those in need, and that I put acts of service before my ego. It is, on occasion, surprisingly difficult to tell the difference between the two, but I very much hope that what I have done for you is worthy of your gratitude."

"You are quite certain nothing can go wrong with this . . . magic potion of yours?" Mercutio grunts, eyeing the glass bottle on the table by Valentine's bed with palpable resentment. Understandably, he harbors no particular enthusiasm for our plan—but his brother has persuaded him to support it anyway. "It will not hurt him, will it?"

"It is not magic; it is alchemy. Or medicine, if you prefer," Laurence returns, and I feel the weight of the second bottle in the pouch at my belt. "I have spent a great deal of my life learning how plants, minerals, and metals can be used for healing— and how, if transmuted under the proper conditions, they can be useful in other ways as well."

Mercutio's brow furrows in suspicion. "That does not answer my question."

"No harm will come to Valentine." Friar Laurence looks him in the eye. "It simulates death; its effects may be understandably upsetting to you, and it is natural you should have doubts. But so long as Romeo has the reviving tonic and a key to the crypt, your brother will rise again—hale and hearty—in two days' time. I promise."

Mercutio twitches unhappily. "And I shall never see him again, just the same."

"That is not true," Valentine protests. "Brescia is only a two-day ride from Verona—one, if you change horses. And you will be welcome there as often as you like." Mercutio does not answer, casting his eyes down at his feet in a sulk. "Please do not be unhappy. We are about to right a terrible wrong, and save Romeo's life. I know you are sad that I am leaving Verona again, but . . . this is just something I must do."

"I never said that I was sad about your leaving." Mercutio sniffs, squaring his shoulders, but his brother sees right through him.

"But you *are* sad, nevertheless," Valentine replies, gloating. "I can tell."

"I am not sad! If anything, I am relieved." Smoothing his hair, Mercutio continues, "No longer will I have to worry about you getting underfoot when I am trying to woo an attractive girl. And besides, you snore at night, and it keeps me awake."

"I do not!"

"He does." Mercutio turns to me, and I see the glint in his eyes. "Romeo, I am telling you this so that you cannot say I didn't warn you: He snores *terribly*. Like a barrel of gravel being poured through a gristmill. It's a wonder he's not been run out of town alr—"

"Not a word of that is true!" Valentine is laughing so hard he can barely protest. "Especially the part about the attractive girls. The only women in Verona who are susceptible to my brother's charms are either half-dead or half-drunk."

"Or both," I point out.

"Oh, piss off—both of you!" Mercutio exclaims, but there is finally a smile on his face. "I only hope Valentine does not begin to snore while lying in the crypt, or he may crack the foundations and cause it to cave in." He grins at his own joke—but then his chin trembles, and he hides his face, trying not to let us see him cry. "Oh, damn it all, I *am* sad. I love you, you know? You're the only brother I've got, and now I must lose you a second time."

"We were reunited once, and we can be again." Valentine swipes at his own eyes. "After all, Brescia needs carpenters as much as any other city. Perhaps someday you will wish to live there, near us."

"Perhaps." Mercutio manages a weak smile—but I am not convinced. It is hard to imagine Verona without him, or him without Verona. He would be lost anywhere else.

"I love you, too, Mercutio," Valentine says, ignoring their audience. "And I will not say goodbye, because we will see each other soon enough."

Mercutio nods, his face blotchy and his mouth clamped shut against emotions that threaten his own foundations. When it is clear there will be nothing more said, Friar Laurence steps forward. "The sun will be up soon. I think it best if we proceed."

There is no fanfare, no final speeches. Uncorking the bottle, Valentine drinks the contents quickly, making a face. "It tastes like . . . licorice."

"Yes, it is deceptively pleasant," Friar Laurence remarks.

"I despise licorice." Valentine lies back against the pillows. "Next time, see if you can make one that tastes of figs."

"I . . . do not believe it comes in other flavors." Laurence smiles. "And I sincerely hope this is the only time my skill in making this particular concoction shall be called for."

But Valentine does not answer.

No part of me wishes to linger as Valentine's heart slows until its beating is imperceptible, until his breathing appears to stop and his body turns cold. Until he is washed and prepared, as any other corpse might be, for his return to Verona so he may be laid to his supposedly eternal rest.

Wrapping my cloak tight around me, I leave the cloisters in a rush, hurrying through the gardens and into the same field Juliet crossed only a few days ago. I try to distract myself with thoughts of how I will handle the mount that is waiting for me a few miles from here, what measures I can take to avoid detection as I ride for Mantua, what it will feel like three days from now when all of this is over and fading from memory.

But what I feel now is cowardly, my heart aching with the cruel memory of the last time I was forced to leave Valentine's side as he lay dying. I am only taking this flight so that he may live again, so that we might *both* live again, I know.

But the bottle in my pouch strikes against my hip with every stride, reminding me of what's at stake.

All I can think about is the boy I love—cold and abandoned—until my eyes fill and I can see the ground ahead of me no longer.

31

MY FLIGHT TO MANTUA PASSES IN A BLUR, MY HANDS SO TIGHT ON
the reins they begin to cramp. I keep one eye on the road, and
the other fixed over my shoulder—watching for wolves, highwaymen, patrols . . . I do not know which would be worse. Four times
I pass early travelers, ducking my head and kicking my horse
into a gallop, convinced they are part of Capulet's network of
mercenaries.

But no one raises the alarm, and no one gives chase; and,
somehow, I find myself on the outskirts of Mantua when it is
only just past the breakfast hour.

The cottage where I am to hide is a rustic, unadorned structure, with stone walls and a thatched roof, tucked in the back
of a sheep farmer's meadow. A curtain twitches as I ride into
view, and once I have gotten close enough to dismount, the
door flies open.

"Romeo." Juliet is pale, her knuckles white on the doorframe.
"Thank heaven it is you at last. I thought . . . well, I'll not dwell
on what I've thought. But I doubt I've slept more than twenty
minutes in the past twenty hours."

"And I feel as if I have aged twenty years in the same time." I am shaky with nerves and hunger, but she wraps me in a fond embrace, and then guides me inside.

The cottage consists of a single room, with an open hearth and a chimney above. The space is warm and cozy, and a modest spread waits on a rough, wooden table by the window. I fall upon the food, gorging myself on fresh bread, sheep's milk cheese, and dried fruit. There is also a flask of spiced wine, and I drink it until my tongue goes numb.

"I have no news of home," Juliet says, pacing awkwardly in the confined quarters. "I have no news *at all*. After leaving the convent yesterday, I came straight here, and have had no company but the farmer and his wife—who are very kind, but seem convinced I am either the pope's mistress or a runaway concubine."

"I expect that the only real news to tell is just being shared now." The air we breathe seems permanently scented by years of smoke from the fireplace. "It has only been about two hours since the friary sent word to Verona."

"If I could only be a ghost long enough to return home and overhear what my parents will say." A sudden, inappropriate giggle escapes her. "They will be incensed. And the conversation that will have to happen between my father and Count Paris . . . oh, I have gooseflesh!"

I laugh, too dizzy from fatigue and wine to bear the weight of my concerns just now. There is just one bed in the room, and no other furniture beyond the table and two stiff-backed chairs. "Does it feel strange to you that we are married? It feels so strange to me."

"I keep forgetting it's real," she admits, shaking her head. "I keep forgetting that, if all goes according to plan, this is how life shall be from here onward." Following my gaze, she looks around us. "I've never had a room this small, let alone an entire home—let alone one I must share with another person. Are husbands and wives afforded no personal privacy?"

I look out the window at the pasture, a sea of green crashing into a forest at the horizon. "Once we are able to leave here—if all goes according to plan—I think we will be free to make our own decisions about what husbands and wives do."

We share stories for a while, describing how we've spent the past week, and daydreaming about the lives we intend to lead in Brescia. I tell her about Valentine, and she tells me about saying goodbye to her nurse—a woman who has been by her side, day in and day out, since she was a child. As she talks, she begins to weep, and I realize just how many sacrifices of her own she has had to make for this escape.

"Once we are established in Brescia, perhaps we can send for her," I suggest. "I know little about running a household, and you might enjoy having someone around who is not quite so helpless as I am when it comes to womanly concerns."

"Thank you." She blows her nose in her handkerchief. "I would like that very much. Thank you for thinking of it."

As night falls, our conversation becomes more and more abstracted, the both of us talking about anything and everything that might keep our minds occupied. But I cannot help cataloging each hour that passes, all the same, measuring the time passed since Valentine's last conscious moments in bed—the time left until I am to wake him again.

I place the bottle containing the second tonic on a shelf; then, fearing it will fall, I begin to carry it everywhere in my hand; then, fearing I will drop it, I put it back in my pouch; then, fearing I will bump against something and shatter it, I put it back on the shelf. There were not sufficient ingredients to prepare a second dose, and so as far as I am concerned it is more precious than any amount of gold or silk or spices the earth might yield.

When neither of us can stay up a minute longer, I offer to sleep on the floor, but Juliet will not hear of it. "You are being absurd. We are friends, are we not? If we can manage sleep at all, we can surely manage it in respectful proximity."

And so we share a bed on our first night together as man and wife—the both of us wide awake and staring at the wall. After a while, Juliet begins to laugh at the absurdity of it, and I cannot resist joining in.

When the sun rises again, we are barely rested; but we clamber out of bed just the same, resuming our fretful laps of the room.

My stomach aches with worry, the sun inching lethargically across the sky, the afternoon bleeding into still more afternoon until I think I shall lose my senses. At the first hint of evening, I rush to saddle my mount . . . and find that Juliet has beaten me to it. Both horses are watered and groomed, and prepared for riders.

A little confused, I turn to her. "You are coming with me?"

"Of course I am!" She lets out an anxious puff of air. "Do you think I could bear another night in this desolate ruin all by myself, with nothing to do but worry and wonder? I should run wild."

Gratitude spills through me, but still I hesitate. "It will be dangerous . . . in addition to all the normal hazards one faces on the roads after dark, there is no telling how your father will react when the prince declares that I shall not hang for Tybalt's death after all."

"Yes, there is," she counters with a snort. "He will put a bounty on your head, because he is vengeful and shortsighted. So you will be well served by a second pair of eyes and ears as you ride back into his territory—and it will not hurt you to have his daughter between you and any armed men hungry for Capulet gold. My father may have little use for me, but hired assassins will expect to forfeit their reward if they do me any harm."

"You would do that?" My throat feels tight again, and I will be glad when this is over, as I am quite tired of crying all the time. "For me?"

"For you, and for Valentine." She smiles, although her nerves are palpable. "And for Mercutio, and for justice—and for me, as well. We are in this together, Romeo. Partnered, if not truly espoused. I intend to carry my weight."

Unable to sit still, we wander in the pasture until the sun finally begins to sink. When the last shred of it vanishes over the horizon, we climb onto our horses and turn them back north—toward Verona.

It grows dark fast, and we force ourselves to maintain a steady and unhurried pace, both to keep our steeds out of unseen potholes and so we can hear any approaching hoofbeats on the road. My fingers are knotted in the reins, and I constantly check the integrity of Friar Laurence's bottle, my thoughts an ugly quagmire.

What if the death potion was not prepared correctly? I wonder. What if it wears off somehow, and Valentine wakes on his own, freezing on a stone block across from his father's moldering remains? *What if he cannot be woken up at all?* Juliet barely speaks as we travel, but from the way her jaw is set, her lips pressed so tightly together they lose their color, I can tell she is as nervous as I am.

In the end, our caution serves us well. Several times, we divert our mounts just in time to avoid other riders, concealing ourselves among the trees as they gallop past. But the closer we draw to the city, the harder this feat becomes. When we are at last some six miles away, the stench of Verona's tanneries just beginning to sour the air, a man we believed to be a good way ahead of us on the road unexpectedly doubles back—catching us by surprise as we round a bend.

The both of us freeze, our hands moving instinctively to the weapons we have concealed beneath our cloaks, but the rider is too shaken to notice. His eyes wide and his face pale, he says, "If you are on your way to Verona, you might wish to take another route."

Juliet finds her voice first. "Why is that?"

"There is a group of men blocking the road ahead." He

glances over his shoulder. "They claim that they are looking for someone, but will not say who, or on what authority they act." Crossing himself, he utters a silent prayer of thanks. "Obviously, they are bandits, and I am lucky to have had my wits about me. I told them that I carry no money, and was on my way to Verona so I might procure some from a lender. It was a lie, but they must have believed me, for they let me go."

Juliet and I exchange an uneasy glance, a cold sweat carving runnels through the dust and grime now clinging to every inch of my skin. No matter who they are—highwaymen, assassins, or even the prince's guard in disguise—we can take no chances. The first would rob and murder us; the second would murder and then rob us; and the third would arrest me for violating my exile.

When the man is gone from earshot, Juliet breaks the silence. "We will have to leave the horses and continue on foot. If this road is being watched, they are all being watched."

"Has your father truly that much money to spare?"

"And more besides," she says. "But you would be shocked how modest a sum is required to entice certain men to murder."

We leave our mounts in a nearby clearing, tied to a pair of saplings—sturdy enough to resist if the horses pull at their leads, but weak enough to break if we cannot return and the animals grow desperate. It is not a happy thought, and I banish it to the same dark hole where I have sequestered all the other horrors this night has provoked from my lurid imagination.

Setting out across the fields, hunkered low, I try not to count all the precious minutes that are slipping away. We are much slower now, and Friar Laurence's tonic knocks urgently against my hip, reminding me that Valentine's two-and-forty hours are nearing their end. I sweat, hot and cold at the same time under my cloak.

Crawling through the brush near a side road, we pass by another improvised blockade—an overturned wagon, attended by a trio of large men with swords at their hips. I hold my breath, each blade of grass that brushes against my cloak as loud as a thunderstorm to my ears. I only exhale again once we are well past them, when we finally catch our first glimpse of torchlight flickering along the city's fortifications.

"It's breathtaking from here." Juliet wipes her face, her hair disheveled. "I never realized it before. Or maybe I just never appreciated how challenging a task they meant to make entering Verona against the whims of the prince. All that stone, all those men—and so few gates."

"We are just lucky that they trust the dead are as safe as they need to be on *this* side of the battlements," I murmur, daring to pull myself upright for the first time in a half hour, the cemetery spreading out on the far side of the lane—at last. "All we have to contend with is a border wall, the likes of which we have both scaled before, and then a handful of watchmen on the lookout for grave robbers."

"Which we *are*," she murmurs back. "At least on technical grounds."

"We only plan to take what doesn't belong."

Juliet snorts. "That will make a fine epitaph."

"*Halt!* Who goes there?!"

The voice, sharp and loud, comes from somewhere in the

darkness just ahead, and Juliet and I are still scrambling for our weapons when two sword-wielding men burst out from behind a cluster of junipers a scant five yards away. It is not until I finally have my rapier in hand that I realize they are not attacking us— they are *laughing* at us.

"The look on your face!" Benvolio guffaws so enthusiastically he can hardly breathe, popping his eyes open and doing a pantomime of childish terror that I am fairly certain he means to be an imitation of me. "I wish I could preserve that moment in amber, so I might cherish it for decades to come."

"You looked as though you were about to wet your hose," Mercutio interjects, slinging his arm around Ben's shoulders. Then, more respectfully, "And you your skirts, my lady."

"Piss. Off." Juliet narrows her eyes, but there is a clear sense of relief in them nonetheless. Her retort sends them into fresh gales of laughter, though, and we must wait until they have tired of it before speaking again.

"I am glad you made it this far without dying of fright, Cousin." Ben pounds me on the back by way of a greeting, but then gives me a genuine smile. "It is good to see you."

"The feeling is mutual," I tell him honestly—even though if we were not so pressed for time, I might like to punch him in the face. "I did not know you would be joining us."

"You are joking!" he scoffs. "A reckless and irresponsible scheme that involves magic potions and faked deaths and opening a crypt under the full moon? If anything, I am deeply offended that I was not included in this ridiculous adventure from the start!"

"Did you bring the key to the crypt?" Juliet asks Mercutio, her hand still resting on the hilt of her short sword, tracking the lane in both directions. As a rule, Veronese girls are not trained in any art of combat, so I cannot guess how skilled she is with a blade, but I have learned not to underestimate her by now.

"No. I came all this way, intending to free my brother from live entombment, and left it in my other pouch." Mercutio gestures to the leather bag strung from his belt. "Yes, of course I have it!"

"Well, let us not waste time, then." Juliet turns on her heel, marching across the road for the cemetery. "We are running short enough as it is."

Scaling the wall is a task both simple and nerve-racking at the same time. Never in my life did I imagine I would have to sneak into a graveyard by moonlight, to break open a crypt and drag a body out of it—and the fear of being caught, coupled with the superstition of doing it at all in the first place, is enough to make me clumsy.

I am the last to drop to the ground inside the cemetery's limits, and the last to creep forward through the headstones, a heavy mist cast up by the Adige rolling around us and clinging to the earth. Crickets and toads score our arrival, and an owl hoots ominously from the reaches of a gnarled tree that arches against the night sky.

"Lovely atmosphere, don't you think?" Benvolio hisses directly into my left ear, and I nearly leap out of my skin. Cackling, he says, "That face was even better than the first one!"

My heart throbbing so hard I feel it in my fingertips, I glare at him. "I have decided I shall not be missing you when I am in Brescia."

"Yes, you will." He nudges me in the ribs, flashing a cheeky grin. Up close, in the moonlight, I finally notice scratch marks on the backs of his hands, and another just under his jaw—swollen, angry welts that look suspiciously familiar.

Squinting at him, I ask, "Did you get a cat while I've been away?"

"Well, someone had to take charge of Hecate's care while you were frolicking in the countryside with a pack of barefoot monks, didn't they?" His face flushes, brows knitting together. "She was utterly despondent after you fled, I'll have you know. I found her crying in your bedchamber and practically had to drag her out by her tail!"

It strikes me that Ben may be speaking more for himself than for a cat that only ever tolerated me, and I find that I am rather touched. "I can see she has not been terribly appreciative of your efforts."

"Truly, she is the devil's own emissary." Ben snorts, shaking his head. "She will roll onto her back and mewl pitifully for belly rubs, but if I so much as reach in her direction she becomes a furious whirlwind of teeth and claws—and this is how she repays me for procuring fish and cream for her nearly every single day!"

Patting him on the shoulder, I say, "Well, I am glad to know that she has found a new home. You will be a wonderful caretaker, Cousin."

"Oh, no I won't! She is going with the three of you to Brescia if I have to fling her there myself," Ben declares emphatically, huffing out a breath. After a moment, he adds, "I cannot believe you have married Juliet Capulet, by the way! I can honestly say that news took me by no small amount of surprise—and after all the grousing you did when I made you attend that masquerade and dance with all those girls." He laughs, but then grows suspiciously quiet, his expression thoughtful. "Cousin . . . there is something I have been meaning to ask you."

I am so distracted, so concerned with the hour, that I fail to appreciate the gravity in his tone. "What is it?"

"I . . ." He hesitates, looking anywhere but directly at me. "As you know, I have occasionally been frustrated by your skittishness where romance is concerned—"

"*Occasionally'?*" I repeat in disbelief.

"—but I have only meant well, and . . . I am beginning to think that I may have been unfair to you." He scratches the back of his neck. "When I came to see you at the friary, I noticed how . . . pronounced your concern was for Valentine. And now Mercutio says he will be following you to Brescia, although he refuses to say much more about it, which is—"

"Of course I was concerned for him." My face might be hot enough to burn away this accursed fog. "He took a blow that was meant for me, and nearly died for it! And naturally he must come to Brescia; he certainly cannot remain here after returning from the dead."

"It was more than just guilt, Romeo," he says softly. "I know you think I am incapable of focusing on anything other than girls, but I did see the way you looked at Valentine that day in

343

the piazza. I just didn't understand what it meant until . . . well, until recently."

"You said you had a question for me." I can barely force the words out, my skin vibrating with incipient panic. "But I have not heard one yet."

"I am aware that there are men who simply do not desire romance with ladies—I personally cannot fathom it, but I have heard it happens." He tries making a joke of this, but it falls flat. And, finally, he gets to the point: "Are you such a man, Romeo?"

"Say that I am." My hands tremble at my sides. "Do you disapprove?"

To my surprise, Ben snorts. "I have hardly lived the sort of life that affords me the privilege of disapproval where another man's romantic exploits are concerned." Hastily, he then adds, "Although, I feel compelled to remind you, the services I have provided to Verona's unhappily married women have saved more than one union from ending in catastrophe. They ought to name a day after me."

"Or a great number of mysteriously ginger-haired children," I quip. "But you have not answered my question."

"You've not exactly answered mine, either, I'd like to point out." He sighs. "But, no, Romeo—I do not disapprove of you. I do not think that I entirely understand . . . but maybe that does not matter. It touched me deeply when you said I was more like a brother to you than a cousin, for I have always felt the same way."

At last, Ben looks at me, and I can see how much he means this. He has always been quick to laugh and quick to anger, but he has never been good at expressing finer sentiments. "If you mean to Valentine what he clearly seems to mean to you, I am only glad to know that you are happy."

The owl calls again, and the mist sways in the moonlight as a breeze touches the headstones, but it is not the heavy vapor that causes the cemetery to suddenly blur around me. My heart swells as I realize that this is how Ben has chosen to say goodbye.

"Also, I am extremely annoyed about all the time and energy I wasted trying to arrange liaisons for you with all those girls," he adds, leaning against me and clucking his tongue. "At least I had the good sense to save the pretty ones for myself and give you the castoffs."

He is teasing, and deserves a jibe in response, but I am far too overwhelmed to speak. It is all I can do to manage a wet little laugh.

"The crypt is just ahead," Mercutio reports in a strained undertone when we catch up with him and Juliet. They are hunkered behind a wide stone monument, their eyes wary as they peer into the brume. "There is someone out there, though. We just saw—*there*."

A light appears, flickering, its glow diffused by the fog. It's eerie and beautiful, and I think to myself that if I somehow survive this heartrending night, I shall have to remember to appreciate it in hindsight.

Ben squints. "I cannot see a blessed thing out there, but it must be one of the watchmen . . . No grave robber worth his salt would risk carrying a lantern."

The cold feeling in my gut claws its way into my chest, my

jaw clenched, my hand gripping the bottle tight. Anxiety has distorted my sense of time, and I have no idea how long we have left before it's too late—before Valentine can no longer be revived.

"It might also be a mourner." Even though she suggests it, Juliet does not sound convinced. "Someone who could not come by day."

"The only people I can think of who fall under that category, at least where my brother's case is concerned, are present and accounted for," Mercutio whispers. "And Valentine is the first person to be laid to rest in this section of the cemetery in what might be months."

"A watchman, then." Ben sets his jaw. "They make a point to mind the recent burials, as they are the most appealing targets for thieves." Leaning down, without a hint of shame, he snatches a half-withered posy of flowers from the base of the monument before us. "And this, I think, is where I finally make myself useful. Do not wait for me—rescue Valentine, and get to safety, and we will all see one another in a brighter future!"

And with that, he sweeps around the monument and plunges into the mist, vanishing almost instantly from sight. But only a few moments pass before we hear him calling out, "Ahoy there—you, with the light!"

"Who goes there?" comes the response, alarm in the old man's voice. "Stay where you are. What business brings you here in the dead of night, with no lamp of your own?"

"I have only come to pay tribute to my dear, departed

mother," Benvolio replies—rather overdoing the pathos, I think. "You see, I brought a bouquet of her favorite flowers. Um . . . violets."

"Those look to be lilacs."

"Well. She will not know the difference." Breezily, he continues, "In any event, I dropped my lantern, and I'm afraid I've become quite lost . . . I've spent half the past hour wandering among the stones, searching for her name. I was about to give up hope when I caught sight of you." Ben lies with practiced ease. "You are the watchman, are you not? You must know the grounds of this place like the back of your hand."

"Aye, that I am, and that I do," the man grunts.

"Could you find it in your heart to help me seek out my mother's grave?" Ben sounds so piteous he might as well be an orphan begging for alms. "I haven't with me more than a handful of coins, but I will gladly pay them to you for your trouble."

"Oh, very well." The man sounds considerably less irritated. "What is her name?"

"Maria. Maria Alberti."

"*What?*" He is definitely irritated again. "There must be a dozen women buried here by that name—possibly more!"

Ben sighs wistfully. "She may have had a common name, but she was a truly extraordinary woman. She died saving me from a fire as an infant, and I come here every year on the anniversary of that fateful night, at the very hour she took her last breath. It is the only time I feel as if she is still with me."

The old man curses under his breath, but the lantern begins

to move again—drifting away from Mercutio's family crypt and deeper into the reaches of the fog. "Well, what are you waiting for? Keep up with me, or this will take us all night!"

Ben rushes after him, profusely offering his thanks. The moment we can hear them no longer, Juliet turns to me with her eyes cast almost comically wide. "That was . . ."

"Remarkable?" Mercutio suggests.

"Overdone?" I supply, a bit more critically.

"*Shocking*," she concludes. "He stole a nosegay off someone's grave and then lied about his mother being dead—does he have no fear of tempting fate?"

"But his mother *is* dead." Mercutio wiggles his hand in the air. "Perhaps she did not go in quite the manner he described, but grief plays tricks on one's memory."

"Yes. So much so that he even forgot her real name." My tone is dry, but I am duly impressed by how quickly my cousin thinks on his feet. "They will be searching for Maria Alberti— whoever she is or was—until dawn."

"And we will be gone from here within the hour." Mercutio rises then, leaving the monument to dart ahead into the billowing mists, and we follow quickly behind.

As with the oldest crypts in Verona, the one belonging to Mercutio's family is surprisingly modest—a rectangular hut of gray stone, darkened with age, its finer details weathered away by time. But for all of that, it is still grand, its dimensions reeking of importance. There could be no mistaking that it houses the dead of a prominent bloodline.

Wrestling a substantial key from the pouch at his belt, Mercutio whispers to Juliet, "Keep on the lookout, and if you see someone coming, just give us the signal."

"And what signal is that?" She fixes him with an incredulous look. "Shall I clap my hands? Bark like a dog? If we have company close enough to be seen through all of this"—she gestures into the turbid gloom—"they will certainly hear me if I shout, 'Stop breaking into that tomb, there are people coming!'"

"A very good point." Two red spots appear in his cheeks. "Just try not to say that, in particular—nor to get caught in general—and I shall be happy." They glare at each other like a pair of basilisks, until Juliet finally withdraws into the shadows, secreting herself behind a cluster of bushes opposite the crypt. Tugging me the other way, leading me to the locked door, Mercutio grumbles, "She is impossible. I cannot believe you married her."

"You are the one who introduced us," I point out, amused by their antagonism.

"Yes. And after all the witless things I've done, all my indiscreet transgressions, who could have guessed *that* would turn out to be my worst mistake?" Fitting the key into the lock, his hands shake so badly that he has to attempt it three times—and then it will not seem to turn. "This is black magic, I know it; there is no chance this is the wrong key—we used it to open the crypt two days ago. Fate is trying to teach me a lesson!"

I have never heard him so frantic, and I place a hand on his arm. "Let me try. Fate has taught me enough lessons already. It is surely bored of the game by now."

In truth, I am no calmer than he is, my fears whirling like a funnel cloud, and my fingers shake as well. If the key does not work . . .

Adjusting my grip, I jostle it carefully, letting it find where it belongs among the unseen workings of the lock . . . and I struggle to continue breathing. Somewhere in the darkness beyond this door, Valentine waits for me, drawing closer to the point of no return. We are late—I can feel it in my bones—and I am terrified that I am going to find only his corpse inside, just beyond the reach of the tonic at my belt.

Or perhaps he has been dead since the moment he swallowed Laurence's potion, and I shall find him two days along in the process of returning to the earth.

There is a click as the key settles into place, the mechanism revolves, and the latch opens. And then I become aware of a shift in the light, a telltale warmth stealing into the pale silver of moonglow that falls on the crypt, and my back goes rigid even before I hear the voice behind us.

"Well, well, well. Isn't this a cozy sight: two grave robbers, caught in the act—and one of them a fugitive from justice, at that."

I turn slowly, horror creeping up from the soles of my feet to tickle the hair on my scalp. Surrounded by the fog, Count Paris watches us with sinister satisfaction, a swinging lantern casting ghoulish shadows across his face. With him is a hulking manservant I've never seen before, taller than Mercutio and more sturdily built than the crypt we've only just managed to open.

"You call me a grave robber for coming to my only brother's resting place?" There is so much venom in Mercutio's tone, I am surprised my skin does not burn from it. "That's quite the insinuation, coming from the likes of you."

"I say what I see." Paris takes a step closer, still looking pleased. "Opening a crypt at midnight, a wanted man by your side . . . How ever will you explain this to the prince?"

Finding my voice at last, I spit back, "I am no fugitive. Tybalt was a murderer—who slew *your* kinsman—and his death was well earned."

"But you are banished, are you not?" Paris challenges. "And yet, here you are."

"And there Verona is." Mercutio flings his arm in the direction of the city walls, looming in the distance, torchlight flickering along the ramparts above the fog. "Romeo has not entered the city, and is in no violation of the prince's edict."

"He is close enough." Paris narrows his eyes. "These hallowed grounds belong to the good people of Verona, just as much as the piazza or the Arena, and Romeo stands on them—thumbing his nose at the punishment his actions have won him."

"What are you doing here, Paris?" Mercutio takes a step toward his cousin, his hands bunching into fists. "Do not tell me it is to pay your respects to my brother, for you showed him no respect when he was alive. You did not even attend his funeral!"

"How could I, when I knew you and your mother would be there? The greediest and most grasping of my relatives, always turning to me for a solution to your embarrassing poverty." He gives a baleful snort. "For all your swaggering and braggadocio, you are a pathetic representative of our shared blood. The sole reason I waited until so late to make this sorrowful visit was to minimize the chance of another encounter with you after your shameful performance in the piazza before the prince. Valentine, at least, had the good sense to keep his head down and his mouth shut—and, yes, I will pay my respects to him."

"Begone from here!" Mercutio lurches forward, and Paris retreats a step, his manservant reaching instinctively for a sword sheathed at his hip. "When my father died, and Valentine needed your help, you refused him; when Tybalt lied before the prince, you cast doubt on *our* honor; and now that Tybalt has slain the boy you claim to respect, you would apprehend the one who avenged his death?" His face bright red, he thrusts his finger at the darkened hills. "Get out! You have no right to utter his name, let alone visit his grave—you are no blood of mine!"

"Valentine's death was a lamentable tragedy." Paris sets his jaw, refusing to budge. "It was also an accident. Had he not interfered, it would be Romeo lying in this graveyard—as he greatly deserves." His eyes flash as he then turns his anger on me. "This treacherous whelp pressed himself upon Juliet, luring her into sin, and stole from me not just a bride but a *fortune*."

"That is what you choose to dwell on—here, of all places?" Mercutio shakes his head in disgust. "All the money you already have, all the glory and respect, and still it is not enough. You uphold the name of a contemptible murderer—*my brother's murderer*—because you blame Romeo for costing you a chance at becoming slightly richer?"

"I need not explain myself to you," Paris seethes. "Your brother was the last hope your sad little family had at recovering the great dignity your father took with him to the grave—and as far as I am concerned it is Romeo who is at fault for Valentine's death. Not Tybalt." Unsheathing a sword of his own, he levels the point of it in my direction. "And I shall see to it that he is delivered unto justice this night."

Mercutio draws his own blade. "Then you shall have to go through me first."

"That is your choice, then, and I will do so if I must." Paris nods to his silent manservant, who brandishes his blade—leaving me no choice but to follow suit, panic surging in my breast as matters spin suddenly and irrecoverably out of my control.

I have had my fill of violence and bloodshed, *more* than my fill; what I want more than anything is to be in peace, to take the boy I love and vanish from Paris's sight for good—from the Capulets and the Montagues and the all-consuming feud that has destroyed my life once already. The crypt is open, the hourglass running out, and I am mere steps from Valentine's side—and now, as the count and his attendant advance upon us, there is a chance I may never make it there.

Paris comes straight for me, and before he can step between us, Mercutio is intercepted by his cousin's glowering servant. The man is truly formidable, with a thick neck and meaty shoulders that strain the fabric of his shirt, and he attacks with brute force. Mercutio leaps back, dissolving into the fog, and the man gives chase—and just like that, I am alone with yet another vengeful and bloodthirsty villain who holds me personally accountable for his misfortunes.

"You took what was promised to me, you spoiled little brat, and I shall gladly finish what Tybalt began." Paris feints, and then thrusts, quick as a whip. The tip of his rapier very nearly catches the skin of my cheek before I flick it off course, and I dance to the side, away from the crypt.

"I took nothing you had any right to claim as yours," I tell him honestly, checking the weight of my sword, trying to use his rage against him. "There were no banns of marriage announced for you and Juliet. You were just another pitiful, money-grubbing suitor, begging her father's approval, and she laughed at you behind your back."

"But I will have the last laugh tonight!" he declares ferociously, and then lunges forward, his blade moving so fast in the darkness that I almost cannot see it coming. I parry twice, metal clanging sharply—and then, to my shock, I feel the sting of his rapier on the flesh of my ear.

Blood rolls down the side of my neck, hot and slippery, and it refocuses my attention. He is a better swordsman than I expected, and I cannot afford to be so distracted, to keep thinking about how close I am to being reunited with Valentine. I move faster, trying to use the fog and shadows to my advantage, to not give him the upper hand—but he seizes it somehow, nonetheless.

In seconds, he has me on the defensive; in a minute, I am retreating with every step, just barely keeping out of range of his weapon, the bottle bouncing in its pouch. He strikes with the deadly precision of a snake, showing an unerring instinct for which direction I am about to move, where my weaknesses are. He opens the flesh on my cheek at last, and then skewers the fabric of my sleeve, and still I've not managed to land a single blow.

And then, as I reel backward from another of his sudden thrusts, I stumble over a broken headstone and sprawl to the ground. The impact drives the air from my lungs, the bottle digging into the flesh of my thigh, and everything seems to slow. Paris lunges forward, his teeth shining in the moonlight, and I already know I won't be able to counter this attack in time.

But the attack doesn't come. To my shock, Paris simply . . . freezes. His sword outstretched, the tip of it mere inches from my heart, he stops and goes deathly still. It takes me a moment of dumbfounded staring, breathing hard and blinking sweat out of my eyes, to make sense of what I see before me.

The point of a short sword, thrust out of the shadows cast by a cluster of thick bushes opposite Mercutio's family crypt, has found the tender flesh just beneath Paris's chin. He starts to speak, and the blade presses upward, with just enough strength to draw a single drop of blood. The man shuts his mouth again as Juliet steps forth into the moonlight. "Drop your weapon, Count Paris, or this cemetery will claim another dead man tonight."

He sucks a shaky breath through his nose, calculating his odds. Flicking his gaze her way, he tries, "You know not what you are doing, my lady—"

"I am protecting my husband," she returns coldly, his blood making a slow journey along her steel. "What sort of woman would I be if I did not?"

Paris swallows, his eyes still on me. "He murdered your cousin."

"Tybalt slew Valentine, and then he paid for it with his life, as the law directs." She tilts her head. "You did not know him well, but he craved battle, and was always destined to die by the sword. Tell me . . . are you?"

The man licks his lips, still thinking, still not giving up—the end of his sword still within reach of my breast. "Obviously, you are in an emotional state, Juliet, and you are not thinking clearly. But it isn't too late for you to reclaim what you've thrown away for the sake of this . . . this deceitful coward of a boy. I've no doubt your father will understand that you were not yourself when you fell for his lies, and that he will forgive you—"

"Do you never grow tired of hearing your own voice?" Juliet's tone finally becomes heated, anger bringing color to her face. "Are you never done with your meaningless obsequies and manipulative prattle?" Pressing the blade deeper into his flesh, drawing a faint whimper from Paris as more blood spills, she states, "I've not heard you utter one sincere statement during all your time in Verona. Every word out of your mouth is measured and false, and I am astonished by how successful you are in your myriad dishonesties!"

"Juliet—"

"Stay quiet," she orders, vibrating with fury. "You came here not to woo me, not to win me, but to *procure* me. To add me to your treasure chest as you might any other object with appreciating value. But if you truly believe my father would forgive me for disobedience under any circumstance, you do not know him. And if you likewise think I would care to have his forgiveness, it proves how little you know me as well."

"You have not considered your position, my lady." His lip curls, but he keeps his voice neutral in spite of the metal digging

into his neck. "You have been cut off. No more wealth and privilege flow your way as a result of your fortunate parentage. And
as your . . . *husband* is in exile, he can offer you nothing, and will
only entrench the losses you have already incurred."

"How typical, that even with your own neck at the end of
a knife's point, all you can think of are gains and losses. But I
have considered my position, and I would much rather become
a destitute vagabond than your miserable wife." Her free hand
moves to her stomach—a subtle gesture, but one Paris clearly
notices. "Besides, how would history judge me if I chose wealth
and comfort over protecting my family?"

His eyes widen and his face goes pale, a storm of conflicting
emotions toying with his expression. "You are . . . you . . . you
cannot have been so *foolish*—"

"For the last time, drop your sword, and call off your manservant, or I will show you what a woman is capable of when she is
in an 'emotional state.'" Her eyes flash, and she uses her blade
to tip his chin up until he finally relinquishes his rapier with a
shaky hand. Wasting no time, she says to me, "Go—and take his
weapon with you. There are some things I'd like to say to him
that will be awkward with an audience."

I do not hesitate for a moment. Scrambling to my feet,
sheathing my sword and grabbing Paris's blade from the dewy
grass at his feet, I sprint for the crypt again. The mists ring with
the sound of Mercutio's continued duel and the count's voice
calling sharply for his man to yield, but I ignore it all. My neck
is filmed with a cold, nervous sweat, my hands unsteady as I
wrench the door open and plunge inside. It has been more than

357

the two-and-forty hours Friar Laurence said the elixir would permit, and my mind has gone blank with dread.

Grabbing a torch from the wall inside the door, I light it quickly and hurry down the carved steps that lead into the burial chamber. The air is dank and fetid, reeking of mold, decay, and perpetual damp; it clings to me, coats my lungs when I breathe it in, and I fight the reflex to gag as the underground vault at last flickers into view before me.

Stone slabs line the walls, with human forms stretched out across them, draped in stained and rotting shrouds. The tattered fabrics, crusted by age and the absorption of unspeakable moisture, suggest even worse horrors than what they probably conceal. But I cannot escape the notion that they are all merely sleeping, waiting for someone to wake them up, waiting for a chance to rise again as I hope at least one of them will.

Valentine's bier is easy enough to identify, his shroud still pristine. My heart lodges in my throat as I stumble forward, wrestling the bottle free with jerking movements. It is still whole, still sealed, unbroken. Holding my breath, my hands so unsteady I can barely fit the torch into its sconce, I fall to my knees beside him . . . and then I take hold of his shroud and pull it aside.

His face is revealed, pale and unmarked, his coloring impossible to decipher by the wavering orange glow of the torch. It dances over his chest and shoulders, and my breath catches, tears flooding my eyes as I remember the night we met—the night all of this began, when he was dressed as a faun in the moonlight.

Uncorking the bottle, forcing his mouth to open, I pour the

contents past Valentine's pale, cracked lips in as slow a trickle as I can manage.

When it's done, and he still does not move, I find his hand—cold and limp—resting on the slab beside his hip; I squeeze it tight, pressing it to my cheek. Crying too hard to speak, I can offer up only a silent prayer, begging for intercession, for mercy . . . for a happy ending due to a boy who never did anything wrong, but was punished for it nevertheless.

Even in my worst imaginings, I never allowed myself to think about what I would do if I made it this far only to find a corpse waiting for me. How I would turn around and walk back out again, leave Verona behind, start over somewhere else—all with the knowledge of Valentine's sacrifice hanging over me. Despite all the times I imagined the worst possible ending to this story, never did I consider what would happen if the story ended and I yet continued.

I am so lost in my despair that I do not even notice when his hand first twitches in mine, when his lips first part again and a shallow sigh presses forth from his lungs. His throat bobs, his eyes move behind their lids . . . and then they open with sluggish resistance. It takes a moment for them to focus, for me to accept that what I'm seeing is real, and then he coughs. "R-Romeo?"

"*Valentine!*" I gasp his name, my terror crashing into a wall of relief, the impact of it breaking me apart. Reaching for him—unsure if I am laughing or sobbing or both at once—I touch his cheek, his brow, the soft curls of his hair. He is so cold . . . but he is alive.

He is alive.

"You're . . . you're bleeding." His voice is weak and breathy, but his brows knit with concern for me. "What happened?"

"I . . ." Shaking my head, tears streaming, I begin to laugh in earnest. "It is nothing—just a scratch or two. They will heal in no time." And with that word, *time*, I finally realize how much of it we have, how much good fortune we have just snatched from the jaws of fate. For two days, I've not dared to let myself believe in the future, fearing the worst sort of disappointment. But now, it seems, we have one after all. "They don't matter. Nothing matters, except that you are awake and we are together."

"I am awake." It seems to occur to him for the first time, and realization dawns in his expression, his mouth spreading into that smile I feared I might never see again. "It worked?"

"Yes." I press my lips to the back of his hand, shutting my eyes and reveling in his closeness. He will never know how near he came to oblivion, for I do not believe I shall ever have the strength to tell him. "It worked. The prince believes you dead, and I have been officially banished—and we are free, Valentine. Our lives belong to us now. We control our destiny, and no one can force us apart so long as we choose each other."

"And I do." He smiles wider, his eyes sparkling in the firelight, and he reaches back for me. Pressing his hand over my heart, he whispers, "I choose you, Romeo. I love you, and cannot wait to love you more."

Leaning in, touching my forehead gently to his, I whisper, "We will teach the torches to burn."

And then I kiss him, and my heart races as the shadows leap

against the wall around us. The night is not over yet, but outside of this moment, nothing else seems to matter. For this moment, nothing can touch us.

His mouth is sweet, and his skin glows, and I let myself sink into him—to sink into a happiness that turns out to have been meant for me after all.

Boundless as the Sea

The sun in Brescia seems to shine brighter than anywhere else I've ever been—although it is possible I am biased. But every day I awake to birdsong, to warm light spilling over terraced hills covered in grapevines, the fruit growing dark and heavy as the summer passes. I have learned more than I ever thought there was to know about making wine, and I look forward to my daily walks through the vineyard, the time spent with my feet in the earth and green leaves trailing between my fingers.

The house is in a bit of a state, and over our first weeks here, Juliet made a comprehensive tour of the property, assembling a list of repairs that would need to be done. It was long, but we started with the most important ones first—patching a hole in the roof, replacing the cracked and crumbling steps down to the cellar—and have been whittling away at it ever since. Ben and Mercutio have visited twice already, and she has not been shy about putting them to work alongside us.

Valentine has started his own garden. A small one, to begin with, although he has ambitious plans—nothing that will rival what Juliet or I grew up with, or what his uncle had in Vicenza, but one that might feed us well someday in the future. He is finally living out his dream of reviving the dead ground, and has even begun experimenting in the kitchen. So far, every dish has been a disaster, but with each one, I think I fall in love with him a little more.

The night we emerged from the crypt, he was barely able to stand, his legs as rubbery as a newborn foal's. Juliet was waiting for us along with Mercutio—who looked quite the worse for wear, after a pitched and exhausting battle with his oversized opponent—but Count Paris was nowhere to be seen.

"I let him go," Juliet reported, casting her eyes back toward the hulking shadow of Verona's walls. "It took a bit of persuasion, but he finally ordered his manservant to stand down and surrender his blade. And in return, we allowed them to leave."

"Was that wise?" The mist still hugging the ground, melting the shadows together and hiding whatever lay more than a handful of yards in any direction, there might have been countless opportunities for Paris to retaliate.

"We shall see." She did not seem to share my concerns. "They are disarmed now, as well as outnumbered, so I do not think they would risk another attack until they have managed to find new weapons and reinforcements."

"I estimate the better part of an hour before that happens." Mercutio was bloodied, his shirt torn and his face bruised, but he was misty eyed as he watched his brother.

"With luck, Count Paris will take the bait I handed him and begin to spread rumors around Verona that I am with child." Smiling grimly, Juliet added, "I think that shall be the exact impetus Prince Escalus needs to demand that my father release my dowry to you in full."

She was right, as it turned out. And although it was delivered along with a furious letter, disclaiming her and any children she should bear, it brought nothing but relief. Juliet is free now, as well, to live as she pleases and choose her own company. For the present, she seems to enjoy devising solutions for the problems posed by our aging home, and selling flasks of our wine at the market in town. It gives her a purpose—something she says she's never had before—and friends.

As for me, I still spend as much time kissing Valentine as I can, aware of how little time we are promised. Of how lucky we are to shape our lives the way we like them. He is still planning a grand adventure for us, still daydreaming about seeing the world, but for the time being he seems to be content in Brescia. We sit together each twilight—outside in the garden, beneath an overgrown pergola Juliet has plans to repair—so that I may draw the vines spangled with fireflies, the evening sky spreading behind the foothills to the north, and the night-blooming flowers that cling to the ancient garden wall.

Hecate joins us, of course, curling up at our feet and purring loud enough to scare the crickets. True to his word, Ben delivered her to us after all, and she fell madly in love with Valentine at first sight. I cannot say I blame her, although sometimes I have to admit that I am jealous he alone is permitted to rub her belly.

For the first time in as long as I can remember, I have no idea what the future will bring, because I've not decided it yet. Instead, I choose to float in this happiness, and to imagine all the possibilities that lie ahead—for they are as boundless as the sea.

AUTHOR'S NOTE

AS A RECOVERING ACTOR AND FORMER THEATER MAJOR WITH MORE than a few Shakespeare plays under his belt (including *Romeo and Juliet*—I was to play Paris in a doomed production my senior year of high school), I thought that writing this novel would be a walk in the park.

I was wrong.

It turns out that writing a historical fiction novel set in the 1300s, even one based on a separate work of historical fiction that was only ever loosely faithful to a certain idea of the past, is extremely challenging. I had to research everything from the native flora of northern Italy to medieval dance steps to the etymologies of about a hundred or more common phrases. (You'll be fascinated to know that the expression *wild goose chase* originates not in the fourteenth century, as I had hoped, but in a play written two hundred years later—entitled . . . *The Tragedy of Romeo and Juliet*.)

Oh, and that's another thing I should mention: Shakespeare's original play is not a romance meant for young readers to swoon over; it is an urgent warning aimed at adults. It contains some of the bard's most beautiful, lyrical meditations on love . . . but it is, at its core, the story of two young people who are so neglected and manipulated by their selfish, self-involved parents that their lives end in senseless and avoidable tragedy. It is a wake-up call, meant to remind us that life is short and love is precious, and that we disrespect our children's self-determination at great peril to their safety—as well as to our own happiness and moral welfare. It is a message that I think contemporary society could benefit from.

But quite a few queer tragedies have already been written, including ones based on *Romeo and Juliet,* and I was hesitant to tread that particular ground. I wanted to bring something to the table that was a little more hopeful. At this point in history, looking back at where our community came from—at where I came from, as a scared teenager feeling unsafe and misunderstood—I wanted to write *Romeo and Juliet* as if it *had* been intended for a young audience. As if, instead of a dire lesson about two impulsive kids who have been failed by an older generation, it was a story of resilience. A story about found family and forged trust and earned, abiding love.

A story about queer people snatching happiness from the jaws of a world that has been fashioned against them. A tale as old as time.

As the shadows deepen, and old ugliness awakes to shake its loathsome head against the peace we've fought long and hard for, remember this: We cannot be corrected or contained. We are as boundless as the sea, and we will teach the torches to burn bright.

ACKNOWLEDGMENTS

THE JOURNEY OF (NEARLY) A HUNDRED THOUSAND WORDS BEGINS with a single step, and in this case that step is thanks to my editor, Emily Settle. It was Emily who offered me this amazing opportunity, who listened to all my thoughts and concerns, and who provided critical guidance that shaped the book you have in your hands. It was also Emily who made sure that Hecate the cat received a happy ending, and for that reason (among many others), she has my undying thanks.

I would need to throw a Capulet-style party, complete with rented peacocks, to express my gratitude to the rest of the Feiwel and Macmillan teams who helped this book come together. To Samira Iravani, Ilana Worrell, Celeste Cass, Brittany Pearlman, Morgan Rath, Brittany Groves, Melissa Zar, Gaby Salpeter, Kristen Luby, and Elysse Villalobos: Thank you from the bottom of my heart. And to Jean Feiwel and Liz Szabla, thank you from the top of my lungs, as well.

There is nothing quite like the feeling you get when you see your characters brought to life through someone else's eyes, and Julie Dillon took my breath away with the amazing cover art for this book. Thank you so much for your stunning work, and for giving Romeo and Valentine such a perfect, romantic moment.

Without my agent, Rosemary Stimola, my literary ambitions

would be—as Shakespeare himself might have put it—"no more yielding but a dream." Thank you again for helping my words find their wings, and for giving your counsel when I need it most!

I wrote most of this novel in isolation, seeing and talking to no one but my husband. Until the holidays rolled around, anyway, and I became the world's worst houseguest to our friends and family—holed up in isolation, seeing and talking to no one while I scrambled to meet my deadlines. Many, many thanks to my parents; to my sisters Jaime and Ann; to my brothers Dan and Dave; to Nick and Mars and Jennifer; to my many niblings, who impress me more and more every day; to my mother-in-law, Māra, and of course to Todd; and a special thank you to Lelde Gilman, who opened her heart and her home, and who was right there when I hit *send* on the first draft of this book.

It's hard to thank someone who isn't here anymore, but I have to try. Thank you, Debie, for teaching me (the hard way) to take a stand, and for teaching me (the easy way) the joys of sharing comfort. Thank you, Mom, for a lifetime of hilarious stories, for being a capital-*C* Character, and for letting me know in ways great and small (and heartwarming and annoying) that your love was always boundless and unqualified. I miss you both.

And then there is the east, and within it, the sun. Uldis, there is no one I'd rather survive a pandemic with, be locked down in a foreign country with, or be stranded at the border with than you. Thank you for making it so easy to write about being in love. Es tevi mīlu, Ulditi.

The sea and those who sail it are far more dangerous than the legends led them to believe . . .

This remix of *Treasure Island* moves the classic pirate adventure story to the South China Sea in 1826, starring queer girls of color—one Chinese and one Vietnamese—as they hunt down the lost treasure of a legendary pirate queen.

They will face first love, health struggles, heartbreak, and new horizons. But they will face it all together.

In a lyrical celebration of Black love and sisterhood, this remix of *Little Women* takes the iconic March family and reimagines them as a family of Black women building a home and future for themselves in the Freedpeople's Colony of Roanoke Island in 1863.

There seems to be no such thing as home in a war.

A ragtag band of misfits—two loyal Muslim sisters, a kindhearted Mongolian warrior, an eccentric Andalusian scientist, a frustratingly handsome spy, and an unfortunate English chaplain abandoned behind enemy lines—gets swept up in Holy Land politics in this thrilling remix of the legend of Robin Hood.

Sometimes, lost things find their way home . . .

Catherine and Heathcliff—two lost souls, both cut off from their Indian heritage and forced to conform to society's expectations of them—find solace and possibly a future together in this masterful new take on Brontë's *Wuthering Heights*.

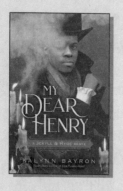

Thank you for reading this Feiwel & Friends book.

The friends who made

Teach the Torches to Burn:

A ROMEO & JULIET REMIX

possible are:

Jean Feiwel, Publisher

Liz Szabla, Associate Publisher

Rich Deas, Senior Creative Director

Anna Roberto, Executive Editor

Holly West, Senior Editor

Kat Brzozowski, Senior Editor

Dawn Ryan, Executive Managing Editor

Celeste Cass, Production Manager

Emily Settle, Editor

Rachel Diebel, Editor

Foyinsi Adegbonmire, Editor

Brittany Groves, Assistant Editor

Samira Iravani, Associate Art Director

Ilana Worrell, Senior Production Editor

Follow us on Facebook or visit us online at mackids.com.

Our books are friends for life.